Tales of the City

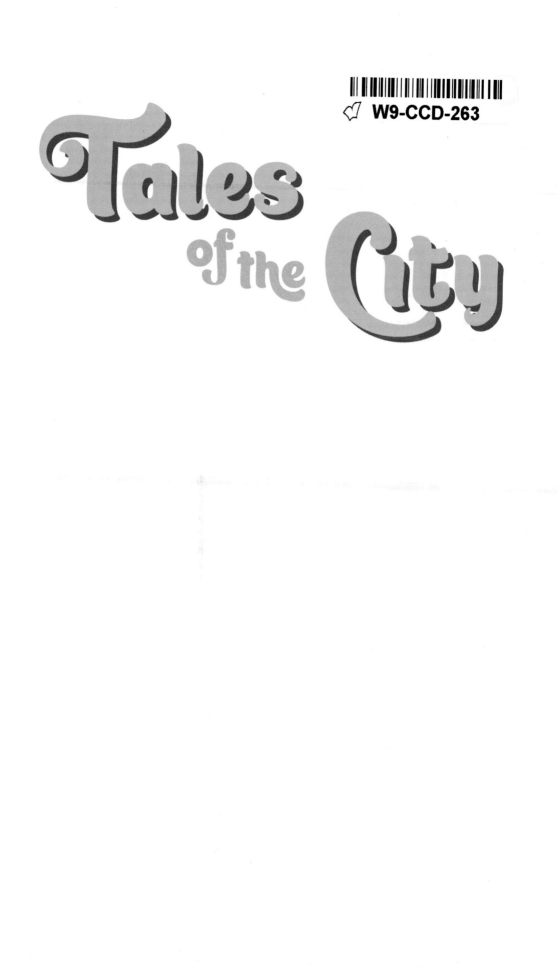

For Ablaze

Managing Editor
Rich Young

Editor
Kevin Ketner

Designer
Rodolfo Muraguchi

Publisher's Cataloging-in-Publication data

Names: Maupin, Armistead, author. | Bauthian, Isabelle, author. |
Revel, Sandrine, illustrator.
Title: Tales of the City / (written by) Armistead Maupin and Isabelle Bauthian;
(illustrated by) Sandrine Revel.
Description: "From the novels of Armistead Maupin"—
Cover. | Portland, OR: Ablaze Publishing, 2022.
Identifiers: ISBN: 978-1-950912-59-9
Subjects: LCSH City and town life—Comic books, strips, etc. | San Francisco (Calif.)—
Comic books, strips, etc. | Humorous stories, American. | Gay comics. | Graphic novels. |
BISAC COMICS & GRAPHIC NOVELS / LGBTQ+
Classification: LCC PN6727 .M378 T35 2022 | DDC 741.5—dc23

10 9 8 7 6 5 4 3 2 1

FROM THE NOVELS OF
ARMISTEAD MAUPIN

Adaptation **Isabelle Bauthian**

Art **Sandrine Revel**

Translation **FairSquare Comics' Lilliah Campagna
and Fabrice Sapolsky**

Lettering **Tom Napolitano**

ABLAZE

To mom.

Sandrine Revel

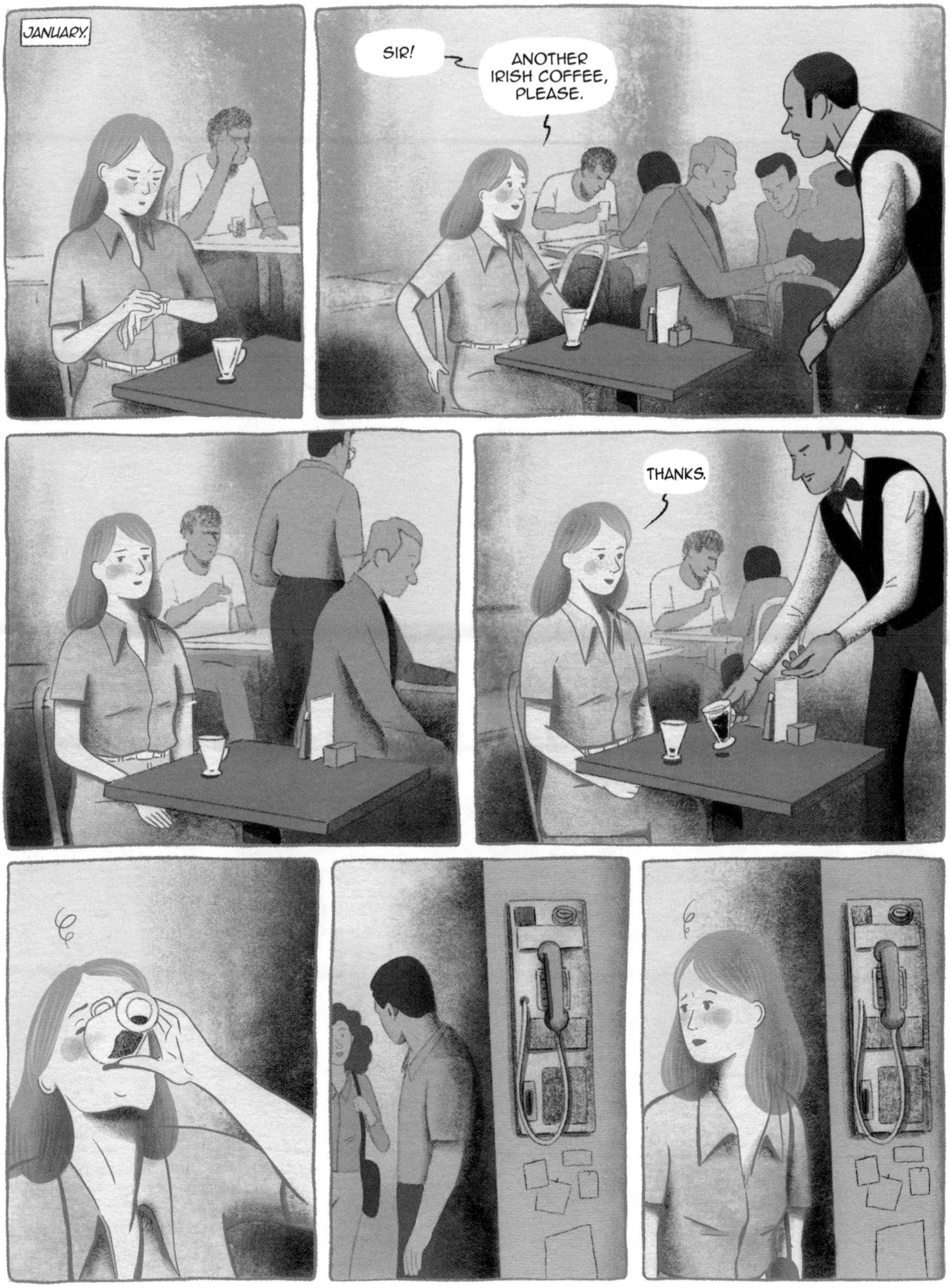
JANUARY.
SIR!
ANOTHER IRISH COFFEE, PLEASE.
THANKS.

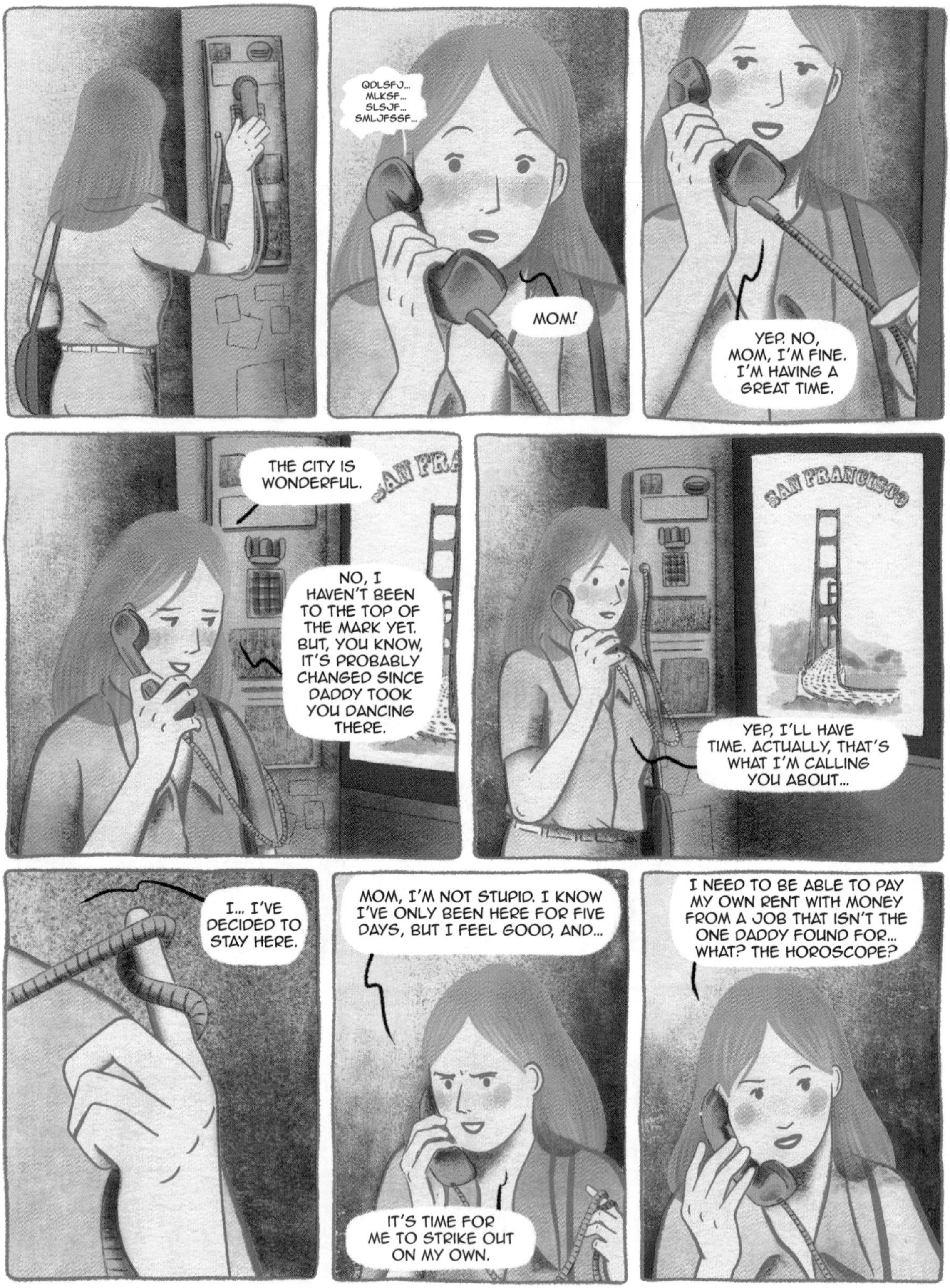
QDLSFJ...
MLKSF...
SLSJF...
SMLJFSSF...
MOM!
YEP. NO, MOM, I'M FINE. I'M HAVING A GREAT TIME.
THE CITY IS WONDERFUL.
SAN FRA
NO, I HAVEN'T BEEN TO THE TOP OF THE MARK YET. BUT, YOU KNOW, IT'S PROBABLY CHANGED SINCE DADDY TOOK YOU DANCING THERE.
SAN FRANCISCO
YEP, I'LL HAVE TIME. ACTUALLY, THAT'S WHAT I'M CALLING YOU ABOUT...
I... I'VE DECIDED TO STAY HERE.
MOM, I'M NOT STUPID. I KNOW I'VE ONLY BEEN HERE FOR FIVE DAYS, BUT I FEEL GOOD, AND...
IT'S TIME FOR ME TO STRIKE OUT ON MY OWN.
I NEED TO BE ABLE TO PAY MY OWN RENT WITH MONEY FROM A JOB THAT ISN'T THE ONE DADDY FOUND FOR... WHAT? THE HOROSCOPE?

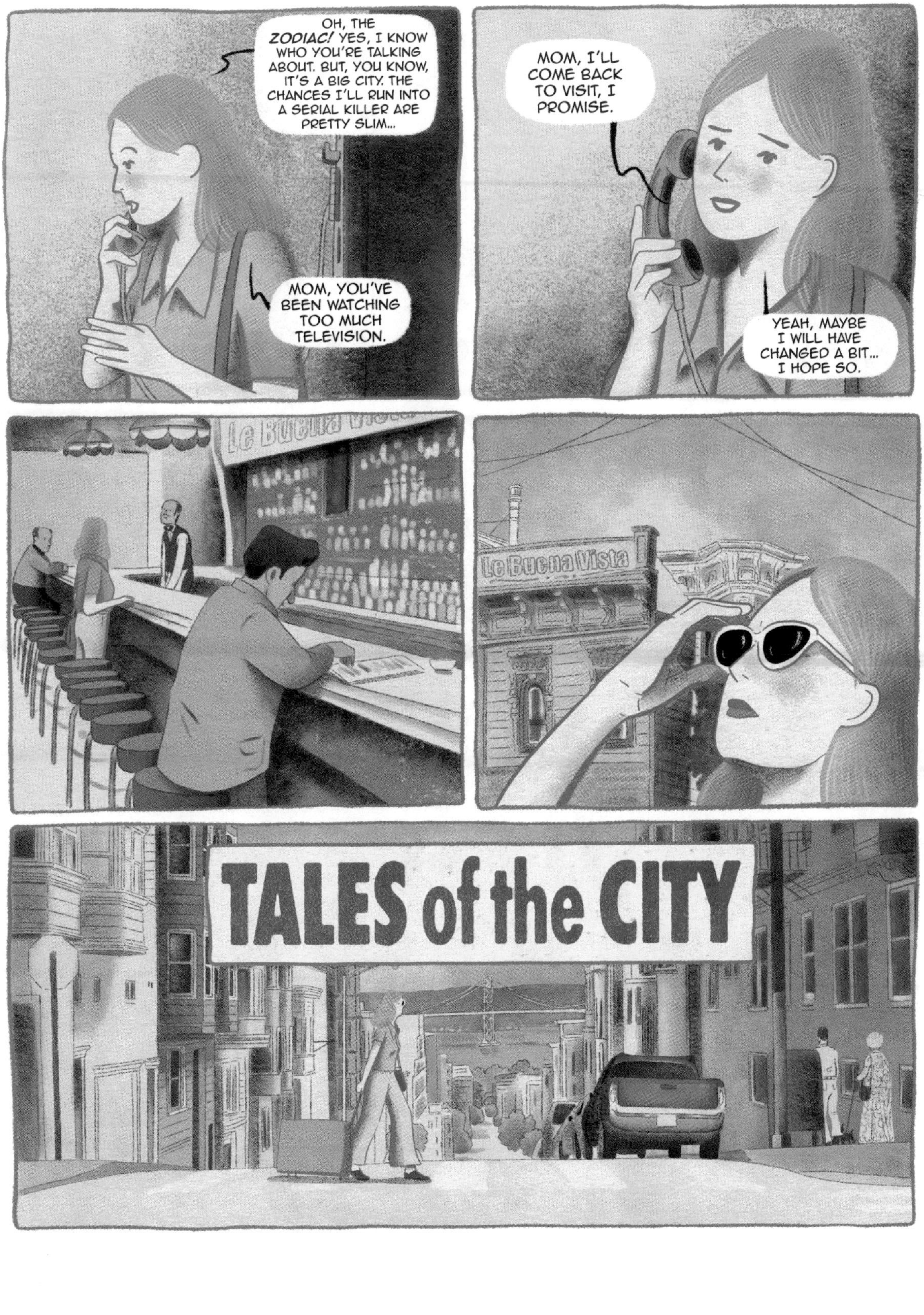
OH, THE *ZODIAC!* YES, I KNOW WHO YOU'RE TALKING ABOUT. BUT, YOU KNOW, IT'S A BIG CITY. THE CHANCES I'LL RUN INTO A SERIAL KILLER ARE PRETTY SLIM...
MOM, YOU'VE BEEN WATCHING TOO MUCH TELEVISION.
MOM, I'LL COME BACK TO VISIT, I PROMISE.
YEAH, MAYBE I WILL HAVE CHANGED A BIT... I HOPE SO.
Le Buena Vista
TALES of the CITY

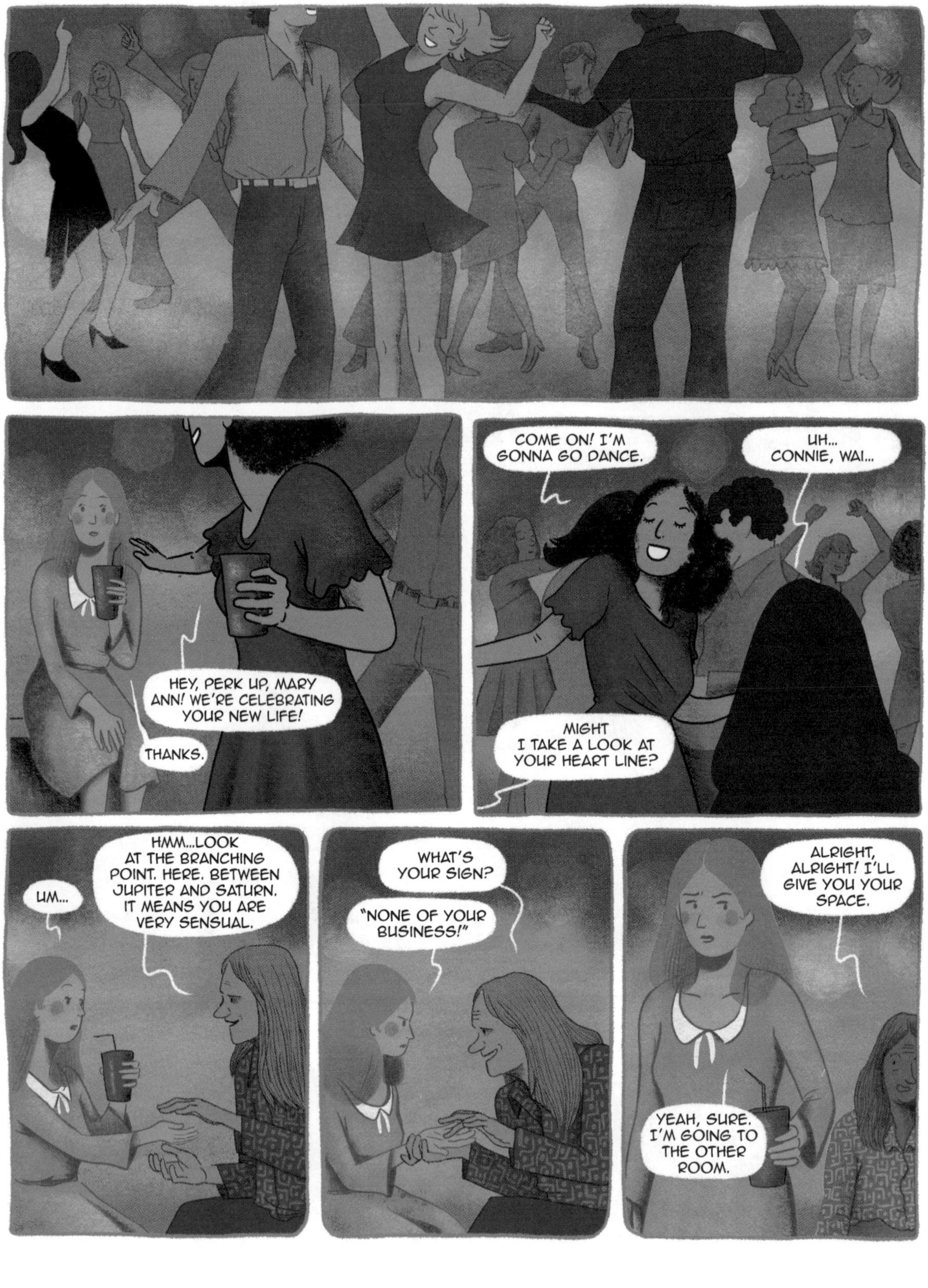
HEY, PERK UP, MARY ANN! WE'RE CELEBRATING YOUR NEW LIFE!
THANKS.
COME ON! I'M GONNA GO DANCE.
UH... CONNIE, WAI...
MIGHT I TAKE A LOOK AT YOUR HEART LINE?
UM...
HMM...LOOK AT THE BRANCHING POINT. HERE. BETWEEN JUPITER AND SATURN. IT MEANS YOU ARE VERY SENSUAL.
WHAT'S YOUR SIGN?
"NONE OF YOUR BUSINESS!"
ALRIGHT, ALRIGHT! I'LL GIVE YOU YOUR SPACE.
YEAH, SURE. I'M GOING TO THE OTHER ROOM.

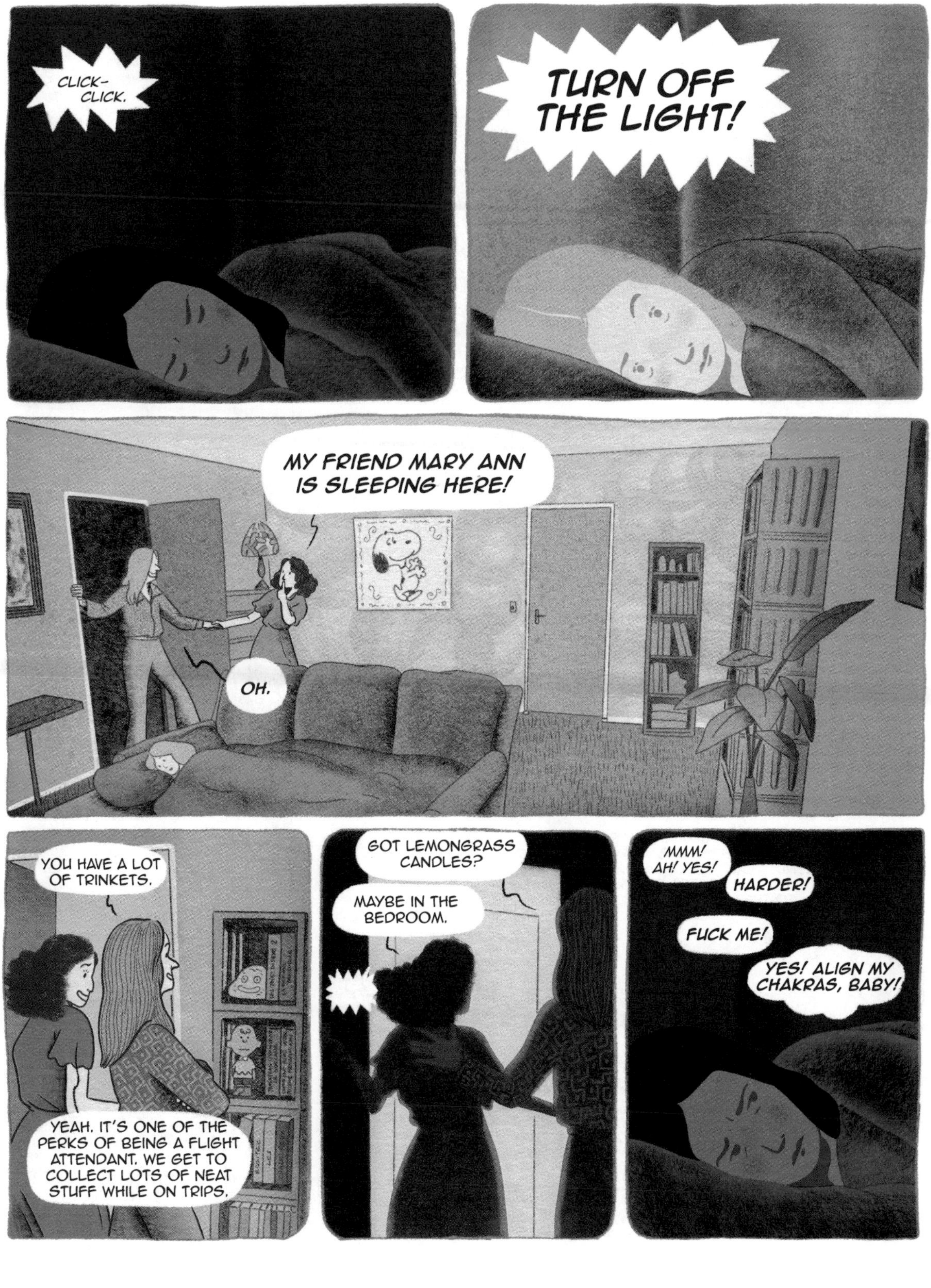
CLICK-CLICK.
TURN OFF THE LIGHT!
MY FRIEND MARY ANN IS SLEEPING HERE!
OH.
YOU HAVE A LOT OF TRINKETS.
YEAH. IT'S ONE OF THE PERKS OF BEING A FLIGHT ATTENDANT. WE GET TO COLLECT LOTS OF NEAT STUFF WHILE ON TRIPS.
GOT LEMONGRASS CANDLES?
MAYBE IN THE BEDROOM.
MMM! AH! YES!
HARDER!
FUCK ME!
YES! ALIGN MY CHAKRAS, BABY!

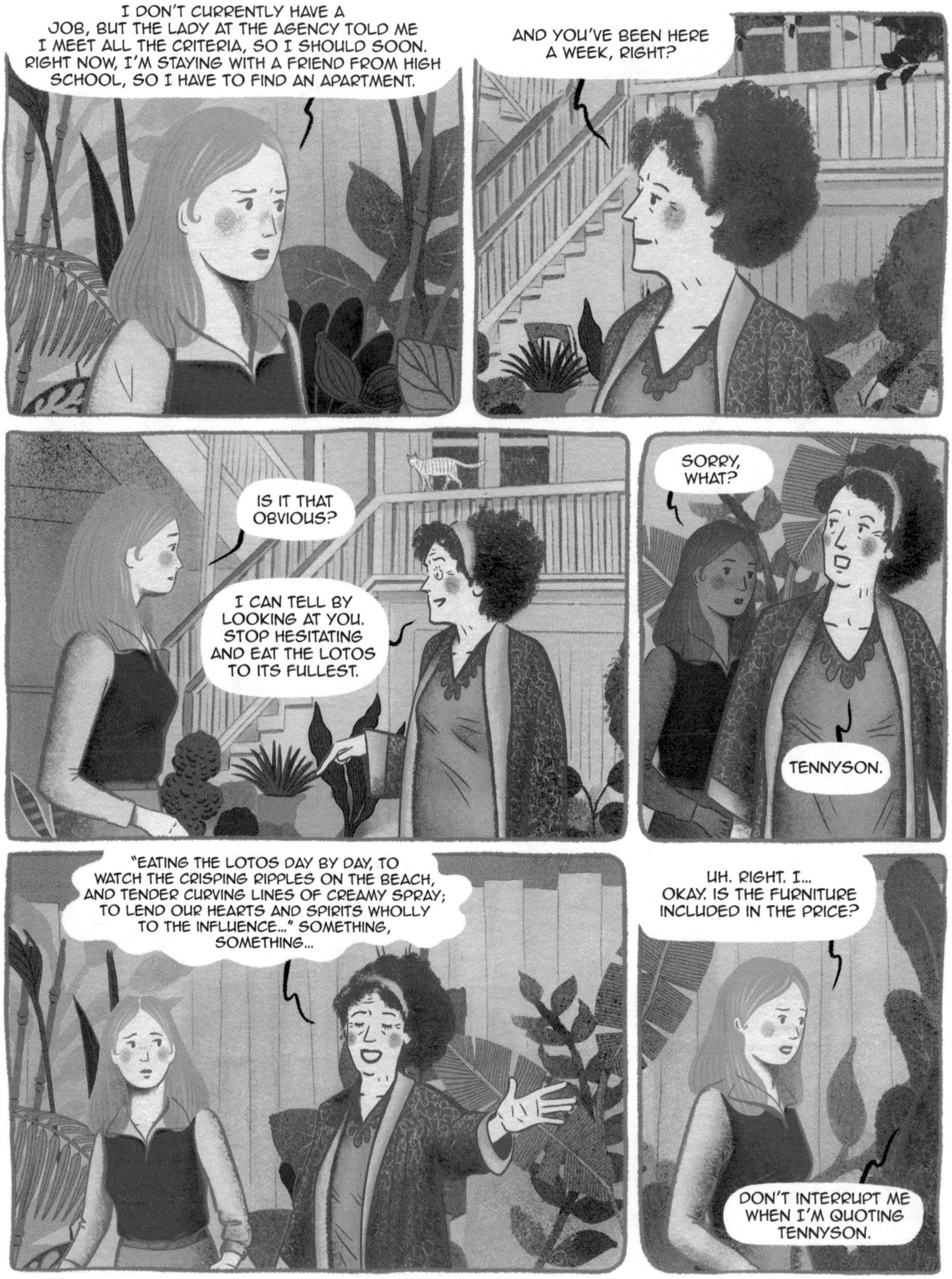
I DON'T CURRENTLY HAVE A JOB, BUT THE LADY AT THE AGENCY TOLD ME I MEET ALL THE CRITERIA, SO I SHOULD SOON. RIGHT NOW, I'M STAYING WITH A FRIEND FROM HIGH SCHOOL, SO I HAVE TO FIND AN APARTMENT.
AND YOU'VE BEEN HERE A WEEK, RIGHT?
IS IT THAT OBVIOUS?
I CAN TELL BY LOOKING AT YOU. STOP HESITATING AND EAT THE LOTOS TO ITS FULLEST.
SORRY, WHAT?
TENNYSON.
"EATING THE LOTOS DAY BY DAY, TO WATCH THE CRISPING RIPPLES ON THE BEACH, AND TENDER CURVING LINES OF CREAMY SPRAY; TO LEND OUR HEARTS AND SPIRITS WHOLLY TO THE INFLUENCE..." SOMETHING, SOMETHING...
UH. RIGHT. I... OKAY. IS THE FURNITURE INCLUDED IN THE PRICE?
DON'T INTERRUPT ME WHEN I'M QUOTING TENNYSON.

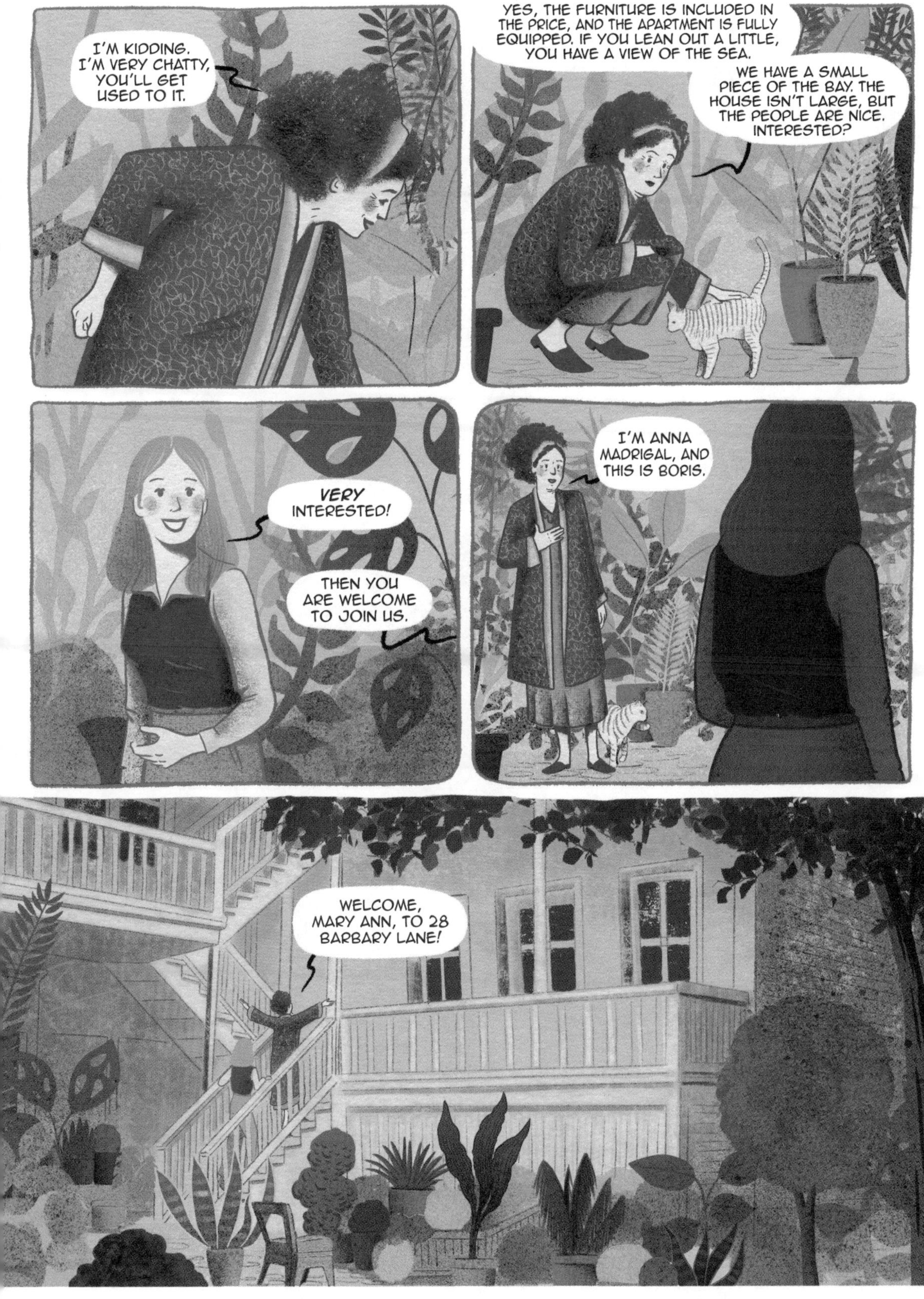
I'M KIDDING. I'M VERY CHATTY, YOU'LL GET USED TO IT.
YES, THE FURNITURE IS INCLUDED IN THE PRICE, AND THE APARTMENT IS FULLY EQUIPPED. IF YOU LEAN OUT A LITTLE, YOU HAVE A VIEW OF THE SEA.
WE HAVE A SMALL PIECE OF THE BAY. THE HOUSE ISN'T LARGE, BUT THE PEOPLE ARE NICE. INTERESTED?
VERY INTERESTED!
THEN YOU ARE WELCOME TO JOIN US.
I'M ANNA MADRIGAL, AND THIS IS BORIS.
WELCOME, MARY ANN, TO 28 BARBARY LANE!

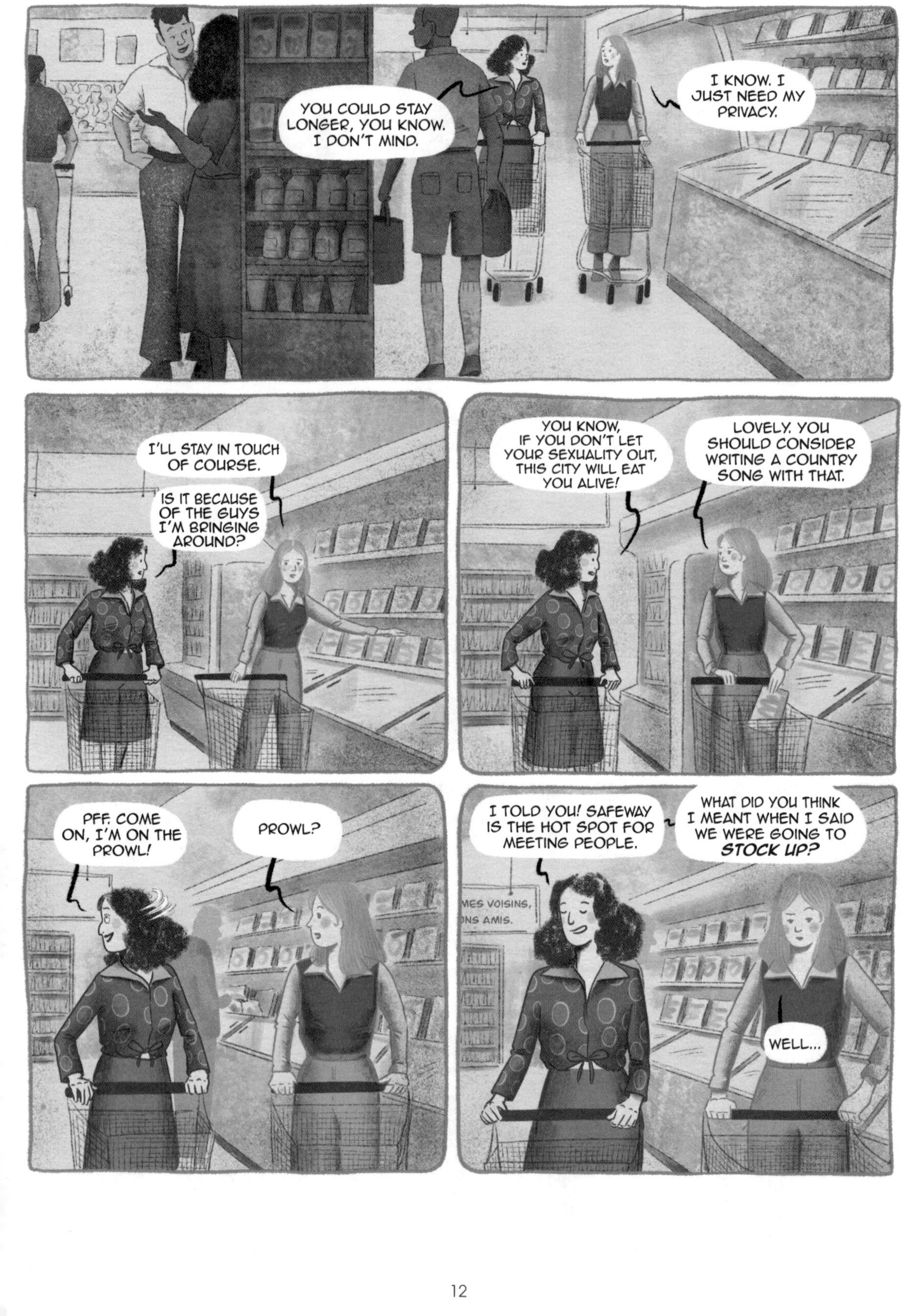

YOU COULD STAY LONGER, YOU KNOW. I DON'T MIND.
I KNOW. I JUST NEED MY PRIVACY.
I'LL STAY IN TOUCH OF COURSE.
IS IT BECAUSE OF THE GUYS I'M BRINGING AROUND?
YOU KNOW, IF YOU DON'T LET YOUR SEXUALITY OUT, THIS CITY WILL EAT YOU ALIVE!
LOVELY. YOU SHOULD CONSIDER WRITING A COUNTRY SONG WITH THAT.
PFF. COME ON, I'M ON THE PROWL!
PROWL?
I TOLD YOU! SAFEWAY IS THE HOT SPOT FOR MEETING PEOPLE.
WHAT DID YOU THINK I MEANT WHEN I SAID WE WERE GOING TO ***STOCK UP?***
WELL...

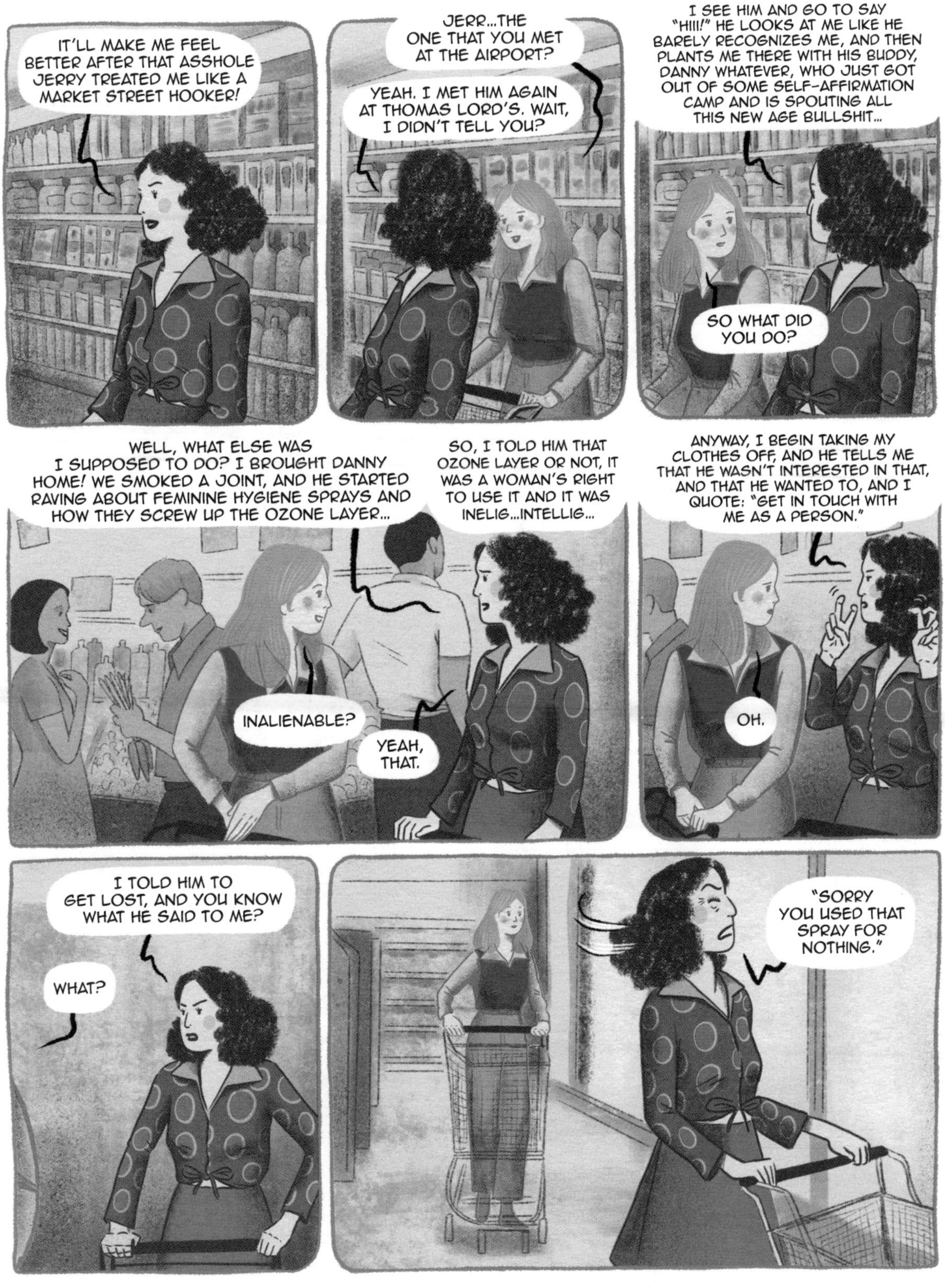
IT'LL MAKE ME FEEL BETTER AFTER THAT ASSHOLE JERRY TREATED ME LIKE A MARKET STREET HOOKER!
JERR...THE ONE THAT YOU MET AT THE AIRPORT?
YEAH. I MET HIM AGAIN AT THOMAS LORD'S. WAIT, I DIDN'T TELL YOU?
I SEE HIM AND GO TO SAY "HIII!" HE LOOKS AT ME LIKE HE BARELY RECOGNIZES ME, AND THEN PLANTS ME THERE WITH HIS BUDDY, DANNY WHATEVER, WHO JUST GOT OUT OF SOME SELF-AFFIRMATION CAMP AND IS SPOUTING ALL THIS NEW AGE BULLSHIT...
SO WHAT DID YOU DO?
WELL, WHAT ELSE WAS I SUPPOSED TO DO? I BROUGHT DANNY HOME! WE SMOKED A JOINT, AND HE STARTED RAVING ABOUT FEMININE HYGIENE SPRAYS AND HOW THEY SCREW UP THE OZONE LAYER...
SO, I TOLD HIM THAT OZONE LAYER OR NOT, IT WAS A WOMAN'S RIGHT TO USE IT AND IT WAS INELIG...INTELLIG...
INALIENABLE?
YEAH, THAT.
ANYWAY, I BEGIN TAKING MY CLOTHES OFF, AND HE TELLS ME THAT HE WASN'T INTERESTED IN THAT, AND THAT HE WANTED TO, AND I QUOTE: "GET IN TOUCH WITH ME AS A PERSON."
OH.
I TOLD HIM TO GET LOST, AND YOU KNOW WHAT HE SAID TO ME?
WHAT?
"SORRY YOU USED THAT SPRAY FOR NOTHING."

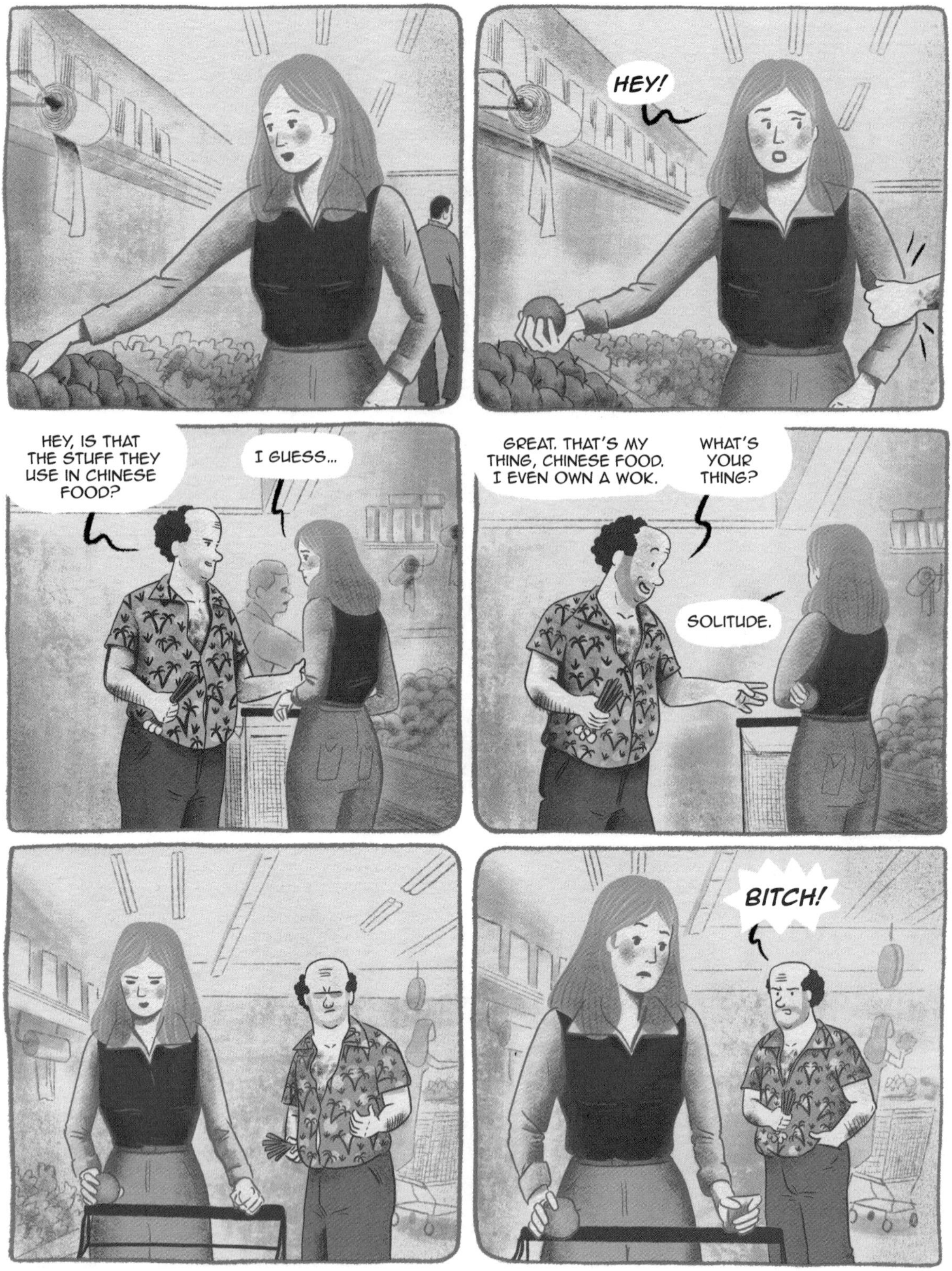
HEY!
HEY, IS THAT THE STUFF THEY USE IN CHINESE FOOD?
I GUESS...
GREAT. THAT'S MY THING, CHINESE FOOD. I EVEN OWN A WOK.
WHAT'S YOUR THING?
SOLITUDE.
BITCH!

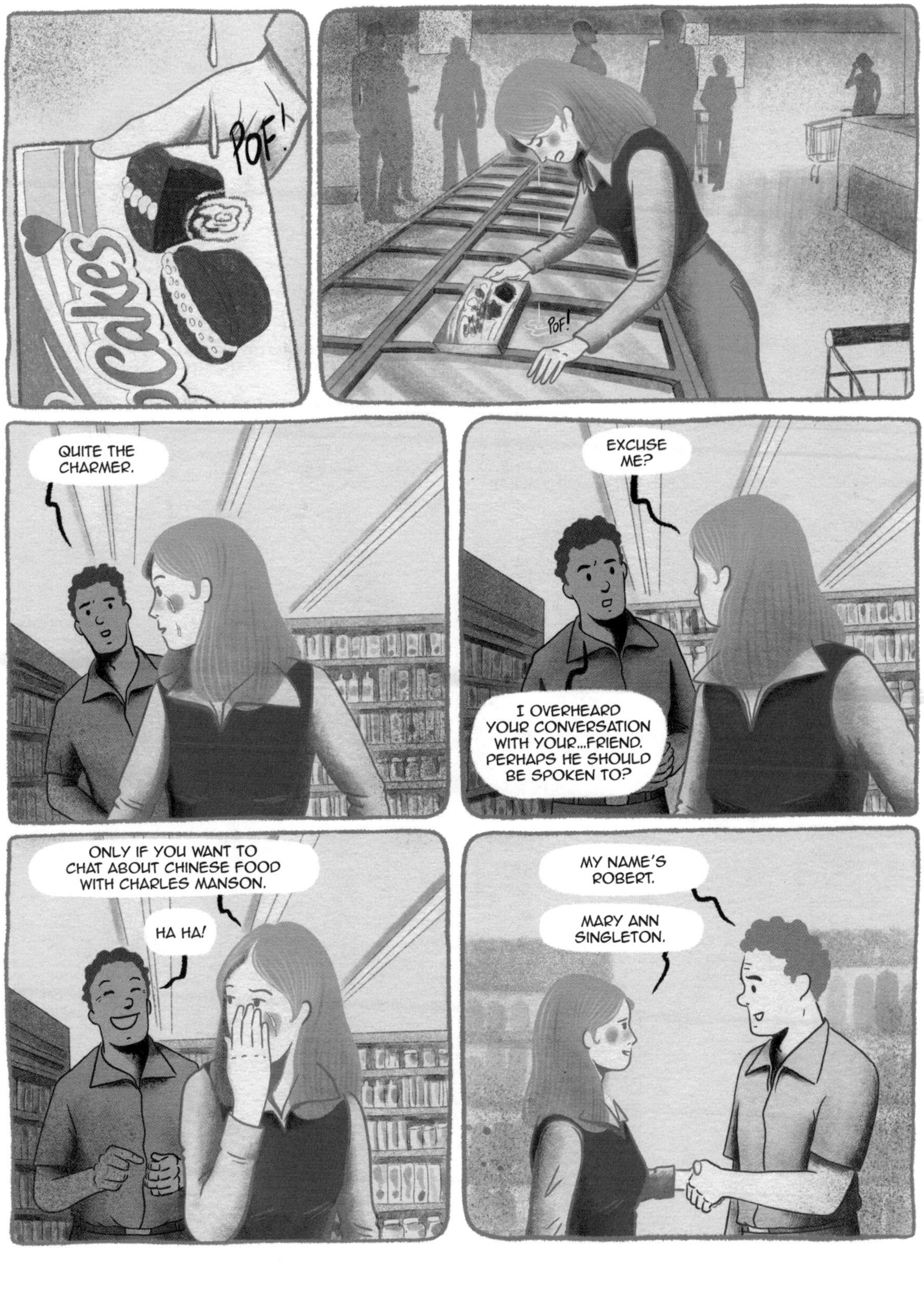
POF!
Cakes
POF!
QUITE THE CHARMER.
EXCUSE ME?
I OVERHEARD YOUR CONVERSATION WITH YOUR...FRIEND. PERHAPS HE SHOULD BE SPOKEN TO?
ONLY IF YOU WANT TO CHAT ABOUT CHINESE FOOD WITH CHARLES MANSON.
HA HA!
MY NAME'S ROBERT.
MARY ANN SINGLETON.

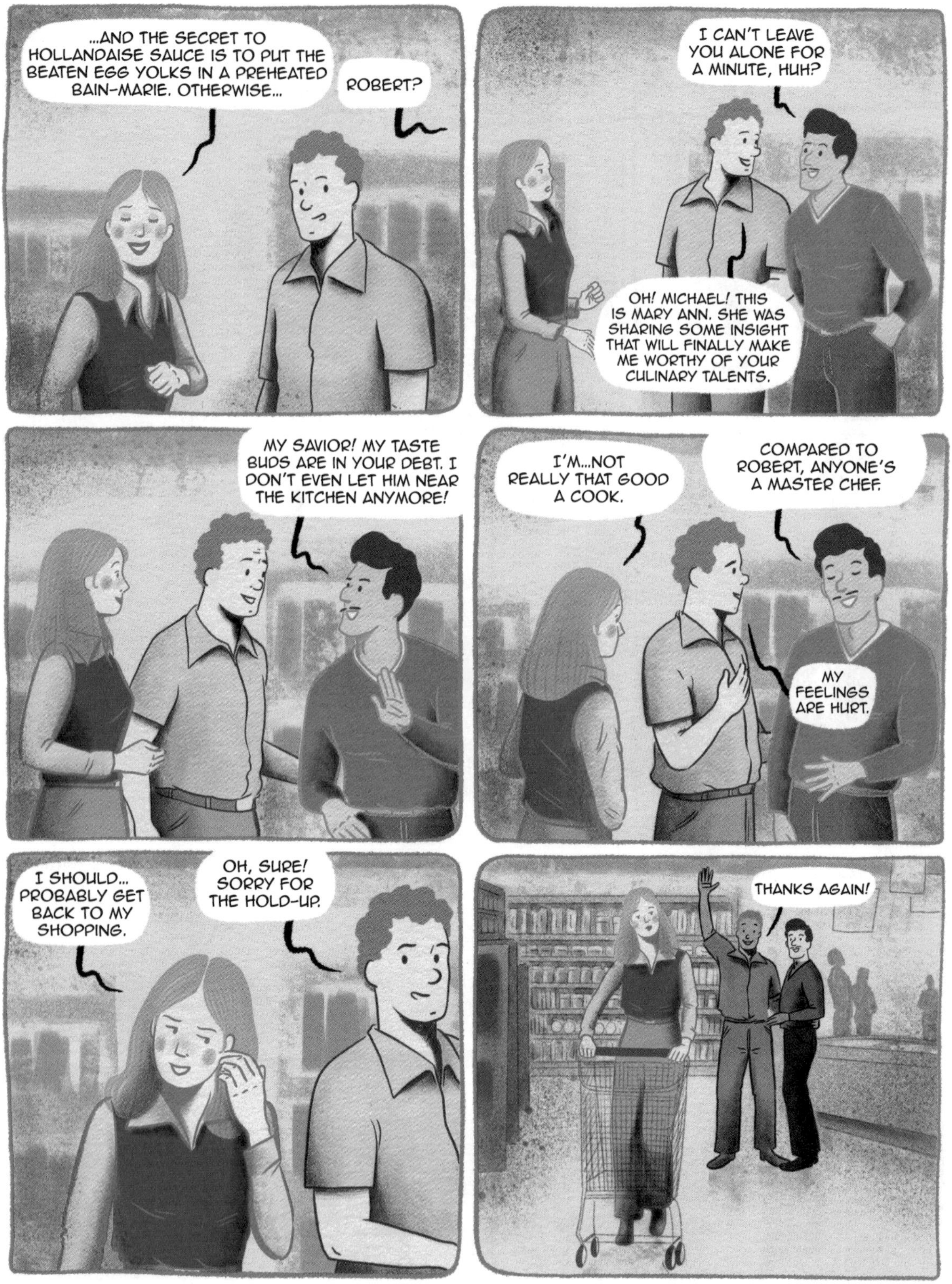
...AND THE SECRET TO HOLLANDAISE SAUCE IS TO PUT THE BEATEN EGG YOLKS IN A PREHEATED BAIN-MARIE. OTHERWISE...
ROBERT?
I CAN'T LEAVE YOU ALONE FOR A MINUTE, HUH?
OH! MICHAEL! THIS IS MARY ANN. SHE WAS SHARING SOME INSIGHT THAT WILL FINALLY MAKE ME WORTHY OF YOUR CULINARY TALENTS.
MY SAVIOR! MY TASTE BUDS ARE IN YOUR DEBT. I DON'T EVEN LET HIM NEAR THE KITCHEN ANYMORE!
I'M...NOT REALLY THAT GOOD A COOK.
COMPARED TO ROBERT, ANYONE'S A MASTER CHEF.
MY FEELINGS ARE HURT.
I SHOULD... PROBABLY GET BACK TO MY SHOPPING.
OH, SURE! SORRY FOR THE HOLD-UP.
THANKS AGAIN!

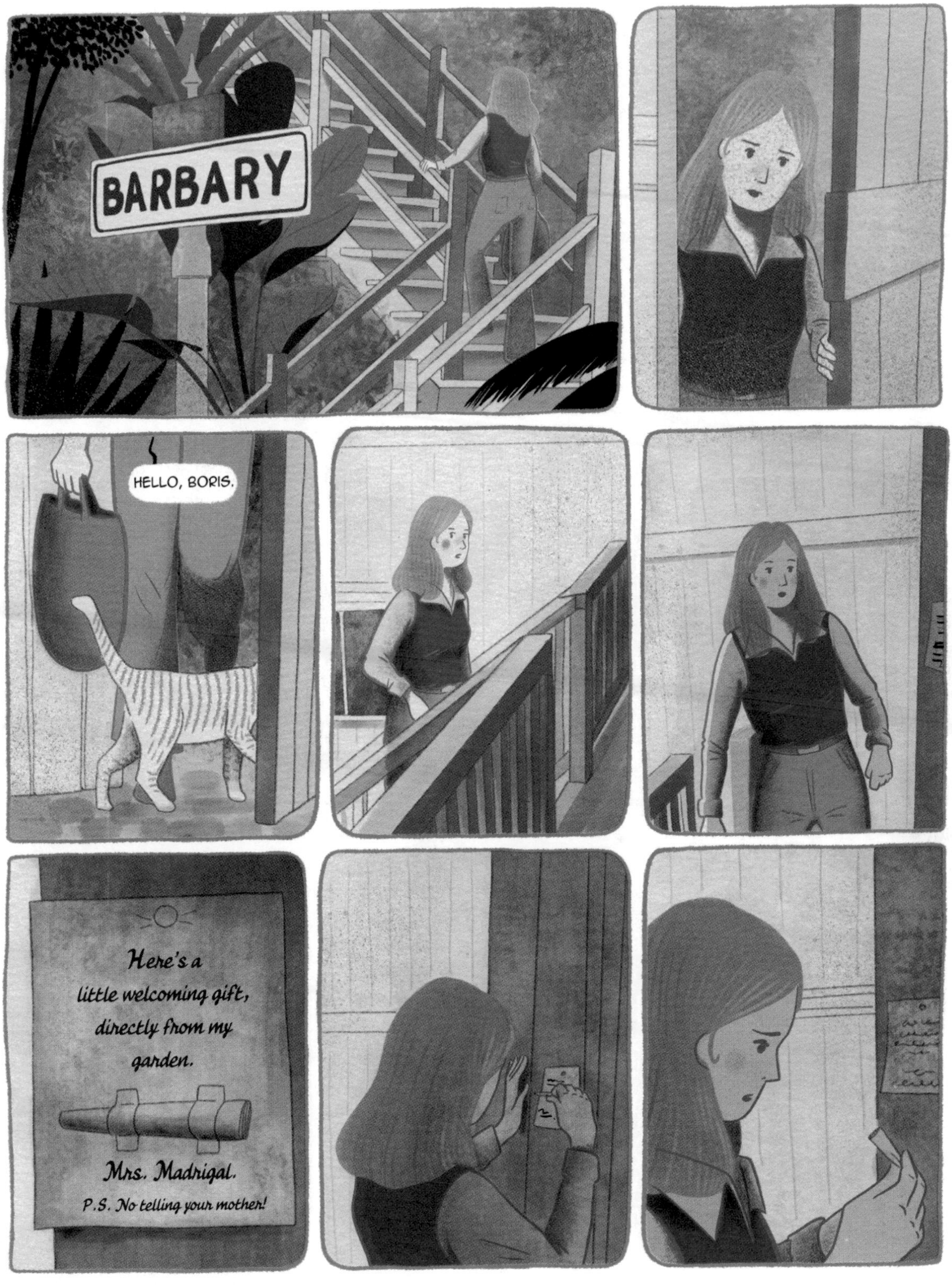
BARBARY
HELLO, BORIS.
Here's a
little welcoming gift,
directly from my
garden.
Mrs. Madrigal.
P.S. No telling your mother!

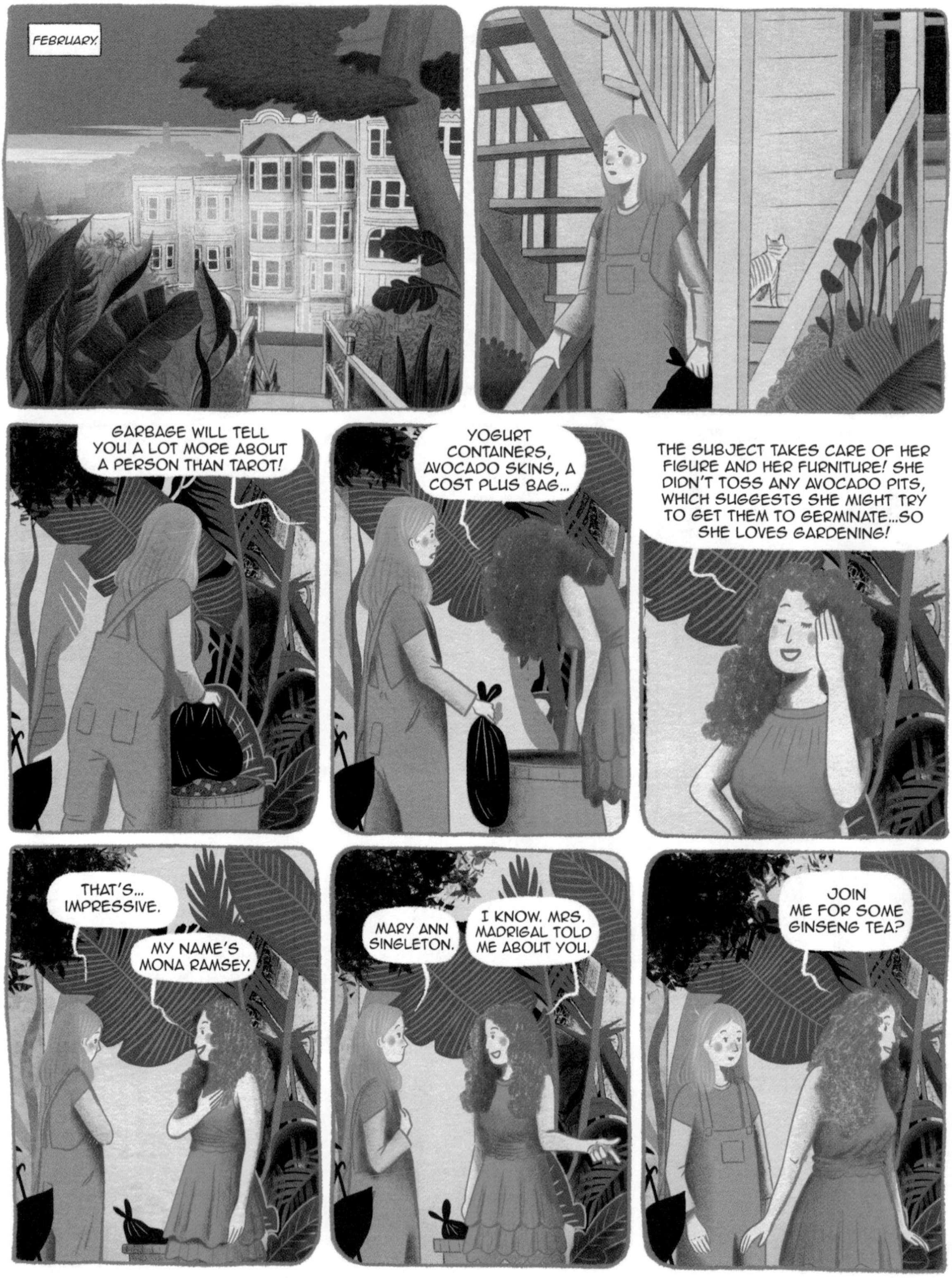
FEBRUARY.
GARBAGE WILL TELL YOU A LOT MORE ABOUT A PERSON THAN TAROT!
YOGURT CONTAINERS, AVOCADO SKINS, A COST PLUS BAG...
THE SUBJECT TAKES CARE OF HER FIGURE AND HER FURNITURE! SHE DIDN'T TOSS ANY AVOCADO PITS, WHICH SUGGESTS SHE MIGHT TRY TO GET THEM TO GERMINATE...SO SHE LOVES GARDENING!
THAT'S... IMPRESSIVE.
MY NAME'S MONA RAMSEY.
MARY ANN SINGLETON.
I KNOW. MRS. MADRIGAL TOLD ME ABOUT YOU.
JOIN ME FOR SOME GINSENG TEA?

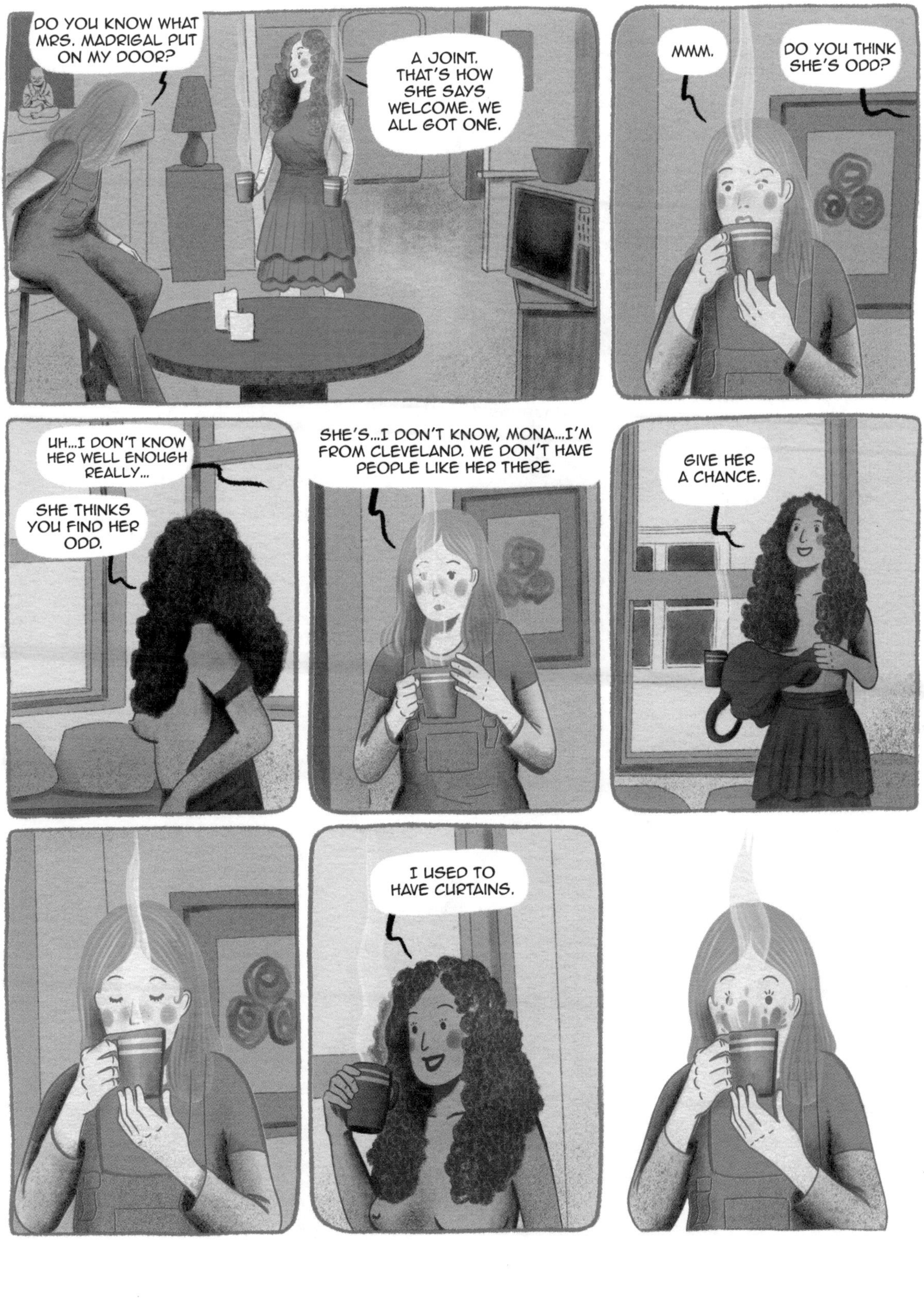
DO YOU KNOW WHAT MRS. MADRIGAL PUT ON MY DOOR?
A JOINT. THAT'S HOW SHE SAYS WELCOME. WE ALL GOT ONE.
MMM.
DO YOU THINK SHE'S ODD?
UH...I DON'T KNOW HER WELL ENOUGH REALLY...
SHE THINKS YOU FIND HER ODD.
SHE'S...I DON'T KNOW, MONA...I'M FROM CLEVELAND. WE DON'T HAVE PEOPLE LIKE HER THERE.
GIVE HER A CHANCE.
I USED TO HAVE CURTAINS.

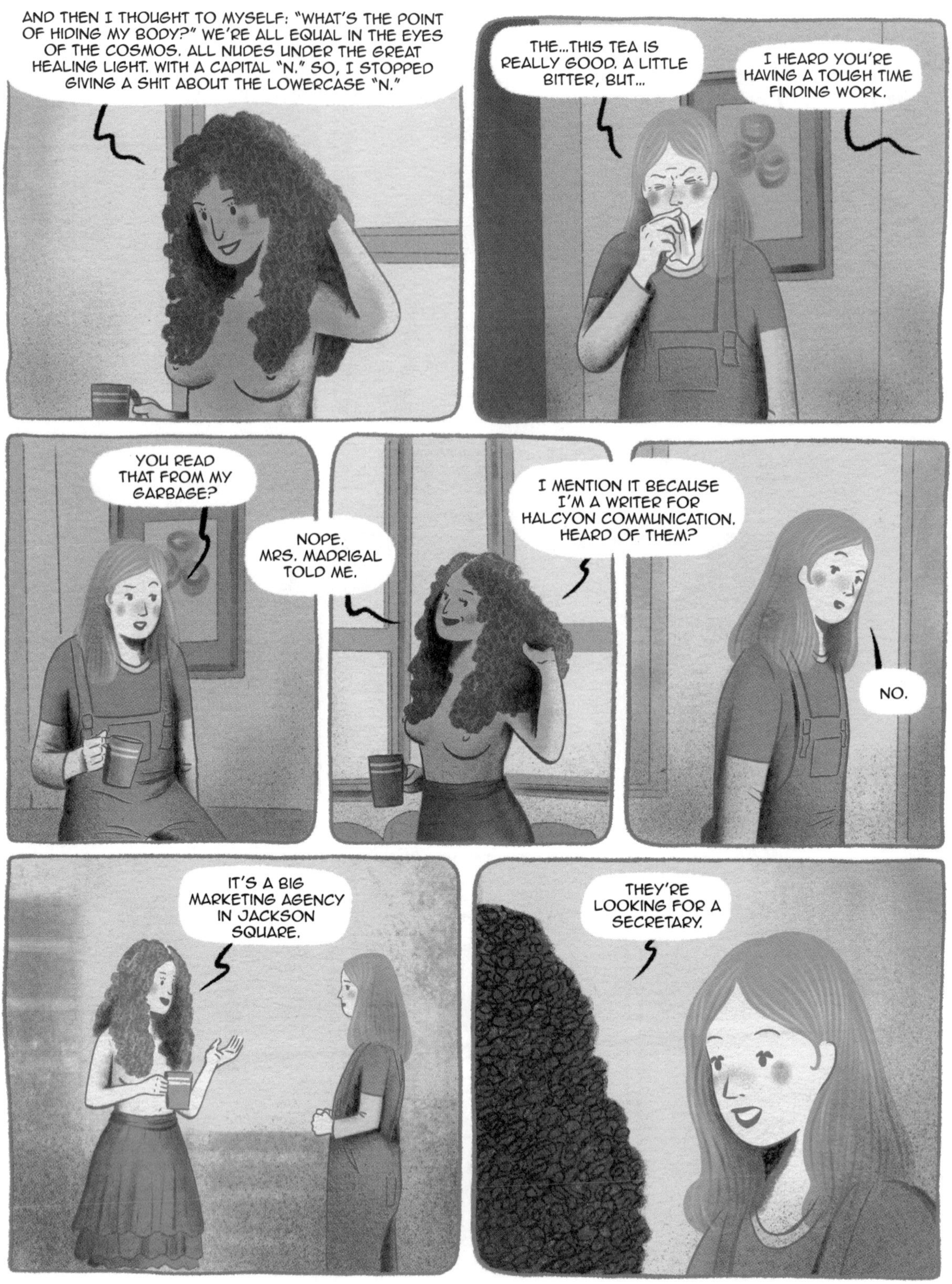
AND THEN I THOUGHT TO MYSELF: "WHAT'S THE POINT OF HIDING MY BODY?" WE'RE ALL EQUAL IN THE EYES OF THE COSMOS. ALL NUDES UNDER THE GREAT HEALING LIGHT. WITH A CAPITAL "N." SO, I STOPPED GIVING A SHIT ABOUT THE LOWERCASE "N."
THE...THIS TEA IS REALLY GOOD. A LITTLE BITTER, BUT...
I HEARD YOU'RE HAVING A TOUGH TIME FINDING WORK.
YOU READ THAT FROM MY GARBAGE?
NOPE. MRS. MADRIGAL TOLD ME.
I MENTION IT BECAUSE I'M A WRITER FOR HALCYON COMMUNICATION. HEARD OF THEM?
NO.
IT'S A BIG MARKETING AGENCY IN JACKSON SQUARE.
THEY'RE LOOKING FOR A SECRETARY.

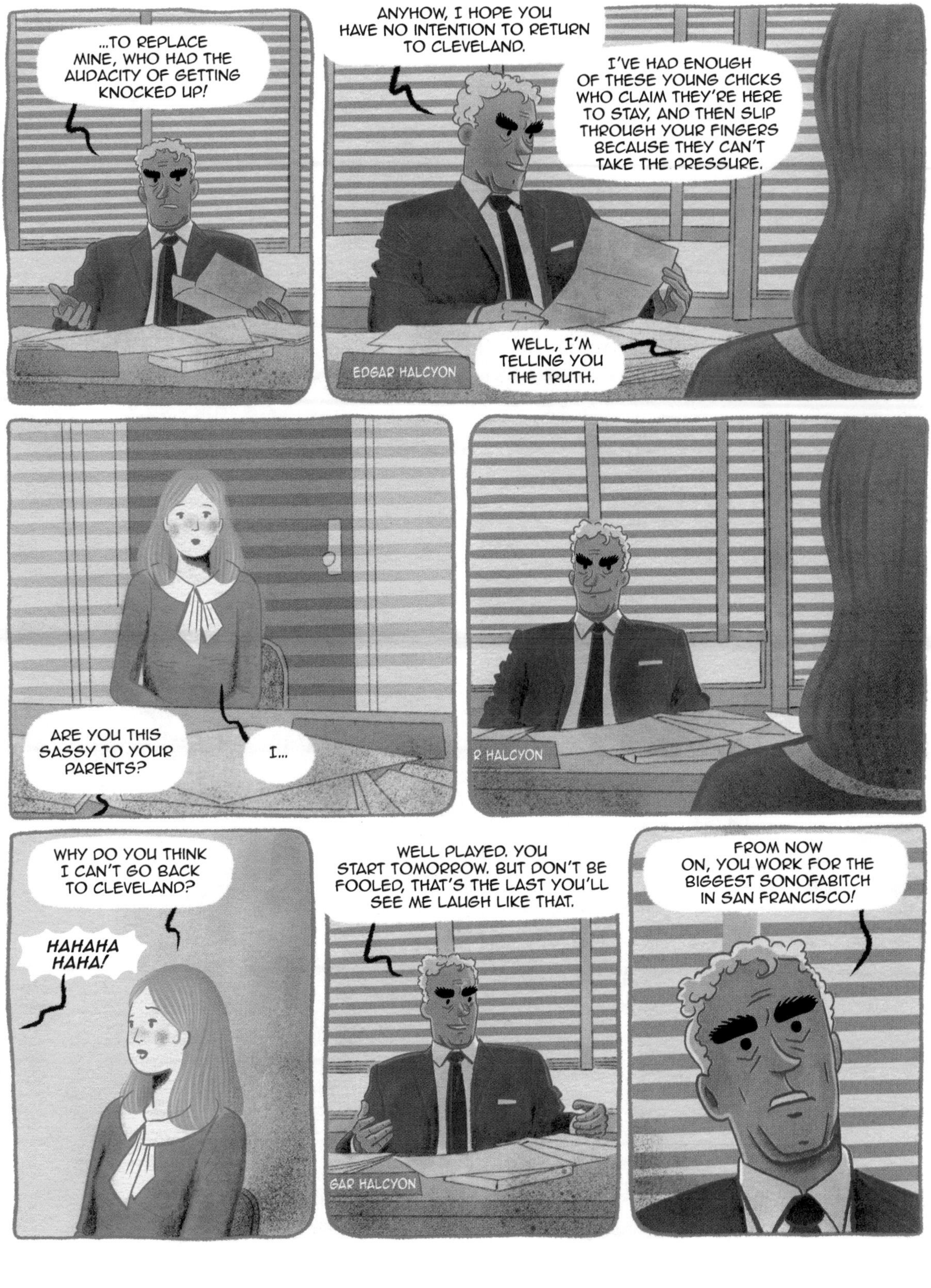
...TO REPLACE MINE, WHO HAD THE AUDACITY OF GETTING KNOCKED UP!
ANYHOW, I HOPE YOU HAVE NO INTENTION TO RETURN TO CLEVELAND.
I'VE HAD ENOUGH OF THESE YOUNG CHICKS WHO CLAIM THEY'RE HERE TO STAY, AND THEN SLIP THROUGH YOUR FINGERS BECAUSE THEY CAN'T TAKE THE PRESSURE.
EDGAR HALCYON
WELL, I'M TELLING YOU THE TRUTH.
ARE YOU THIS SASSY TO YOUR PARENTS?
I...
R HALCYON
WHY DO YOU THINK I CAN'T GO BACK TO CLEVELAND?
HAHAHA HAHA!
WELL PLAYED. YOU START TOMORROW. BUT DON'T BE FOOLED, THAT'S THE LAST YOU'LL SEE ME LAUGH LIKE THAT.
GAR HALCYON
FROM NOW ON, YOU WORK FOR THE BIGGEST SONOFABITCH IN SAN FRANCISCO!

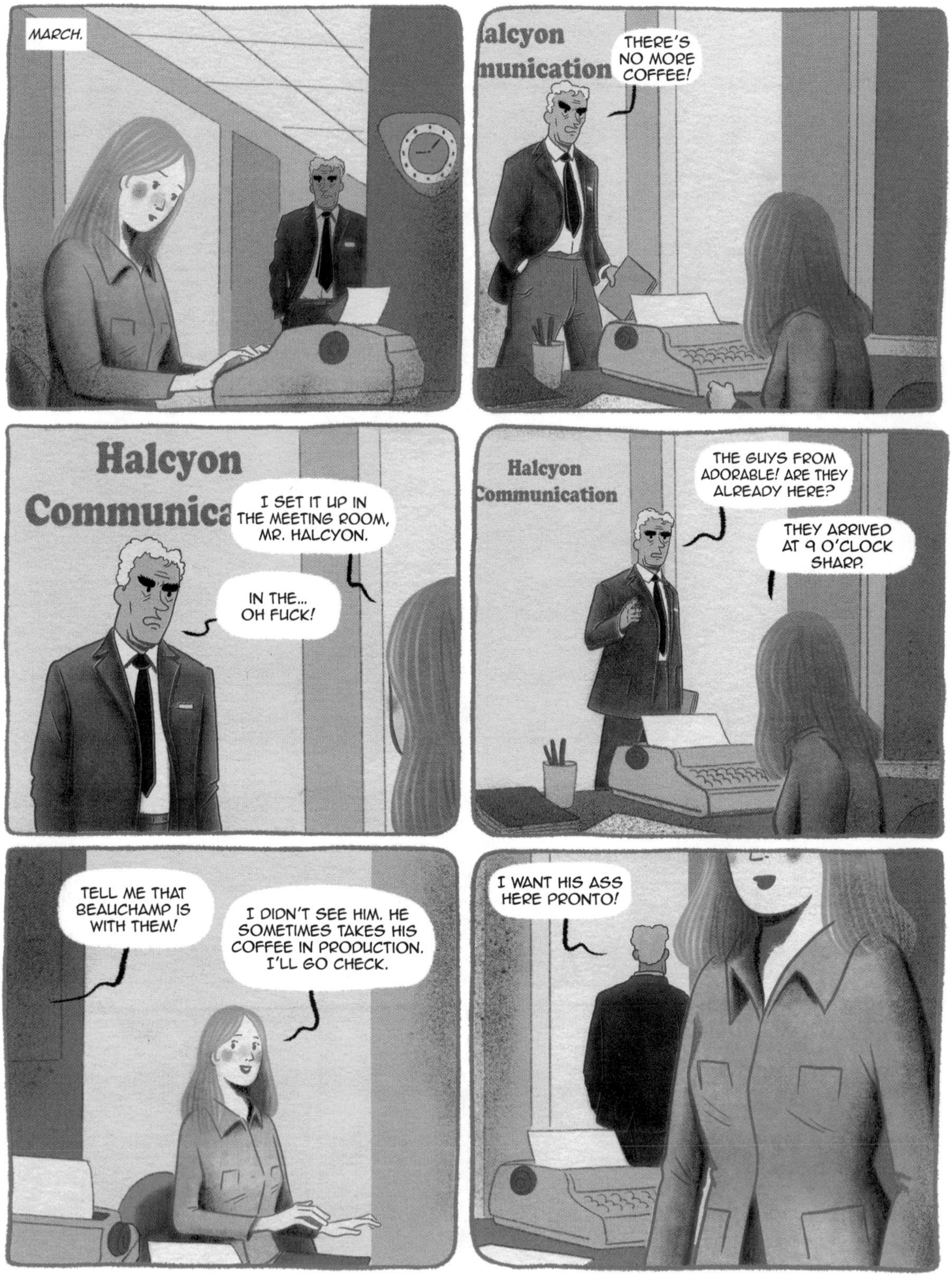
MARCH.
THERE'S NO MORE COFFEE!
I SET IT UP IN THE MEETING ROOM, MR. HALCYON.
IN THE... OH FUCK!
THE GUYS FROM ADORABLE! ARE THEY ALREADY HERE?
THEY ARRIVED AT 9 O'CLOCK SHARP.
TELL ME THAT BEAUCHAMP IS WITH THEM!
I DIDN'T SEE HIM. HE SOMETIMES TAKES HIS COFFEE IN PRODUCTION. I'LL GO CHECK.
I WANT HIS ASS HERE PRONTO!

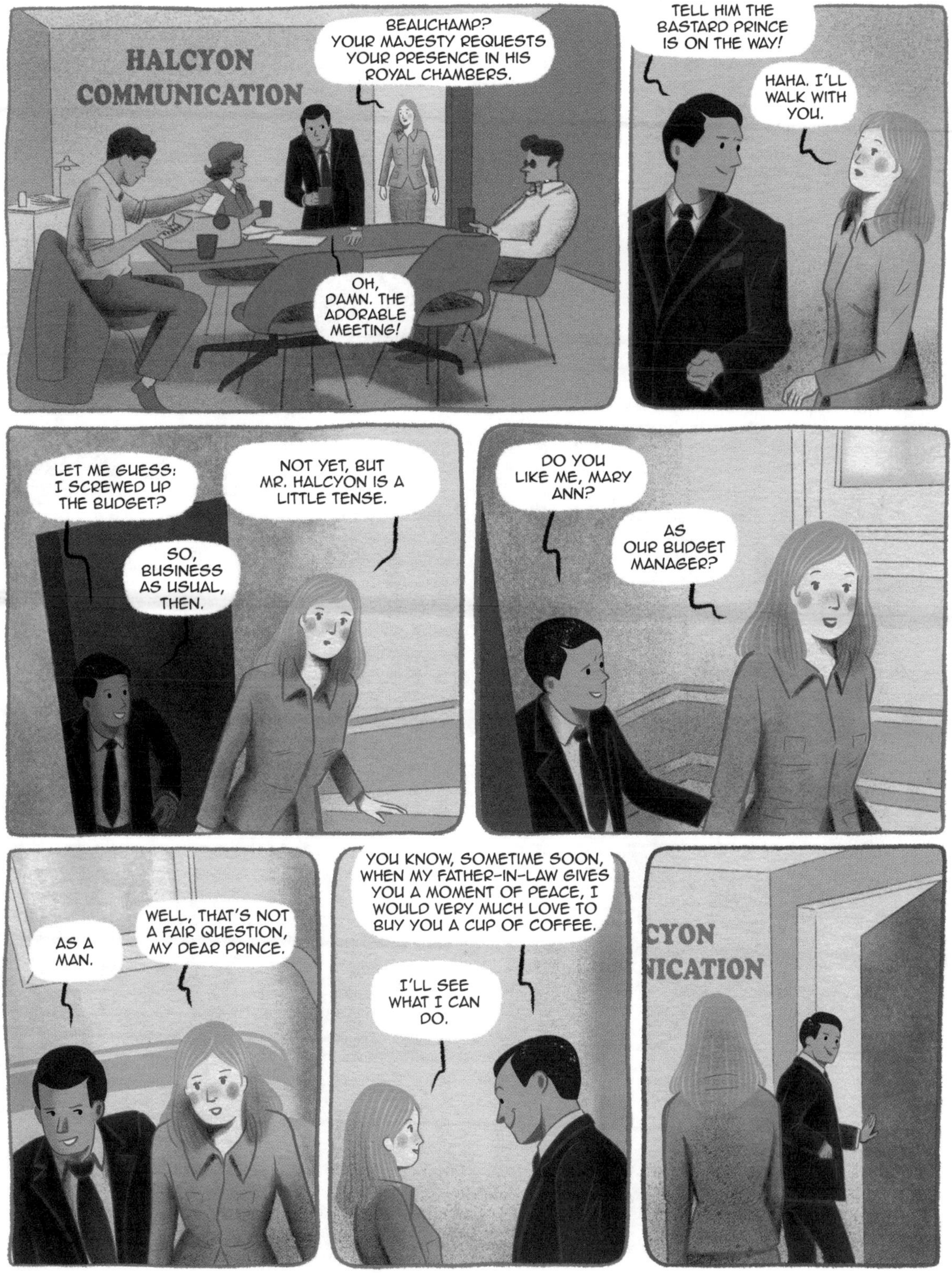
HALCYON
COMMUNICATION
BEAUCHAMP? YOUR MAJESTY REQUESTS YOUR PRESENCE IN HIS ROYAL CHAMBERS.
OH, DAMN. THE ADORABLE MEETING!
TELL HIM THE BASTARD PRINCE IS ON THE WAY!
HAHA. I'LL WALK WITH YOU.
LET ME GUESS: I SCREWED UP THE BUDGET?
NOT YET, BUT MR. HALCYON IS A LITTLE TENSE.
SO, BUSINESS AS USUAL, THEN.
DO YOU LIKE ME, MARY ANN?
AS OUR BUDGET MANAGER?
AS A MAN.
WELL, THAT'S NOT A FAIR QUESTION, MY DEAR PRINCE.
YOU KNOW, SOMETIME SOON, WHEN MY FATHER-IN-LAW GIVES YOU A MOMENT OF PEACE, I WOULD VERY MUCH LOVE TO BUY YOU A CUP OF COFFEE.
I'LL SEE WHAT I CAN DO.
CYON
NICATION

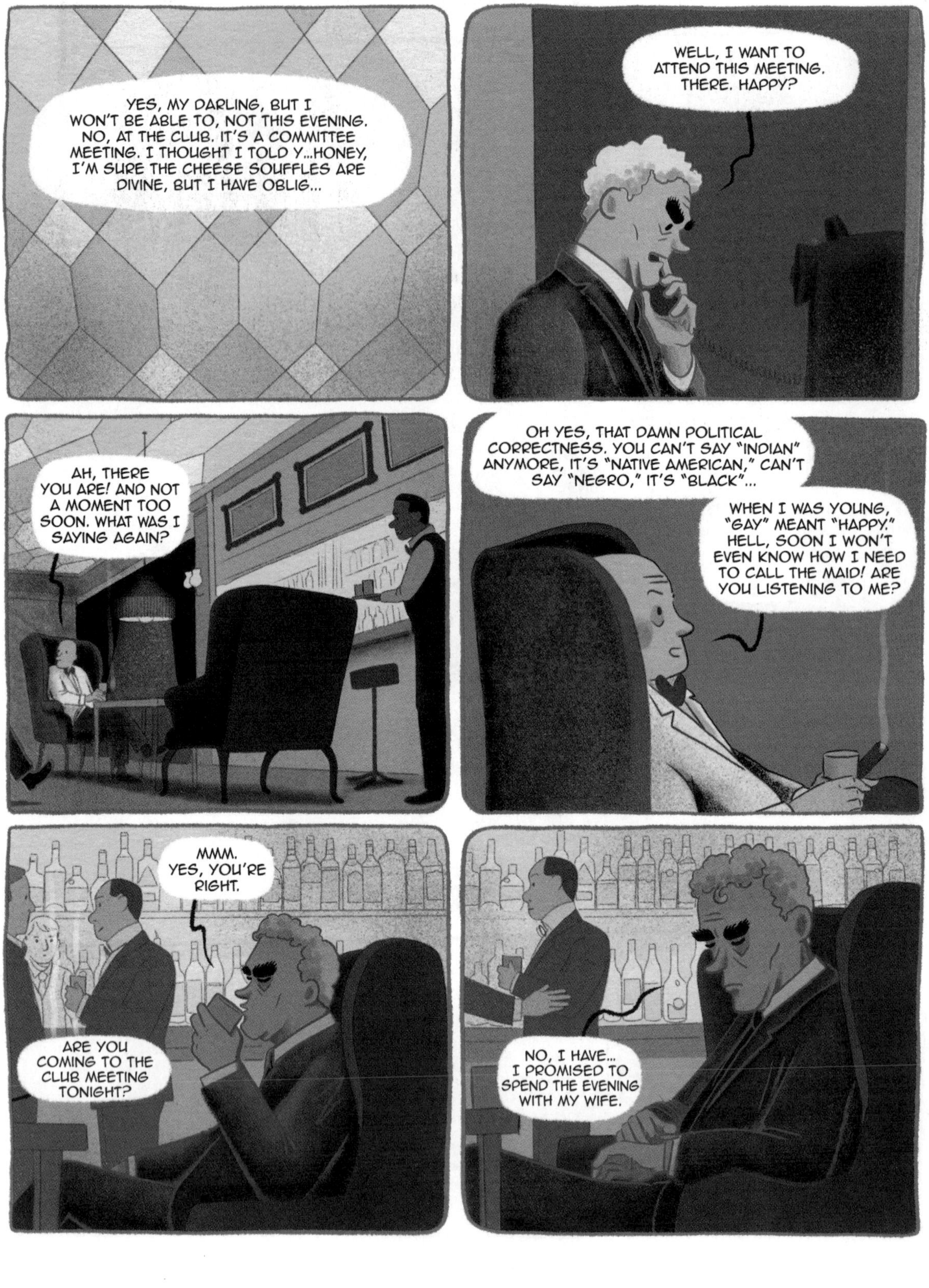
YES, MY DARLING, BUT I WON'T BE ABLE TO, NOT THIS EVENING. NO, AT THE CLUB. IT'S A COMMITTEE MEETING. I THOUGHT I TOLD Y...HONEY, I'M SURE THE CHEESE SOUFFLES ARE DIVINE, BUT I HAVE OBLIG...
WELL, I WANT TO ATTEND THIS MEETING. THERE. HAPPY?
AH, THERE YOU ARE! AND NOT A MOMENT TOO SOON. WHAT WAS I SAYING AGAIN?
OH YES, THAT DAMN POLITICAL CORRECTNESS. YOU CAN'T SAY "INDIAN" ANYMORE, IT'S "NATIVE AMERICAN," CAN'T SAY "NEGRO," IT'S "BLACK"...
WHEN I WAS YOUNG, "GAY" MEANT "HAPPY." HELL, SOON I WON'T EVEN KNOW HOW I NEED TO CALL THE MAID! ARE YOU LISTENING TO ME?
MMM. YES, YOU'RE RIGHT.
ARE YOU COMING TO THE CLUB MEETING TONIGHT?
NO, I HAVE... I PROMISED TO SPEND THE EVENING WITH MY WIFE.

I WAS SO WORRIED ABOUT DEDE. YOU NEED TO SPEAK WITH BEAUCHAMP, EDGAR. HIS BEHAVIOR HAS BEEN...OH, DIDN'T I TELL YOU?

I WAS WITH HELEN AND GLADYS IN THIS LOVELY LITTLE RESTAURANT...PAVILION? ANYHOW, THIS IS WHERE THEY TOLD ME...

NIGEL HUXTABLE, THE CONDUCTOR. YOU KNOW, THE ONE WHO'S MARRIED TO LAURA CUNNINGHAM? YOU FELL ASLEEP DURING THEIR AIDA LAST MONTH. ANYHOW, HE'S IN TOWN, EDGAR!

I MUST INVITE HIM TO MY PARTY! VIOLA WILL BE GREEN WITH JEALOUSY. SHE'LL THROW A FIT! JUST THINK OF IT! EDGAR?

HMM?

HUH? UH. FRANNIE, I DON'T...OH, YES, GO AHEAD. JUST TRY TO AVOID MAKING IT TOO EXPENSIVE.

SSSSNNNK...

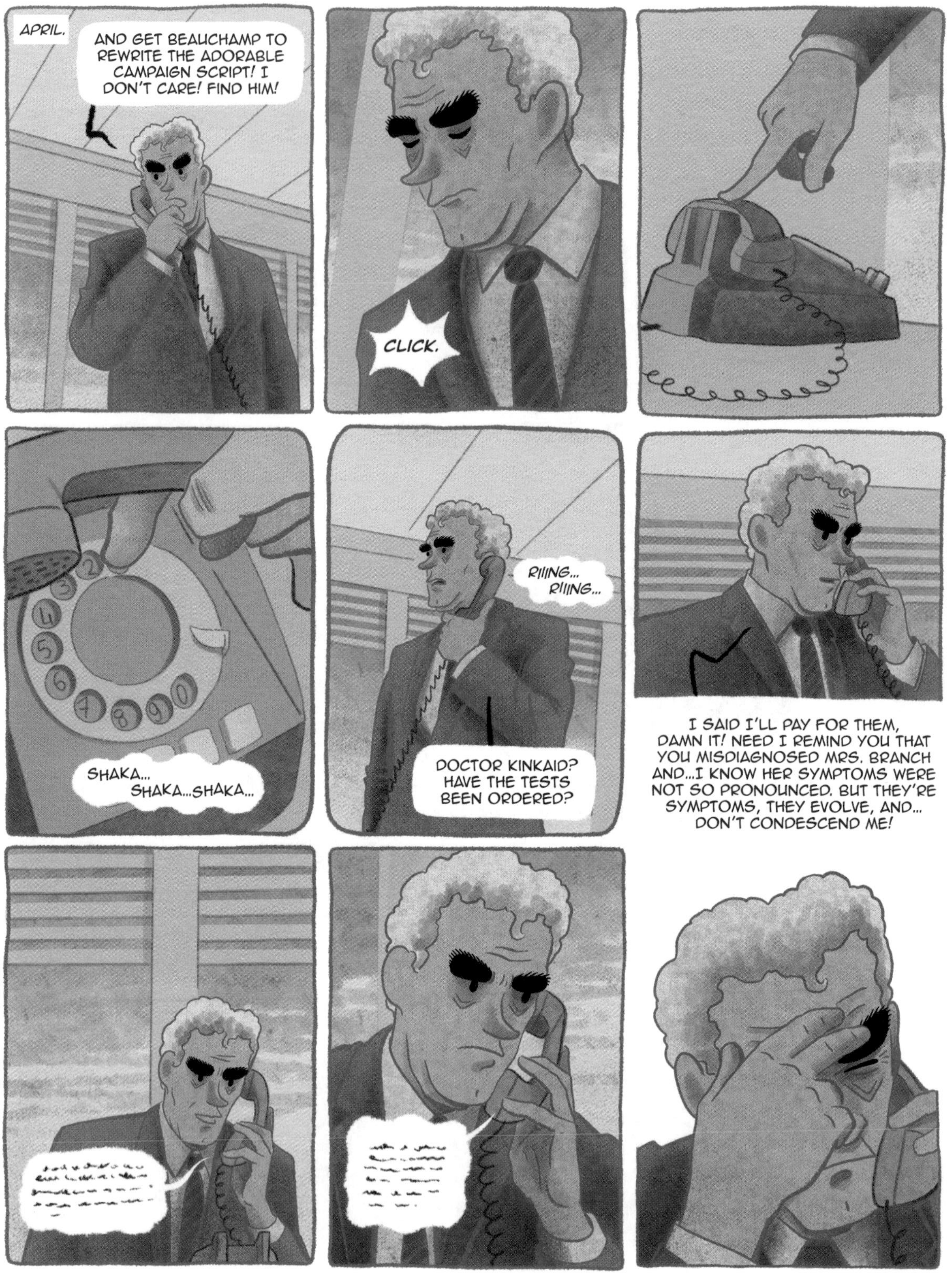
APRIL.
AND GET BEAUCHAMP TO REWRITE THE ADORABLE CAMPAIGN SCRIPT! I DON'T CARE! FIND HIM!
CLICK.
SHAKA... SHAKA...SHAKA...
RIIING... RIIING...
DOCTOR KINKAID? HAVE THE TESTS BEEN ORDERED?
I SAID I'LL PAY FOR THEM, DAMN IT! NEED I REMIND YOU THAT YOU MISDIAGNOSED MRS. BRANCH AND...I KNOW HER SYMPTOMS WERE NOT SO PRONOUNCED. BUT THEY'RE SYMPTOMS, THEY EVOLVE, AND... DON'T CONDESCEND ME!

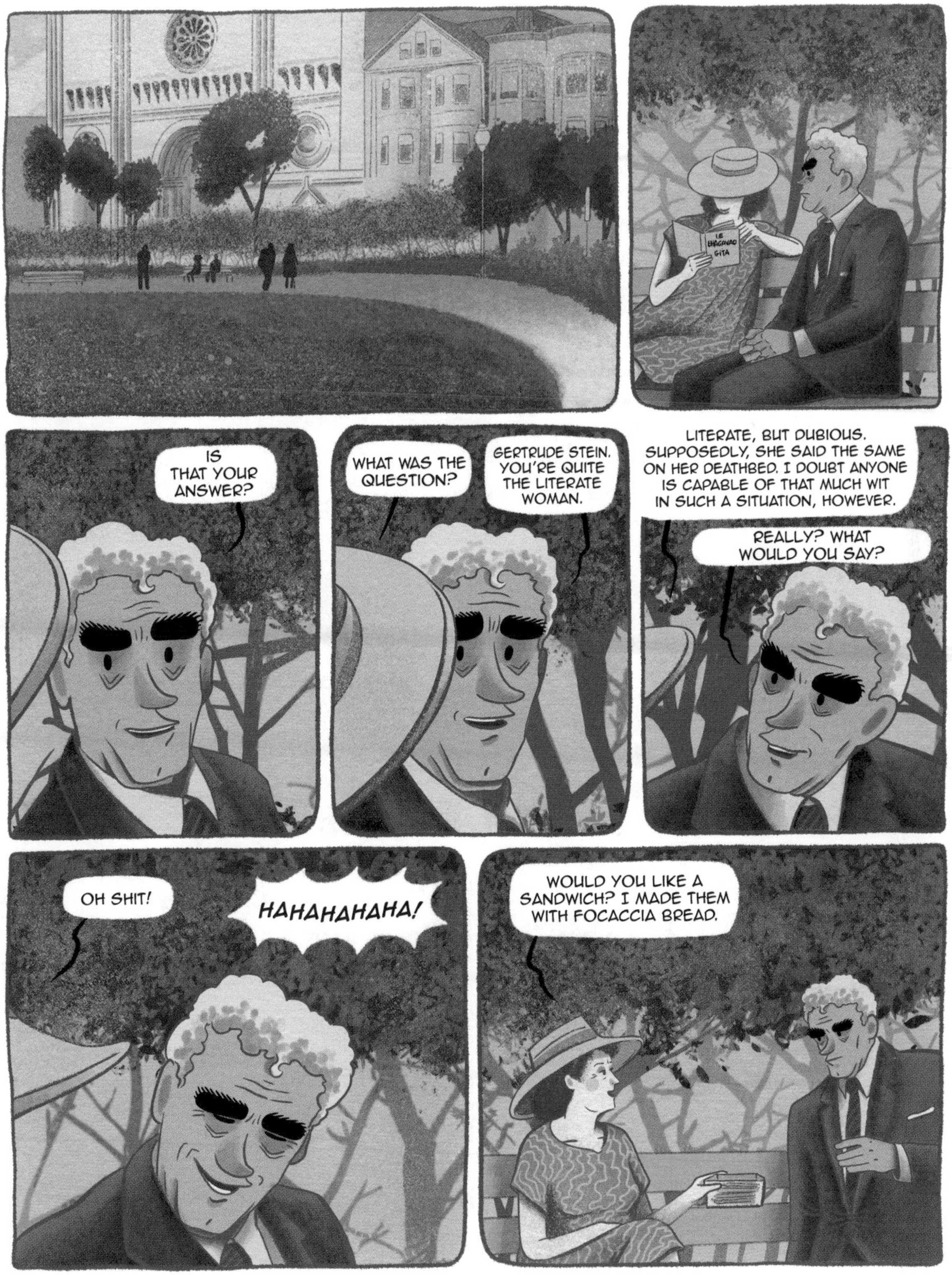
LE BHAGAVAD GITA
IS THAT YOUR ANSWER?
WHAT WAS THE QUESTION?
GERTRUDE STEIN. YOU'RE QUITE THE LITERATE WOMAN.
LITERATE, BUT DUBIOUS. SUPPOSEDLY, SHE SAID THE SAME ON HER DEATHBED. I DOUBT ANYONE IS CAPABLE OF THAT MUCH WIT IN SUCH A SITUATION, HOWEVER.
REALLY? WHAT WOULD YOU SAY?
OH SHIT!
HAHAHAHAHA!
WOULD YOU LIKE A SANDWICH? I MADE THEM WITH FOCACCIA BREAD.

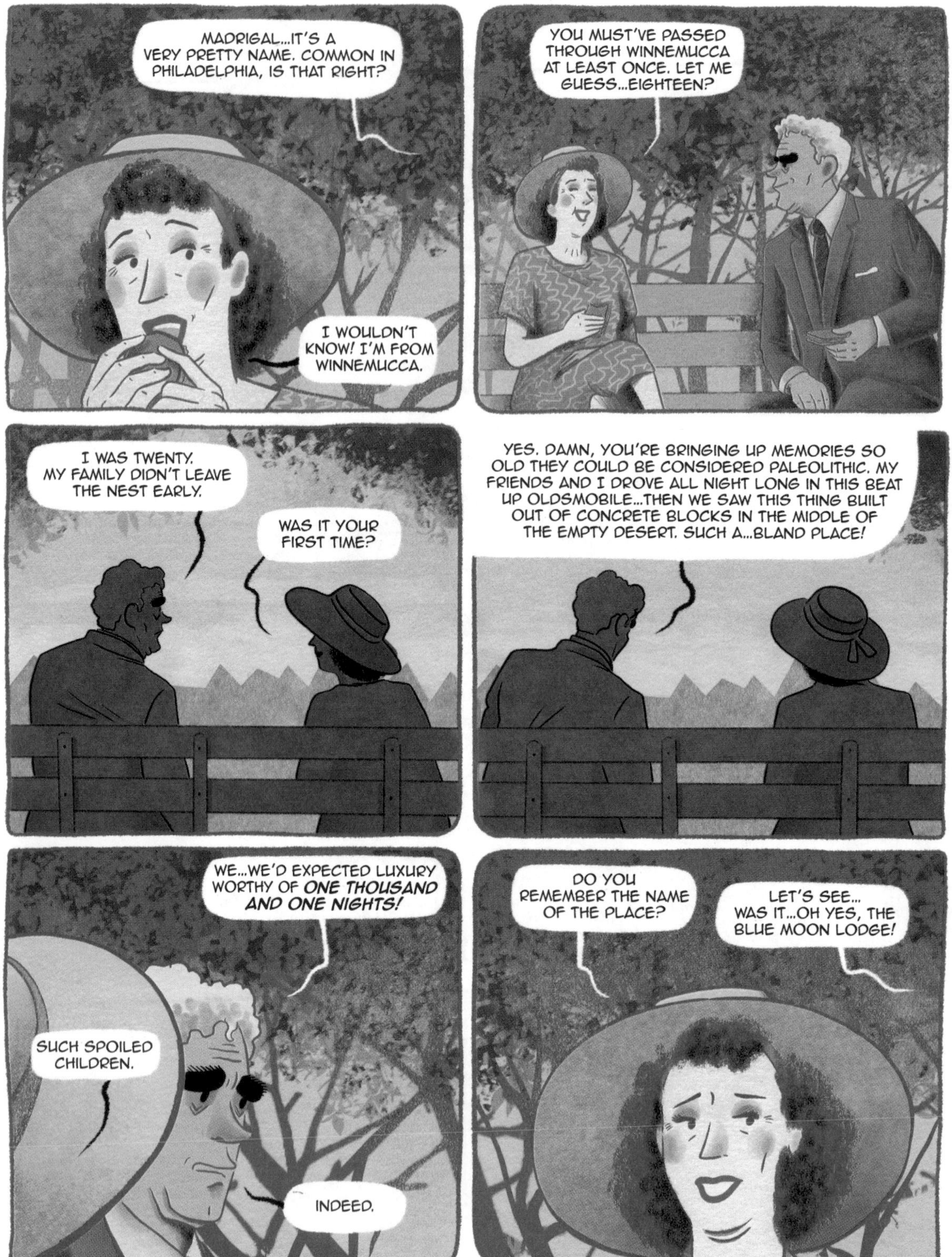
MADRIGAL...IT'S A VERY PRETTY NAME. COMMON IN PHILADELPHIA, IS THAT RIGHT?
I WOULDN'T KNOW! I'M FROM WINNEMUCCA.
YOU MUST'VE PASSED THROUGH WINNEMUCCA AT LEAST ONCE. LET ME GUESS...EIGHTEEN?
I WAS TWENTY. MY FAMILY DIDN'T LEAVE THE NEST EARLY.
WAS IT YOUR FIRST TIME?
YES. DAMN, YOU'RE BRINGING UP MEMORIES SO OLD THEY COULD BE CONSIDERED PALEOLITHIC. MY FRIENDS AND I DROVE ALL NIGHT LONG IN THIS BEAT UP OLDSMOBILE...THEN WE SAW THIS THING BUILT OUT OF CONCRETE BLOCKS IN THE MIDDLE OF THE EMPTY DESERT. SUCH A...BLAND PLACE!
WE...WE'D EXPECTED LUXURY WORTHY OF ***ONE THOUSAND AND ONE NIGHTS!***
SUCH SPOILED CHILDREN.
INDEED.
DO YOU REMEMBER THE NAME OF THE PLACE?
LET'S SEE... WAS IT...OH YES, THE BLUE MOON LODGE!

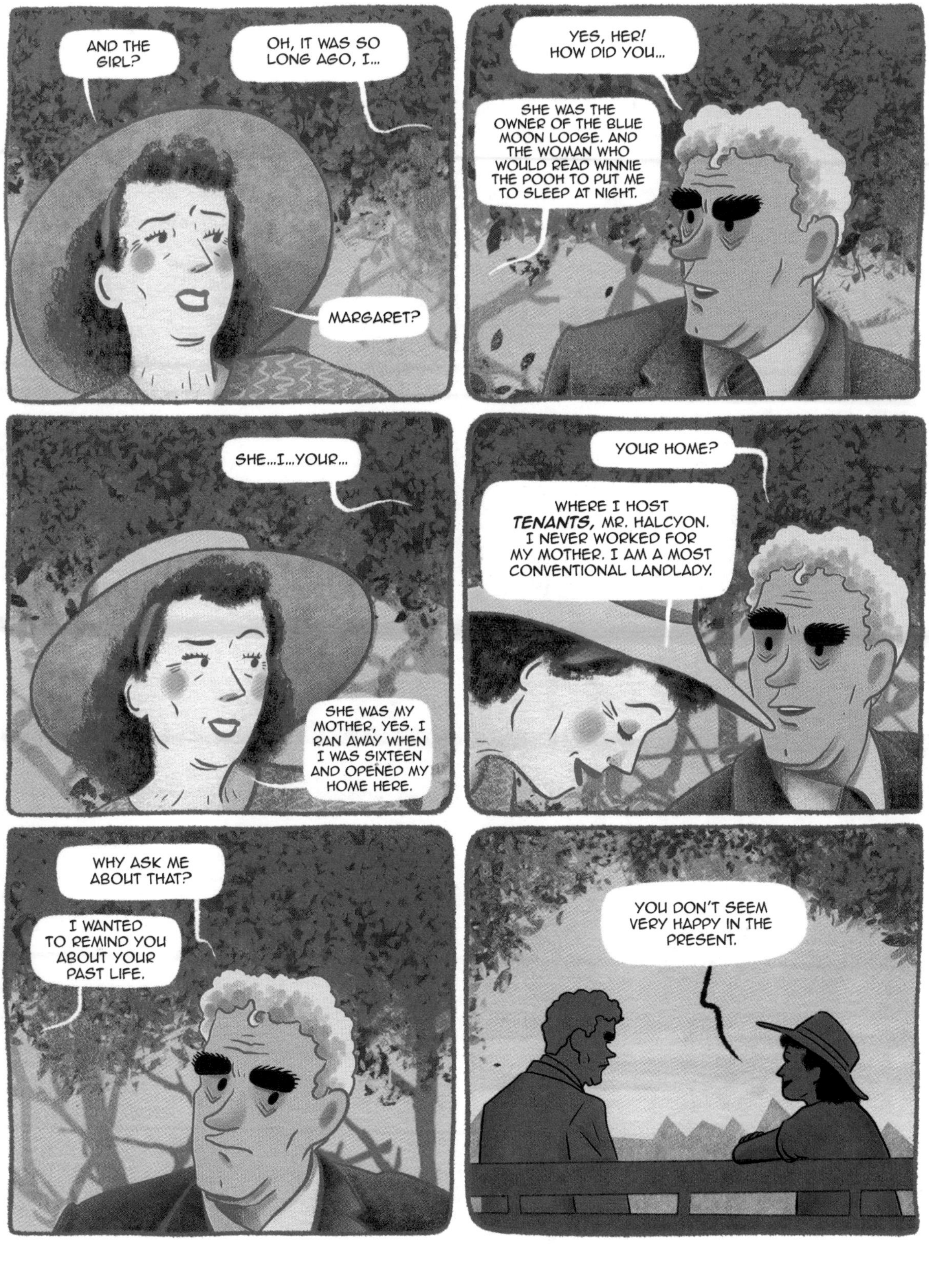
AND THE GIRL?
OH, IT WAS SO LONG AGO, I...
MARGARET?
YES, HER! HOW DID YOU...
SHE WAS THE OWNER OF THE BLUE MOON LODGE. AND THE WOMAN WHO WOULD READ WINNIE THE POOH TO PUT ME TO SLEEP AT NIGHT.
SHE...I...YOUR...
SHE WAS MY MOTHER, YES. I RAN AWAY WHEN I WAS SIXTEEN AND OPENED MY HOME HERE.
YOUR HOME?
WHERE I HOST *TENANTS,* MR. HALCYON. I NEVER WORKED FOR MY MOTHER. I AM A MOST CONVENTIONAL LANDLADY.
WHY ASK ME ABOUT THAT?
I WANTED TO REMIND YOU ABOUT YOUR PAST LIFE.
YOU DON'T SEEM VERY HAPPY IN THE PRESENT.

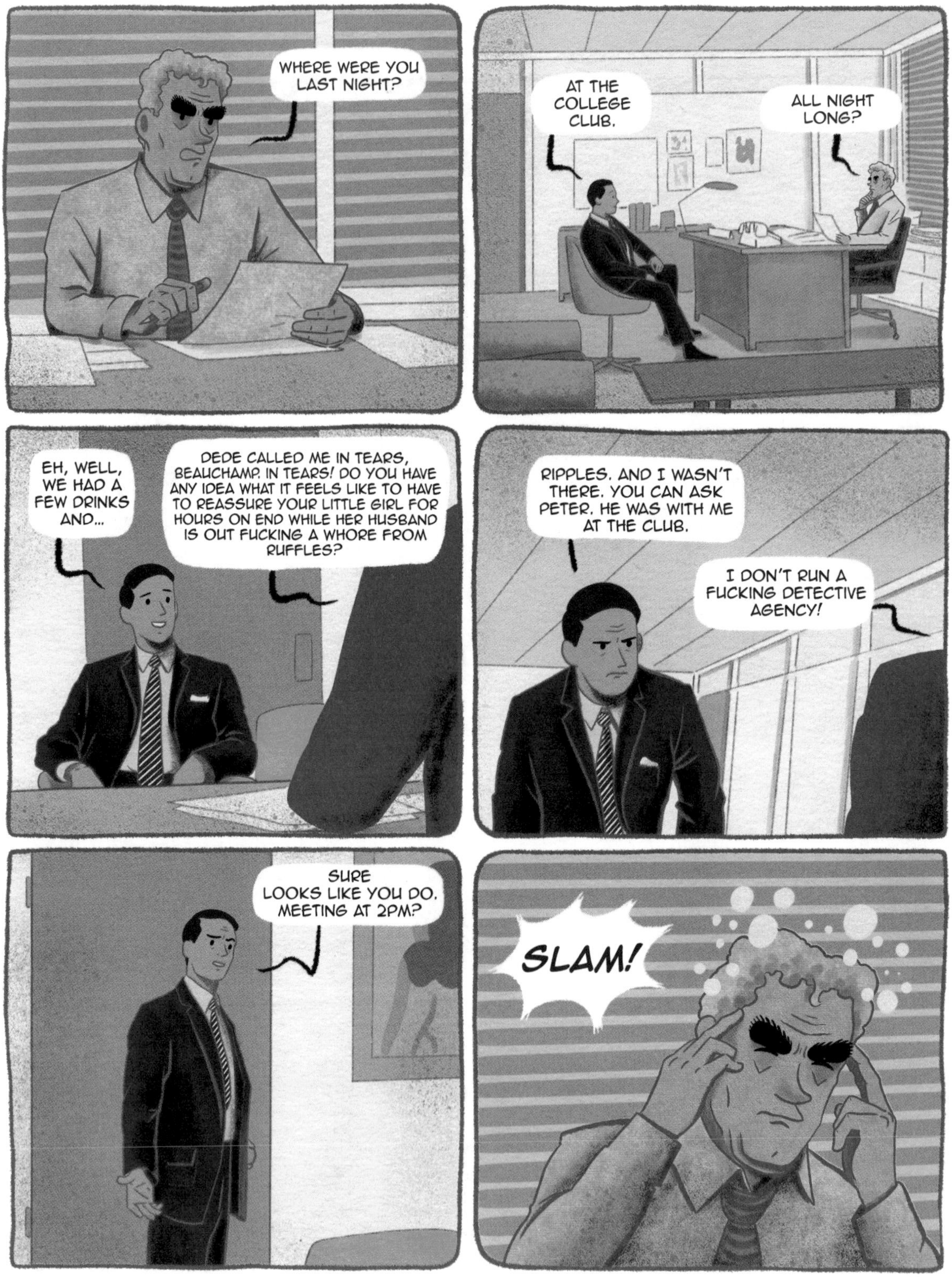
WHERE WERE YOU LAST NIGHT?
AT THE COLLEGE CLUB.
ALL NIGHT LONG?
EH, WELL, WE HAD A FEW DRINKS AND...
DEDE CALLED ME IN TEARS, BEAUCHAMP. IN TEARS! DO YOU HAVE ANY IDEA WHAT IT FEELS LIKE TO HAVE TO REASSURE YOUR LITTLE GIRL FOR HOURS ON END WHILE HER HUSBAND IS OUT FUCKING A WHORE FROM RUFFLES?
RIPPLES. AND I WASN'T THERE. YOU CAN ASK PETER. HE WAS WITH ME AT THE CLUB.
I DON'T RUN A FUCKING DETECTIVE AGENCY!
SURE LOOKS LIKE YOU DO. MEETING AT 2PM?
SLAM!

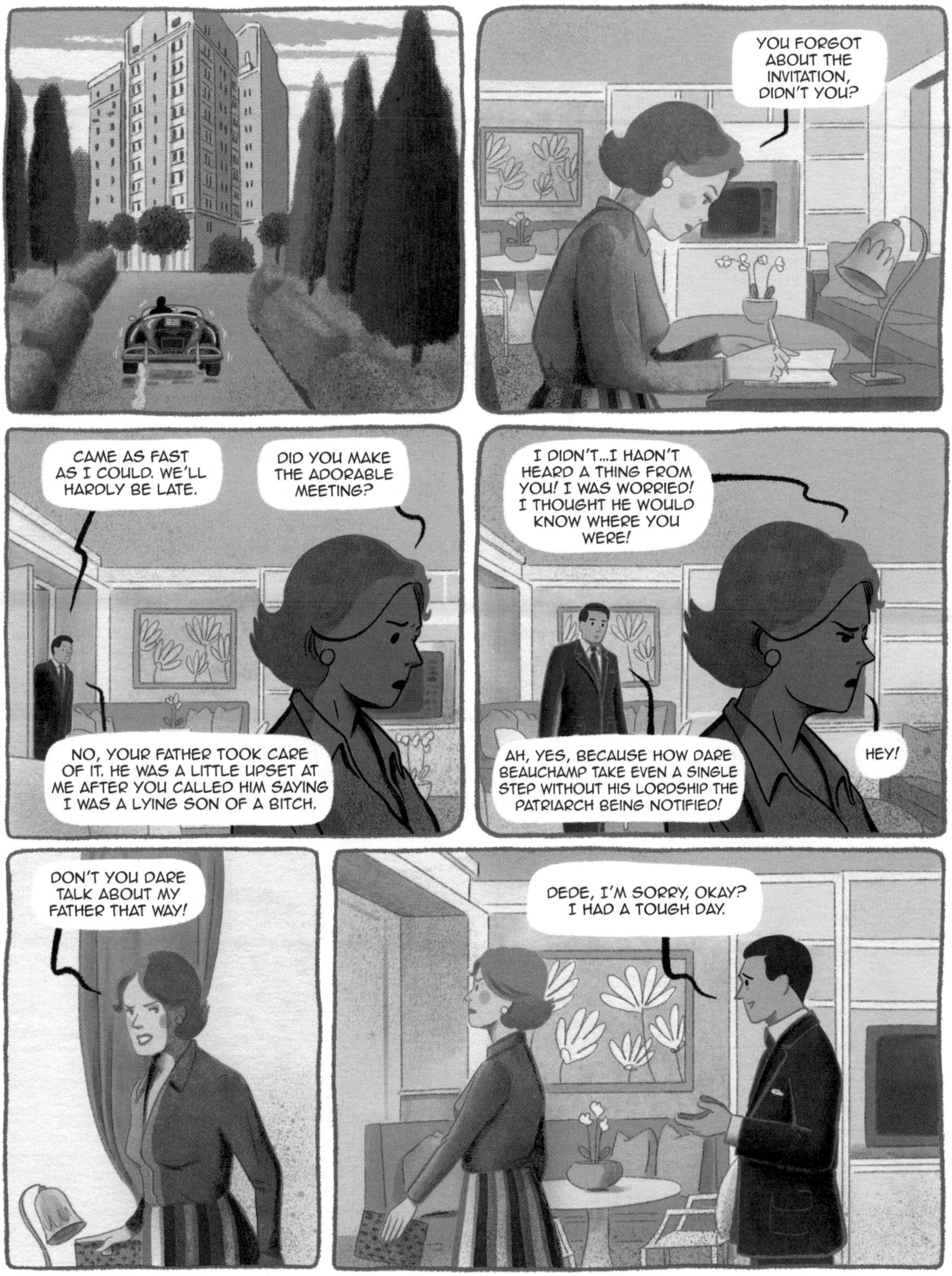

YOU FORGOT ABOUT THE INVITATION, DIDN'T YOU?
CAME AS FAST AS I COULD. WE'LL HARDLY BE LATE.
DID YOU MAKE THE ADORABLE MEETING?
NO, YOUR FATHER TOOK CARE OF IT. HE WAS A LITTLE UPSET AT ME AFTER YOU CALLED HIM SAYING I WAS A LYING SON OF A BITCH.
I DIDN'T...I HADN'T HEARD A THING FROM YOU! I WAS WORRIED! I THOUGHT HE WOULD KNOW WHERE YOU WERE!
AH, YES, BECAUSE HOW DARE BEAUCHAMP TAKE EVEN A SINGLE STEP WITHOUT HIS LORDSHIP THE PATRIARCH BEING NOTIFIED!
HEY!
DON'T YOU DARE TALK ABOUT MY FATHER THAT WAY!
DEDE, I'M SORRY, OKAY? I HAD A TOUGH DAY.

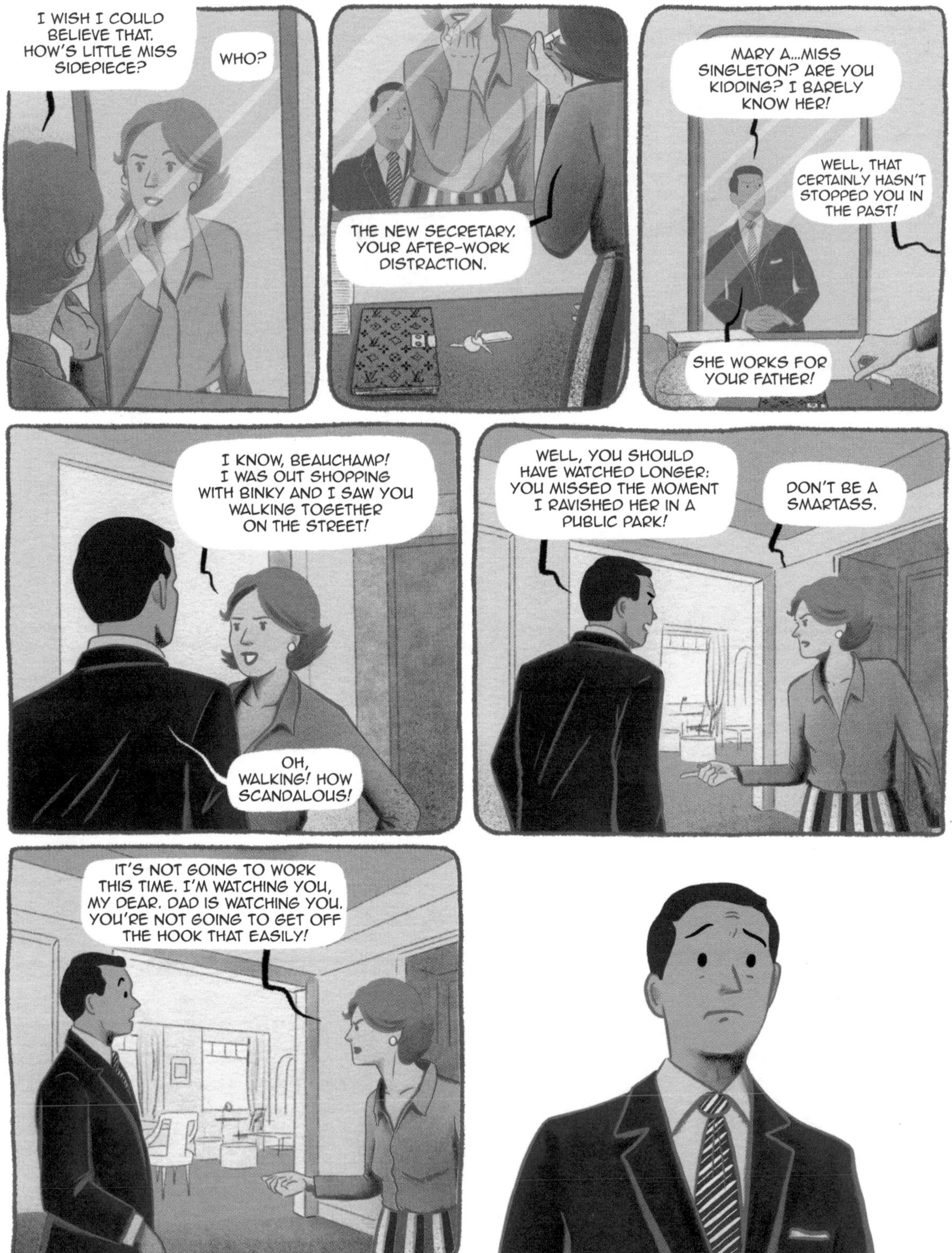
I WISH I COULD BELIEVE THAT. HOW'S LITTLE MISS SIDEPIECE?
WHO?
THE NEW SECRETARY. YOUR AFTER-WORK DISTRACTION.
MARY A...MISS SINGLETON? ARE YOU KIDDING? I BARELY KNOW HER!
WELL, THAT CERTAINLY HASN'T STOPPED YOU IN THE PAST!
SHE WORKS FOR YOUR FATHER!
I KNOW, BEAUCHAMP! I WAS OUT SHOPPING WITH BINKY AND I SAW YOU WALKING TOGETHER ON THE STREET!
OH, WALKING! HOW SCANDALOUS!
WELL, YOU SHOULD HAVE WATCHED LONGER: YOU MISSED THE MOMENT I RAVISHED HER IN A PUBLIC PARK!
DON'T BE A SMARTASS.
IT'S NOT GOING TO WORK THIS TIME. I'M WATCHING YOU, MY DEAR. DAD IS WATCHING YOU. YOU'RE NOT GOING TO GET OFF THE HOOK THAT EASILY!

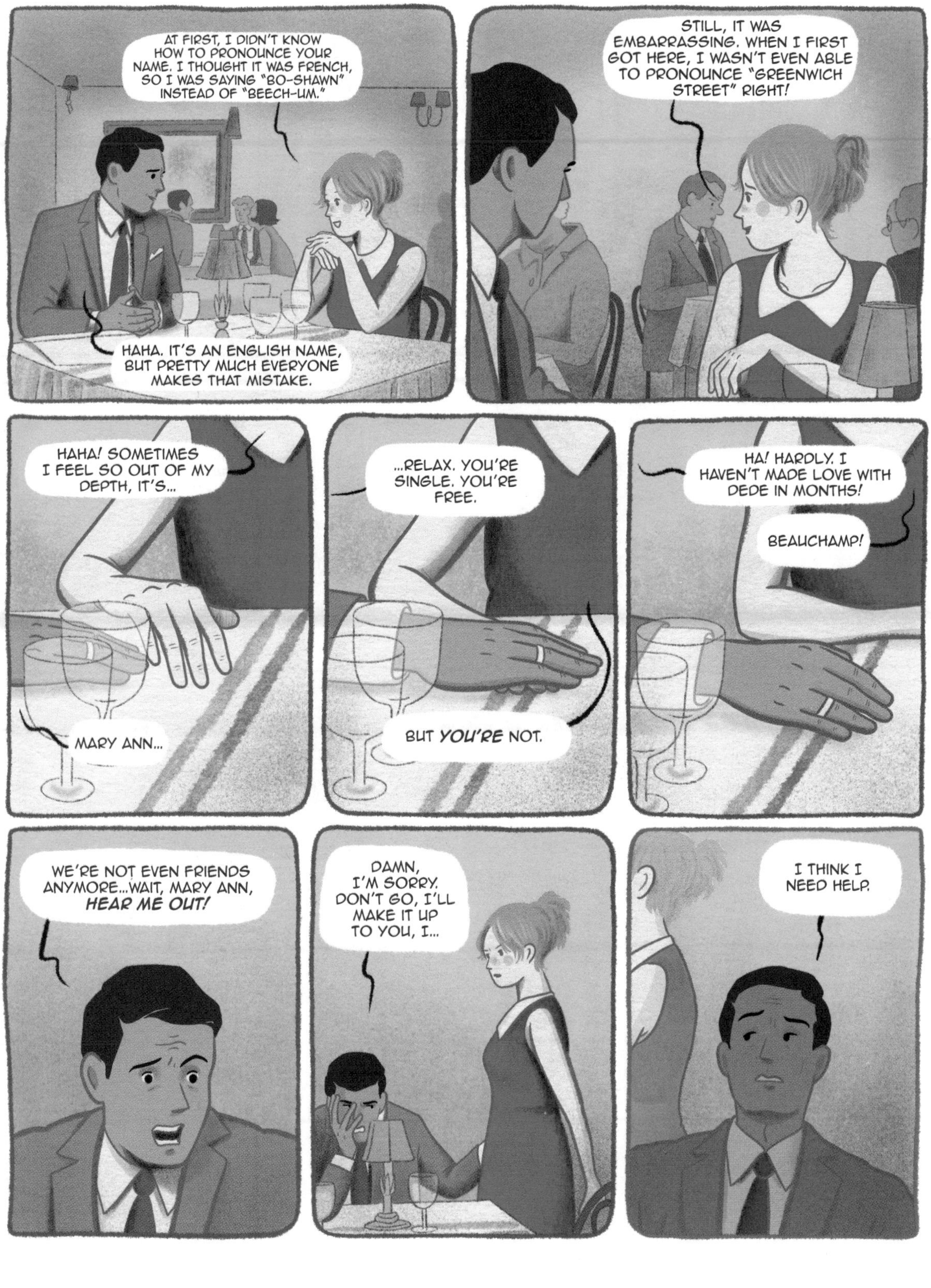
AT FIRST, I DIDN'T KNOW HOW TO PRONOUNCE YOUR NAME. I THOUGHT IT WAS FRENCH, SO I WAS SAYING "BO-SHAWN" INSTEAD OF "BEECH-UM."
HAHA. IT'S AN ENGLISH NAME, BUT PRETTY MUCH EVERYONE MAKES THAT MISTAKE.
STILL, IT WAS EMBARRASSING. WHEN I FIRST GOT HERE, I WASN'T EVEN ABLE TO PRONOUNCE "GREENWICH STREET" RIGHT!
HAHA! SOMETIMES I FEEL SO OUT OF MY DEPTH, IT'S...
MARY ANN...
...RELAX. YOU'RE SINGLE. YOU'RE FREE.
BUT *YOU'RE* NOT.
HA! HARDLY. I HAVEN'T MADE LOVE WITH DEDE IN MONTHS!
BEAUCHAMP!
WE'RE NOT EVEN FRIENDS ANYMORE...WAIT, MARY ANN, **HEAR ME OUT!**
DAMN, I'M SORRY. DON'T GO, I'LL MAKE IT UP TO YOU, I...
I THINK I NEED HELP.

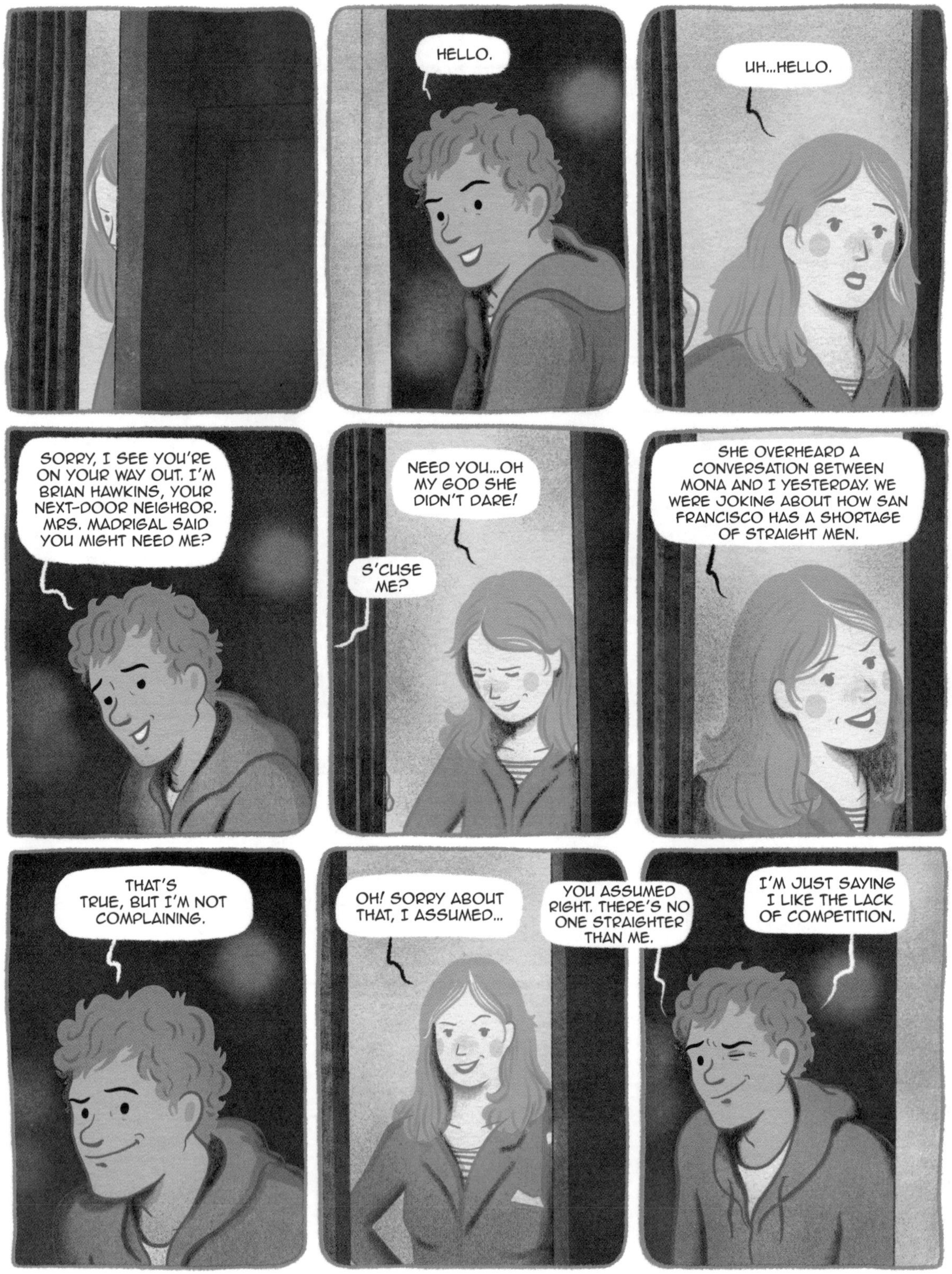
HELLO.
UH...HELLO.
SORRY, I SEE YOU'RE ON YOUR WAY OUT. I'M BRIAN HAWKINS, YOUR NEXT-DOOR NEIGHBOR. MRS. MADRIGAL SAID YOU MIGHT NEED ME?
NEED YOU...OH MY GOD SHE DIDN'T DARE!
S'CUSE ME?
SHE OVERHEARD A CONVERSATION BETWEEN MONA AND I YESTERDAY. WE WERE JOKING ABOUT HOW SAN FRANCISCO HAS A SHORTAGE OF STRAIGHT MEN.
THAT'S TRUE, BUT I'M NOT COMPLAINING.
OH! SORRY ABOUT THAT, I ASSUMED...
YOU ASSUMED RIGHT. THERE'S NO ONE STRAIGHTER THAN ME.
I'M JUST SAYING I LIKE THE LACK OF COMPETITION.

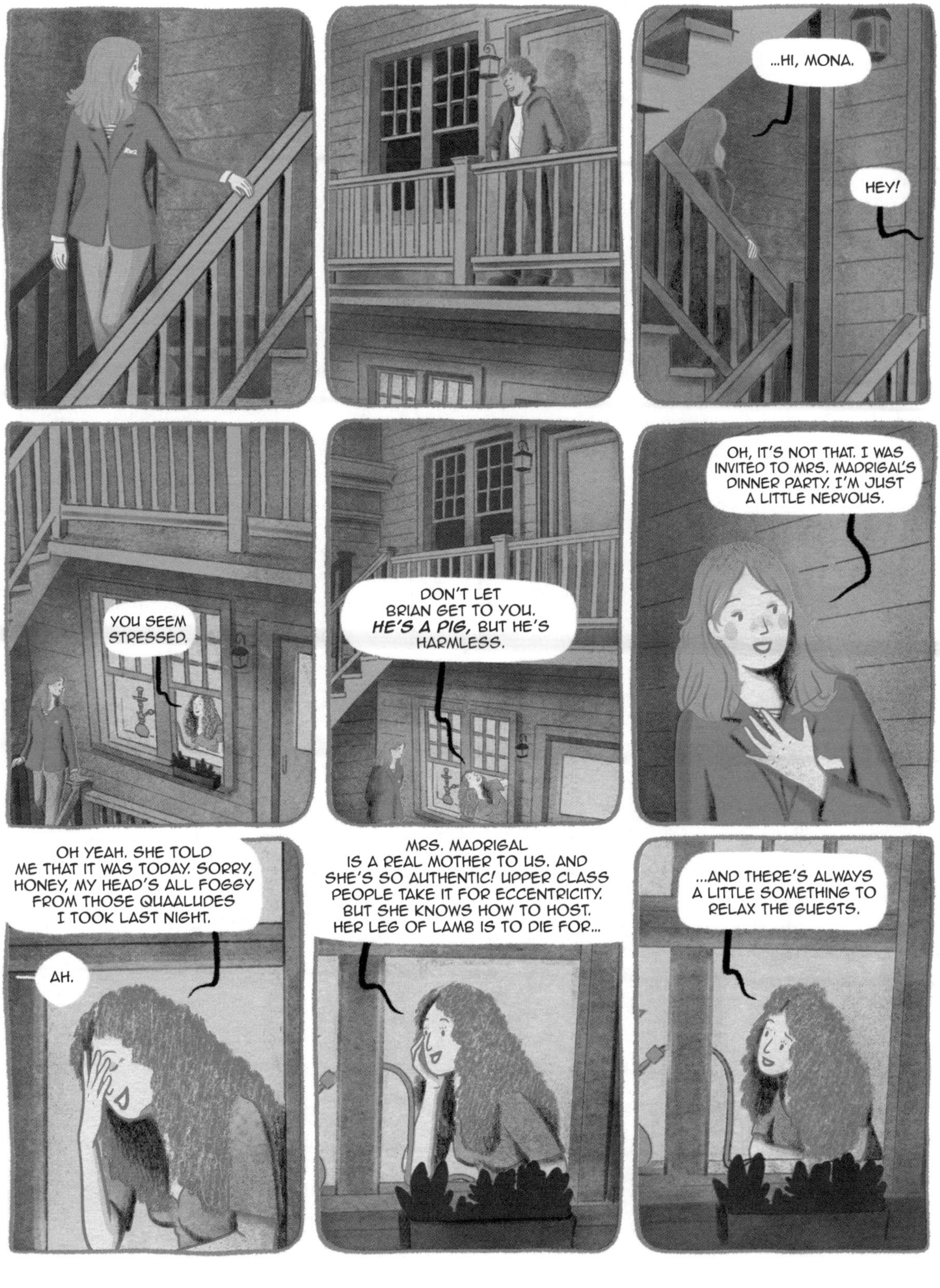
...HI, MONA.
HEY!
YOU SEEM STRESSED.
DON'T LET BRIAN GET TO YOU. HE'S A PIG, BUT HE'S HARMLESS.
OH, IT'S NOT THAT. I WAS INVITED TO MRS. MADRIGAL'S DINNER PARTY. I'M JUST A LITTLE NERVOUS.
OH YEAH. SHE TOLD ME THAT IT WAS TODAY. SORRY, HONEY, MY HEAD'S ALL FOGGY FROM THOSE QUAALUDES I TOOK LAST NIGHT.
AH.
MRS. MADRIGAL IS A REAL MOTHER TO US. AND SHE'S SO AUTHENTIC! UPPER CLASS PEOPLE TAKE IT FOR ECCENTRICITY. BUT SHE KNOWS HOW TO HOST. HER LEG OF LAMB IS TO DIE FOR...
...AND THERE'S ALWAYS A LITTLE SOMETHING TO RELAX THE GUESTS.

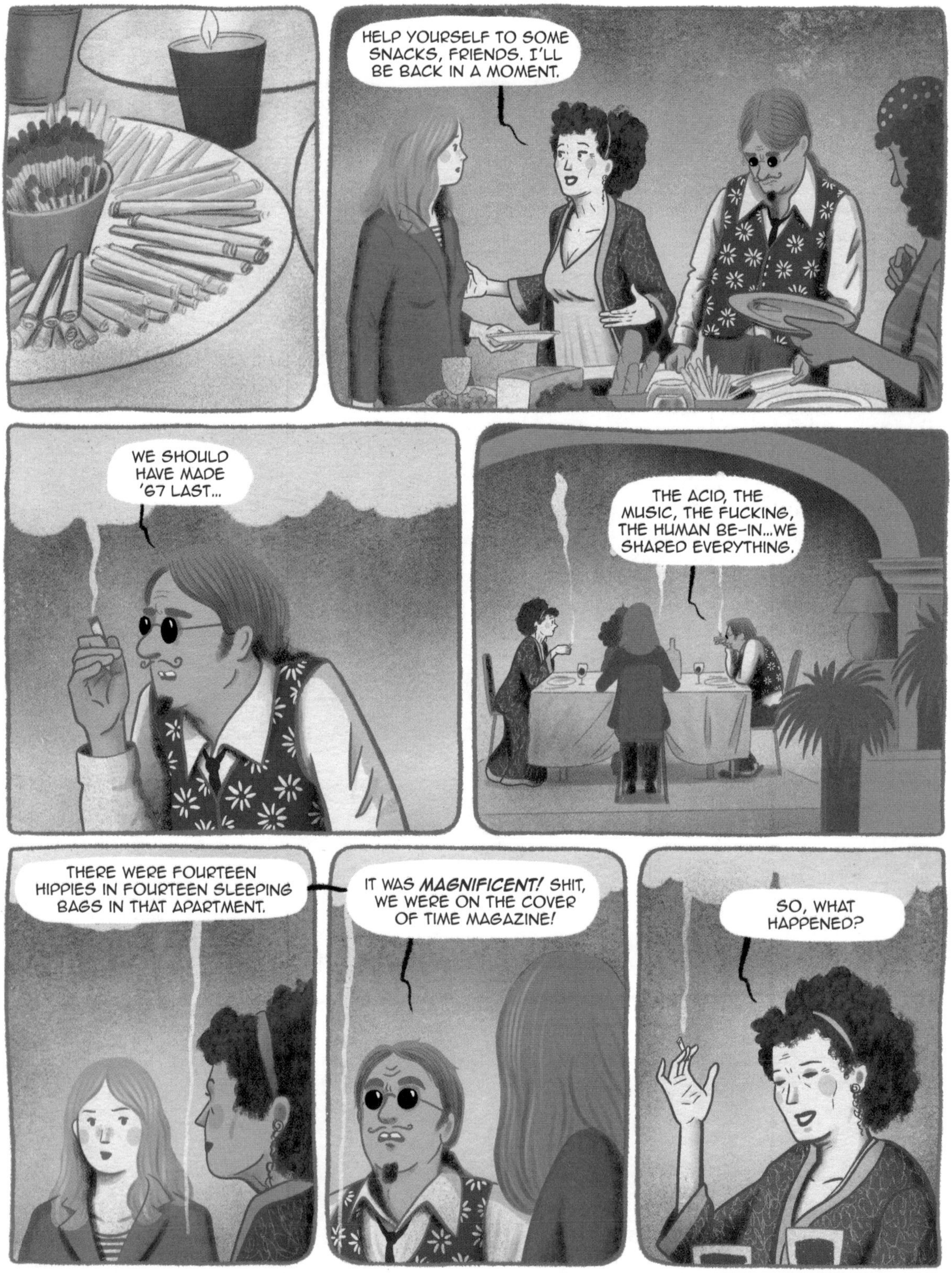
HELP YOURSELF TO SOME SNACKS, FRIENDS. I'LL BE BACK IN A MOMENT.
WE SHOULD HAVE MADE '67 LAST...
THE ACID, THE MUSIC, THE FUCKING, THE HUMAN BE-IN...WE SHARED EVERYTHING.
THERE WERE FOURTEEN HIPPIES IN FOURTEEN SLEEPING BAGS IN THAT APARTMENT.
IT WAS *MAGNIFICENT!* SHIT, WE WERE ON THE COVER OF TIME MAGAZINE!
SO, WHAT HAPPENED?

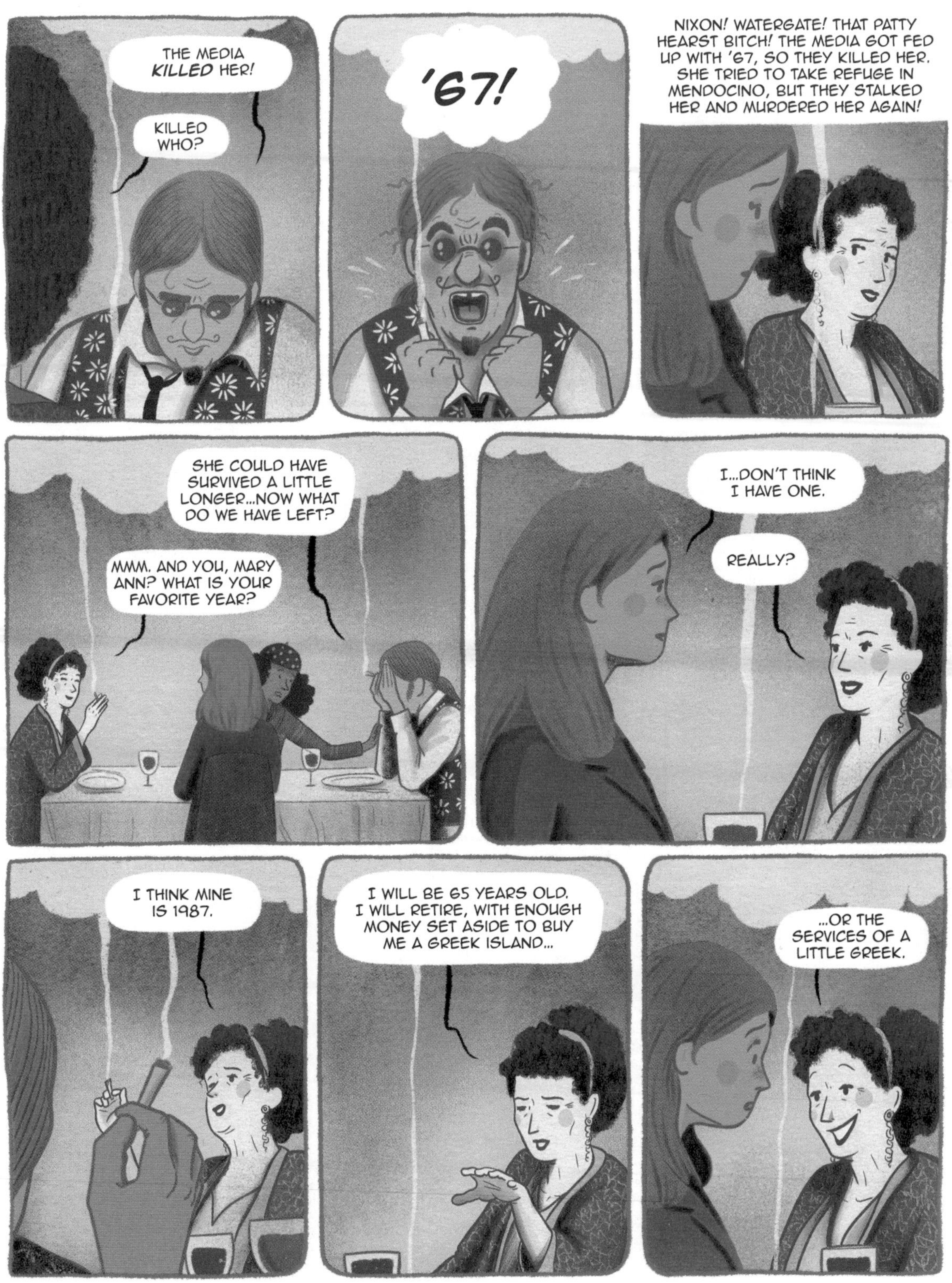
THE MEDIA *KILLED* HER!
KILLED WHO?
'67!
NIXON! WATERGATE! THAT PATTY HEARST BITCH! THE MEDIA GOT FED UP WITH '67, SO THEY KILLED HER. SHE TRIED TO TAKE REFUGE IN MENDOCINO, BUT THEY STALKED HER AND MURDERED HER AGAIN!
SHE COULD HAVE SURVIVED A LITTLE LONGER...NOW WHAT DO WE HAVE LEFT?
MMM. AND YOU, MARY ANN? WHAT IS YOUR FAVORITE YEAR?
I...DON'T THINK I HAVE ONE.
REALLY?
I THINK MINE IS 1987.
I WILL BE 65 YEARS OLD. I WILL RETIRE, WITH ENOUGH MONEY SET ASIDE TO BUY ME A GREEK ISLAND...
...OR THE SERVICES OF A LITTLE GREEK.

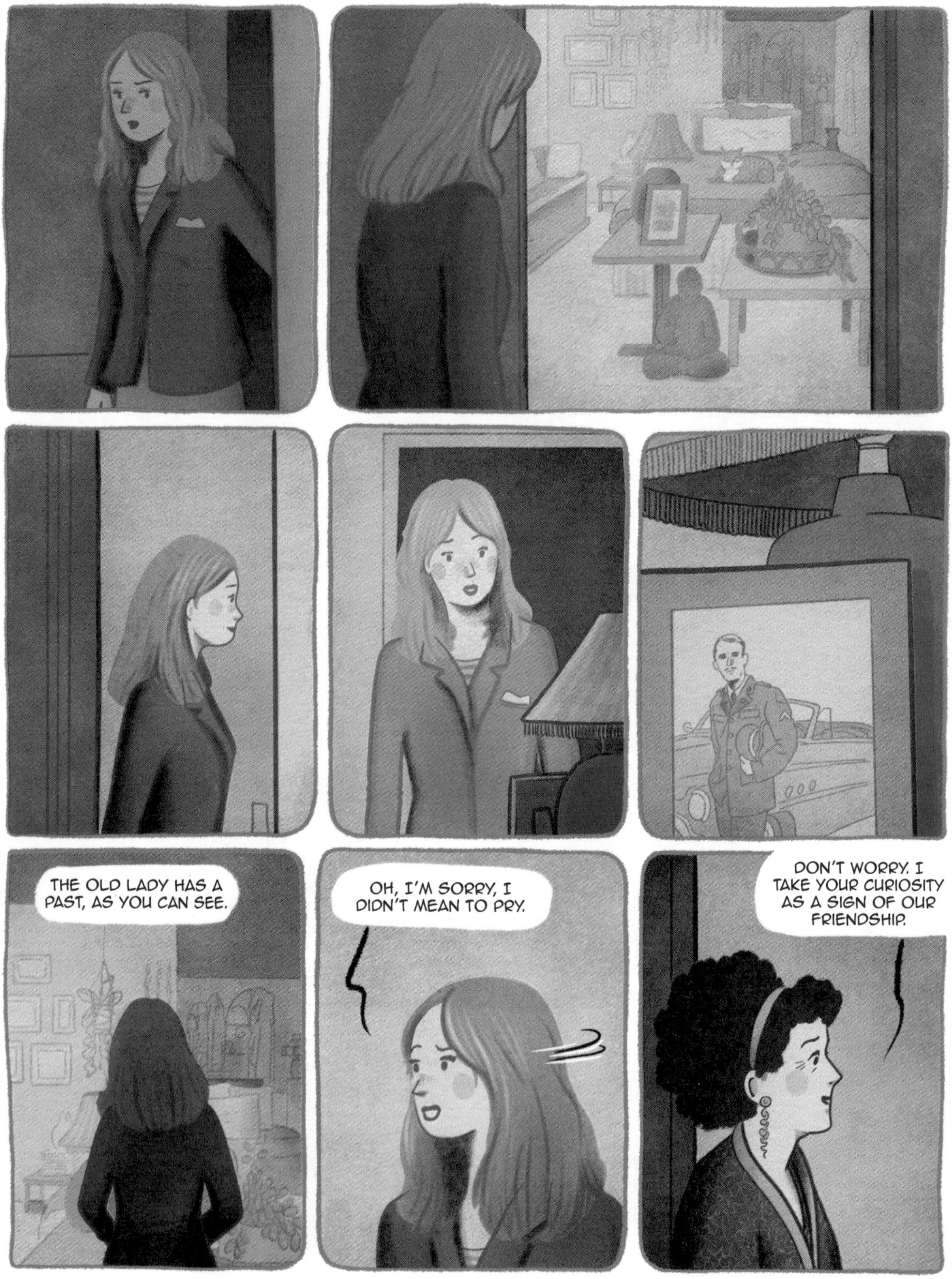
THE OLD LADY HAS A PAST, AS YOU CAN SEE.
OH, I'M SORRY, I DIDN'T MEAN TO PRY.
DON'T WORRY. I TAKE YOUR CURIOSITY AS A SIGN OF OUR FRIENDSHIP.

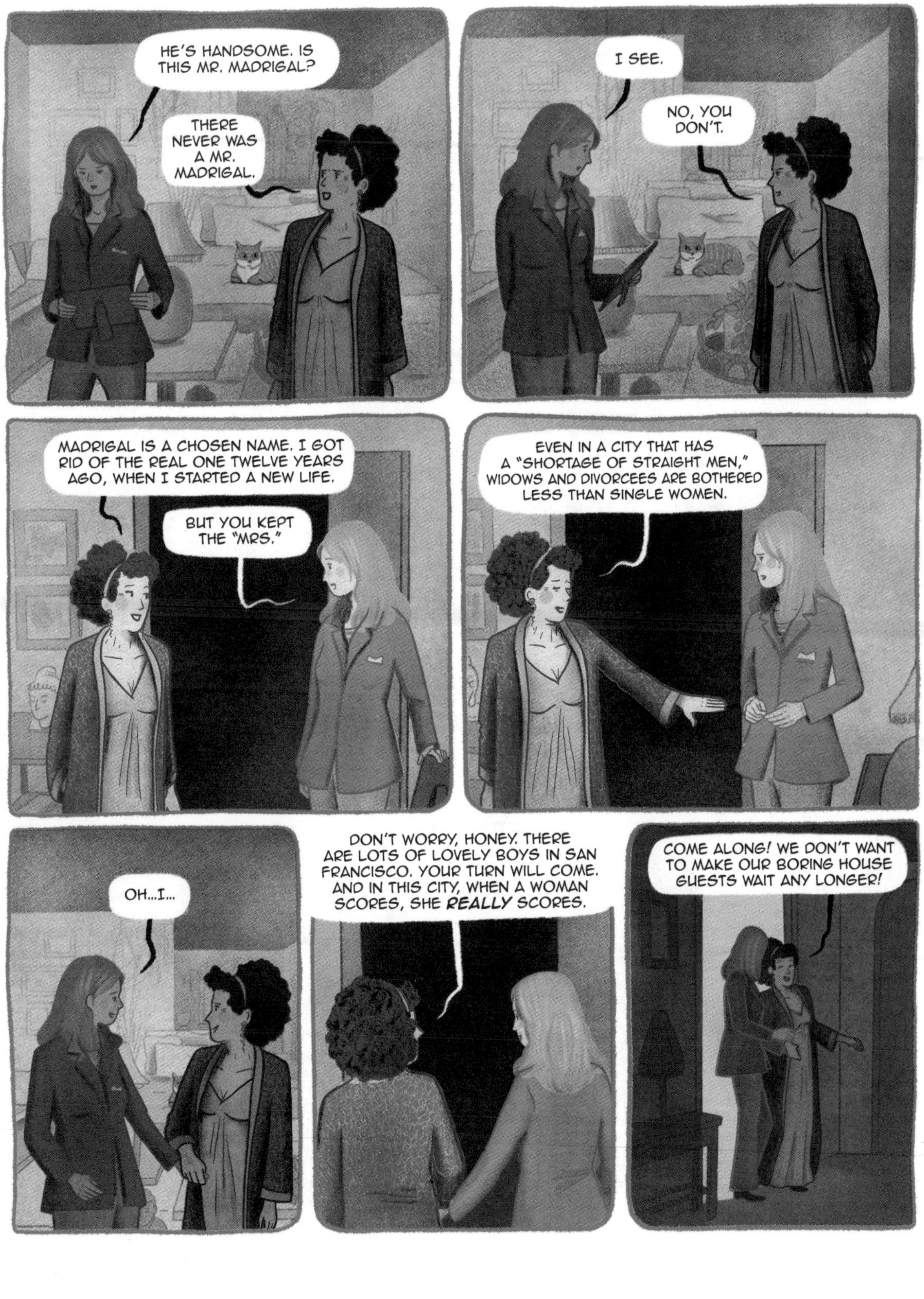
HE'S HANDSOME. IS THIS MR. MADRIGAL?
THERE NEVER WAS A MR. MADRIGAL.
I SEE.
NO, YOU DON'T.
MADRIGAL IS A CHOSEN NAME. I GOT RID OF THE REAL ONE TWELVE YEARS AGO, WHEN I STARTED A NEW LIFE.
BUT YOU KEPT THE "MRS."
EVEN IN A CITY THAT HAS A "SHORTAGE OF STRAIGHT MEN," WIDOWS AND DIVORCEES ARE BOTHERED LESS THAN SINGLE WOMEN.
OH...I...
DON'T WORRY, HONEY. THERE ARE LOTS OF LOVELY BOYS IN SAN FRANCISCO. YOUR TURN WILL COME. AND IN THIS CITY, WHEN A WOMAN SCORES, SHE ***REALLY*** SCORES.
COME ALONG! WE DON'T WANT TO MAKE OUR BORING HOUSE GUESTS WAIT ANY LONGER!

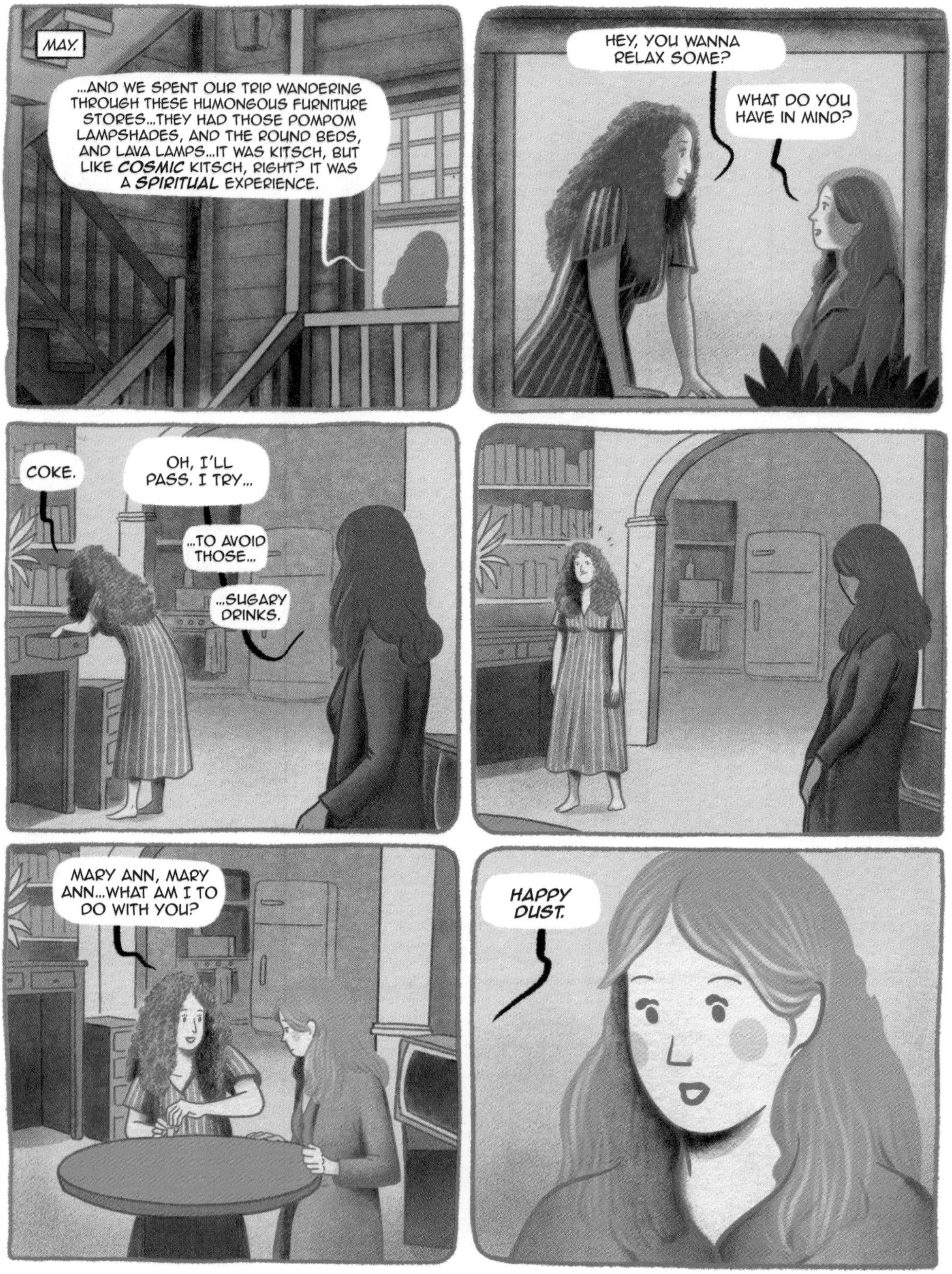
MAY.
...AND WE SPENT OUR TRIP WANDERING THROUGH THESE HUMONGOUS FURNITURE STORES...THEY HAD THOSE POMPOM LAMPSHADES, AND THE ROUND BEDS, AND LAVA LAMPS...IT WAS KITSCH, BUT LIKE COSMIC KITSCH, RIGHT? IT WAS A SPIRITUAL EXPERIENCE.
HEY, YOU WANNA RELAX SOME?
WHAT DO YOU HAVE IN MIND?
COKE.
OH, I'LL PASS. I TRY...
...TO AVOID THOSE...
...SUGARY DRINKS.
MARY ANN, MARY ANN...WHAT AM I TO DO WITH YOU?
HAPPY DUST.

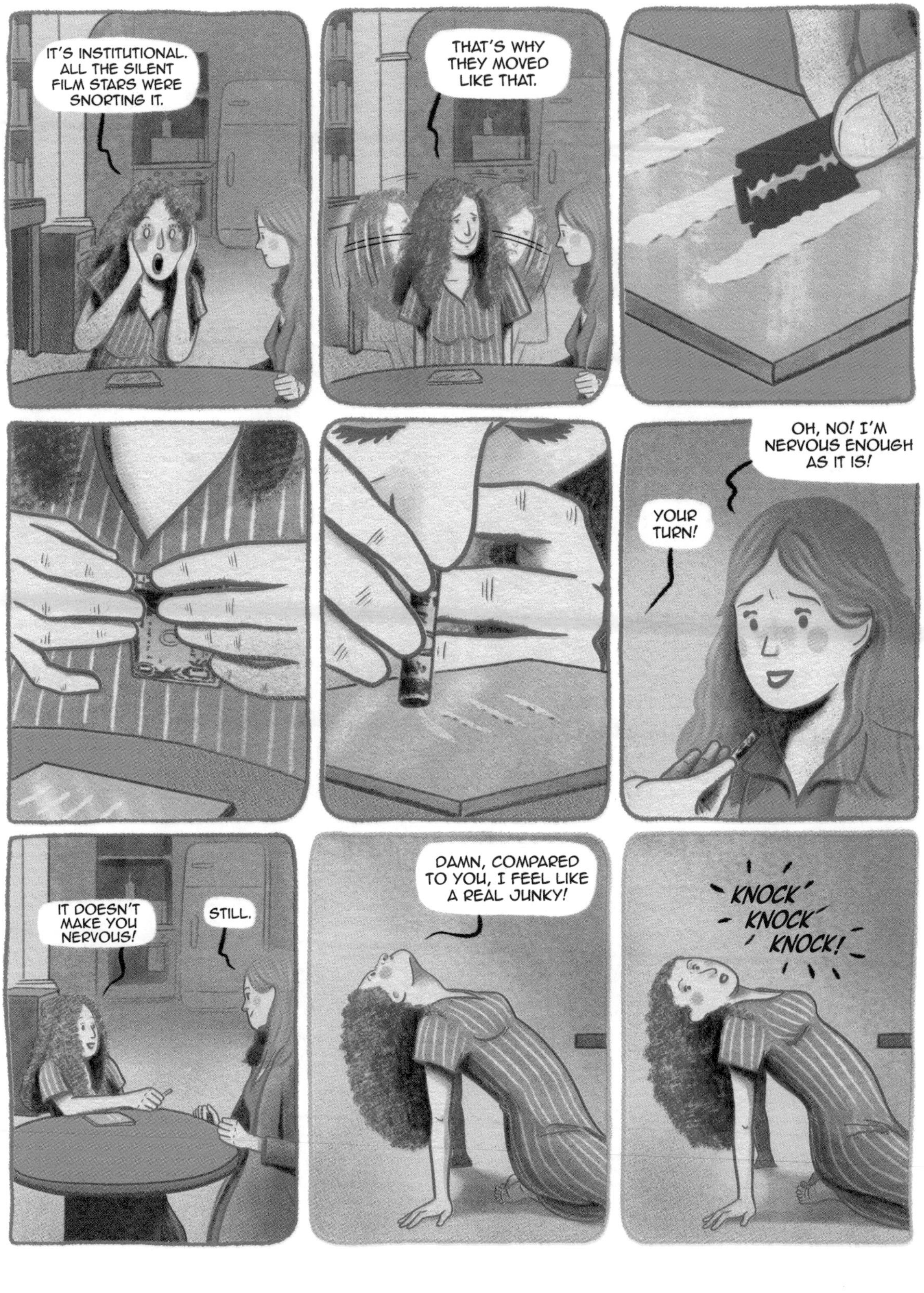
IT'S INSTITUTIONAL. ALL THE SILENT FILM STARS WERE SNORTING IT.
THAT'S WHY THEY MOVED LIKE THAT.
OH, NO! I'M NERVOUS ENOUGH AS IT IS!
YOUR TURN!
IT DOESN'T MAKE YOU NERVOUS!
STILL.
DAMN, COMPARED TO YOU, I FEEL LIKE A REAL JUNKY!
KNOCK KNOCK KNOCK!

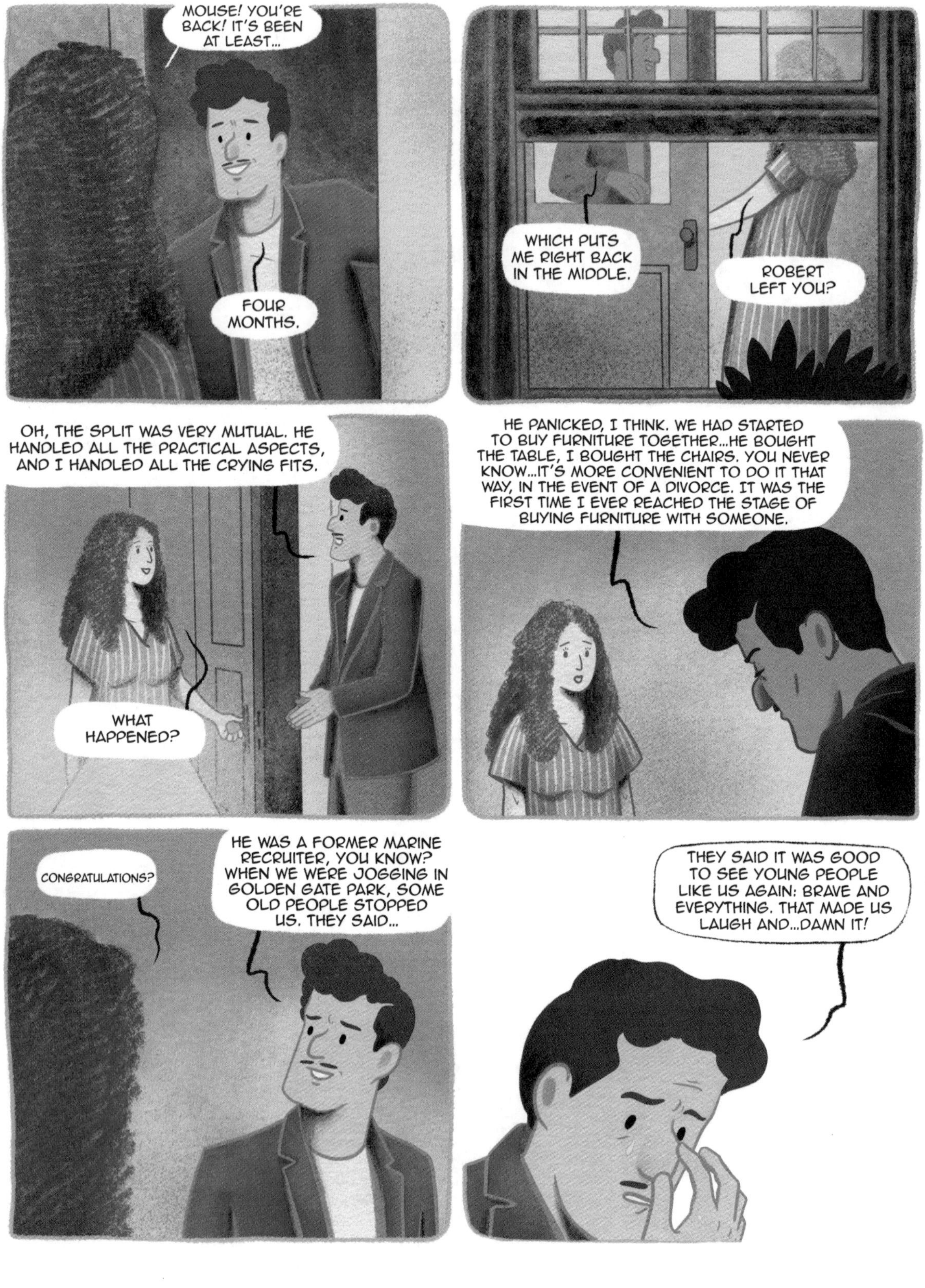
MOUSE! YOU'RE BACK! IT'S BEEN AT LEAST...
FOUR MONTHS.
WHICH PUTS ME RIGHT BACK IN THE MIDDLE.
ROBERT LEFT YOU?
OH, THE SPLIT WAS VERY MUTUAL. HE HANDLED ALL THE PRACTICAL ASPECTS, AND I HANDLED ALL THE CRYING FITS.
WHAT HAPPENED?
HE PANICKED, I THINK. WE HAD STARTED TO BUY FURNITURE TOGETHER...HE BOUGHT THE TABLE, I BOUGHT THE CHAIRS. YOU NEVER KNOW...IT'S MORE CONVENIENT TO DO IT THAT WAY, IN THE EVENT OF A DIVORCE. IT WAS THE FIRST TIME I EVER REACHED THE STAGE OF BUYING FURNITURE WITH SOMEONE.
CONGRATULATIONS?
HE WAS A FORMER MARINE RECRUITER, YOU KNOW? WHEN WE WERE JOGGING IN GOLDEN GATE PARK, SOME OLD PEOPLE STOPPED US. THEY SAID...
THEY SAID IT WAS GOOD TO SEE YOUNG PEOPLE LIKE US AGAIN: BRAVE AND EVERYTHING. THAT MADE US LAUGH AND...DAMN IT!

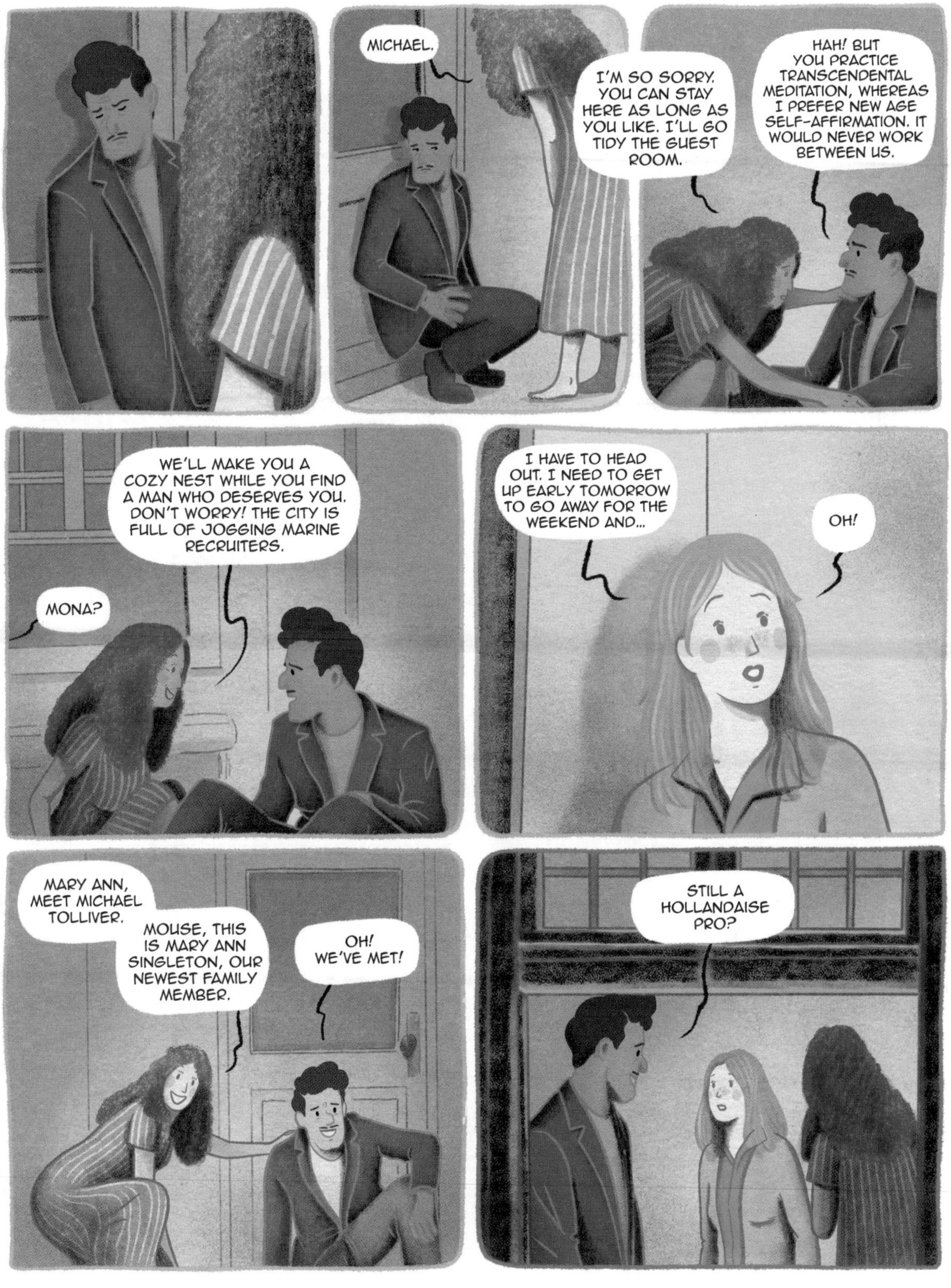
MICHAEL.
I'M SO SORRY. YOU CAN STAY HERE AS LONG AS YOU LIKE. I'LL GO TIDY THE GUEST ROOM.
HAH! BUT YOU PRACTICE TRANSCENDENTAL MEDITATION, WHEREAS I PREFER NEW AGE SELF-AFFIRMATION. IT WOULD NEVER WORK BETWEEN US.
WE'LL MAKE YOU A COZY NEST WHILE YOU FIND A MAN WHO DESERVES YOU. DON'T WORRY! THE CITY IS FULL OF JOGGING MARINE RECRUITERS.
MONA?
I HAVE TO HEAD OUT. I NEED TO GET UP EARLY TOMORROW TO GO AWAY FOR THE WEEKEND AND...
OH!
MARY ANN, MEET MICHAEL TOLLIVER.
MOUSE, THIS IS MARY ANN SINGLETON, OUR NEWEST FAMILY MEMBER.
OH! WE'VE MET!
STILL A HOLLANDAISE PRO?

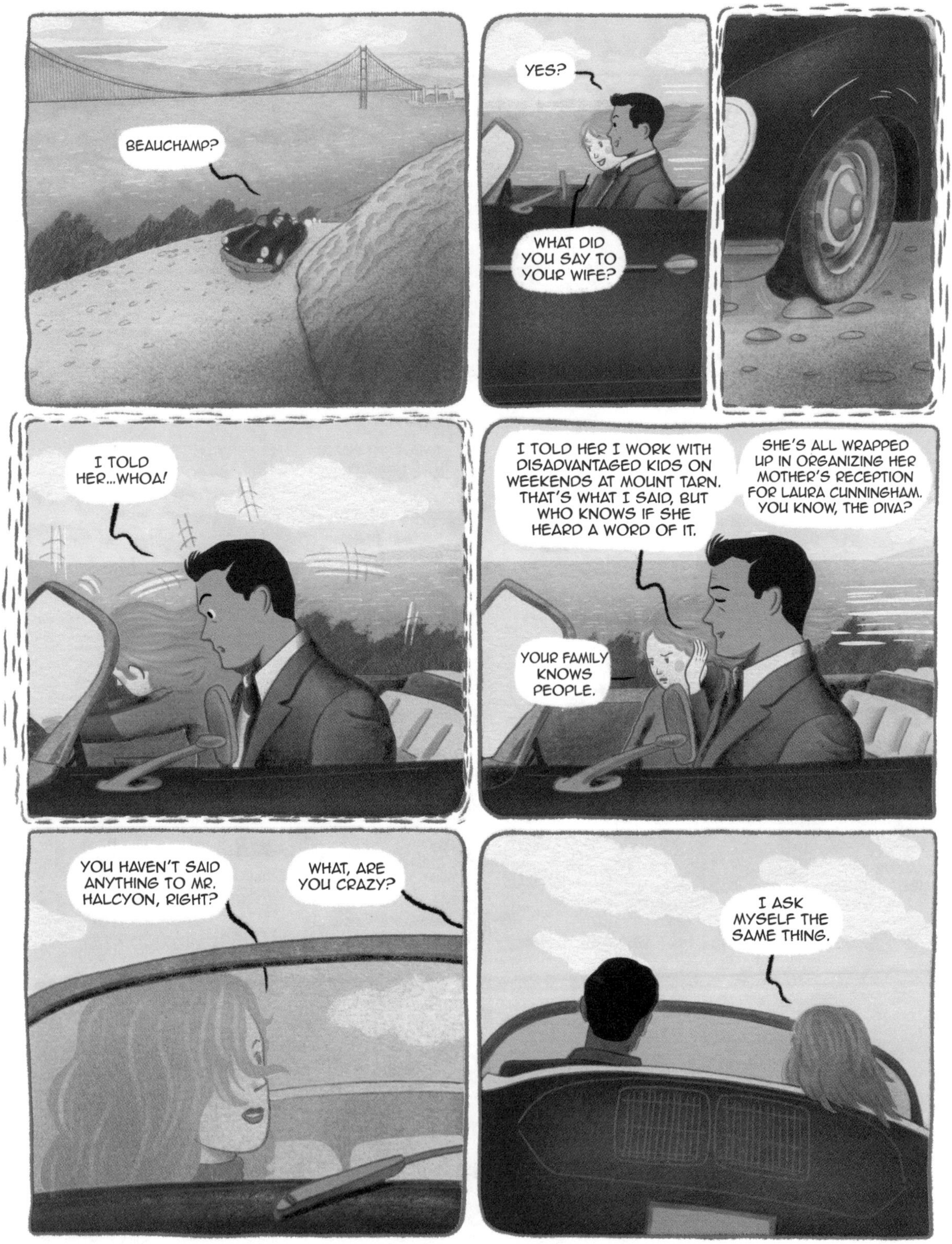
BEAUCHAMP?
YES?
WHAT DID YOU SAY TO YOUR WIFE?
I TOLD HER...WHOA!
I TOLD HER I WORK WITH DISADVANTAGED KIDS ON WEEKENDS AT MOUNT TARN. THAT'S WHAT I SAID, BUT WHO KNOWS IF SHE HEARD A WORD OF IT.
SHE'S ALL WRAPPED UP IN ORGANIZING HER MOTHER'S RECEPTION FOR LAURA CUNNINGHAM. YOU KNOW, THE DIVA?
YOUR FAMILY KNOWS PEOPLE.
YOU HAVEN'T SAID ANYTHING TO MR. HALCYON, RIGHT?
WHAT, ARE YOU CRAZY?
I ASK MYSELF THE SAME THING.

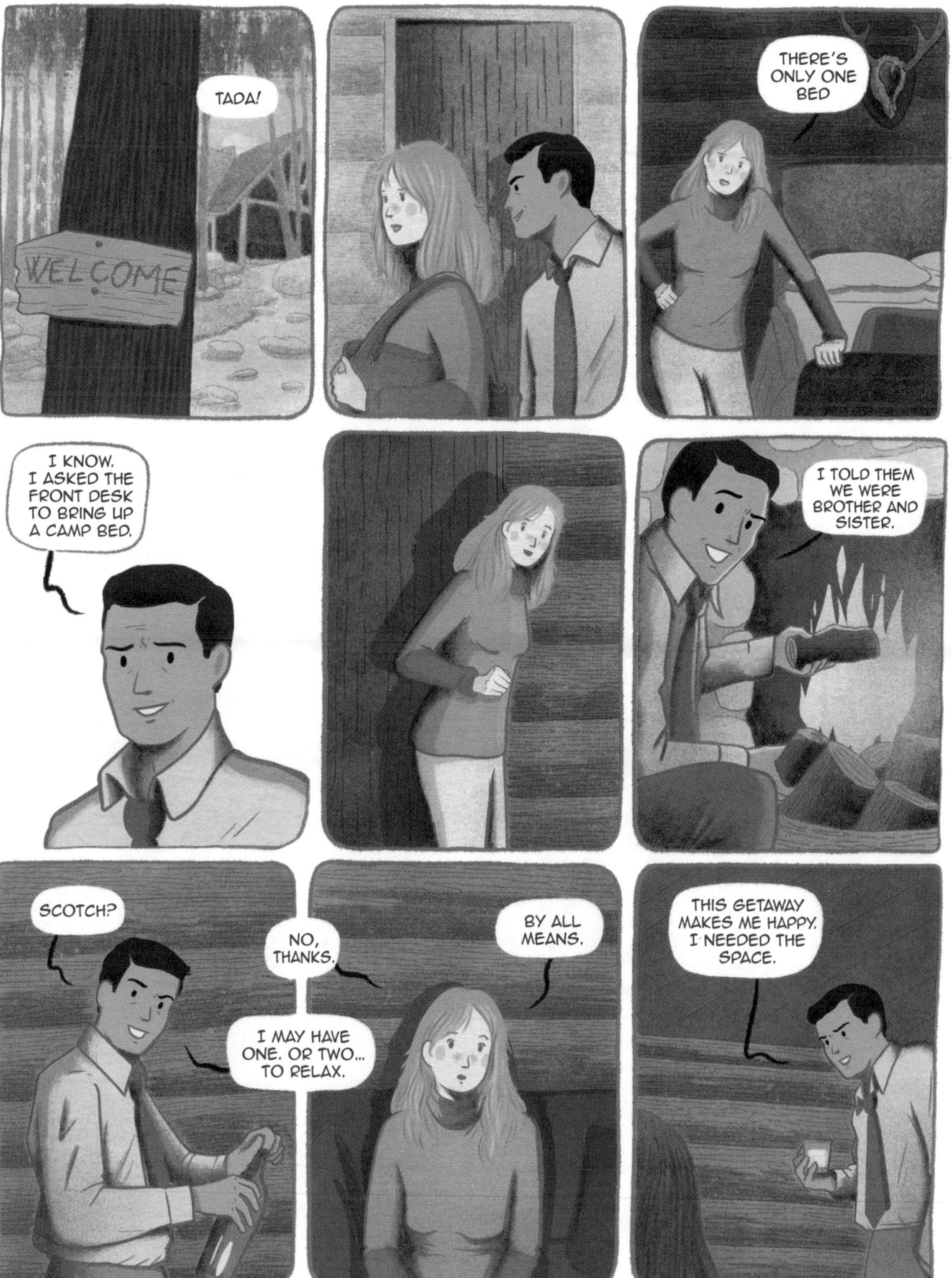
TADA!
WELCOME
THERE'S ONLY ONE BED
I KNOW. I ASKED THE FRONT DESK TO BRING UP A CAMP BED.
I TOLD THEM WE WERE BROTHER AND SISTER.
SCOTCH?
I MAY HAVE ONE. OR TWO... TO RELAX.
NO, THANKS.
BY ALL MEANS.
THIS GETAWAY MAKES ME HAPPY. I NEEDED THE SPACE.

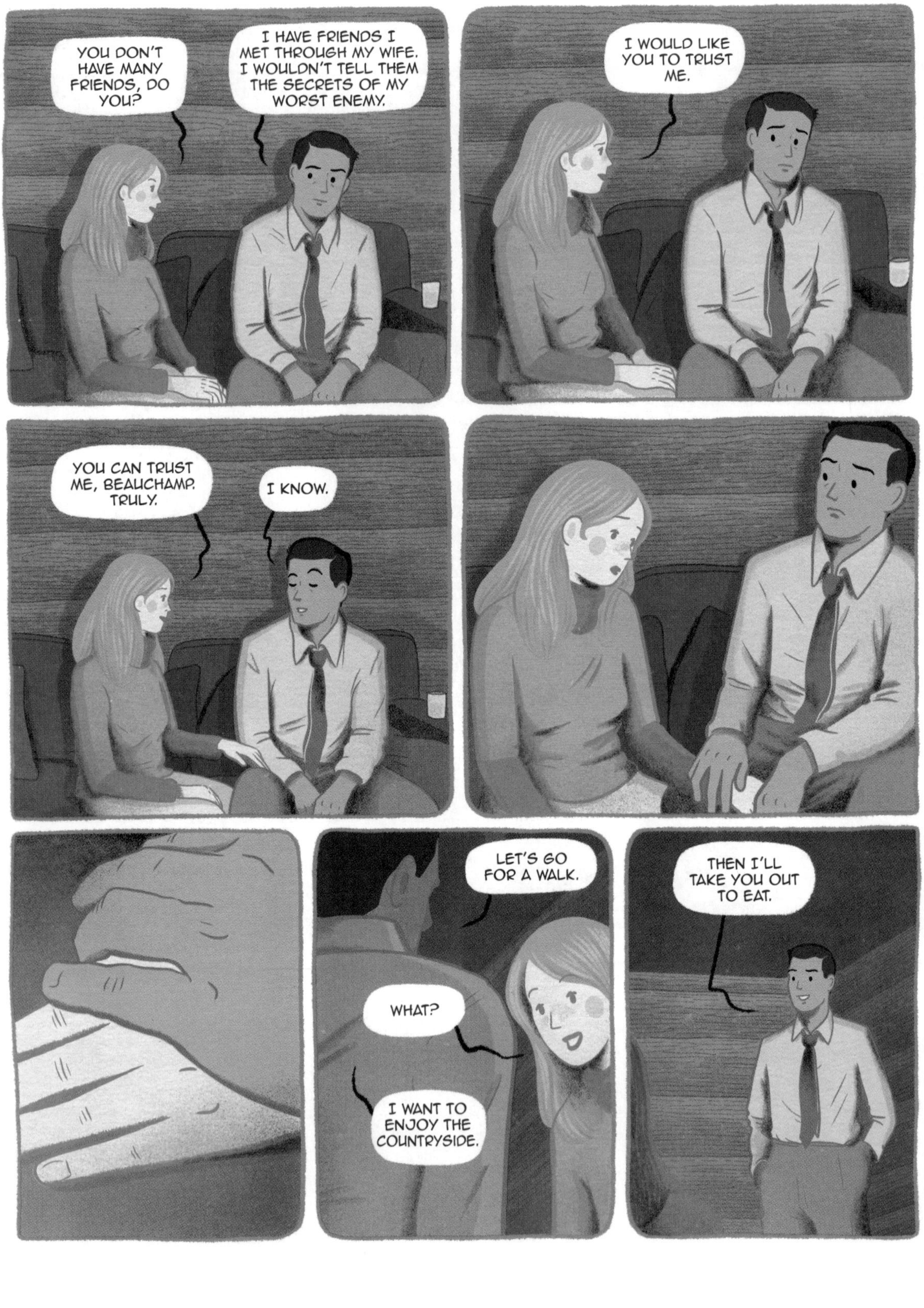
YOU DON'T HAVE MANY FRIENDS, DO YOU?
I HAVE FRIENDS I MET THROUGH MY WIFE. I WOULDN'T TELL THEM THE SECRETS OF MY WORST ENEMY.
I WOULD LIKE YOU TO TRUST ME.
YOU CAN TRUST ME, BEAUCHAMP. TRULY.
I KNOW.
LET'S GO FOR A WALK.
WHAT?
I WANT TO ENJOY THE COUNTRYSIDE.
THEN I'LL TAKE YOU OUT TO EAT.

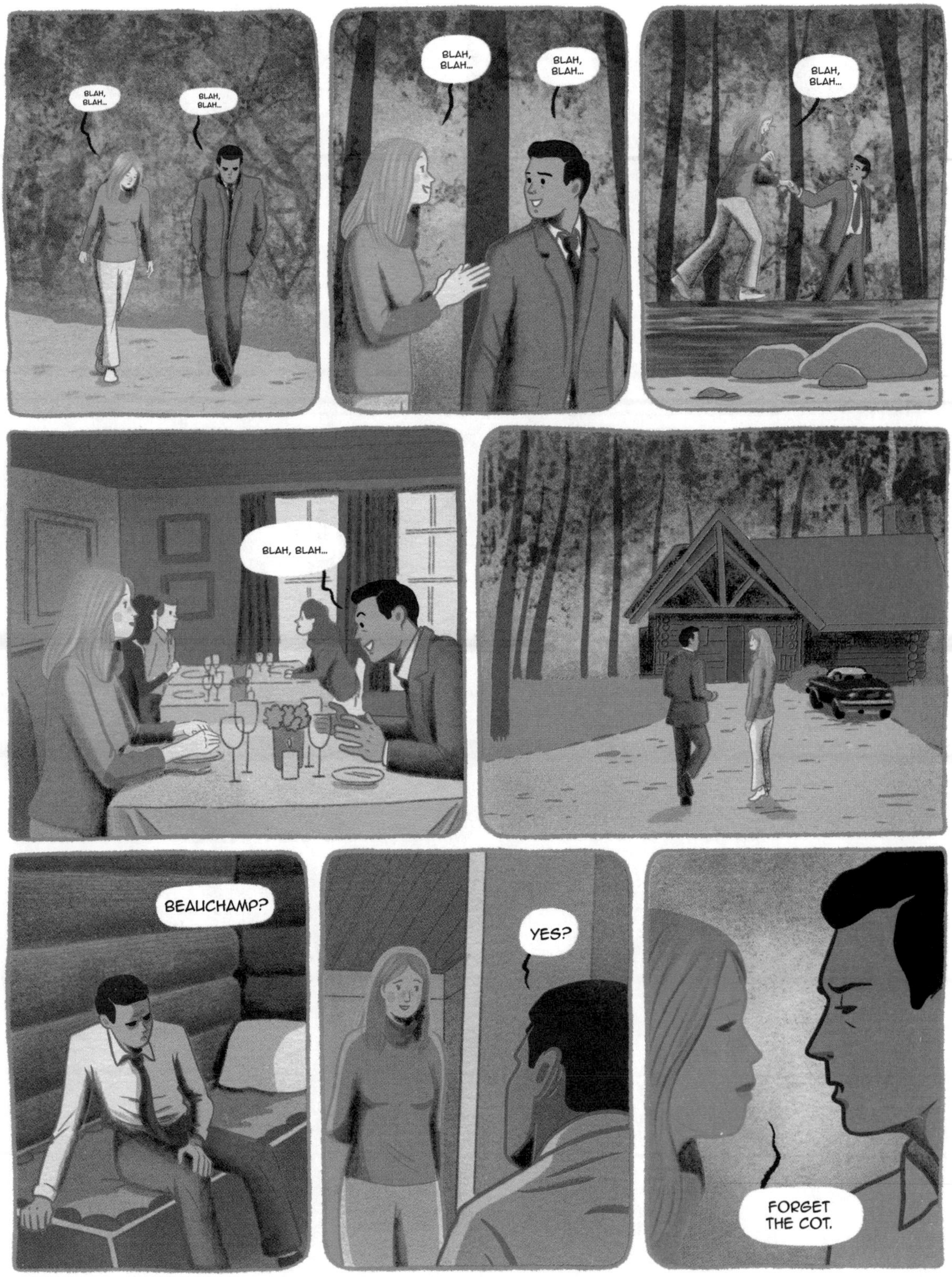
BLAH,
BLAH...
BLAH,
BLAH...
BLAH,
BLAH...
BLAH,
BLAH...
BLAH,
BLAH...
BLAH, BLAH...
BEAUCHAMP?
YES?
FORGET
THE COT.

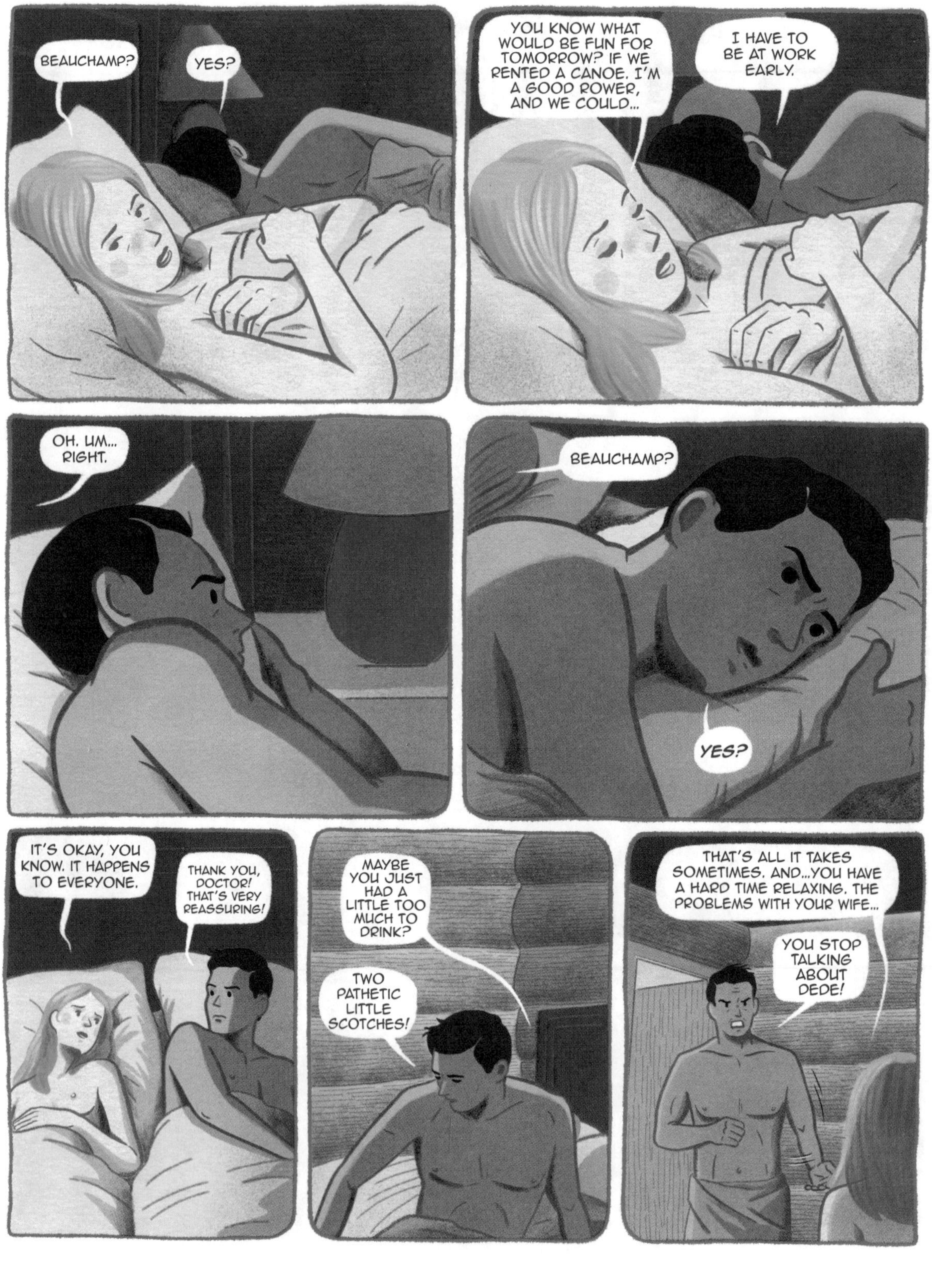
BEAUCHAMP?
YES?
YOU KNOW WHAT WOULD BE FUN FOR TOMORROW? IF WE RENTED A CANOE. I'M A GOOD ROWER, AND WE COULD...
I HAVE TO BE AT WORK EARLY.
OH. UM... RIGHT.
BEAUCHAMP?
YES?
IT'S OKAY, YOU KNOW. IT HAPPENS TO EVERYONE.
THANK YOU, DOCTOR! THAT'S VERY REASSURING!
MAYBE YOU JUST HAD A LITTLE TOO MUCH TO DRINK?
TWO PATHETIC LITTLE SCOTCHES!
THAT'S ALL IT TAKES SOMETIMES. AND...YOU HAVE A HARD TIME RELAXING. THE PROBLEMS WITH YOUR WIFE...
YOU STOP TALKING ABOUT DEDE!

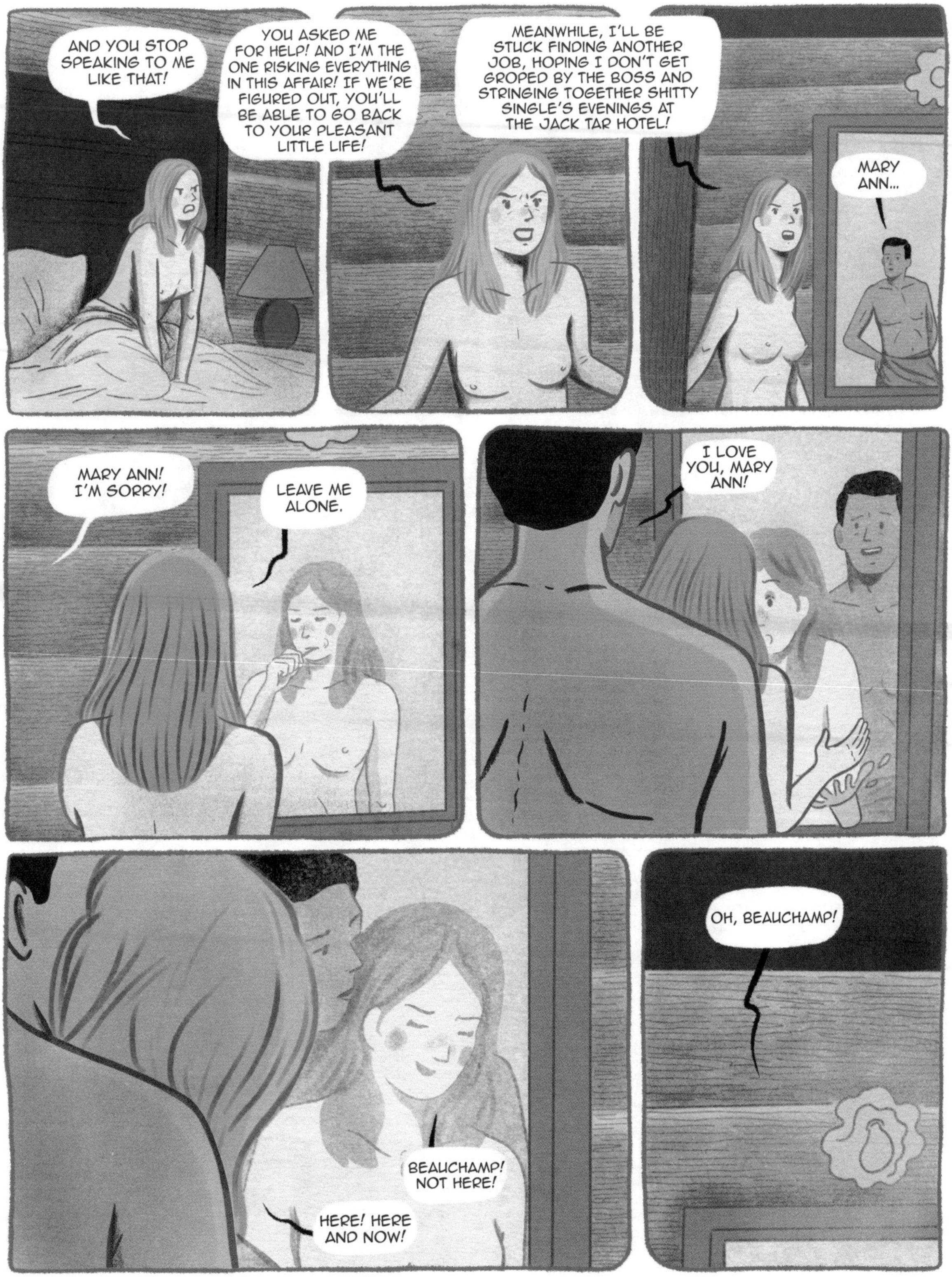
AND YOU STOP SPEAKING TO ME LIKE THAT!
YOU ASKED ME FOR HELP! AND I'M THE ONE RISKING EVERYTHING IN THIS AFFAIR! IF WE'RE FIGURED OUT, YOU'LL BE ABLE TO GO BACK TO YOUR PLEASANT LITTLE LIFE!
MEANWHILE, I'LL BE STUCK FINDING ANOTHER JOB, HOPING I DON'T GET GROPED BY THE BOSS AND STRINGING TOGETHER SHITTY SINGLE'S EVENINGS AT THE JACK TAR HOTEL!
MARY ANN...
MARY ANN! I'M SORRY!
LEAVE ME ALONE.
I LOVE YOU, MARY ANN!
BEAUCHAMP! NOT HERE!
HERE! HERE AND NOW!
OH, BEAUCHAMP!

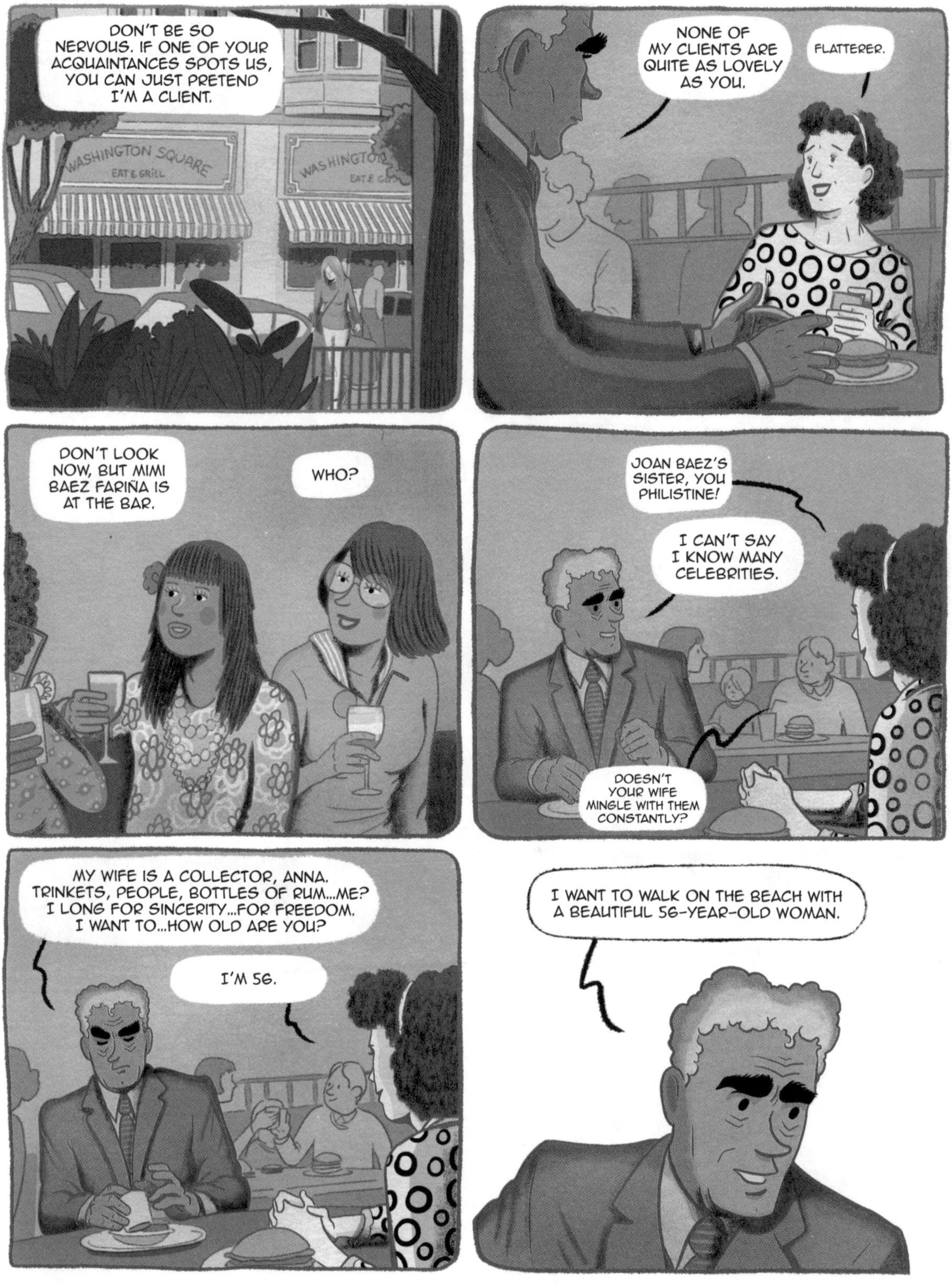
DON'T BE SO NERVOUS. IF ONE OF YOUR ACQUAINTANCES SPOTS US, YOU CAN JUST PRETEND I'M A CLIENT.
WASHINGTON SQUARE EAT & GRILL
NONE OF MY CLIENTS ARE QUITE AS LOVELY AS YOU.
FLATTERER.
DON'T LOOK NOW, BUT MIMI BAEZ FARIÑA IS AT THE BAR.
WHO?
JOAN BAEZ'S SISTER, YOU PHILISTINE!
I CAN'T SAY I KNOW MANY CELEBRITIES.
DOESN'T YOUR WIFE MINGLE WITH THEM CONSTANTLY?
MY WIFE IS A COLLECTOR, ANNA. TRINKETS, PEOPLE, BOTTLES OF RUM...ME? I LONG FOR SINCERITY...FOR FREEDOM. I WANT TO...HOW OLD ARE YOU?
I'M 56.
I WANT TO WALK ON THE BEACH WITH A BEAUTIFUL 56-YEAR-OLD WOMAN.

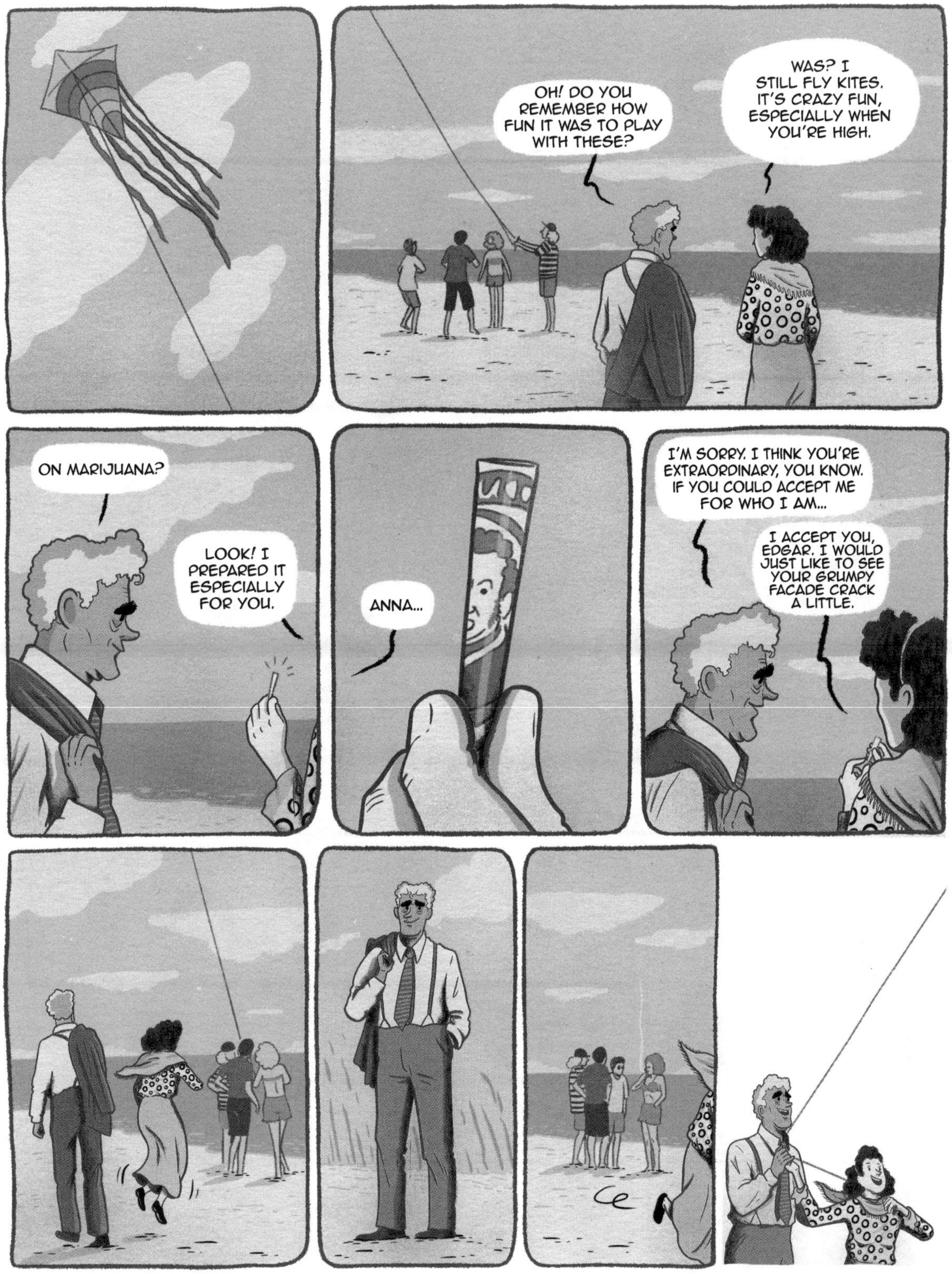
OH! DO YOU REMEMBER HOW FUN IT WAS TO PLAY WITH THESE?
WAS? I STILL FLY KITES. IT'S CRAZY FUN, ESPECIALLY WHEN YOU'RE HIGH.
ON MARIJUANA?
LOOK! I PREPARED IT ESPECIALLY FOR YOU.
ANNA...
I'M SORRY. I THINK YOU'RE EXTRAORDINARY, YOU KNOW. IF YOU COULD ACCEPT ME FOR WHO I AM...
I ACCEPT YOU, EDGAR. I WOULD JUST LIKE TO SEE YOUR GRUMPY FACADE CRACK A LITTLE.

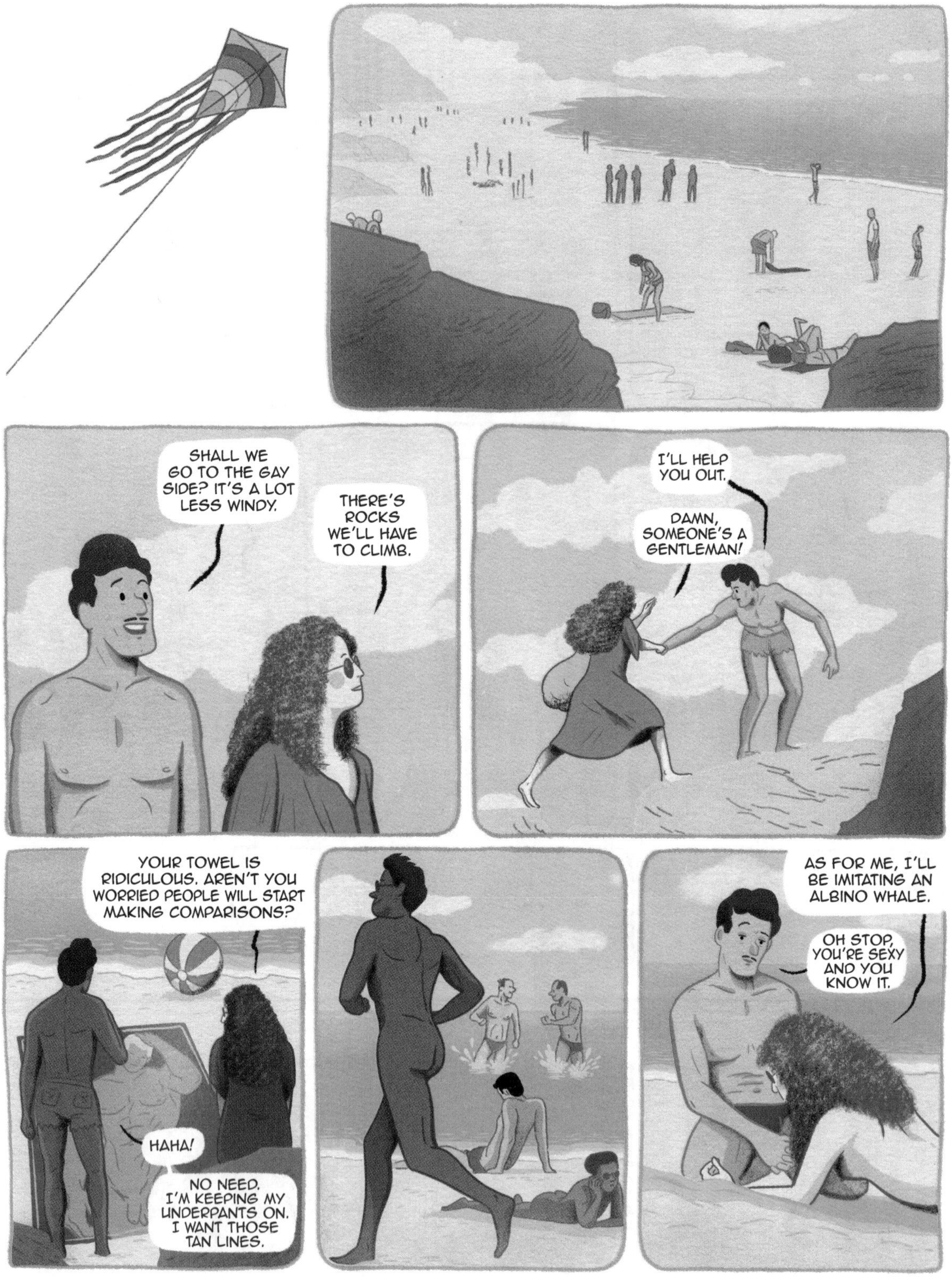
SHALL WE GO TO THE GAY SIDE? IT'S A LOT LESS WINDY.
THERE'S ROCKS WE'LL HAVE TO CLIMB.
I'LL HELP YOU OUT.
DAMN, SOMEONE'S A GENTLEMAN!
YOUR TOWEL IS RIDICULOUS. AREN'T YOU WORRIED PEOPLE WILL START MAKING COMPARISONS?
HAHA!
NO NEED. I'M KEEPING MY UNDERPANTS ON. I WANT THOSE TAN LINES.
AS FOR ME, I'LL BE IMITATING AN ALBINO WHALE.
OH STOP, YOU'RE SEXY AND YOU KNOW IT.

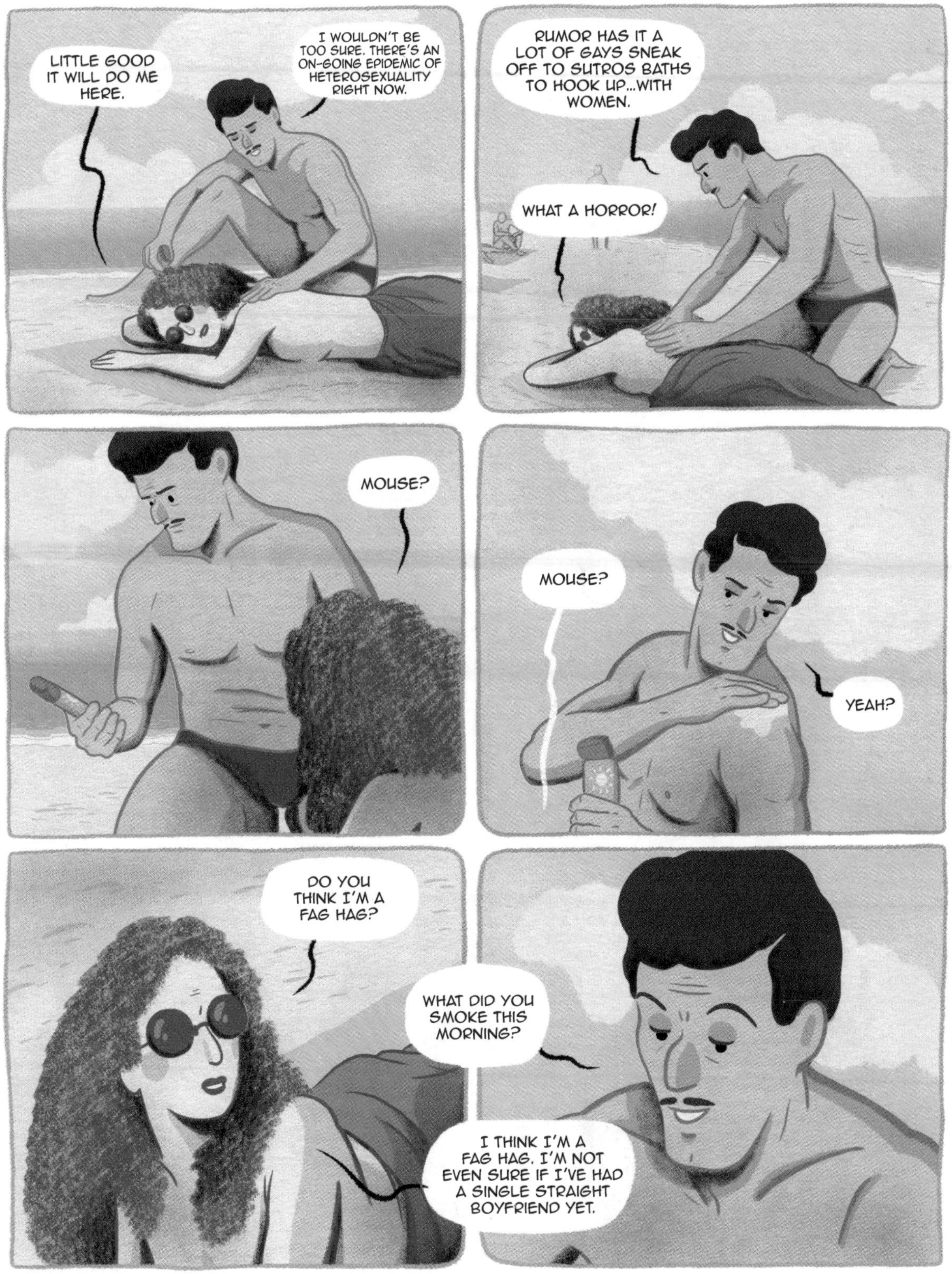
LITTLE GOOD IT WILL DO ME HERE.
I WOULDN'T BE TOO SURE. THERE'S AN ON-GOING EPIDEMIC OF HETEROSEXUALITY RIGHT NOW.
RUMOR HAS IT A LOT OF GAYS SNEAK OFF TO SUTROS BATHS TO HOOK UP...WITH WOMEN.
WHAT A HORROR!
MOUSE?
MOUSE?
YEAH?
DO YOU THINK I'M A FAG HAG?
WHAT DID YOU SMOKE THIS MORNING?
I THINK I'M A FAG HAG. I'M NOT EVEN SURE IF I'VE HAD A SINGLE STRAIGHT BOYFRIEND YET.

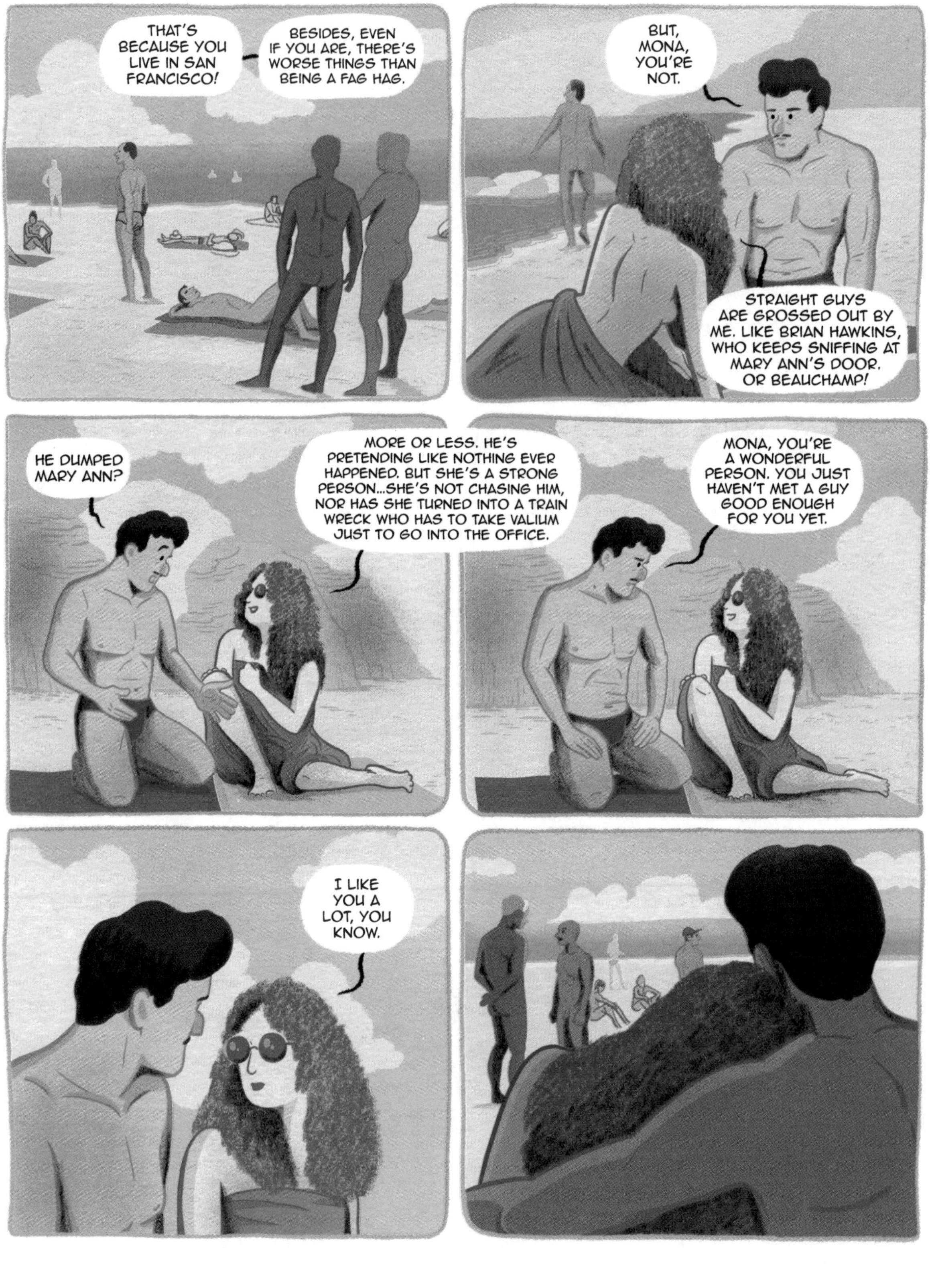
THAT'S BECAUSE YOU LIVE IN SAN FRANCISCO!
BESIDES, EVEN IF YOU ARE, THERE'S WORSE THINGS THAN BEING A FAG HAG.
BUT, MONA, YOU'RE NOT.
STRAIGHT GUYS ARE GROSSED OUT BY ME. LIKE BRIAN HAWKINS, WHO KEEPS SNIFFING AT MARY ANN'S DOOR. OR BEAUCHAMP!
HE DUMPED MARY ANN?
MORE OR LESS. HE'S PRETENDING LIKE NOTHING EVER HAPPENED. BUT SHE'S A STRONG PERSON...SHE'S NOT CHASING HIM, NOR HAS SHE TURNED INTO A TRAIN WRECK WHO HAS TO TAKE VALIUM JUST TO GO INTO THE OFFICE.
MONA, YOU'RE A WONDERFUL PERSON. YOU JUST HAVEN'T MET A GUY GOOD ENOUGH FOR YOU YET.
I LIKE YOU A LOT, YOU KNOW.

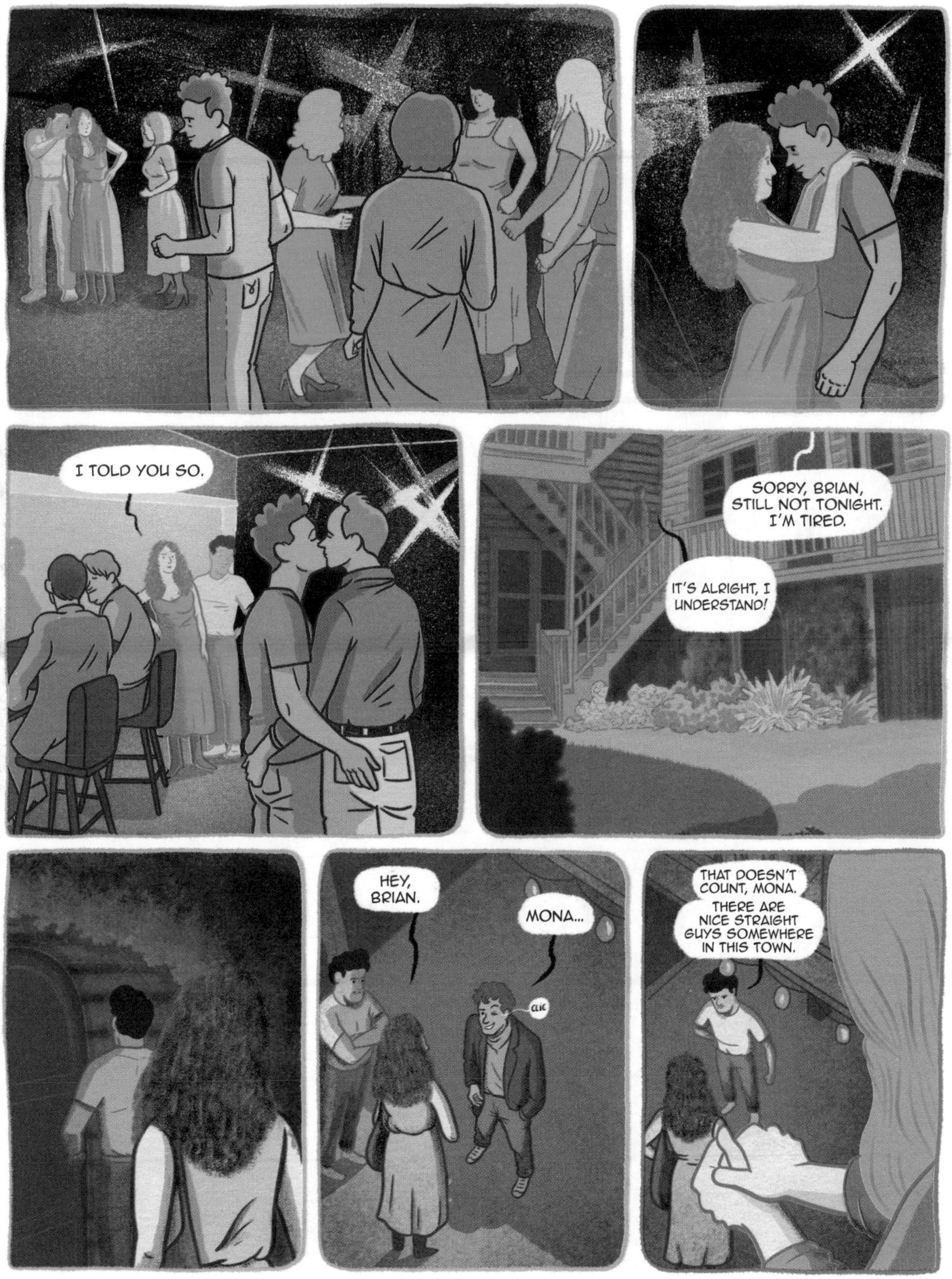
I TOLD YOU SO.
SORRY, BRIAN, STILL NOT TONIGHT. I'M TIRED.
IT'S ALRIGHT, I UNDERSTAND!
HEY, BRIAN.
MONA...
CLIC
THAT DOESN'T COUNT, MONA.
THERE ARE NICE STRAIGHT GUYS SOMEWHERE IN THIS TOWN.

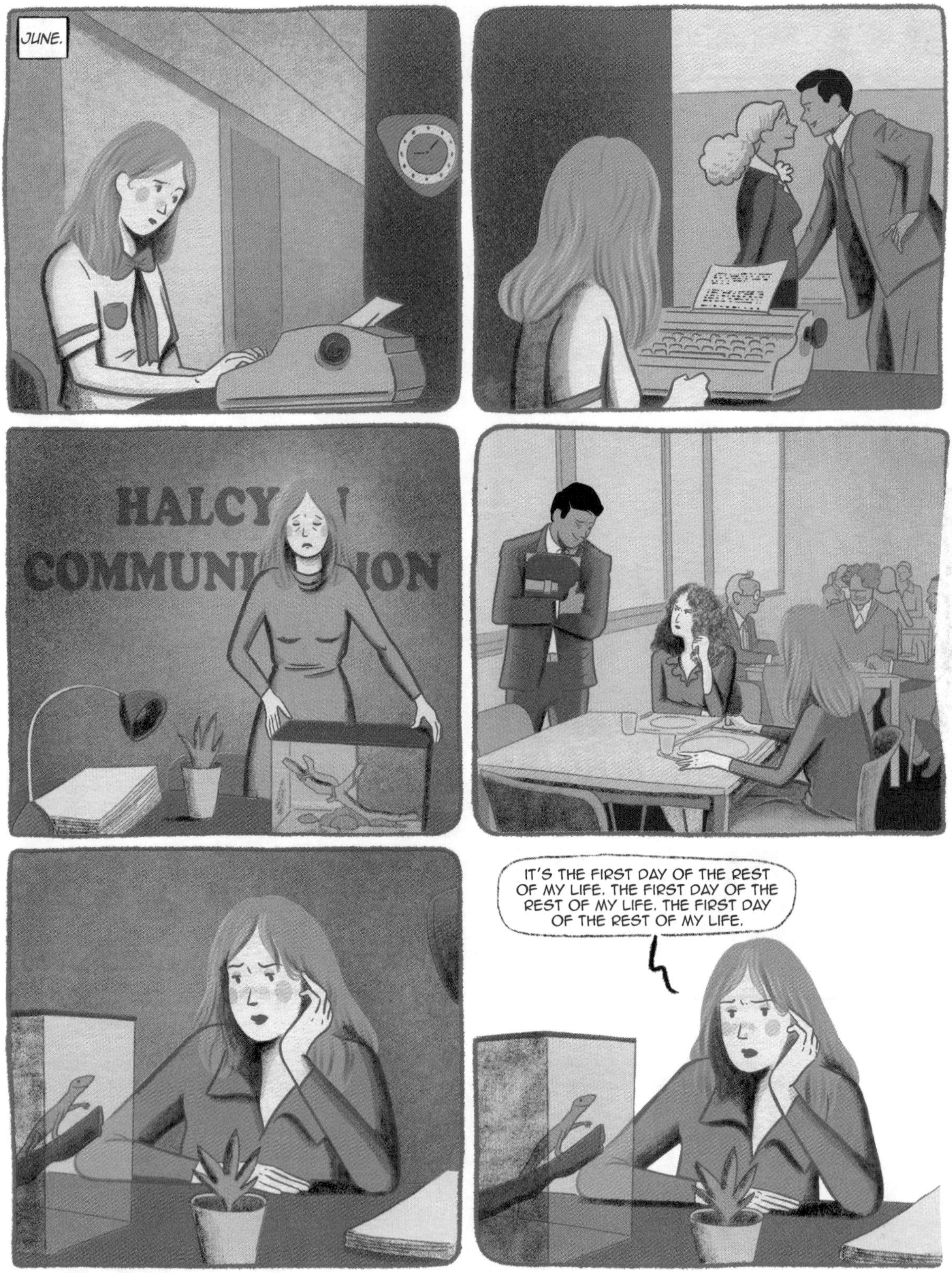
JUNE.
HALCY
COMMUNI ION
IT'S THE FIRST DAY OF THE REST OF MY LIFE. THE FIRST DAY OF THE REST OF MY LIFE. THE FIRST DAY OF THE REST OF MY LIFE.

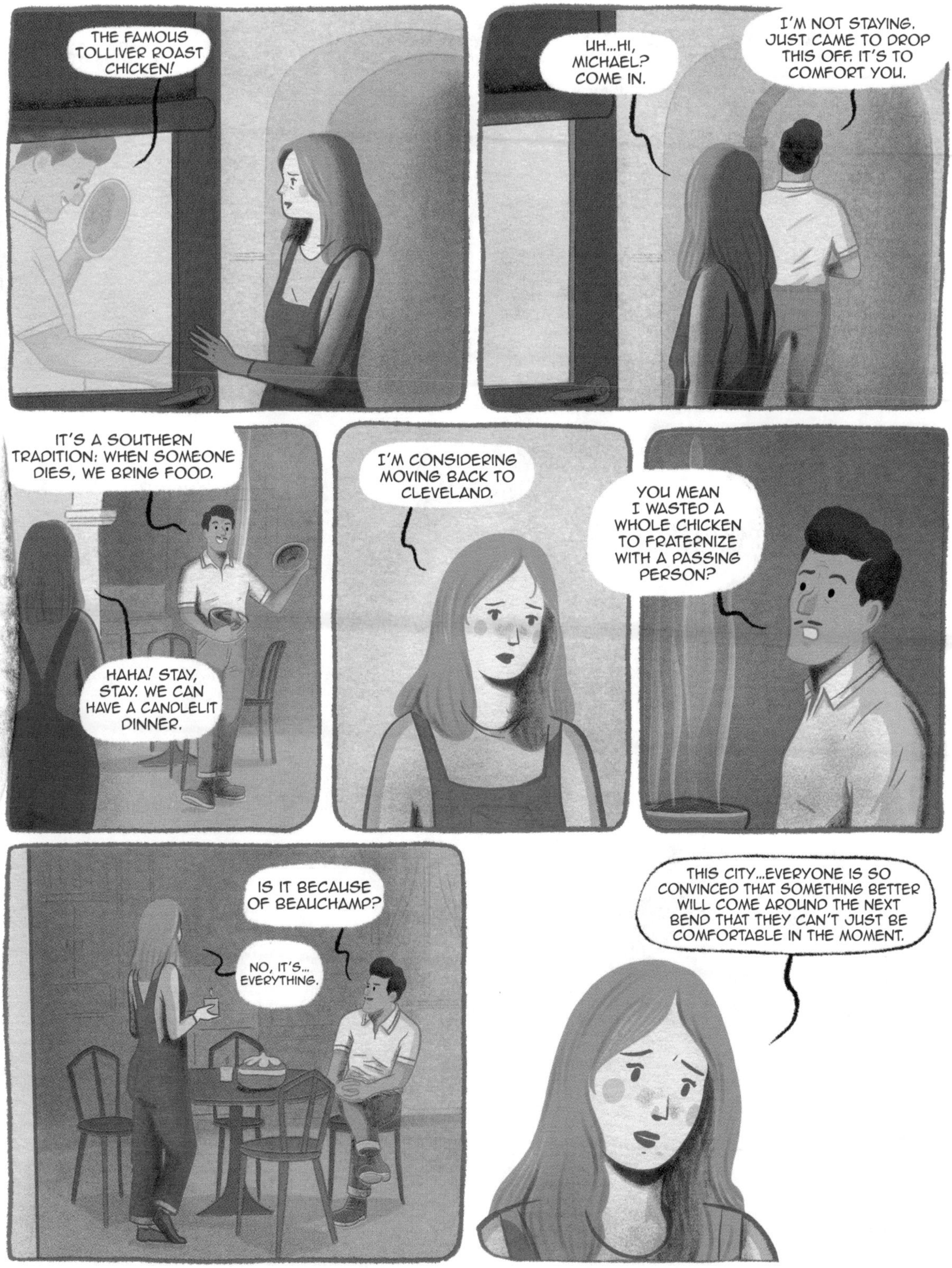
THE FAMOUS TOLLIVER ROAST CHICKEN!
UH...HI, MICHAEL? COME IN.
I'M NOT STAYING. JUST CAME TO DROP THIS OFF. IT'S TO COMFORT YOU.
IT'S A SOUTHERN TRADITION: WHEN SOMEONE DIES, WE BRING FOOD.
HAHA! STAY, STAY. WE CAN HAVE A CANDLELIT DINNER.
I'M CONSIDERING MOVING BACK TO CLEVELAND.
YOU MEAN I WASTED A WHOLE CHICKEN TO FRATERNIZE WITH A PASSING PERSON?
IS IT BECAUSE OF BEAUCHAMP?
NO, IT'S... EVERYTHING.
THIS CITY...EVERYONE IS SO CONVINCED THAT SOMETHING BETTER WILL COME AROUND THE NEXT BEND THAT THEY CAN'T JUST BE COMFORTABLE IN THE MOMENT.

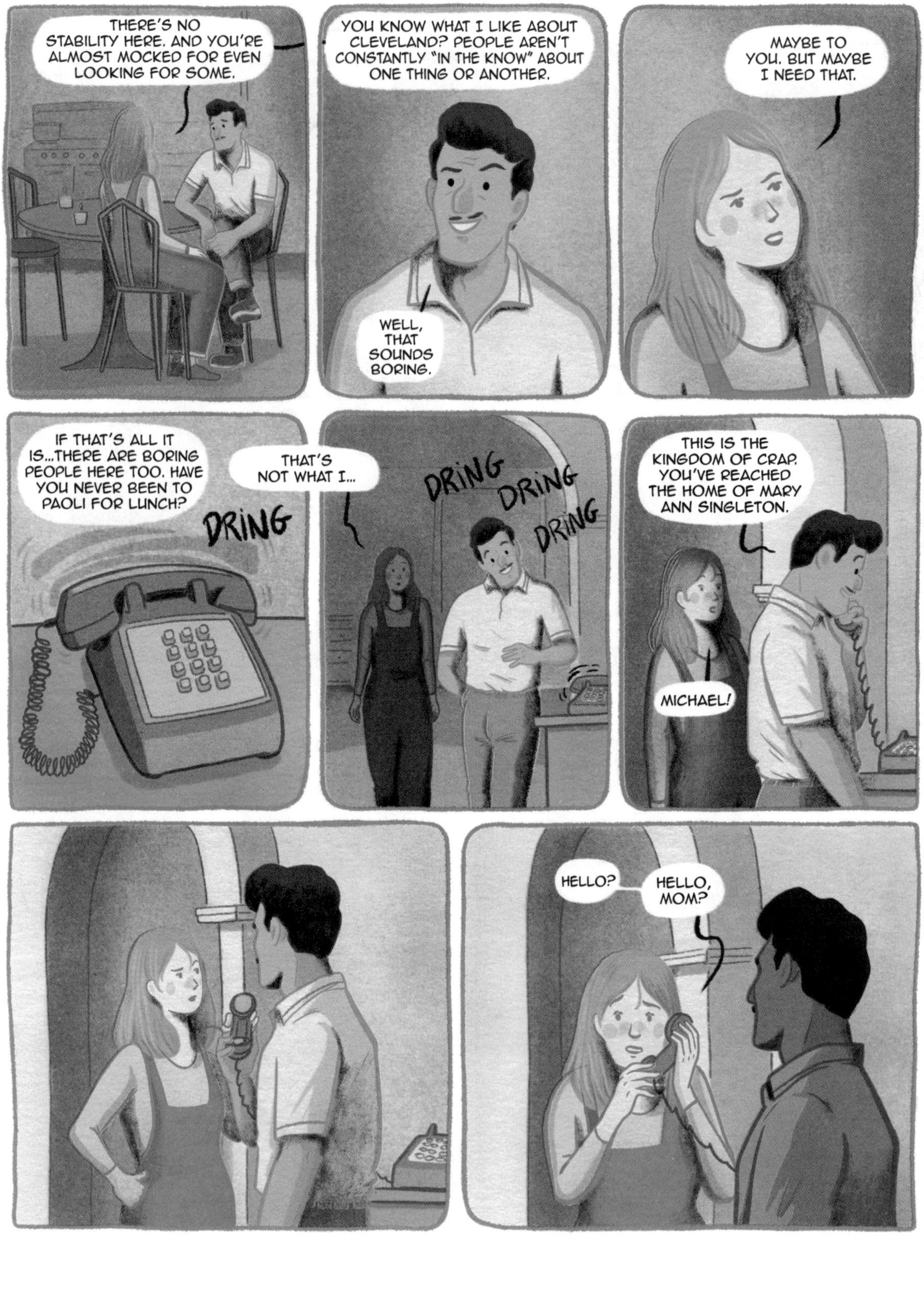
THERE'S NO STABILITY HERE. AND YOU'RE ALMOST MOCKED FOR EVEN LOOKING FOR SOME.
YOU KNOW WHAT I LIKE ABOUT CLEVELAND? PEOPLE AREN'T CONSTANTLY "IN THE KNOW" ABOUT ONE THING OR ANOTHER.
WELL, THAT SOUNDS BORING.
MAYBE TO YOU. BUT MAYBE I NEED THAT.
IF THAT'S ALL IT IS...THERE ARE BORING PEOPLE HERE TOO. HAVE YOU NEVER BEEN TO PAOLI FOR LUNCH?
DRING
THAT'S NOT WHAT I...
DRING
DRING
DRING
THIS IS THE KINGDOM OF CRAP. YOU'VE REACHED THE HOME OF MARY ANN SINGLETON.
MICHAEL!
HELLO?
HELLO, MOM?

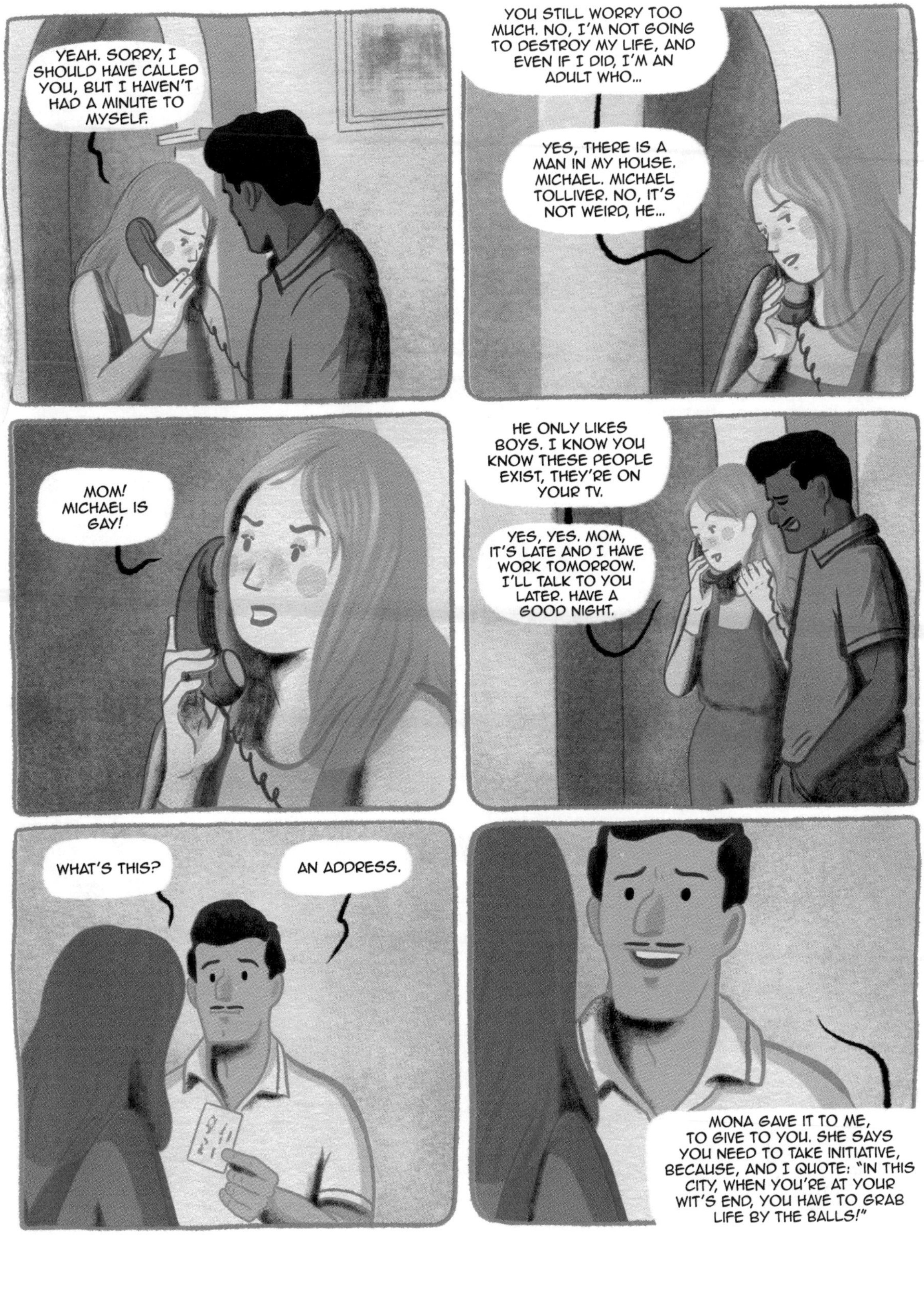
YEAH. SORRY, I SHOULD HAVE CALLED YOU, BUT I HAVEN'T HAD A MINUTE TO MYSELF.
YOU STILL WORRY TOO MUCH. NO, I'M NOT GOING TO DESTROY MY LIFE, AND EVEN IF I DID, I'M AN ADULT WHO...
YES, THERE IS A MAN IN MY HOUSE. MICHAEL. MICHAEL TOLLIVER. NO, IT'S NOT WEIRD, HE...
MOM! MICHAEL IS GAY!
HE ONLY LIKES BOYS. I KNOW YOU KNOW THESE PEOPLE EXIST, THEY'RE ON YOUR TV.
YES, YES. MOM, IT'S LATE AND I HAVE WORK TOMORROW. I'LL TALK TO YOU LATER. HAVE A GOOD NIGHT.
WHAT'S THIS?
AN ADDRESS.
MONA GAVE IT TO ME, TO GIVE TO YOU. SHE SAYS YOU NEED TO TAKE INITIATIVE, BECAUSE, AND I QUOTE: "IN THIS CITY, WHEN YOU'RE AT YOUR WIT'S END, YOU HAVE TO GRAB LIFE BY THE BALLS!"

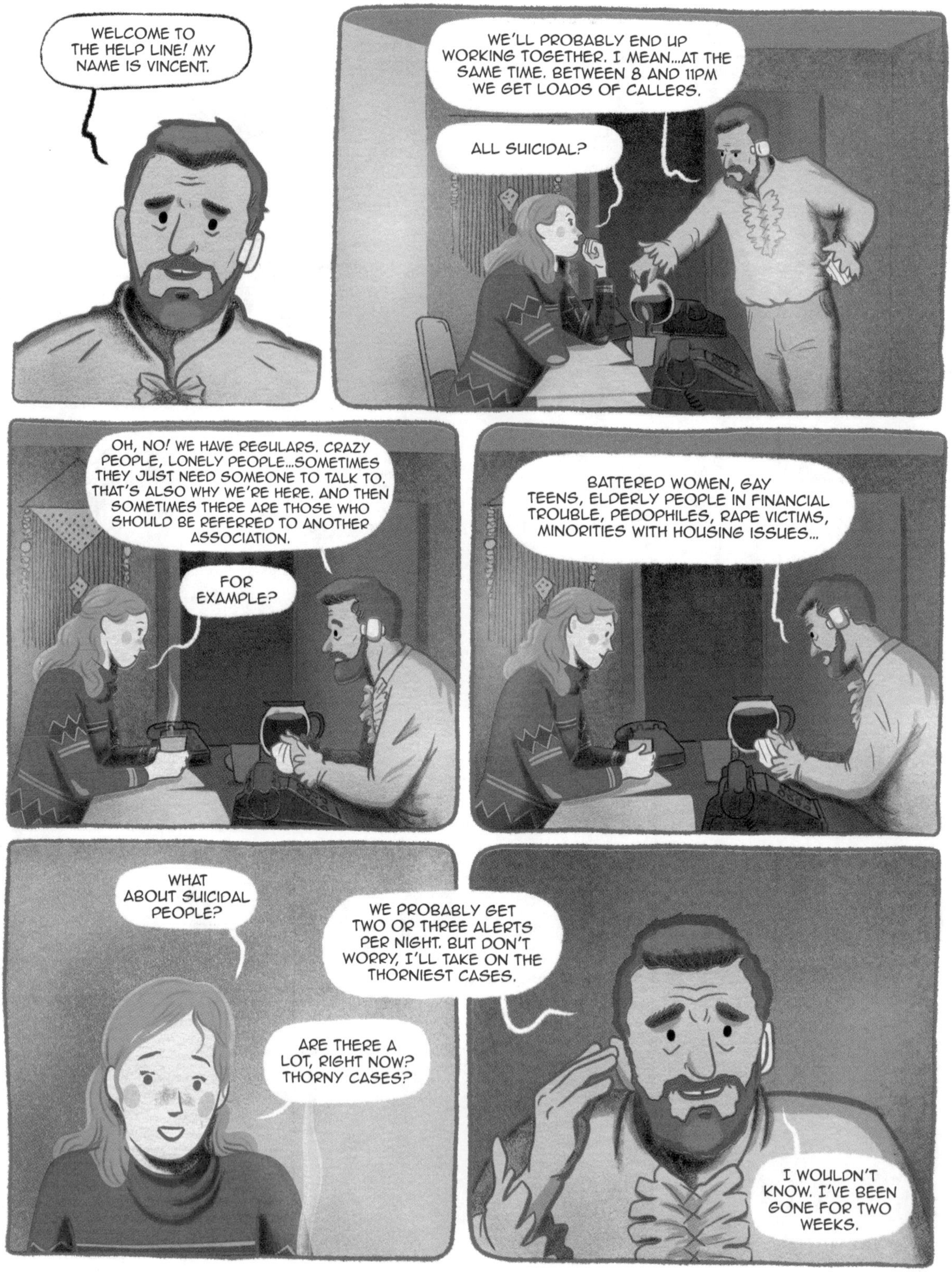
WELCOME TO THE HELP LINE! MY NAME IS VINCENT.
WE'LL PROBABLY END UP WORKING TOGETHER. I MEAN...AT THE SAME TIME. BETWEEN 8 AND 11PM WE GET LOADS OF CALLERS.
ALL SUICIDAL?
OH, NO! WE HAVE REGULARS. CRAZY PEOPLE, LONELY PEOPLE...SOMETIMES THEY JUST NEED SOMEONE TO TALK TO. THAT'S ALSO WHY WE'RE HERE. AND THEN SOMETIMES THERE ARE THOSE WHO SHOULD BE REFERRED TO ANOTHER ASSOCIATION.
FOR EXAMPLE?
BATTERED WOMEN, GAY TEENS, ELDERLY PEOPLE IN FINANCIAL TROUBLE, PEDOPHILES, RAPE VICTIMS, MINORITIES WITH HOUSING ISSUES...
WHAT ABOUT SUICIDAL PEOPLE?
WE PROBABLY GET TWO OR THREE ALERTS PER NIGHT. BUT DON'T WORRY, I'LL TAKE ON THE THORNIEST CASES.
ARE THERE A LOT, RIGHT NOW? THORNY CASES?
I WOULDN'T KNOW. I'VE BEEN GONE FOR TWO WEEKS.

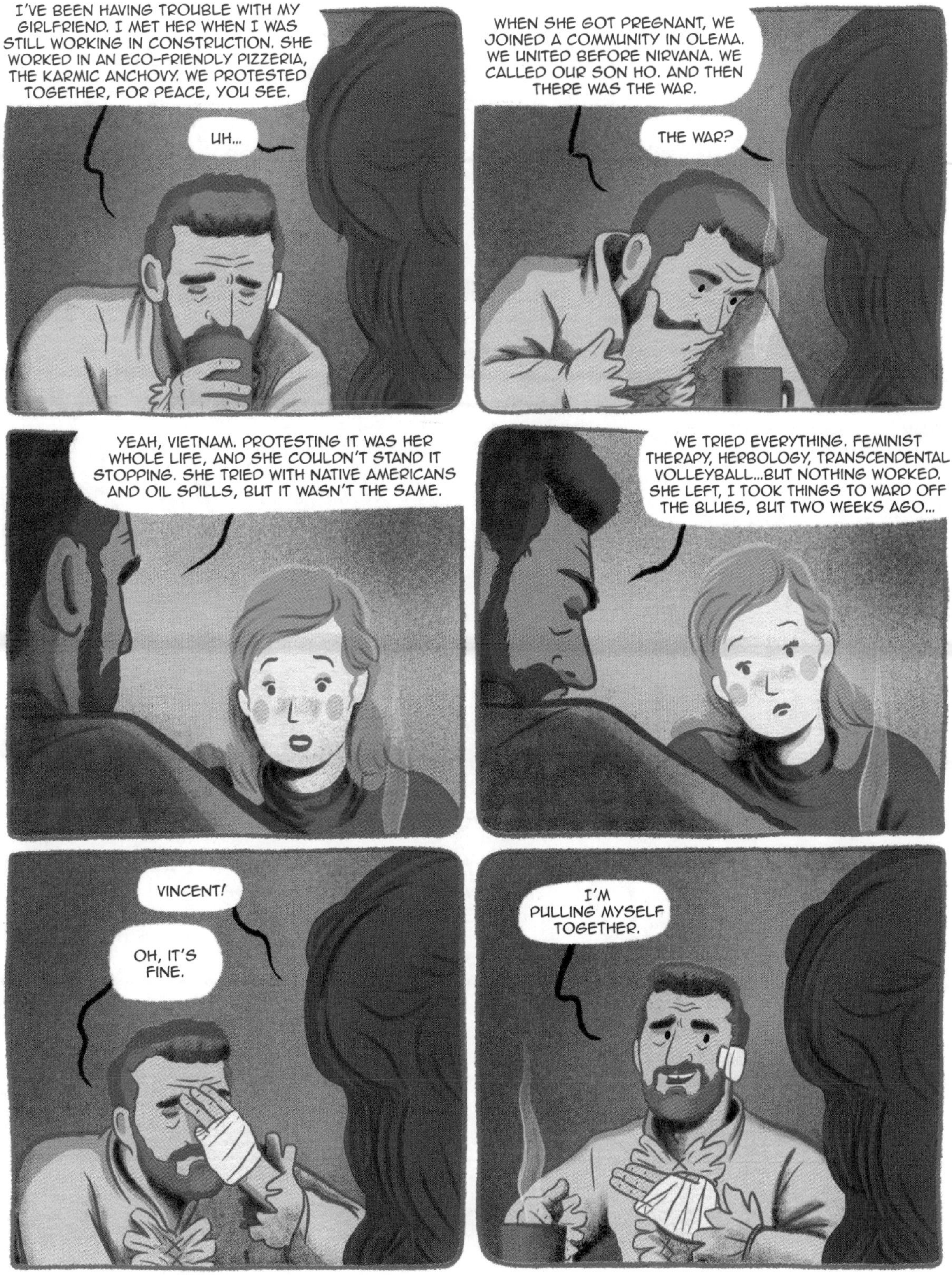
I'VE BEEN HAVING TROUBLE WITH MY GIRLFRIEND. I MET HER WHEN I WAS STILL WORKING IN CONSTRUCTION. SHE WORKED IN AN ECO-FRIENDLY PIZZERIA, THE KARMIC ANCHOVY. WE PROTESTED TOGETHER, FOR PEACE, YOU SEE.
UH...
WHEN SHE GOT PREGNANT, WE JOINED A COMMUNITY IN OLEMA. WE UNITED BEFORE NIRVANA. WE CALLED OUR SON HO. AND THEN THERE WAS THE WAR.
THE WAR?
YEAH, VIETNAM. PROTESTING IT WAS HER WHOLE LIFE, AND SHE COULDN'T STAND IT STOPPING. SHE TRIED WITH NATIVE AMERICANS AND OIL SPILLS, BUT IT WASN'T THE SAME.
WE TRIED EVERYTHING. FEMINIST THERAPY, HERBOLOGY, TRANSCENDENTAL VOLLEYBALL...BUT NOTHING WORKED. SHE LEFT, I TOOK THINGS TO WARD OFF THE BLUES, BUT TWO WEEKS AGO...
VINCENT!
OH, IT'S FINE.
I'M PULLING MYSELF TOGETHER.

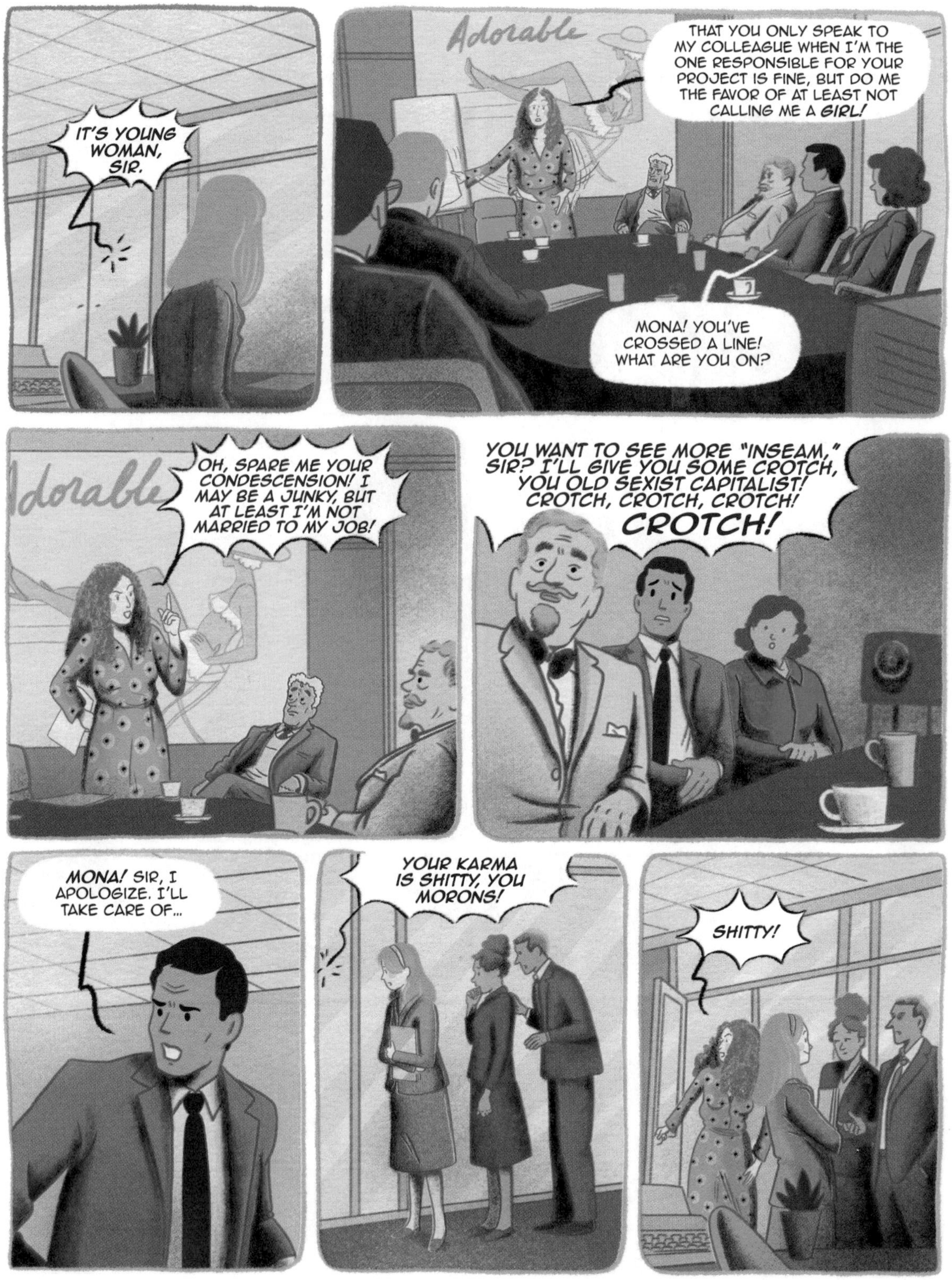
IT'S YOUNG WOMAN, SIR.
THAT YOU ONLY SPEAK TO MY COLLEAGUE WHEN I'M THE ONE RESPONSIBLE FOR YOUR PROJECT IS FINE, BUT DO ME THE FAVOR OF AT LEAST NOT CALLING ME A GIRL!
Adorable
MONA! YOU'VE CROSSED A LINE! WHAT ARE YOU ON?
OH, SPARE ME YOUR CONDESCENSION! I MAY BE A JUNKY, BUT AT LEAST I'M NOT MARRIED TO MY JOB!
YOU WANT TO SEE MORE "INSEAM," SIR? I'LL GIVE YOU SOME CROTCH, YOU OLD SEXIST CAPITALIST! CROTCH, CROTCH, CROTCH! CROTCH!
MONA! SIR, I APOLOGIZE. I'LL TAKE CARE OF...
YOUR KARMA IS SHITTY, YOU MORONS!
SHITTY!

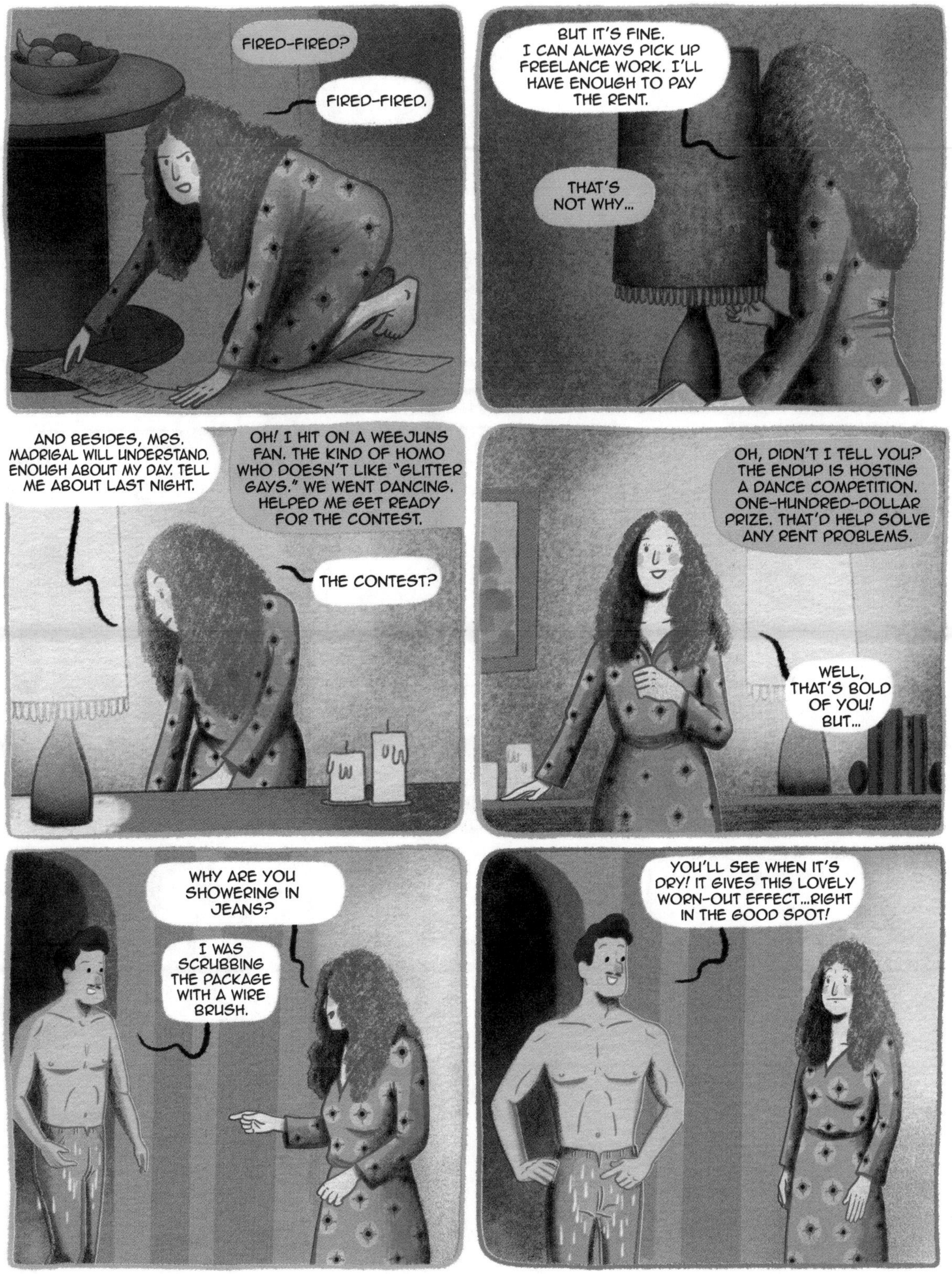
FIRED-FIRED?
FIRED-FIRED.
BUT IT'S FINE. I CAN ALWAYS PICK UP FREELANCE WORK. I'LL HAVE ENOUGH TO PAY THE RENT.
THAT'S NOT WHY...
AND BESIDES, MRS. MADRIGAL WILL UNDERSTAND. ENOUGH ABOUT MY DAY. TELL ME ABOUT LAST NIGHT.
OH! I HIT ON A WEEJUNS FAN. THE KIND OF HOMO WHO DOESN'T LIKE "GLITTER GAYS." WE WENT DANCING. HELPED ME GET READY FOR THE CONTEST.
THE CONTEST?
OH, DIDN'T I TELL YOU? THE ENDUP IS HOSTING A DANCE COMPETITION. ONE-HUNDRED-DOLLAR PRIZE. THAT'D HELP SOLVE ANY RENT PROBLEMS.
WELL, THAT'S BOLD OF YOU! BUT...
WHY ARE YOU SHOWERING IN JEANS?
I WAS SCRUBBING THE PACKAGE WITH A WIRE BRUSH.
YOU'LL SEE WHEN IT'S DRY! IT GIVES THIS LOVELY WORN-OUT EFFECT...RIGHT IN THE GOOD SPOT!

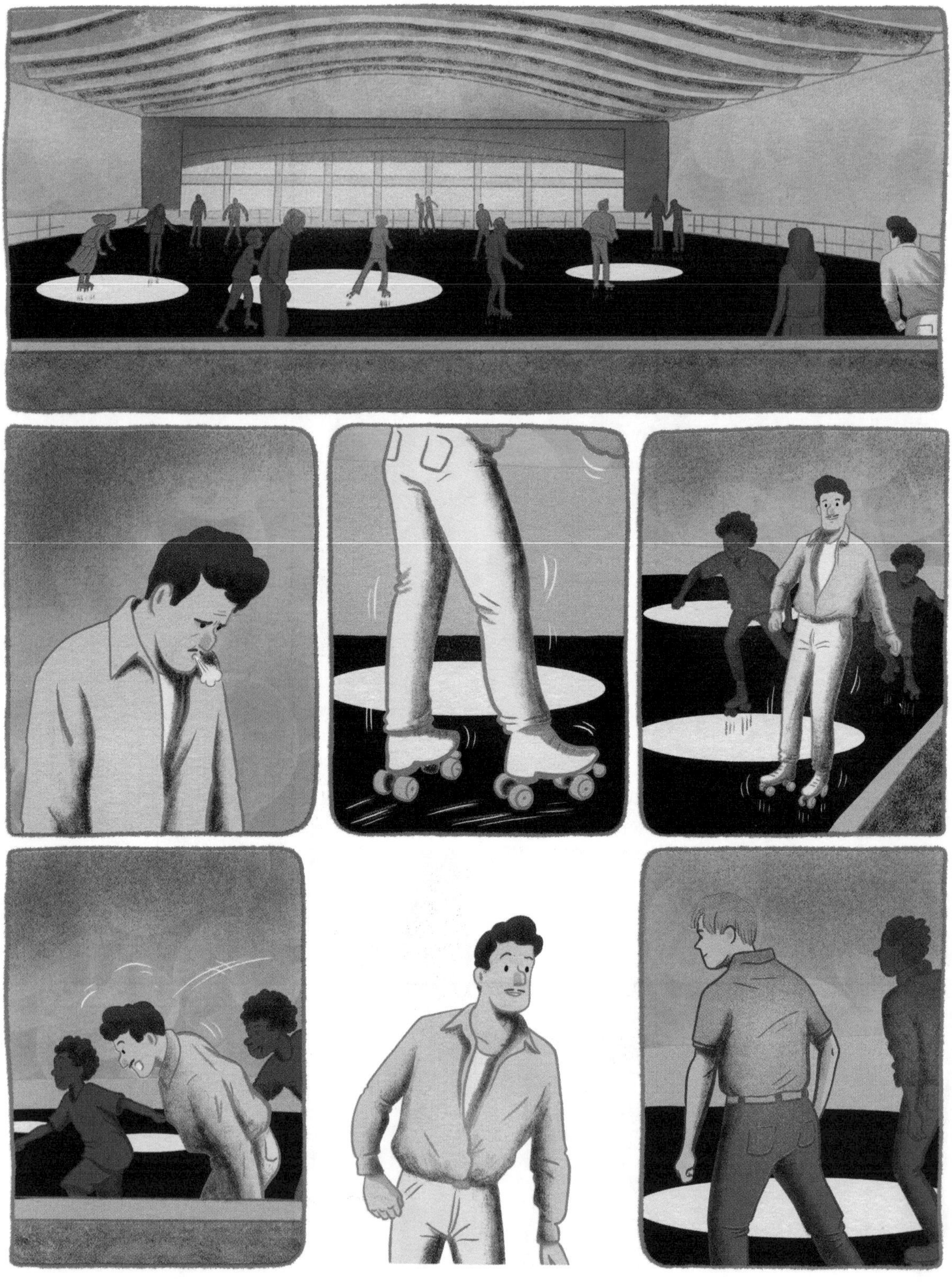

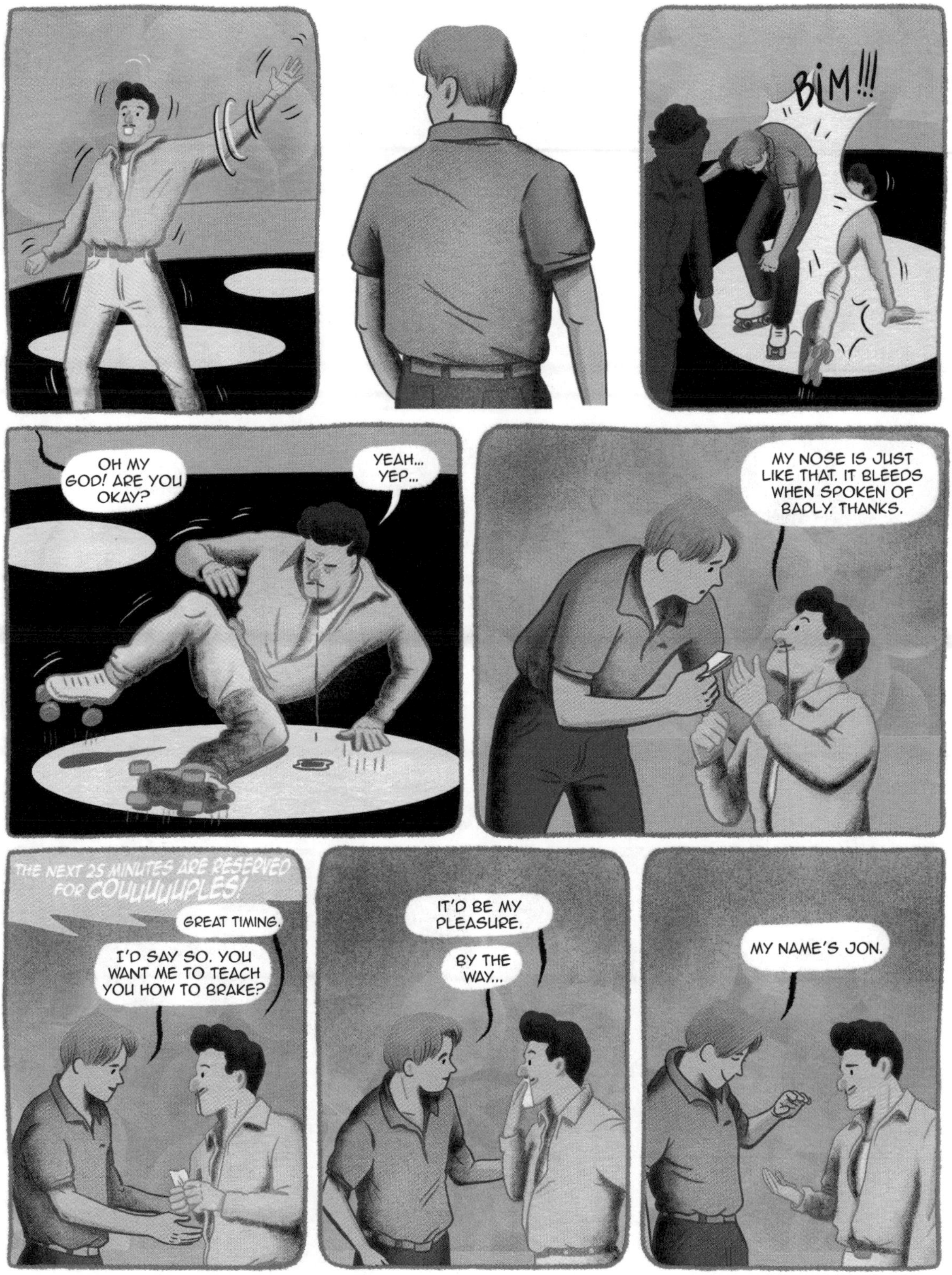
BIM!!!
OH MY GOD! ARE YOU OKAY?
YEAH... YEP...
MY NOSE IS JUST LIKE THAT. IT BLEEDS WHEN SPOKEN OF BADLY. THANKS.
THE NEXT 25 MINUTES ARE RESERVED FOR COUUUUUPLES!
GREAT TIMING.
I'D SAY SO. YOU WANT ME TO TEACH YOU HOW TO BRAKE?
IT'D BE MY PLEASURE.
BY THE WAY...
MY NAME'S JON.

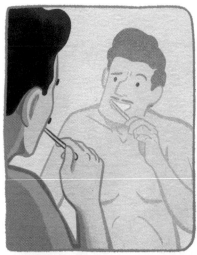
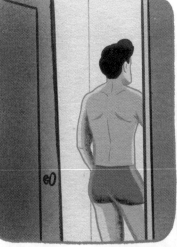
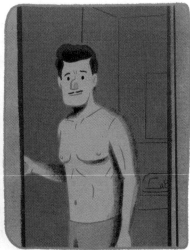

CHEATER.

NOW I'LL HAVE TO FRESHEN UP TOO.

NO NEED.

IT'S MY BREATH THAT WORRIES ME, DR. JON FIELDING, NOT YOURS.

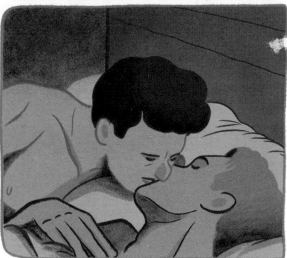

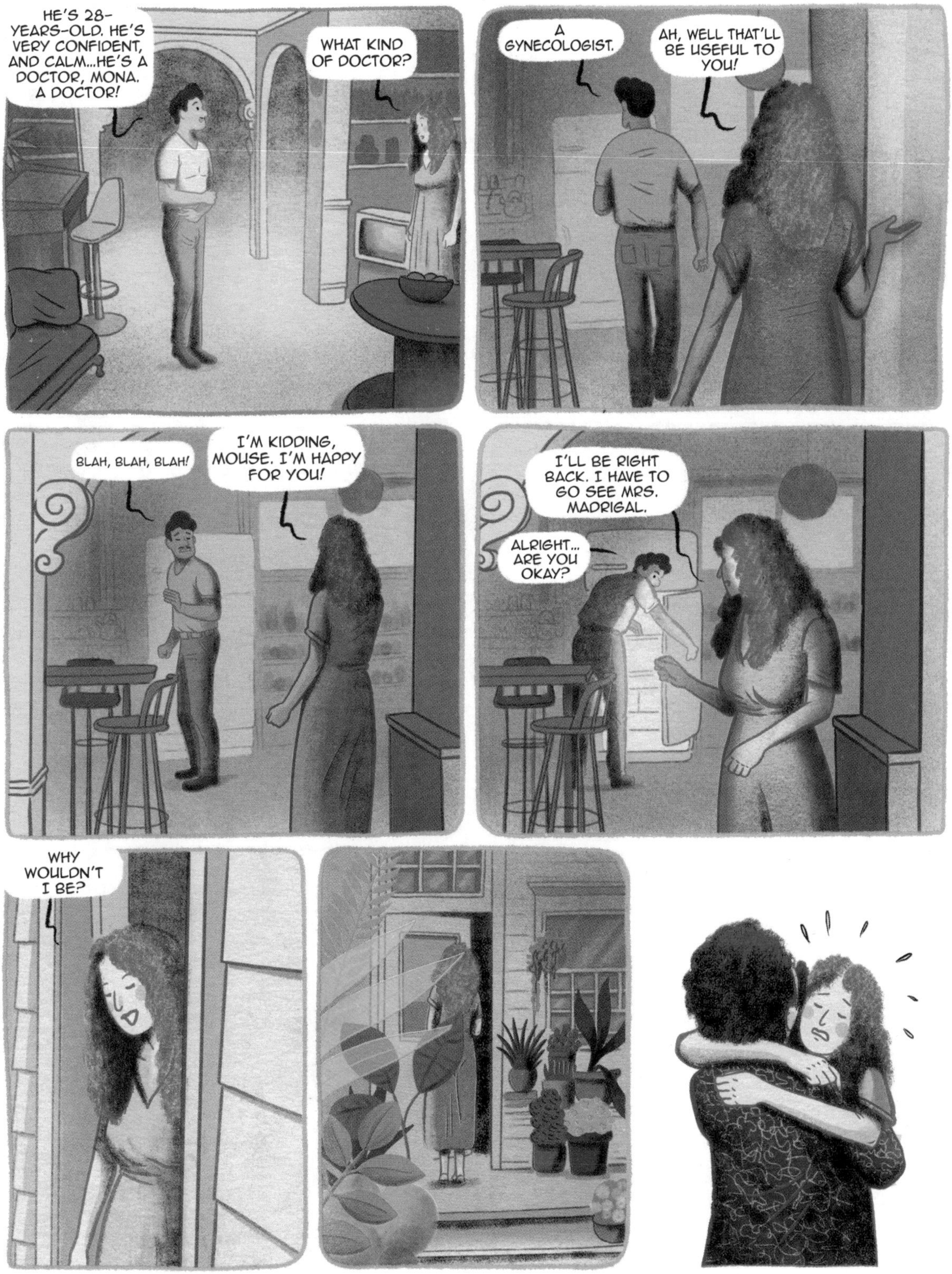
HE'S 28-YEARS-OLD. HE'S VERY CONFIDENT, AND CALM...HE'S A DOCTOR, MONA. A DOCTOR!
WHAT KIND OF DOCTOR?
A GYNECOLOGIST.
AH, WELL THAT'LL BE USEFUL TO YOU!
BLAH, BLAH, BLAH!
I'M KIDDING, MOUSE. I'M HAPPY FOR YOU!
I'LL BE RIGHT BACK. I HAVE TO GO SEE MRS. MADRIGAL.
ALRIGHT... ARE YOU OKAY?
WHY WOULDN'T I BE?

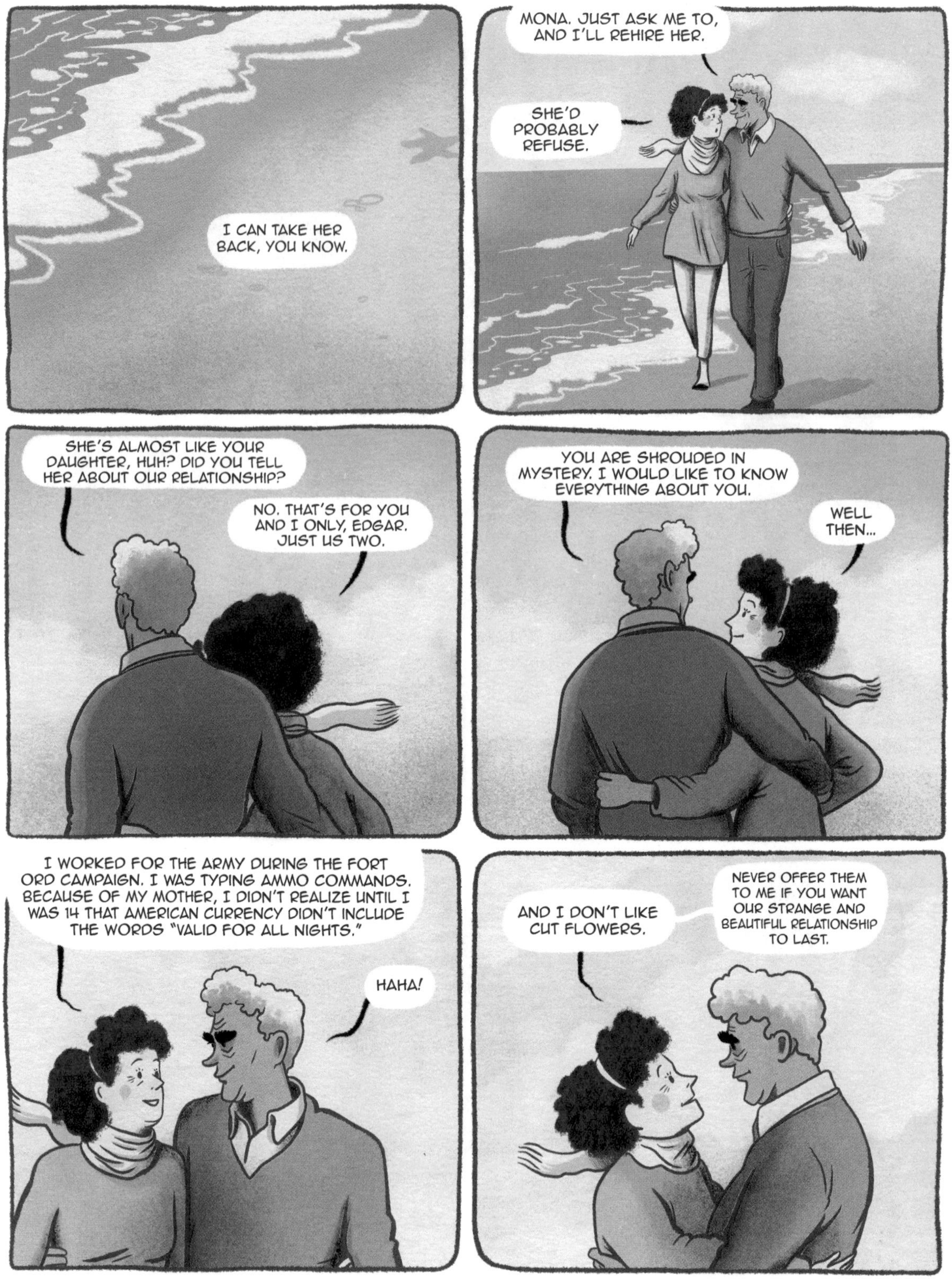
I CAN TAKE HER BACK, YOU KNOW.
MONA. JUST ASK ME TO, AND I'LL REHIRE HER.
SHE'D PROBABLY REFUSE.
SHE'S ALMOST LIKE YOUR DAUGHTER, HUH? DID YOU TELL HER ABOUT OUR RELATIONSHIP?
NO. THAT'S FOR YOU AND I ONLY, EDGAR. JUST US TWO.
YOU ARE SHROUDED IN MYSTERY. I WOULD LIKE TO KNOW EVERYTHING ABOUT YOU.
WELL THEN...
I WORKED FOR THE ARMY DURING THE FORT ORD CAMPAIGN. I WAS TYPING AMMO COMMANDS. BECAUSE OF MY MOTHER, I DIDN'T REALIZE UNTIL I WAS 14 THAT AMERICAN CURRENCY DIDN'T INCLUDE THE WORDS "VALID FOR ALL NIGHTS."
HAHA!
AND I DON'T LIKE CUT FLOWERS.
NEVER OFFER THEM TO ME IF YOU WANT OUR STRANGE AND BEAUTIFUL RELATIONSHIP TO LAST.

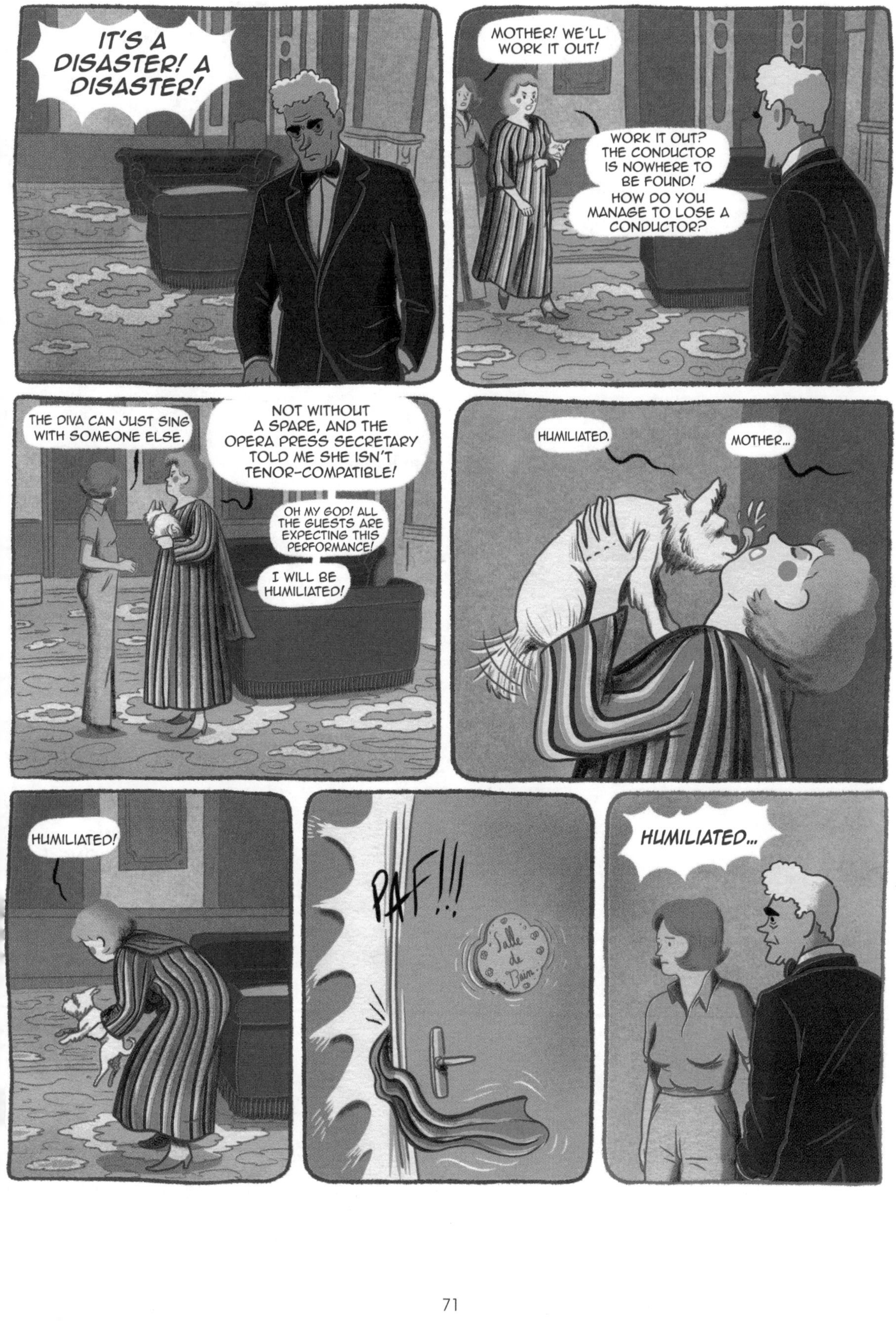
IT'S A DISASTER! A DISASTER!
MOTHER! WE'LL WORK IT OUT!
WORK IT OUT? THE CONDUCTOR IS NOWHERE TO BE FOUND!
HOW DO YOU MANAGE TO LOSE A CONDUCTOR?
THE DIVA CAN JUST SING WITH SOMEONE ELSE.
NOT WITHOUT A SPARE, AND THE OPERA PRESS SECRETARY TOLD ME SHE ISN'T TENOR-COMPATIBLE!
OH MY GOD! ALL THE GUESTS ARE EXPECTING THIS PERFORMANCE!
I WILL BE HUMILIATED!
HUMILIATED.
MOTHER...
HUMILIATED!
PAF!!!
Salle de Bain
HUMILIATED...

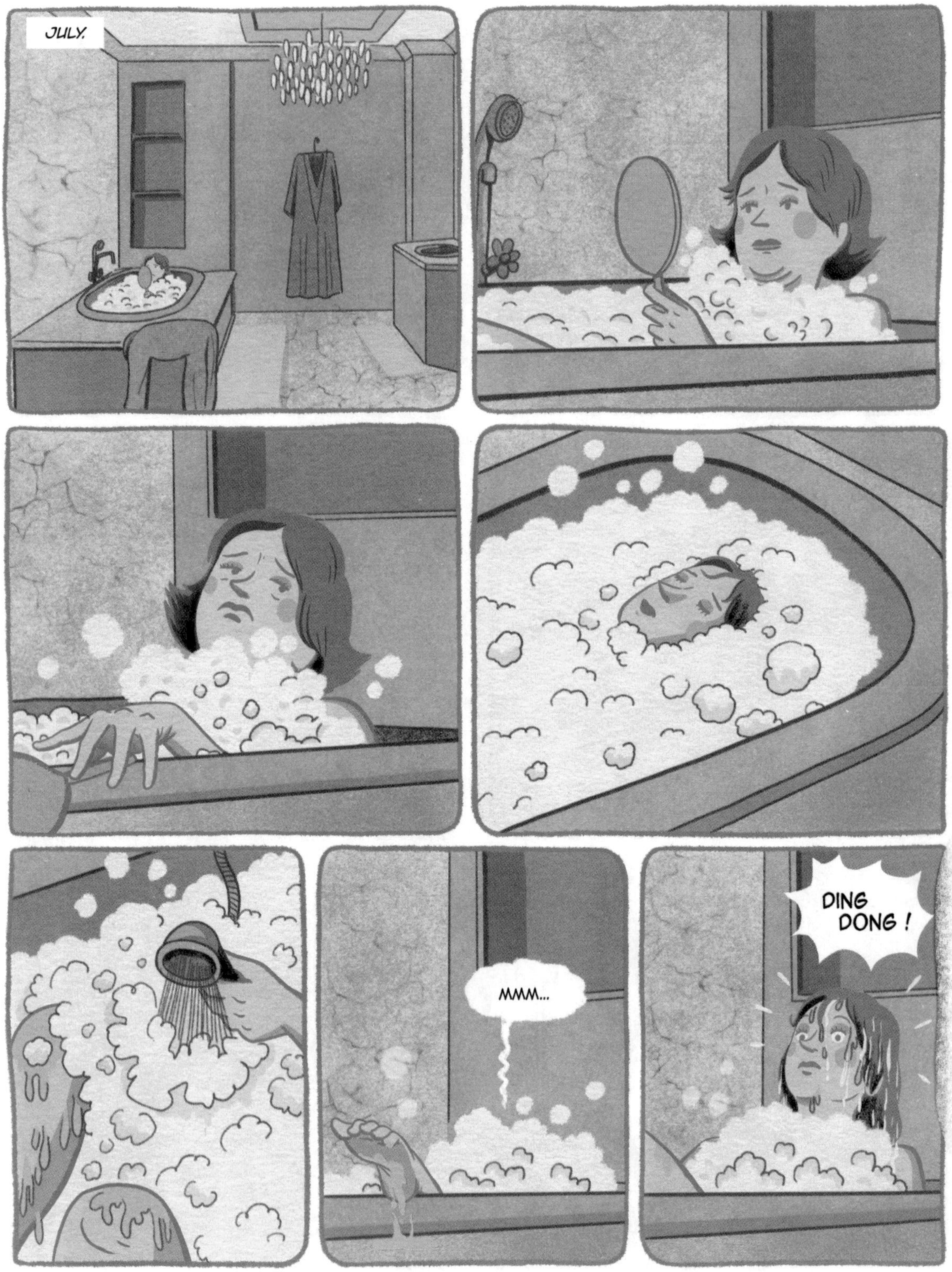
JULY.
MMM...
DING DONG !

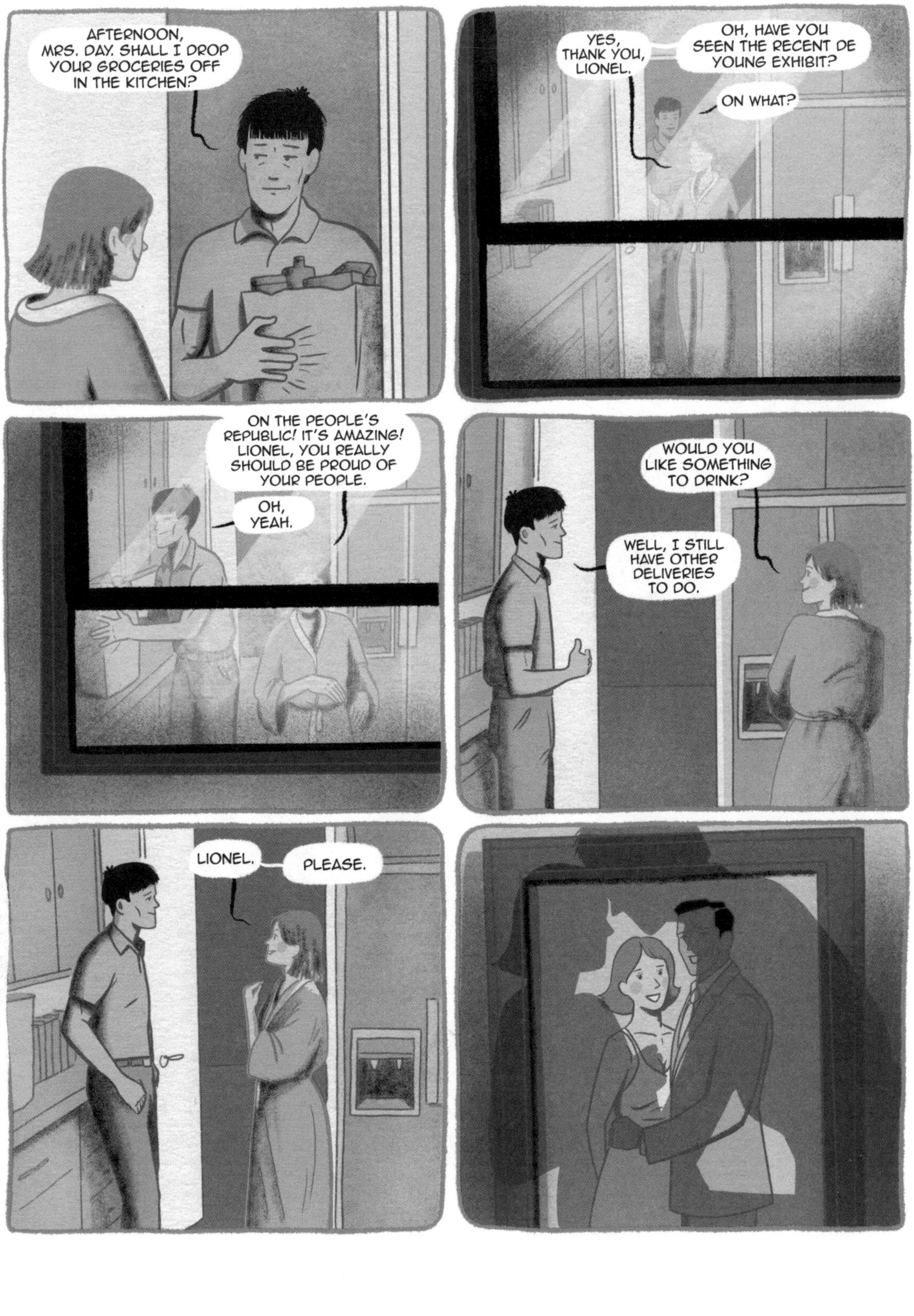
AFTERNOON, MRS. DAY. SHALL I DROP YOUR GROCERIES OFF IN THE KITCHEN?
YES, THANK YOU, LIONEL.
OH, HAVE YOU SEEN THE RECENT DE YOUNG EXHIBIT?
ON WHAT?
ON THE PEOPLE'S REPUBLIC! IT'S AMAZING! LIONEL, YOU REALLY SHOULD BE PROUD OF YOUR PEOPLE.
OH, YEAH.
WOULD YOU LIKE SOMETHING TO DRINK?
WELL, I STILL HAVE OTHER DELIVERIES TO DO.
LIONEL.
PLEASE.

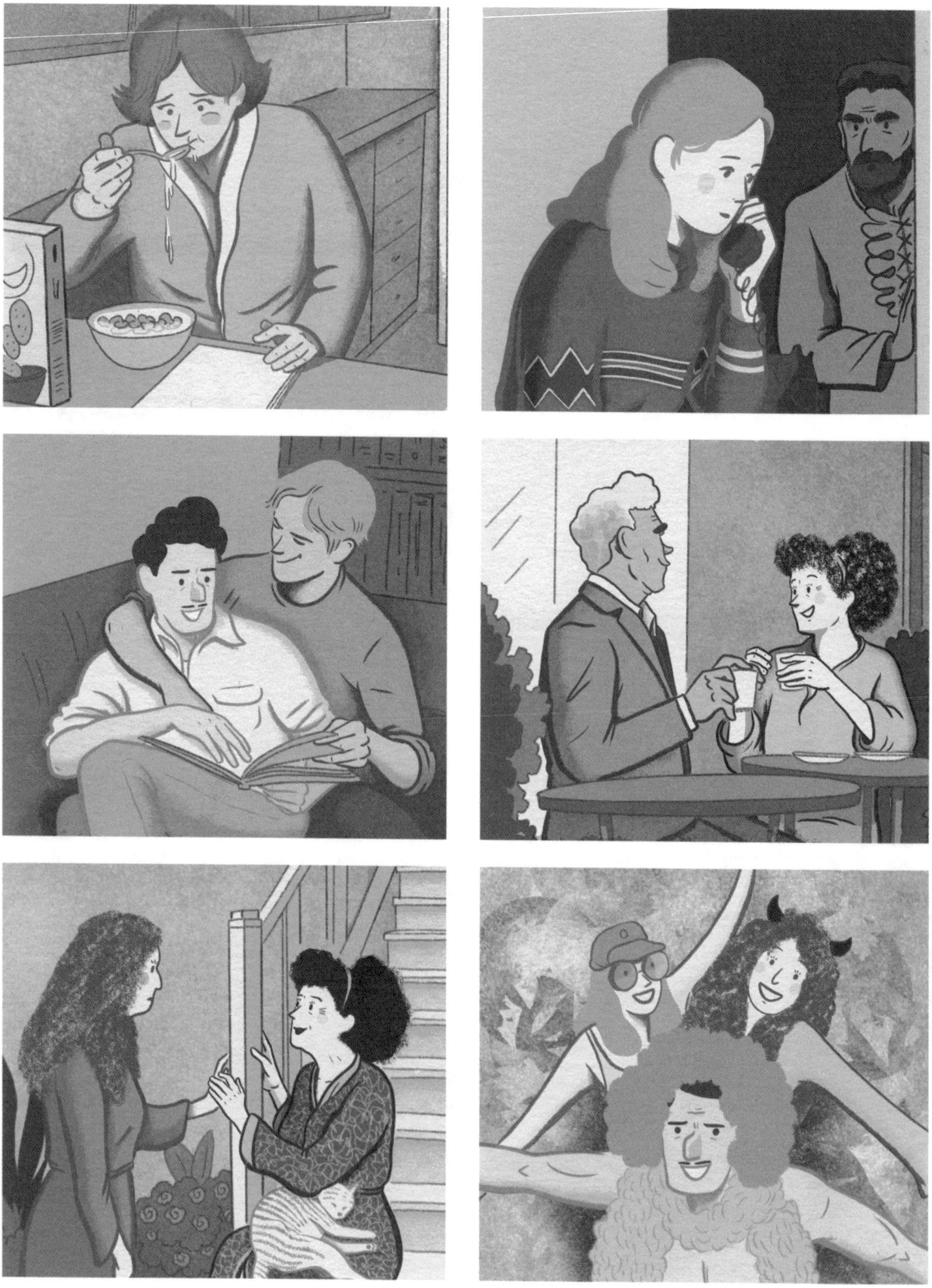

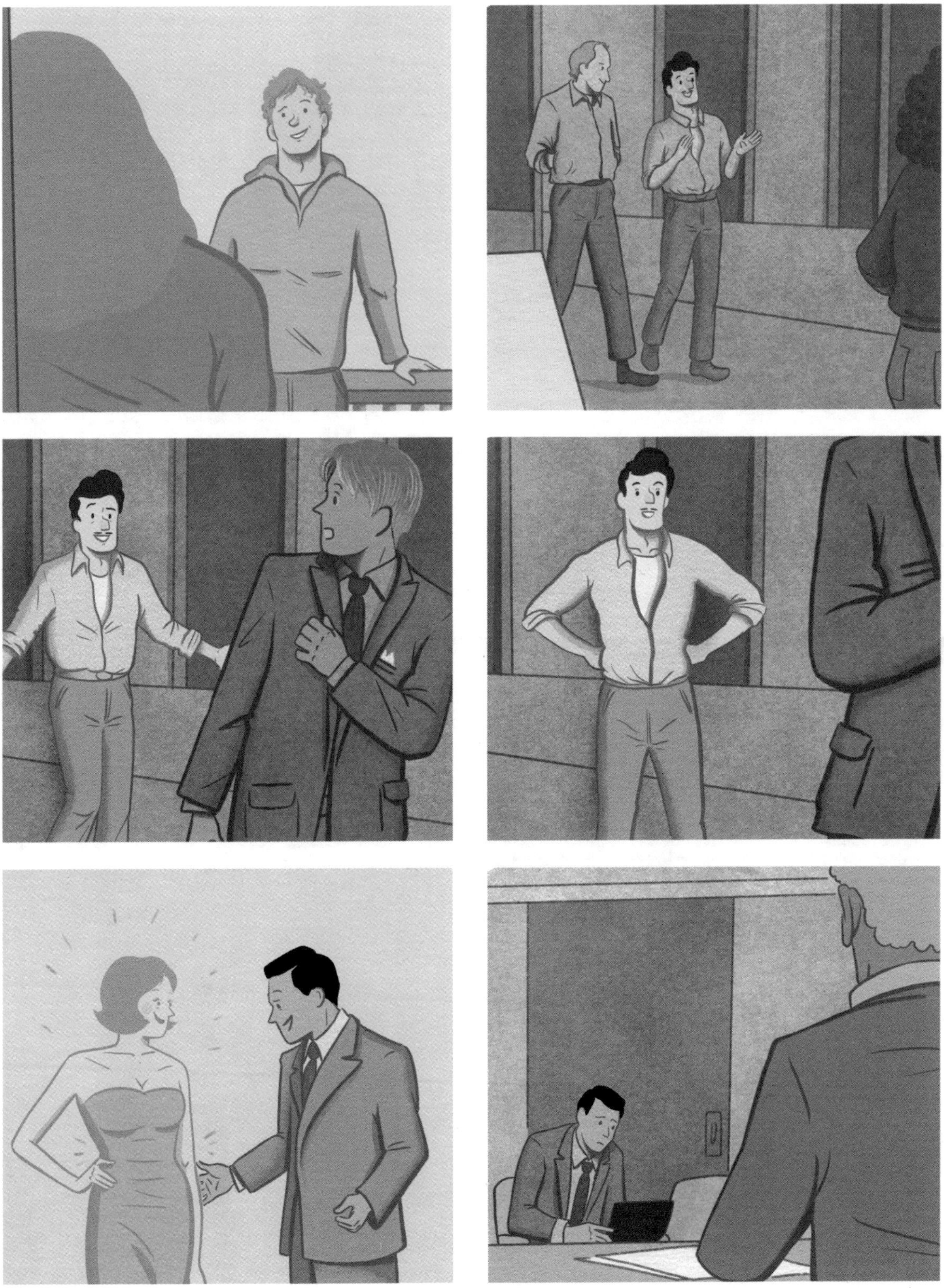

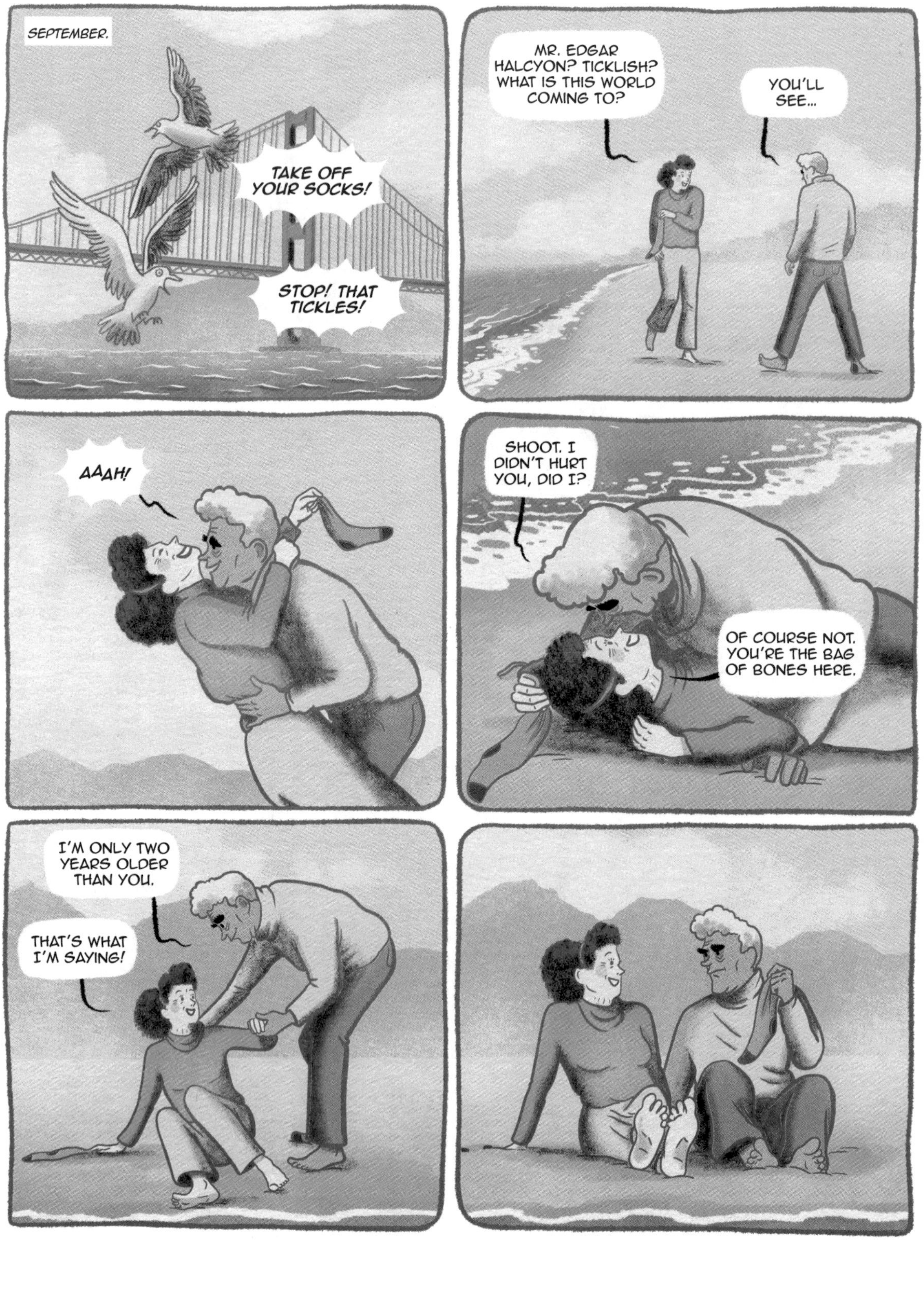
SEPTEMBER.
TAKE OFF YOUR SOCKS!
STOP! THAT TICKLES!
MR. EDGAR HALCYON? TICKLISH? WHAT IS THIS WORLD COMING TO?
YOU'LL SEE...
AAAH!
SHOOT. I DIDN'T HURT YOU, DID I?
OF COURSE NOT. YOU'RE THE BAG OF BONES HERE.
I'M ONLY TWO YEARS OLDER THAN YOU.
THAT'S WHAT I'M SAYING!

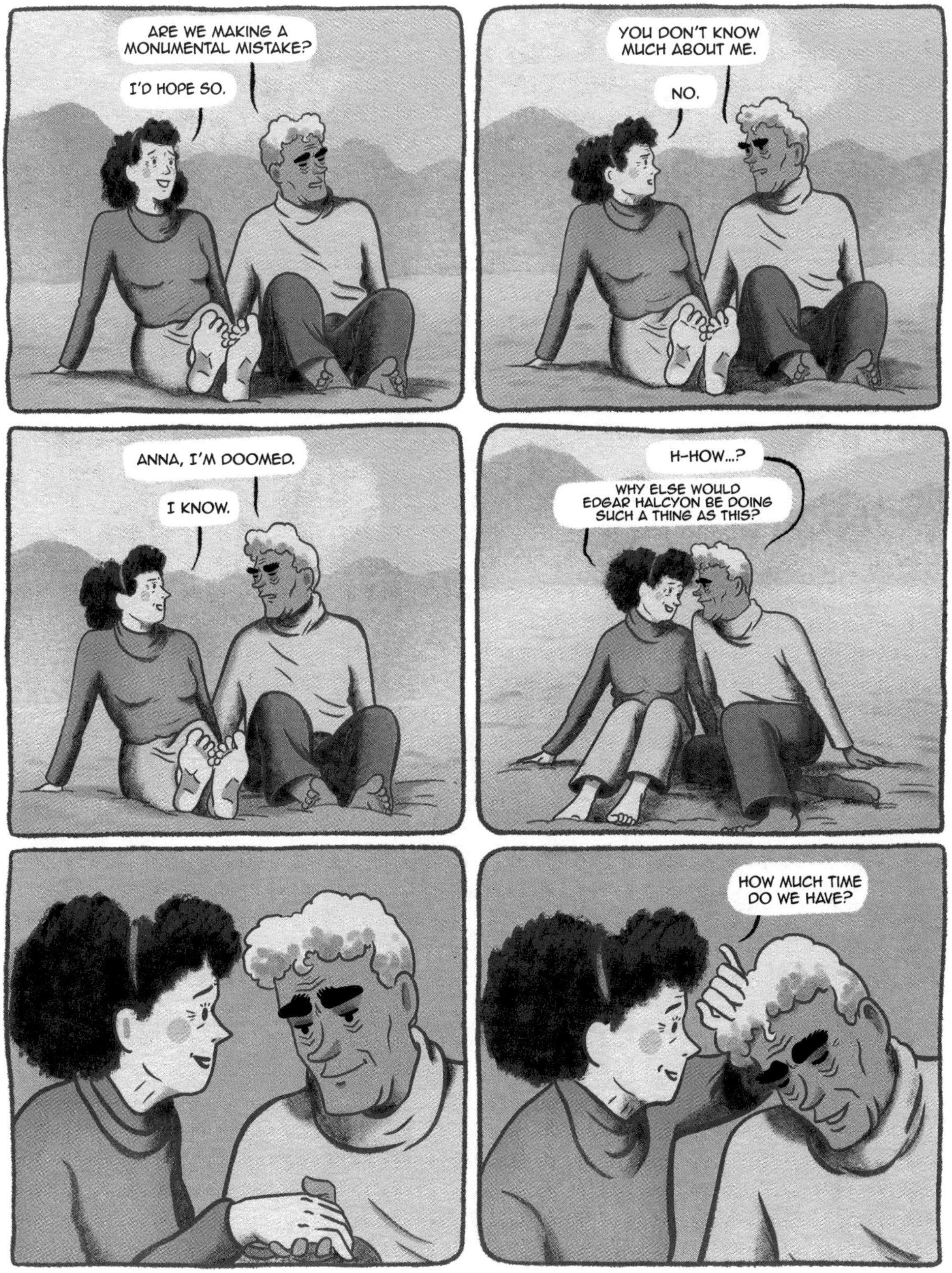
ARE WE MAKING A MONUMENTAL MISTAKE?
I'D HOPE SO.
YOU DON'T KNOW MUCH ABOUT ME.
NO.
ANNA, I'M DOOMED.
I KNOW.
H-HOW...?
WHY ELSE WOULD EDGAR HALCYON BE DOING SUCH A THING AS THIS?
HOW MUCH TIME DO WE HAVE?

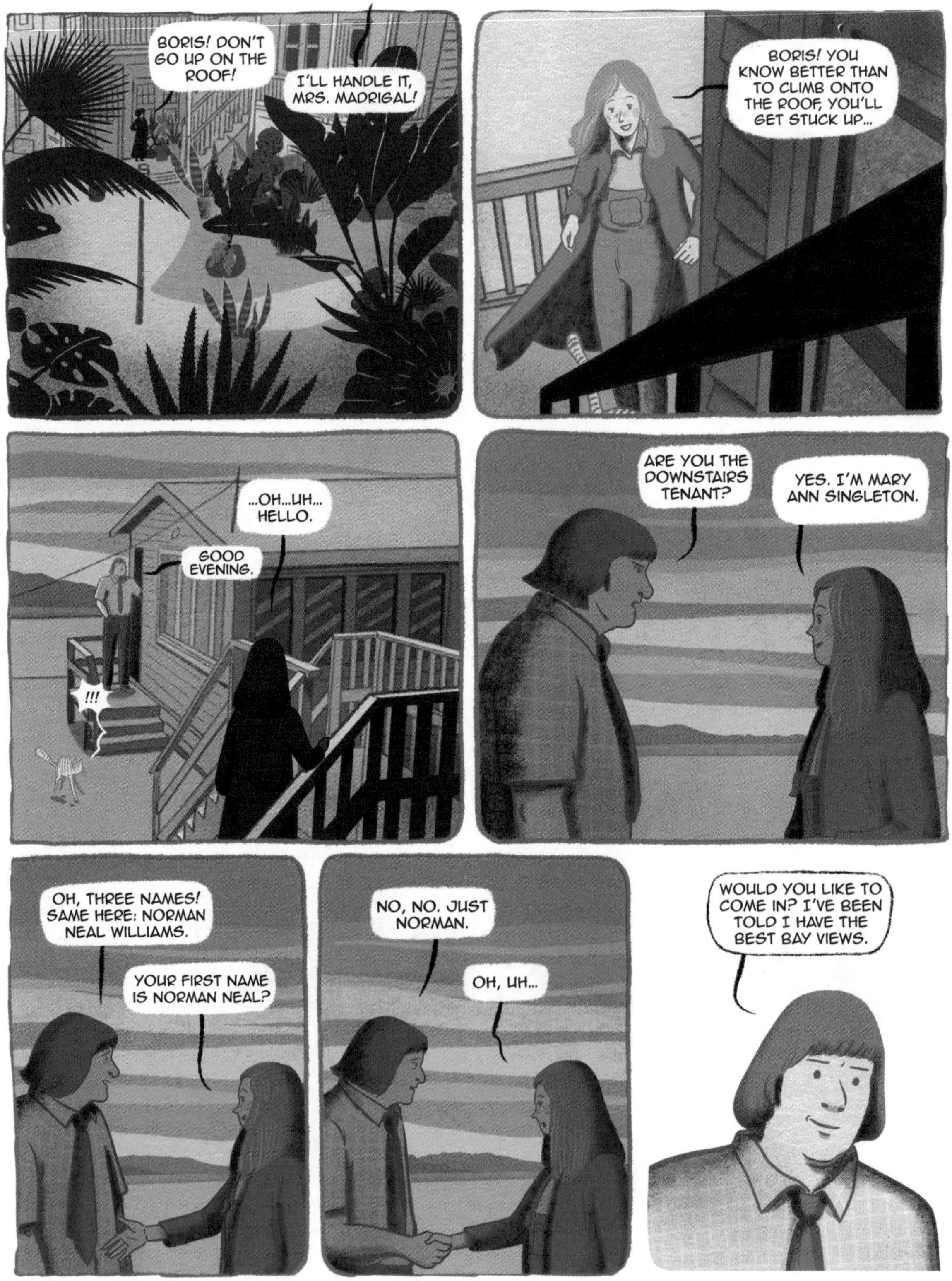
BORIS! DON'T GO UP ON THE ROOF!
I'LL HANDLE IT, MRS. MADRIGAL!
BORIS! YOU KNOW BETTER THAN TO CLIMB ONTO THE ROOF, YOU'LL GET STUCK UP...
GOOD EVENING.
...OH...UH... HELLO.
!!!
ARE YOU THE DOWNSTAIRS TENANT?
YES. I'M MARY ANN SINGLETON.
OH, THREE NAMES! SAME HERE: NORMAN NEAL WILLIAMS.
YOUR FIRST NAME IS NORMAN NEAL?
NO, NO. JUST NORMAN.
OH, UH...
WOULD YOU LIKE TO COME IN? I'VE BEEN TOLD I HAVE THE BEST BAY VIEWS.

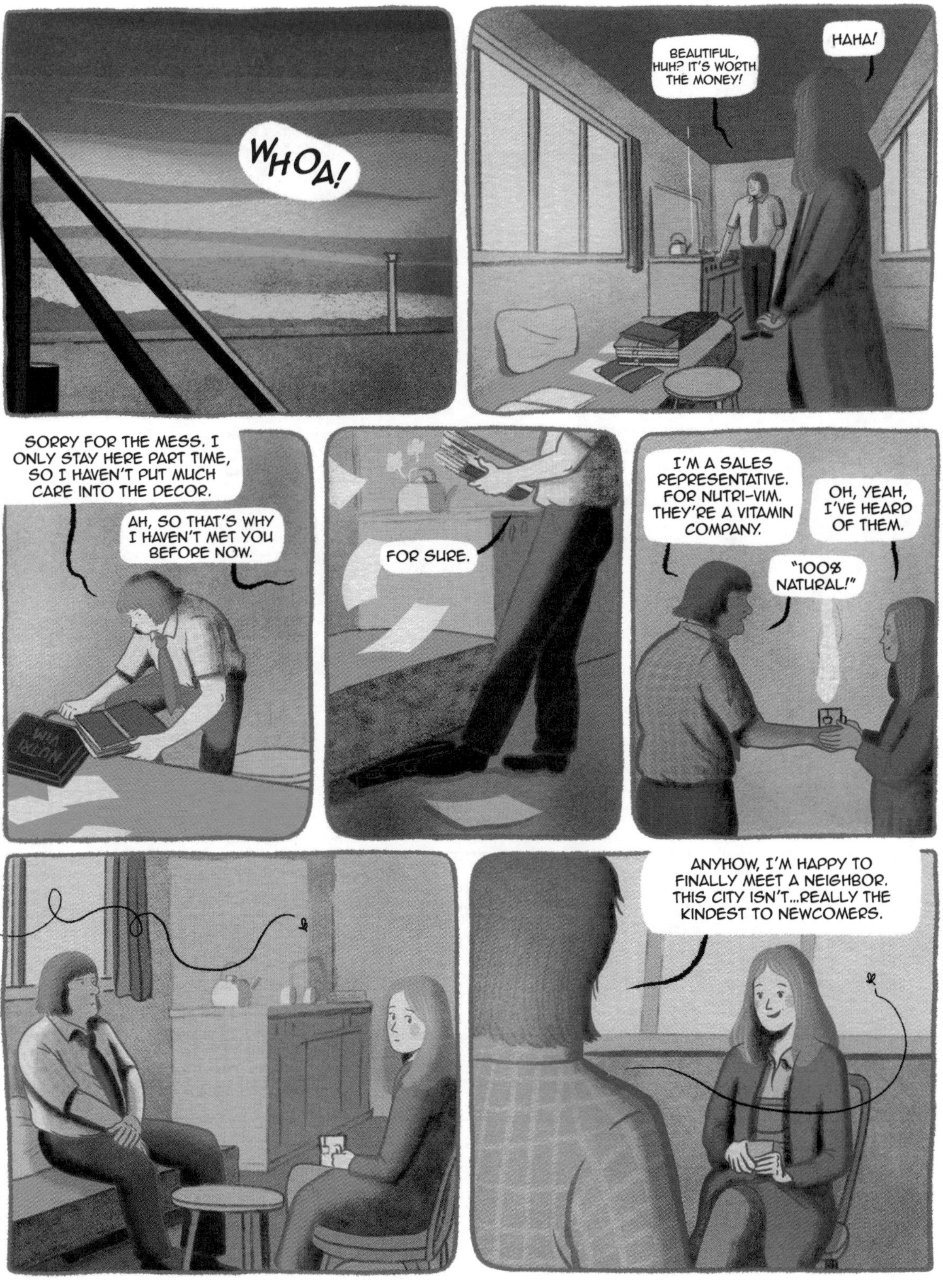
WHOA!
BEAUTIFUL, HUH? IT'S WORTH THE MONEY!
HAHA!
SORRY FOR THE MESS. I ONLY STAY HERE PART TIME, SO I HAVEN'T PUT MUCH CARE INTO THE DECOR.
AH, SO THAT'S WHY I HAVEN'T MET YOU BEFORE NOW.
NUTRI VIM
FOR SURE.
I'M A SALES REPRESENTATIVE. FOR NUTRI-VIM. THEY'RE A VITAMIN COMPANY.
OH, YEAH, I'VE HEARD OF THEM.
"100% NATURAL!"
ANYHOW, I'M HAPPY TO FINALLY MEET A NEIGHBOR. THIS CITY ISN'T...REALLY THE KINDEST TO NEWCOMERS.

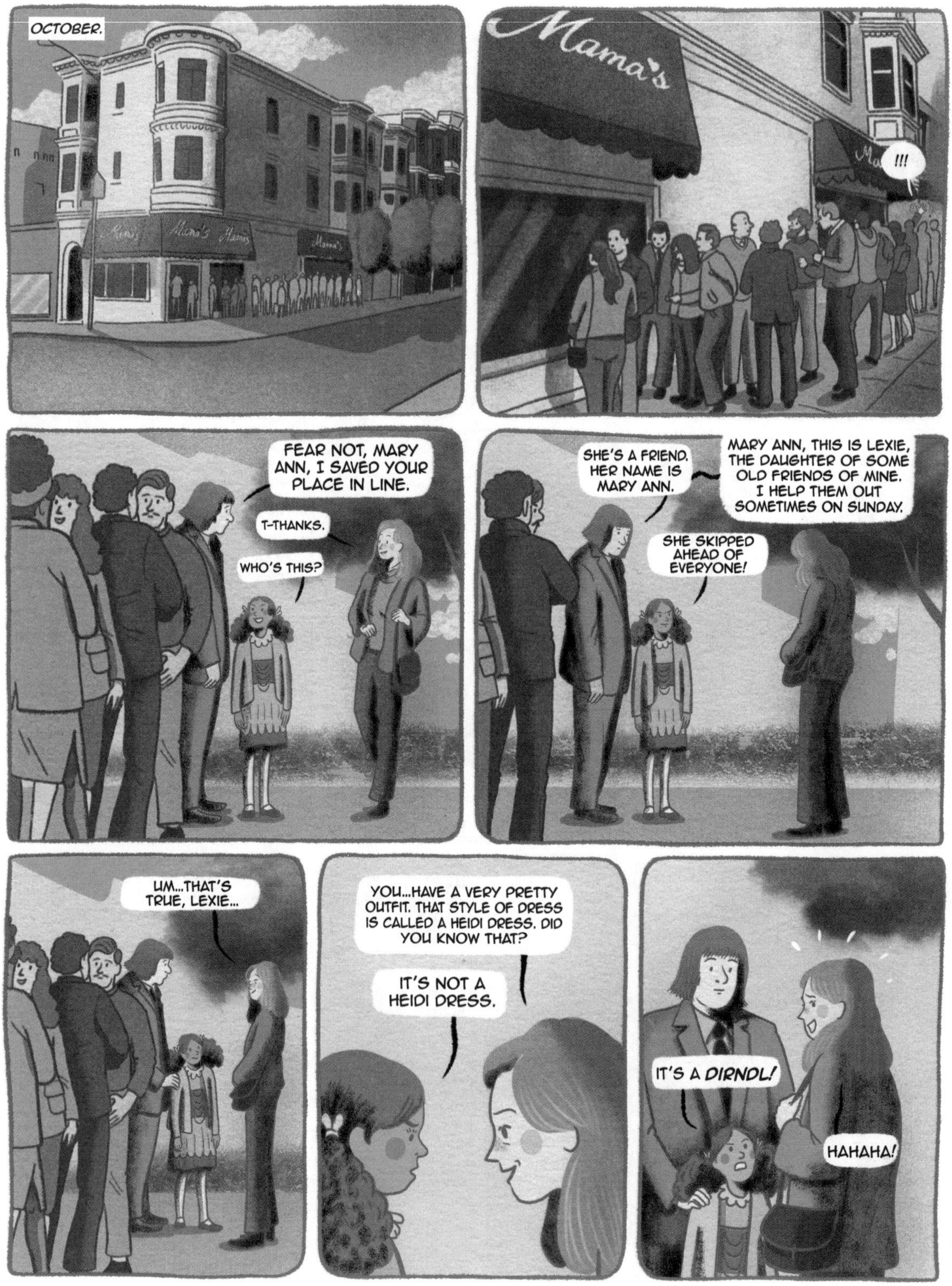
OCTOBER.
Mama's
!!!
FEAR NOT, MARY ANN, I SAVED YOUR PLACE IN LINE.
T-THANKS.
WHO'S THIS?
SHE'S A FRIEND. HER NAME IS MARY ANN.
MARY ANN, THIS IS LEXIE, THE DAUGHTER OF SOME OLD FRIENDS OF MINE. I HELP THEM OUT SOMETIMES ON SUNDAY.
SHE SKIPPED AHEAD OF EVERYONE!
UM...THAT'S TRUE, LEXIE...
YOU...HAVE A VERY PRETTY OUTFIT. THAT STYLE OF DRESS IS CALLED A HEIDI DRESS. DID YOU KNOW THAT?
IT'S NOT A HEIDI DRESS.
IT'S A *DIRNDL!*
HAHAHA!

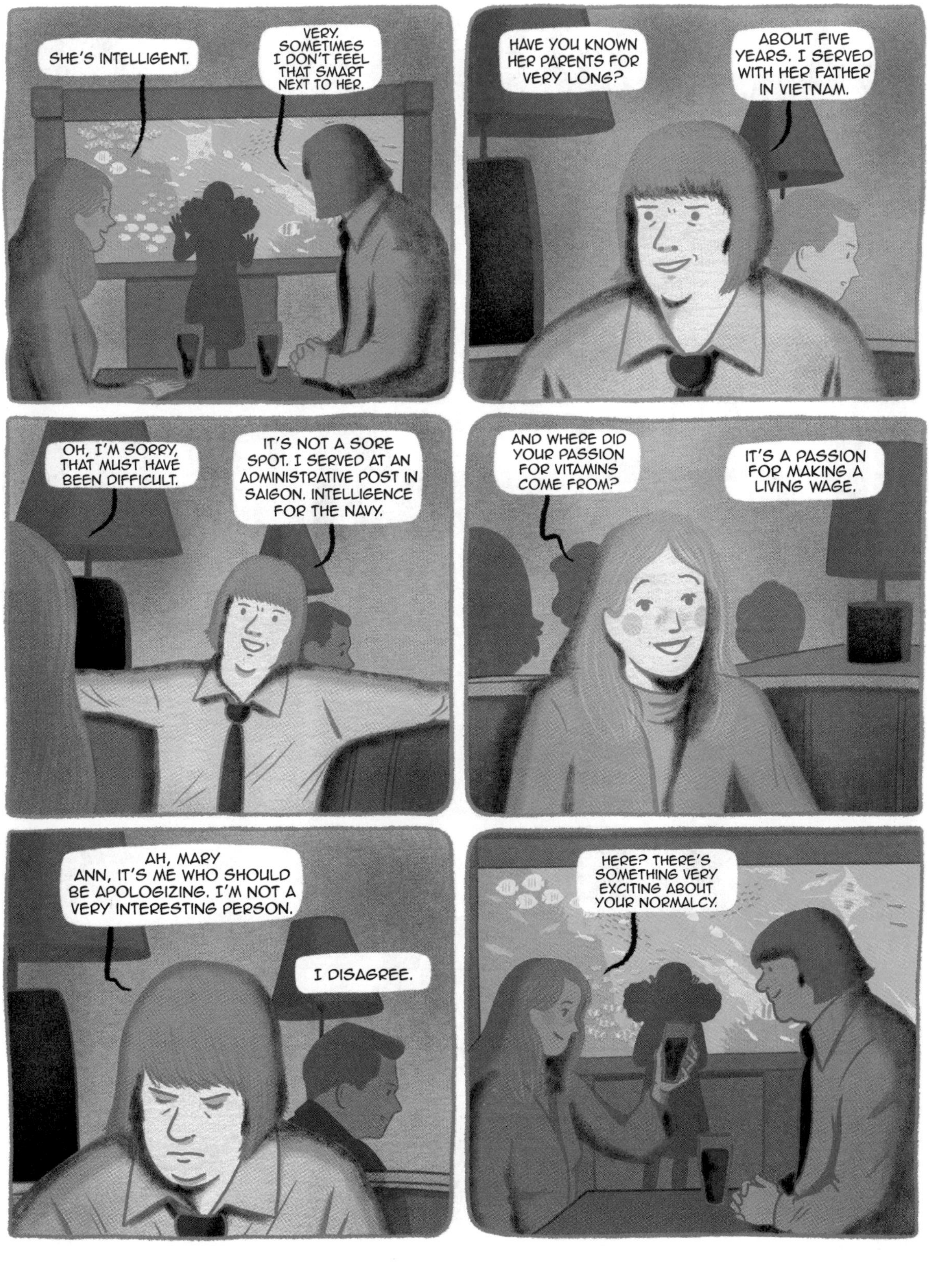
SHE'S INTELLIGENT.
VERY. SOMETIMES I DON'T FEEL THAT SMART NEXT TO HER.
HAVE YOU KNOWN HER PARENTS FOR VERY LONG?
ABOUT FIVE YEARS. I SERVED WITH HER FATHER IN VIETNAM.
OH, I'M SORRY, THAT MUST HAVE BEEN DIFFICULT.
IT'S NOT A SORE SPOT. I SERVED AT AN ADMINISTRATIVE POST IN SAIGON. INTELLIGENCE FOR THE NAVY.
AND WHERE DID YOUR PASSION FOR VITAMINS COME FROM?
IT'S A PASSION FOR MAKING A LIVING WAGE.
AH, MARY ANN, IT'S ME WHO SHOULD BE APOLOGIZING. I'M NOT A VERY INTERESTING PERSON.
I DISAGREE.
HERE? THERE'S SOMETHING VERY EXCITING ABOUT YOUR NORMALCY.

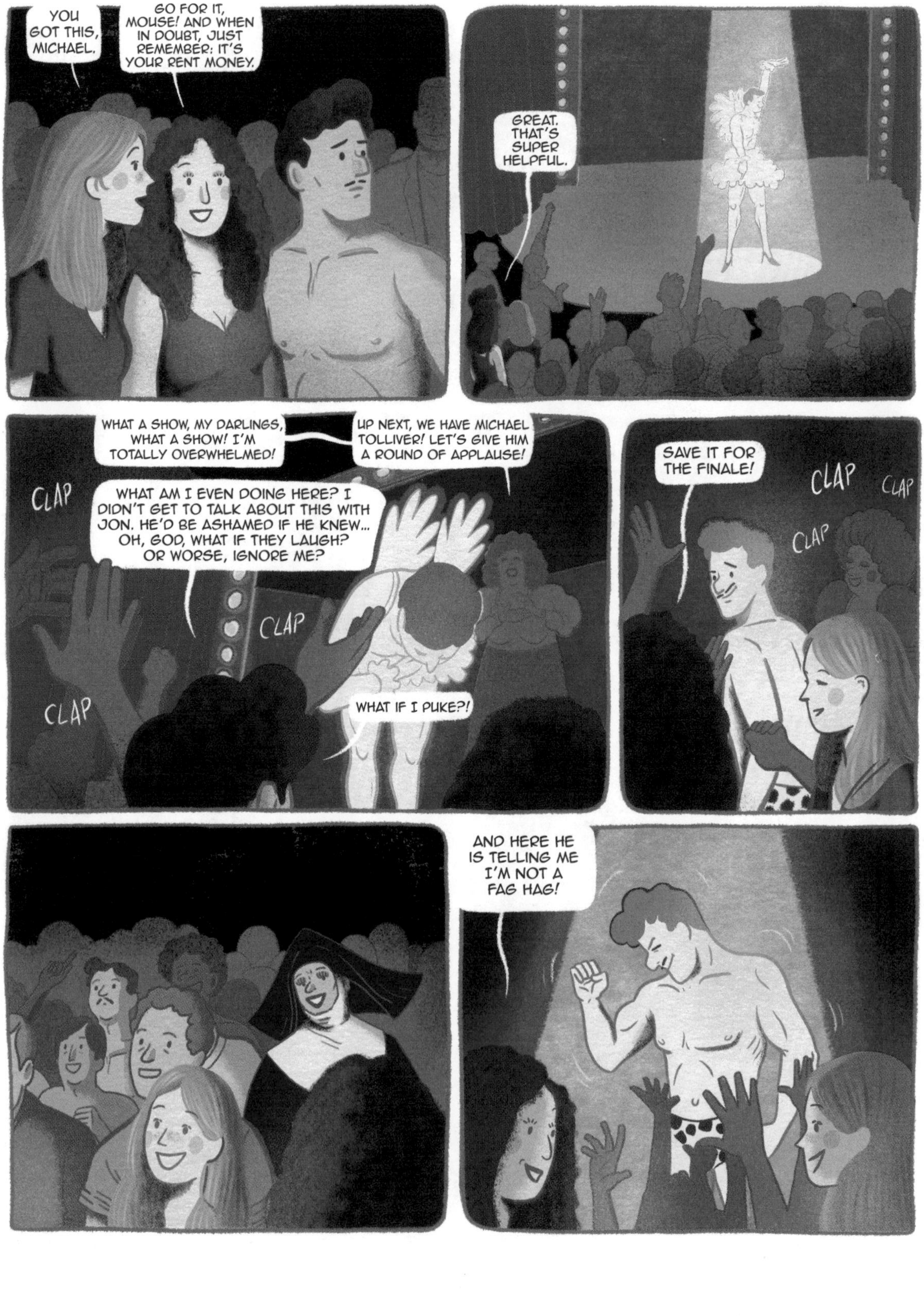
YOU GOT THIS, MICHAEL.
GO FOR IT, MOUSE! AND WHEN IN DOUBT, JUST REMEMBER: IT'S YOUR RENT MONEY.
GREAT. THAT'S SUPER HELPFUL.
WHAT A SHOW, MY DARLINGS, WHAT A SHOW! I'M TOTALLY OVERWHELMED!
UP NEXT, WE HAVE MICHAEL TOLLIVER! LET'S GIVE HIM A ROUND OF APPLAUSE!
CLAP
WHAT AM I EVEN DOING HERE? I DIDN'T GET TO TALK ABOUT THIS WITH JON. HE'D BE ASHAMED IF HE KNEW... OH, GOD, WHAT IF THEY LAUGH? OR WORSE, IGNORE ME?
CLAP
CLAP
WHAT IF I PUKE?!
SAVE IT FOR THE FINALE!
CLAP
CLAP
CLAP
AND HERE HE IS TELLING ME I'M NOT A FAG HAG!

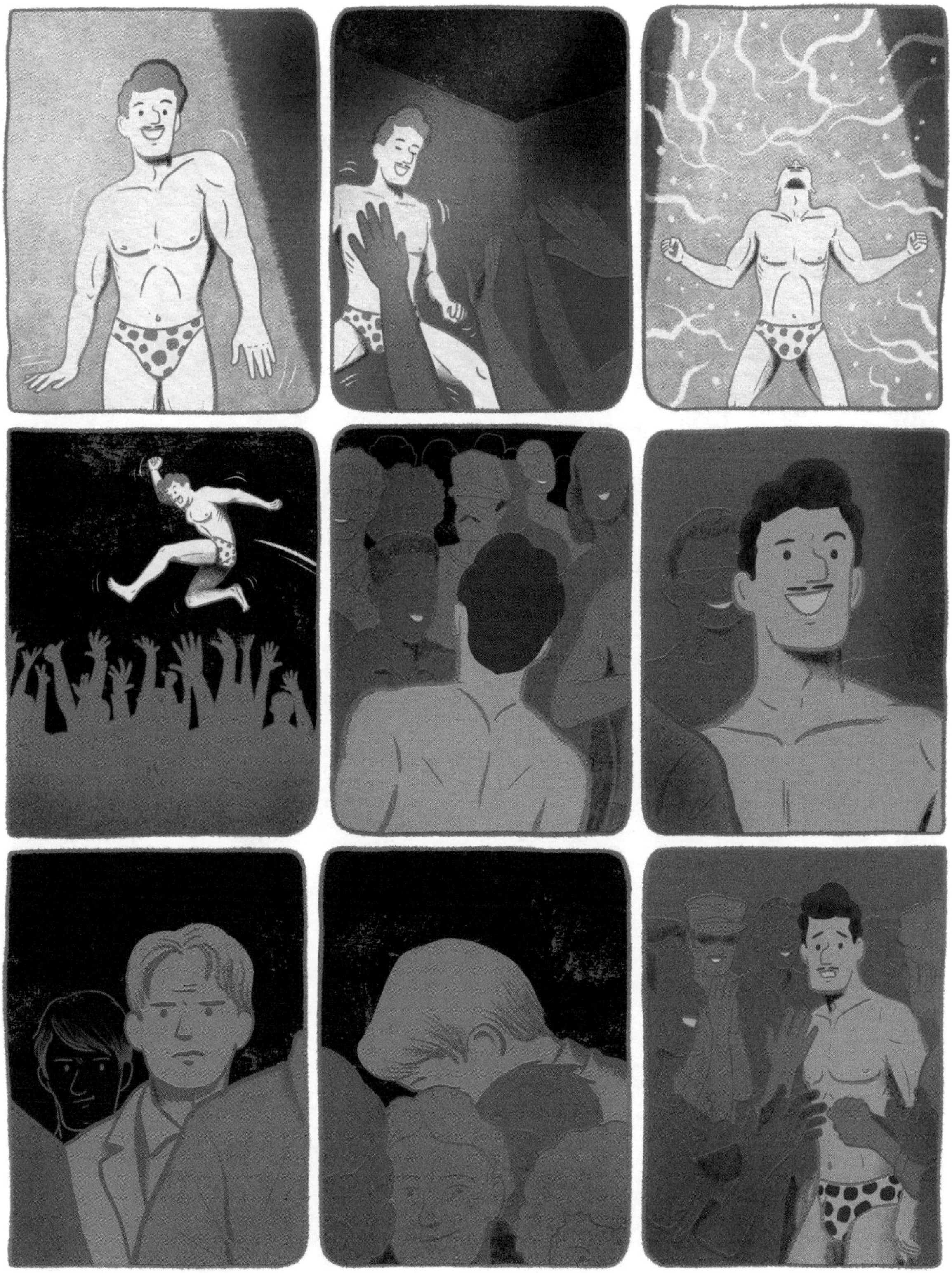

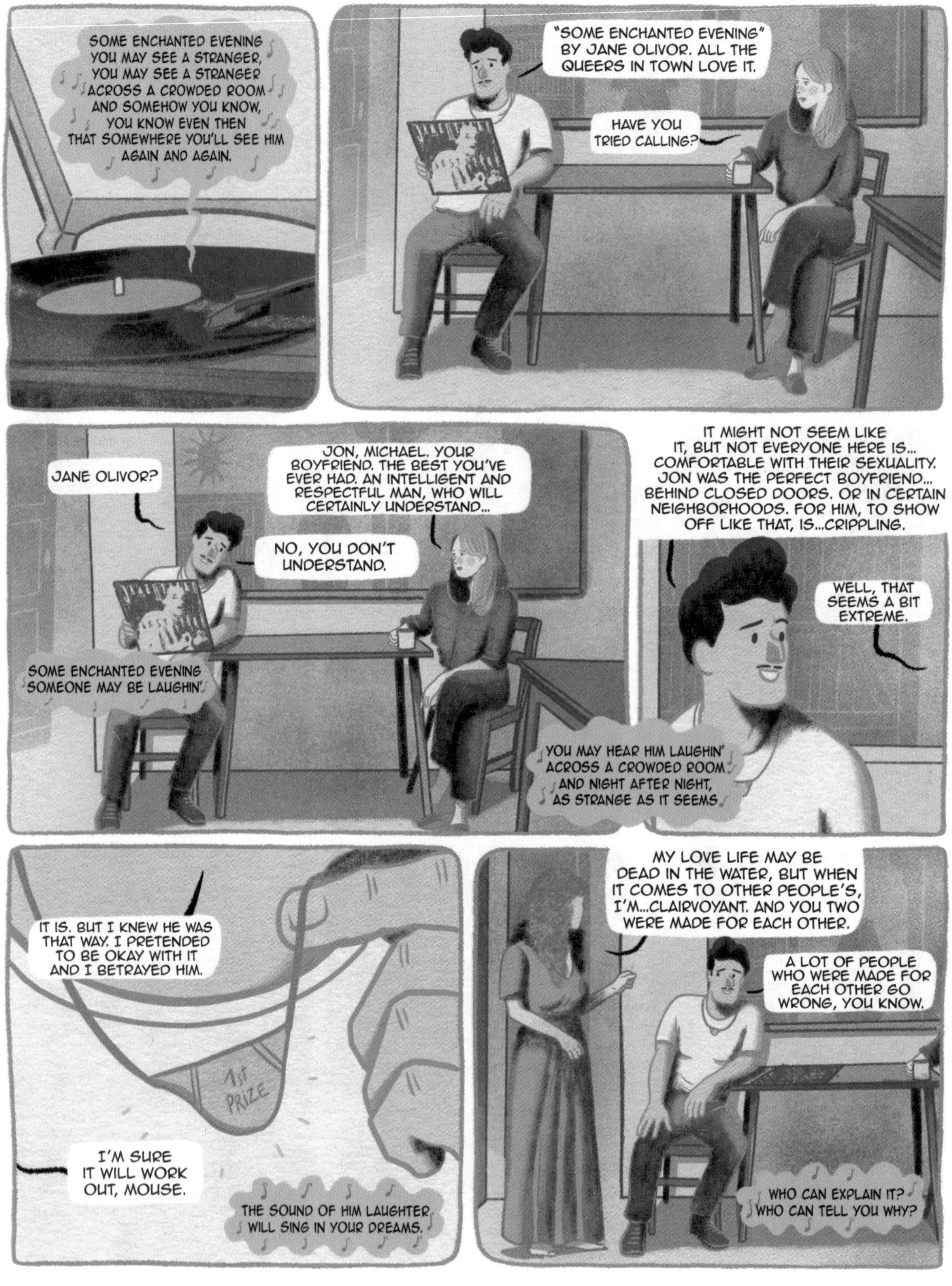
SOME ENCHANTED EVENING YOU MAY SEE A STRANGER, YOU MAY SEE A STRANGER ACROSS A CROWDED ROOM AND SOMEHOW YOU KNOW, YOU KNOW EVEN THEN THAT SOMEWHERE YOU'LL SEE HIM AGAIN AND AGAIN.
"SOME ENCHANTED EVENING" BY JANE OLIVOR. ALL THE QUEERS IN TOWN LOVE IT.
HAVE YOU TRIED CALLING?
JANE OLIVOR?
JON, MICHAEL. YOUR BOYFRIEND. THE BEST YOU'VE EVER HAD. AN INTELLIGENT AND RESPECTFUL MAN, WHO WILL CERTAINLY UNDERSTAND...
NO, YOU DON'T UNDERSTAND.
SOME ENCHANTED EVENING SOMEONE MAY BE LAUGHIN'
IT MIGHT NOT SEEM LIKE IT, BUT NOT EVERYONE HERE IS... COMFORTABLE WITH THEIR SEXUALITY. JON WAS THE PERFECT BOYFRIEND... BEHIND CLOSED DOORS. OR IN CERTAIN NEIGHBORHOODS. FOR HIM, TO SHOW OFF LIKE THAT, IS...CRIPPLING.
WELL, THAT SEEMS A BIT EXTREME.
YOU MAY HEAR HIM LAUGHIN' ACROSS A CROWDED ROOM AND NIGHT AFTER NIGHT, AS STRANGE AS IT SEEMS
IT IS. BUT I KNEW HE WAS THAT WAY. I PRETENDED TO BE OKAY WITH IT AND I BETRAYED HIM.
1st PRIZE
I'M SURE IT WILL WORK OUT, MOUSE.
THE SOUND OF HIM LAUGHTER WILL SING IN YOUR DREAMS.
MY LOVE LIFE MAY BE DEAD IN THE WATER, BUT WHEN IT COMES TO OTHER PEOPLE'S, I'M...CLAIRVOYANT. AND YOU TWO WERE MADE FOR EACH OTHER.
A LOT OF PEOPLE WHO WERE MADE FOR EACH OTHER GO WRONG, YOU KNOW.
WHO CAN EXPLAIN IT? WHO CAN TELL YOU WHY?

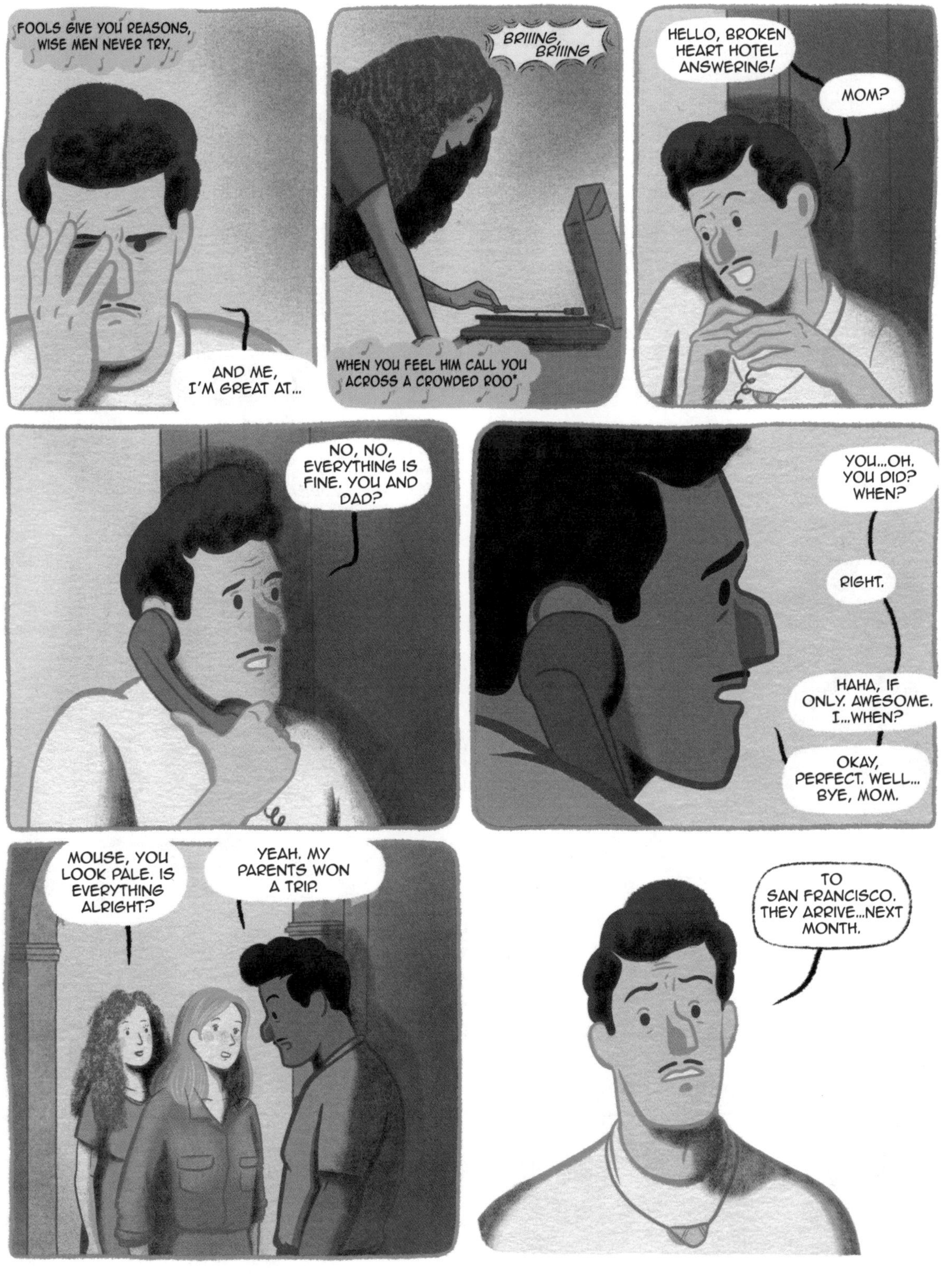
FOOLS GIVE YOU REASONS, WISE MEN NEVER TRY.
AND ME, I'M GREAT AT...
BRIIING, BRIIING
WHEN YOU FEEL HIM CALL YOU ACROSS A CROWDED ROO*
HELLO, BROKEN HEART HOTEL ANSWERING!
MOM?
NO, NO, EVERYTHING IS FINE. YOU AND DAD?
YOU...OH. YOU DID? WHEN?
RIGHT.
HAHA, IF ONLY. AWESOME. I...WHEN?
OKAY, PERFECT. WELL... BYE, MOM.
MOUSE, YOU LOOK PALE. IS EVERYTHING ALRIGHT?
YEAH. MY PARENTS WON A TRIP.
TO SAN FRANCISCO. THEY ARRIVE...NEXT MONTH.

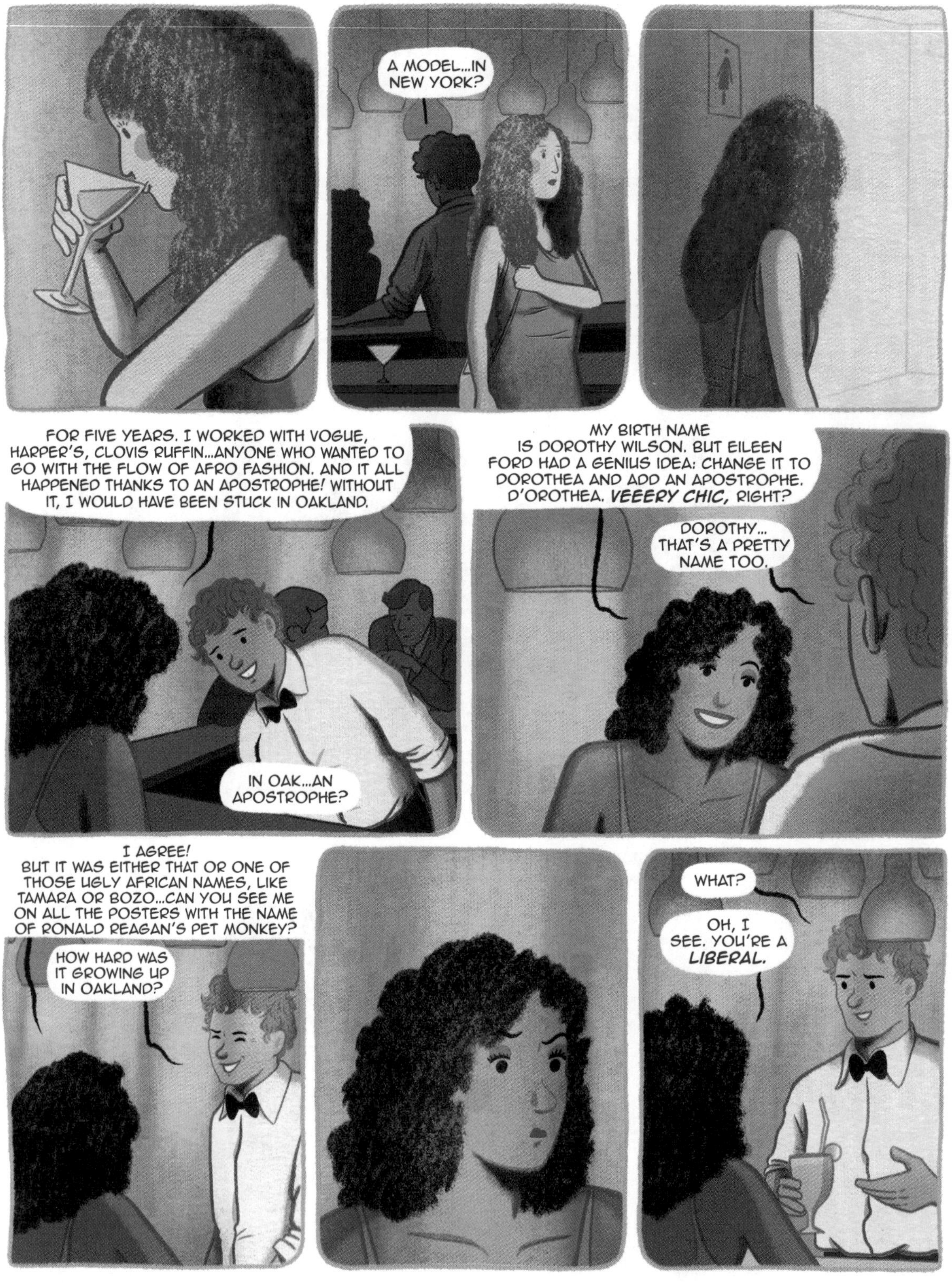

A MODEL...IN NEW YORK?
FOR FIVE YEARS. I WORKED WITH VOGUE, HARPER'S, CLOVIS RUFFIN...ANYONE WHO WANTED TO GO WITH THE FLOW OF AFRO FASHION. AND IT ALL HAPPENED THANKS TO AN APOSTROPHE! WITHOUT IT, I WOULD HAVE BEEN STUCK IN OAKLAND.
IN OAK...AN APOSTROPHE?
MY BIRTH NAME IS DOROTHY WILSON. BUT EILEEN FORD HAD A GENIUS IDEA: CHANGE IT TO DOROTHEA AND ADD AN APOSTROPHE. D'OROTHEA. VEEERY CHIC, RIGHT?
DOROTHY... THAT'S A PRETTY NAME TOO.
I AGREE! BUT IT WAS EITHER THAT OR ONE OF THOSE UGLY AFRICAN NAMES, LIKE TAMARA OR BOZO...CAN YOU SEE ME ON ALL THE POSTERS WITH THE NAME OF RONALD REAGAN'S PET MONKEY?
HOW HARD WAS IT GROWING UP IN OAKLAND?
WHAT?
OH, I SEE. YOU'RE A LIBERAL.

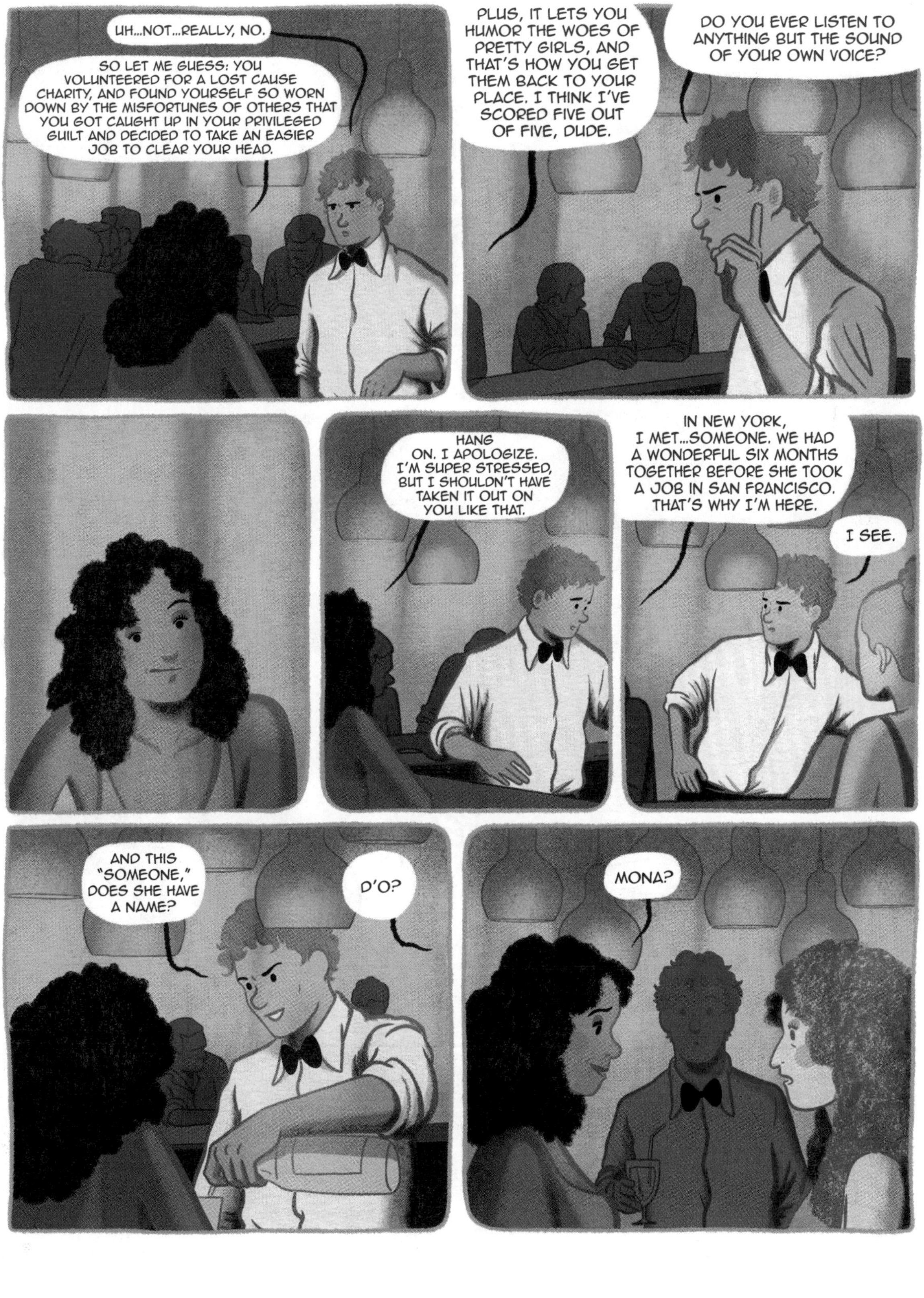
UH...NOT...REALLY, NO.
SO LET ME GUESS: YOU VOLUNTEERED FOR A LOST CAUSE CHARITY, AND FOUND YOURSELF SO WORN DOWN BY THE MISFORTUNES OF OTHERS THAT YOU GOT CAUGHT UP IN YOUR PRIVILEGED GUILT AND DECIDED TO TAKE AN EASIER JOB TO CLEAR YOUR HEAD.
PLUS, IT LETS YOU HUMOR THE WOES OF PRETTY GIRLS, AND THAT'S HOW YOU GET THEM BACK TO YOUR PLACE. I THINK I'VE SCORED FIVE OUT OF FIVE, DUDE.
DO YOU EVER LISTEN TO ANYTHING BUT THE SOUND OF YOUR OWN VOICE?
HANG ON. I APOLOGIZE. I'M SUPER STRESSED, BUT I SHOULDN'T HAVE TAKEN IT OUT ON YOU LIKE THAT.
IN NEW YORK, I MET...SOMEONE. WE HAD A WONDERFUL SIX MONTHS TOGETHER BEFORE SHE TOOK A JOB IN SAN FRANCISCO. THAT'S WHY I'M HERE.
I SEE.
AND THIS "SOMEONE," DOES SHE HAVE A NAME?
D'O?
MONA?

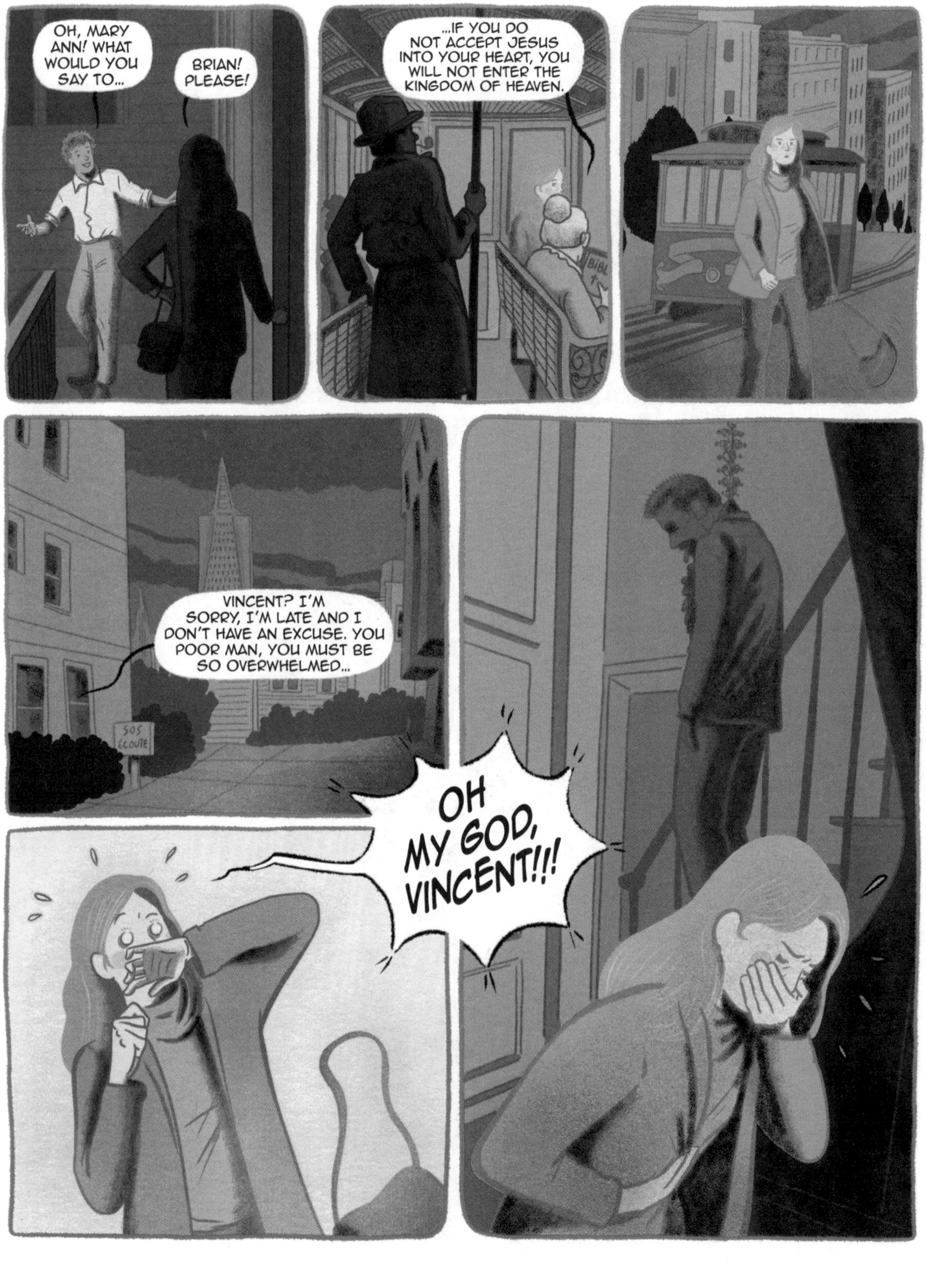
OH, MARY ANN! WHAT WOULD YOU SAY TO...
BRIAN! PLEASE!
...IF YOU DO NOT ACCEPT JESUS INTO YOUR HEART, YOU WILL NOT ENTER THE KINGDOM OF HEAVEN.
VINCENT? I'M SORRY, I'M LATE AND I DON'T HAVE AN EXCUSE. YOU POOR MAN, YOU MUST BE SO OVERWHELMED...
OH MY GOD, VINCENT!!!

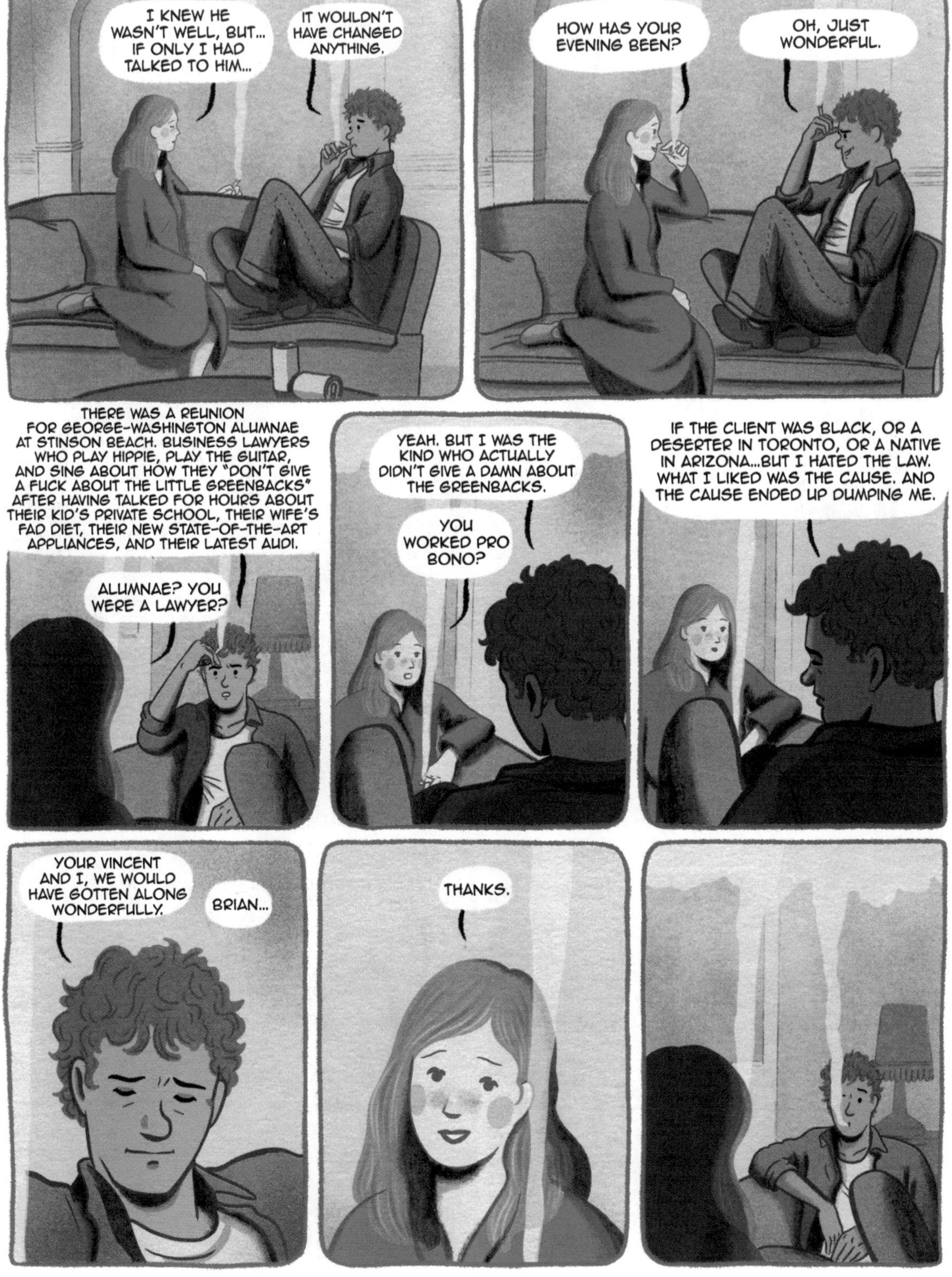
I KNEW HE WASN'T WELL, BUT... IF ONLY I HAD TALKED TO HIM...
IT WOULDN'T HAVE CHANGED ANYTHING.
HOW HAS YOUR EVENING BEEN?
OH, JUST WONDERFUL.
THERE WAS A REUNION FOR GEORGE-WASHINGTON ALUMNAE AT STINSON BEACH. BUSINESS LAWYERS WHO PLAY HIPPIE, PLAY THE GUITAR, AND SING ABOUT HOW THEY "DON'T GIVE A FUCK ABOUT THE LITTLE GREENBACKS" AFTER HAVING TALKED FOR HOURS ABOUT THEIR KID'S PRIVATE SCHOOL, THEIR WIFE'S FAD DIET, THEIR NEW STATE-OF-THE-ART APPLIANCES, AND THEIR LATEST AUDI.
ALUMNAE? YOU WERE A LAWYER?
YEAH. BUT I WAS THE KIND WHO ACTUALLY DIDN'T GIVE A DAMN ABOUT THE GREENBACKS.
YOU WORKED PRO BONO?
IF THE CLIENT WAS BLACK, OR A DESERTER IN TORONTO, OR A NATIVE IN ARIZONA...BUT I HATED THE LAW. WHAT I LIKED WAS THE CAUSE. AND THE CAUSE ENDED UP DUMPING ME.
YOUR VINCENT AND I, WE WOULD HAVE GOTTEN ALONG WONDERFULLY.
BRIAN...
THANKS.

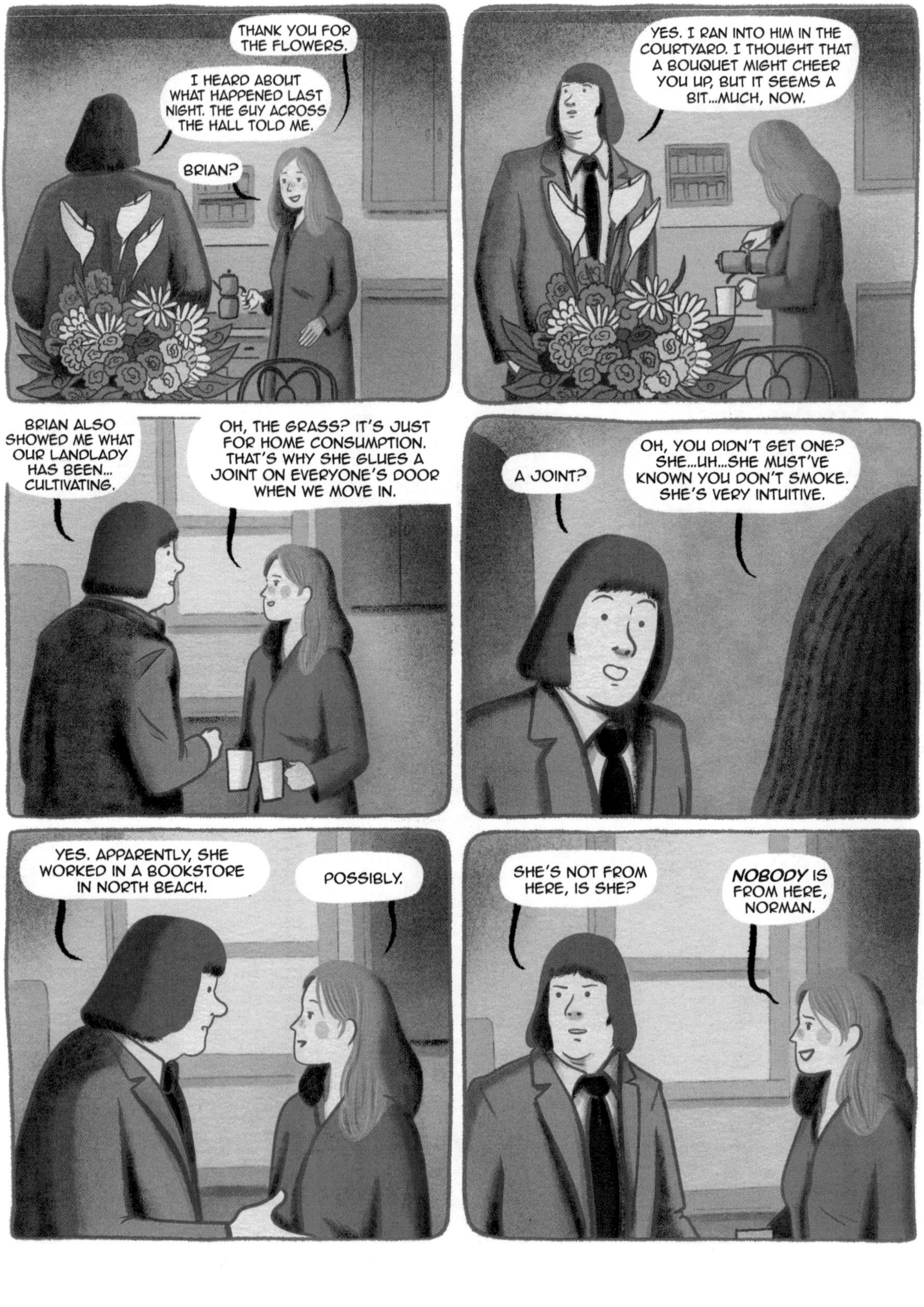
THANK YOU FOR THE FLOWERS.
I HEARD ABOUT WHAT HAPPENED LAST NIGHT. THE GUY ACROSS THE HALL TOLD ME.
BRIAN?
YES. I RAN INTO HIM IN THE COURTYARD. I THOUGHT THAT A BOUQUET MIGHT CHEER YOU UP, BUT IT SEEMS A BIT...MUCH, NOW.
BRIAN ALSO SHOWED ME WHAT OUR LANDLADY HAS BEEN... CULTIVATING.
OH, THE GRASS? IT'S JUST FOR HOME CONSUMPTION. THAT'S WHY SHE GLUES A JOINT ON EVERYONE'S DOOR WHEN WE MOVE IN.
A JOINT?
OH, YOU DIDN'T GET ONE? SHE...UH...SHE MUST'VE KNOWN YOU DON'T SMOKE. SHE'S VERY INTUITIVE.
YES. APPARENTLY, SHE WORKED IN A BOOKSTORE IN NORTH BEACH.
POSSIBLY.
SHE'S NOT FROM HERE, IS SHE?
NOBODY IS FROM HERE, NORMAN.

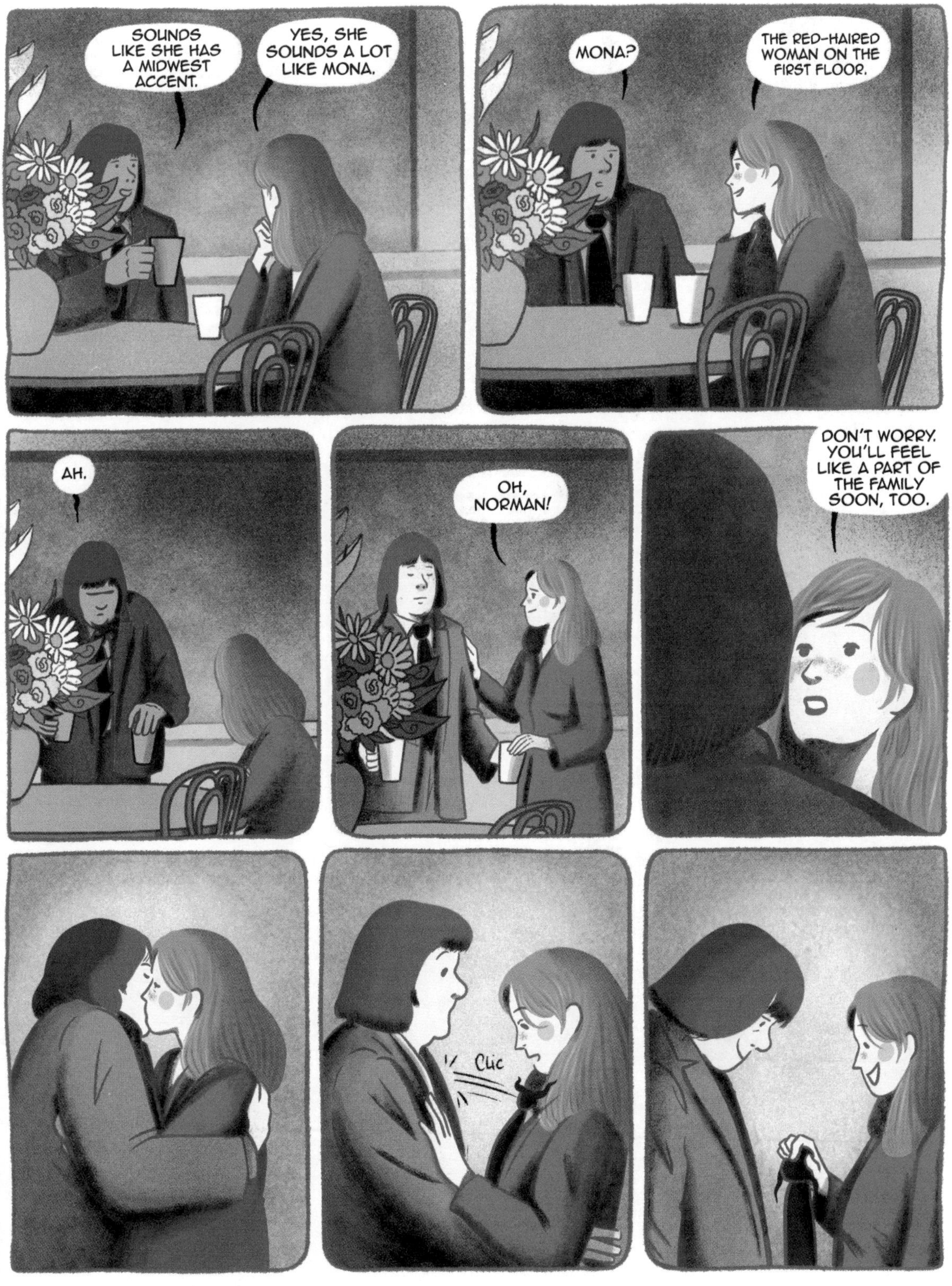
SOUNDS LIKE SHE HAS A MIDWEST ACCENT.
YES, SHE SOUNDS A LOT LIKE MONA.
MONA?
THE RED-HAIRED WOMAN ON THE FIRST FLOOR.
AH.
OH, NORMAN!
DON'T WORRY. YOU'LL FEEL LIKE A PART OF THE FAMILY SOON, TOO.
Clic

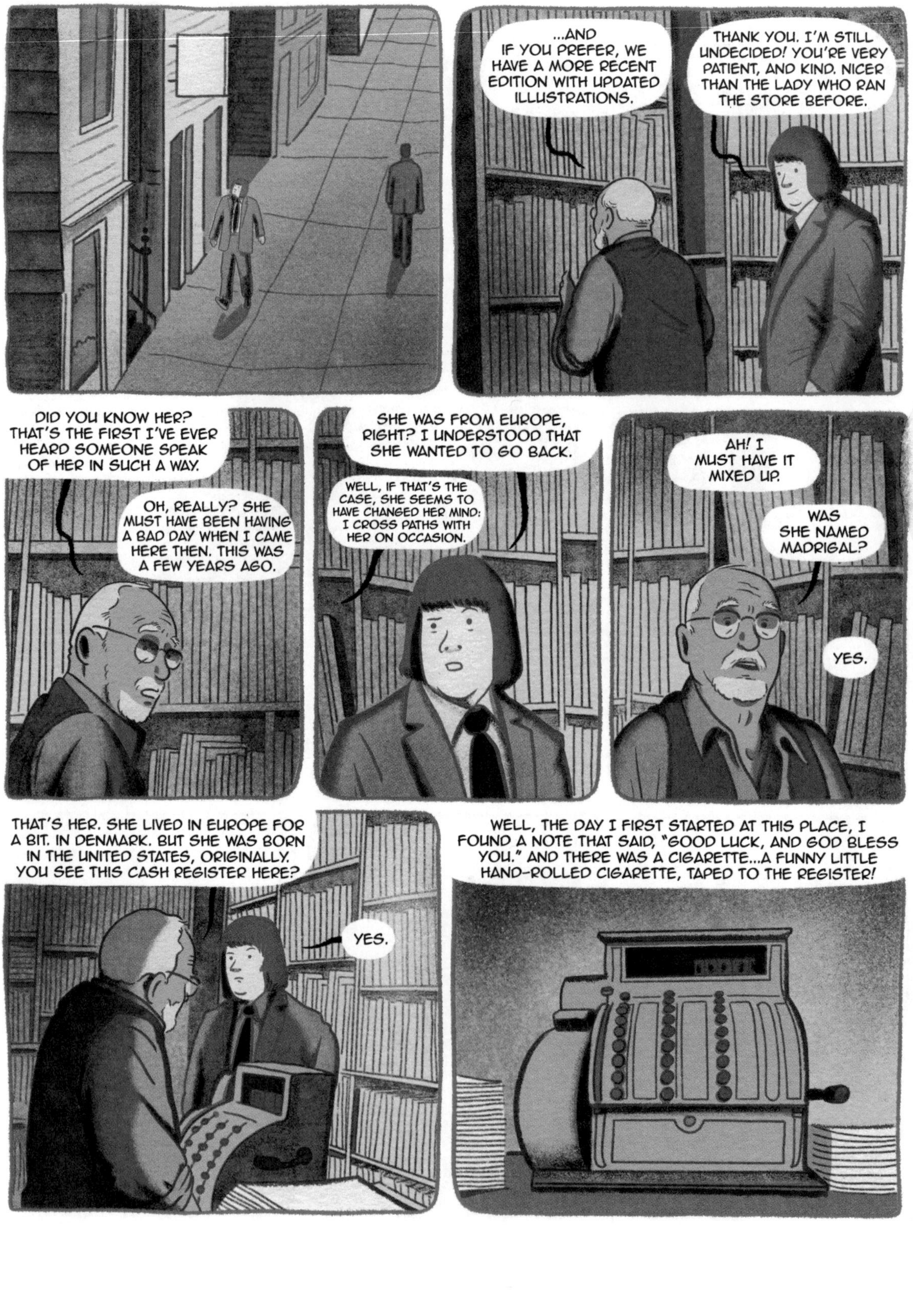
...AND IF YOU PREFER, WE HAVE A MORE RECENT EDITION WITH UPDATED ILLUSTRATIONS.
THANK YOU. I'M STILL UNDECIDED! YOU'RE VERY PATIENT, AND KIND. NICER THAN THE LADY WHO RAN THE STORE BEFORE.
DID YOU KNOW HER? THAT'S THE FIRST I'VE EVER HEARD SOMEONE SPEAK OF HER IN SUCH A WAY.
OH, REALLY? SHE MUST HAVE BEEN HAVING A BAD DAY WHEN I CAME HERE THEN. THIS WAS A FEW YEARS AGO.
SHE WAS FROM EUROPE, RIGHT? I UNDERSTOOD THAT SHE WANTED TO GO BACK.
WELL, IF THAT'S THE CASE, SHE SEEMS TO HAVE CHANGED HER MIND: I CROSS PATHS WITH HER ON OCCASION.
AH! I MUST HAVE IT MIXED UP.
WAS SHE NAMED MADRIGAL?
YES.
THAT'S HER. SHE LIVED IN EUROPE FOR A BIT. IN DENMARK. BUT SHE WAS BORN IN THE UNITED STATES, ORIGINALLY. YOU SEE THIS CASH REGISTER HERE?
YES.
WELL, THE DAY I FIRST STARTED AT THIS PLACE, I FOUND A NOTE THAT SAID, "GOOD LUCK, AND GOD BLESS YOU." AND THERE WAS A CIGARETTE...A FUNNY LITTLE HAND-ROLLED CIGARETTE, TAPED TO THE REGISTER!

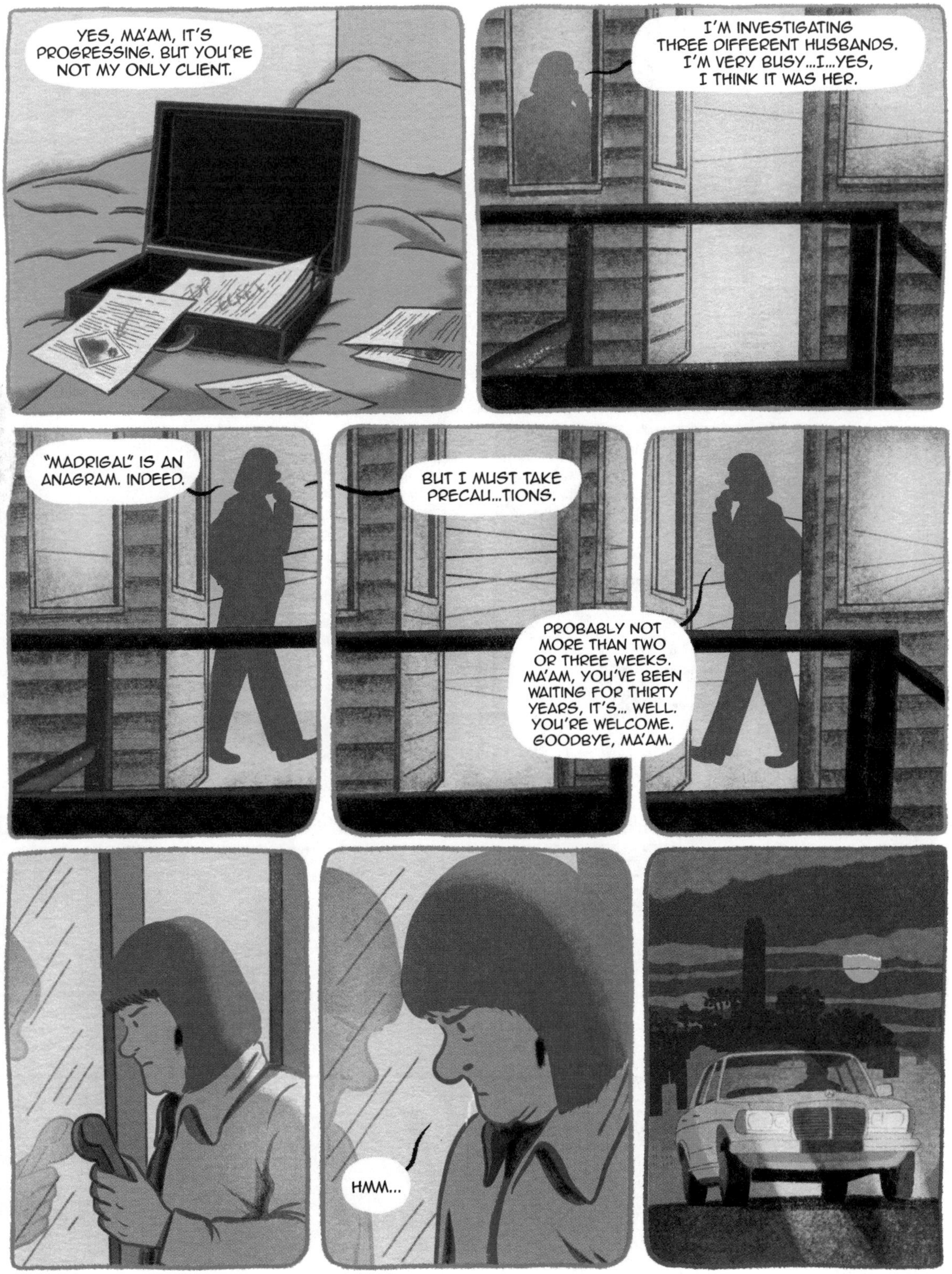
YES, MA'AM, IT'S PROGRESSING. BUT YOU'RE NOT MY ONLY CLIENT.
I'M INVESTIGATING THREE DIFFERENT HUSBANDS. I'M VERY BUSY...I...YES, I THINK IT WAS HER.
"MADRIGAL" IS AN ANAGRAM. INDEED.
BUT I MUST TAKE PRECAU...TIONS.
PROBABLY NOT MORE THAN TWO OR THREE WEEKS. MA'AM, YOU'VE BEEN WAITING FOR THIRTY YEARS, IT'S... WELL. YOU'RE WELCOME. GOODBYE, MA'AM.
HMM...

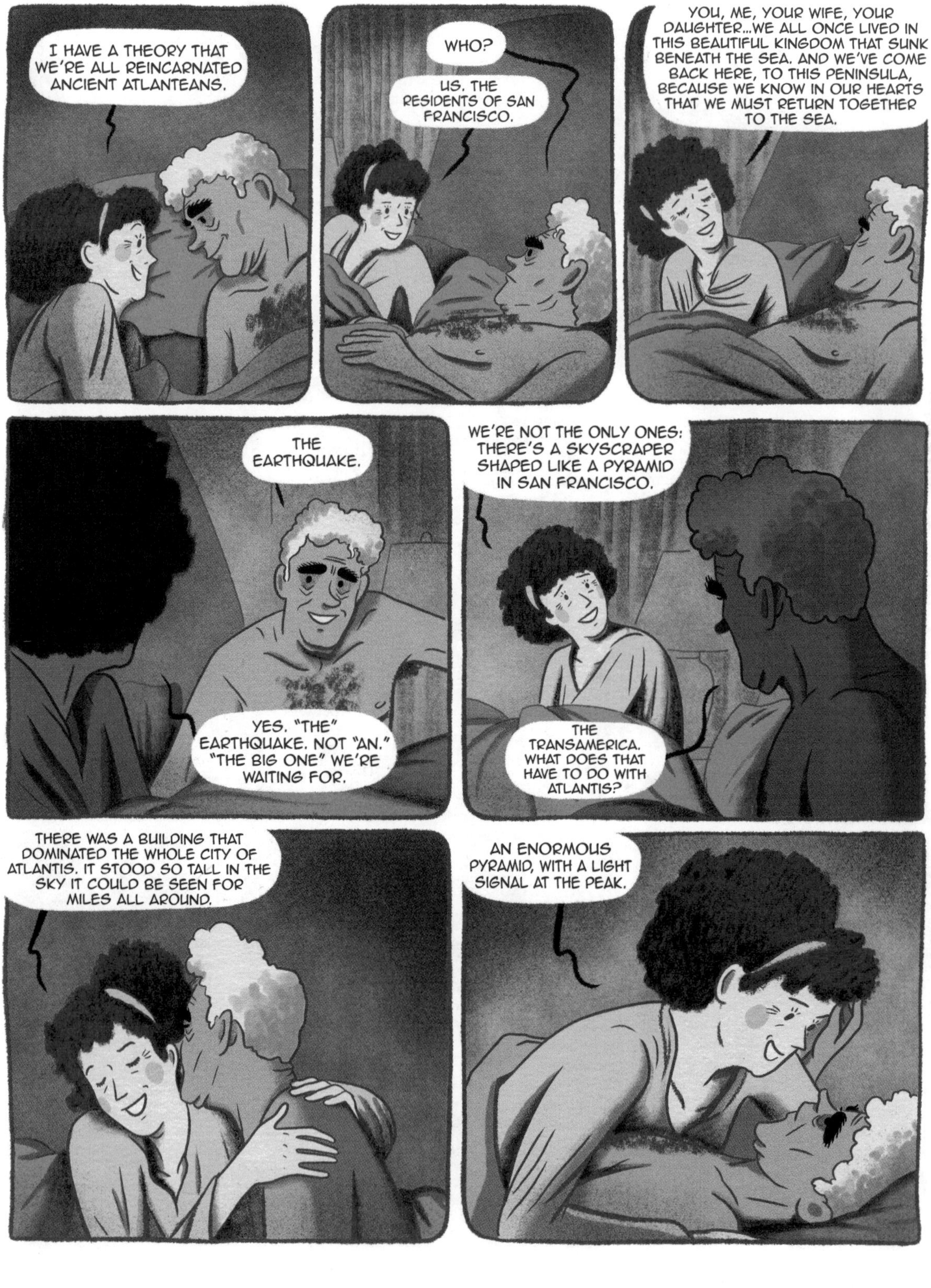
I HAVE A THEORY THAT WE'RE ALL REINCARNATED ANCIENT ATLANTEANS.
WHO?
US. THE RESIDENTS OF SAN FRANCISCO.
YOU, ME, YOUR WIFE, YOUR DAUGHTER...WE ALL ONCE LIVED IN THIS BEAUTIFUL KINGDOM THAT SUNK BENEATH THE SEA. AND WE'VE COME BACK HERE, TO THIS PENINSULA, BECAUSE WE KNOW IN OUR HEARTS THAT WE MUST RETURN TOGETHER TO THE SEA.
THE EARTHQUAKE.
YES. "THE" EARTHQUAKE. NOT "AN." "THE BIG ONE" WE'RE WAITING FOR.
WE'RE NOT THE ONLY ONES: THERE'S A SKYSCRAPER SHAPED LIKE A PYRAMID IN SAN FRANCISCO.
THE TRANSAMERICA. WHAT DOES THAT HAVE TO DO WITH ATLANTIS?
THERE WAS A BUILDING THAT DOMINATED THE WHOLE CITY OF ATLANTIS. IT STOOD SO TALL IN THE SKY IT COULD BE SEEN FOR MILES ALL AROUND.
AN ENORMOUS PYRAMID, WITH A LIGHT SIGNAL AT THE PEAK.

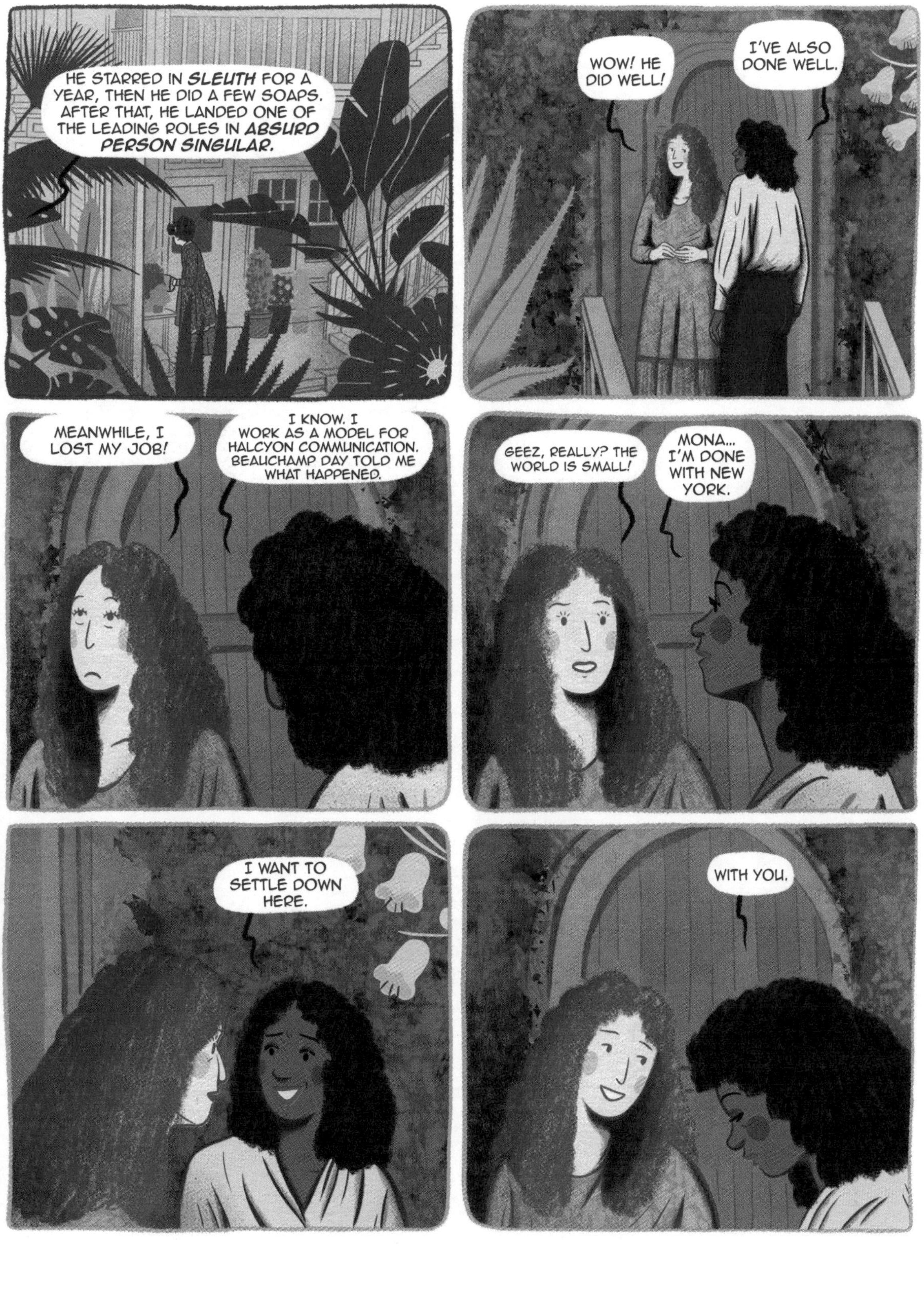
HE STARRED IN ***SLEUTH*** FOR A YEAR, THEN HE DID A FEW SOAPS. AFTER THAT, HE LANDED ONE OF THE LEADING ROLES IN ***ABSURD PERSON SINGULAR.***
WOW! HE DID WELL!
I'VE ALSO DONE WELL.
MEANWHILE, I LOST MY JOB!
I KNOW. I WORK AS A MODEL FOR HALCYON COMMUNICATION. BEAUCHAMP DAY TOLD ME WHAT HAPPENED.
GEEZ, REALLY? THE WORLD IS SMALL!
MONA... I'M DONE WITH NEW YORK.
I WANT TO SETTLE DOWN HERE.
WITH YOU.

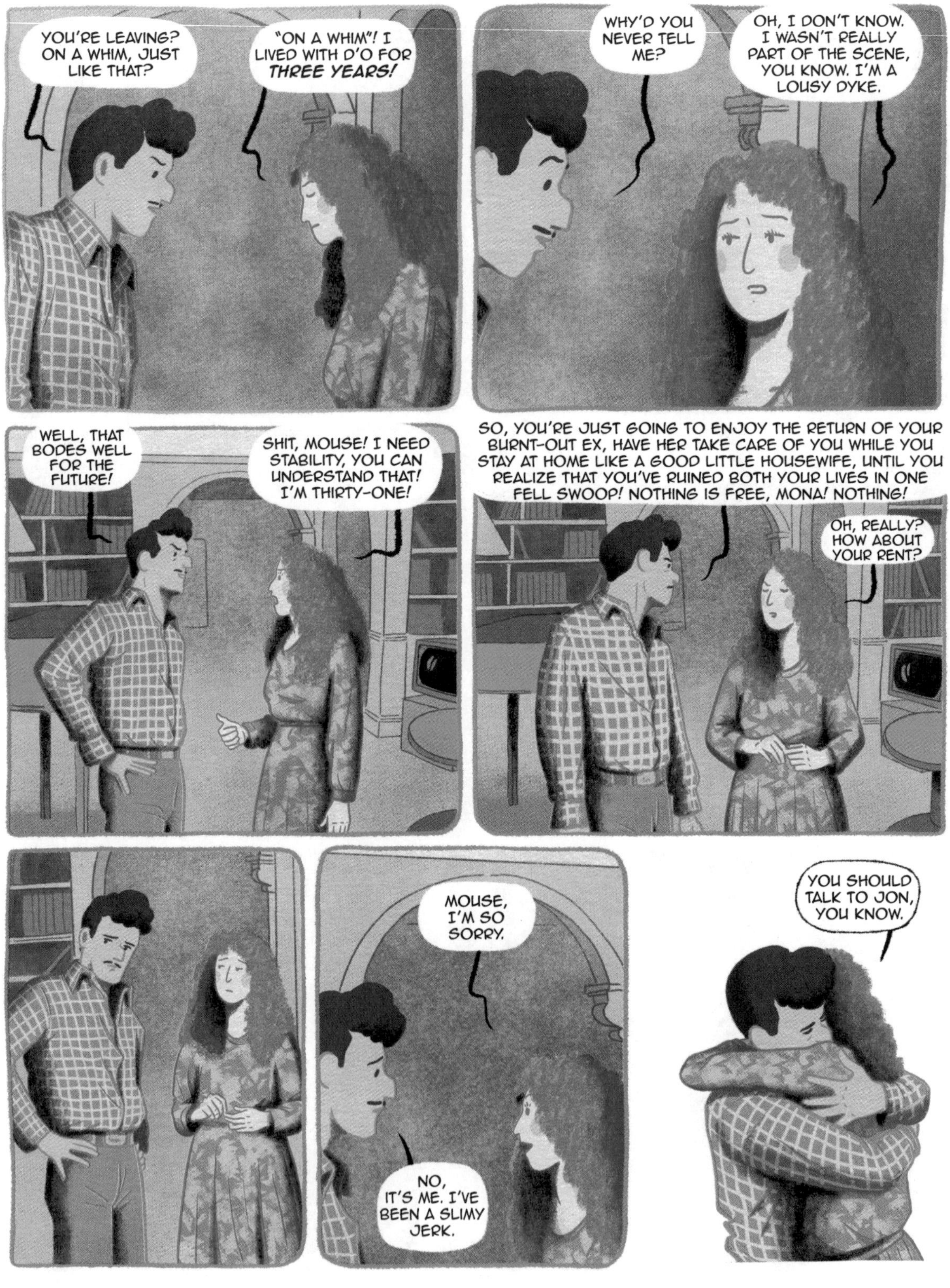
YOU'RE LEAVING? ON A WHIM, JUST LIKE THAT?
"ON A WHIM"! I LIVED WITH D'O FOR THREE YEARS!
WHY'D YOU NEVER TELL ME?
OH, I DON'T KNOW. I WASN'T REALLY PART OF THE SCENE, YOU KNOW. I'M A LOUSY DYKE.
WELL, THAT BODES WELL FOR THE FUTURE!
SHIT, MOUSE! I NEED STABILITY, YOU CAN UNDERSTAND THAT! I'M THIRTY-ONE!
SO, YOU'RE JUST GOING TO ENJOY THE RETURN OF YOUR BURNT-OUT EX, HAVE HER TAKE CARE OF YOU WHILE YOU STAY AT HOME LIKE A GOOD LITTLE HOUSEWIFE, UNTIL YOU REALIZE THAT YOU'VE RUINED BOTH YOUR LIVES IN ONE FELL SWOOP! NOTHING IS FREE, MONA! NOTHING!
OH, REALLY? HOW ABOUT YOUR RENT?
MOUSE, I'M SO SORRY.
NO, IT'S ME. I'VE BEEN A SLIMY JERK.
YOU SHOULD TALK TO JON, YOU KNOW.

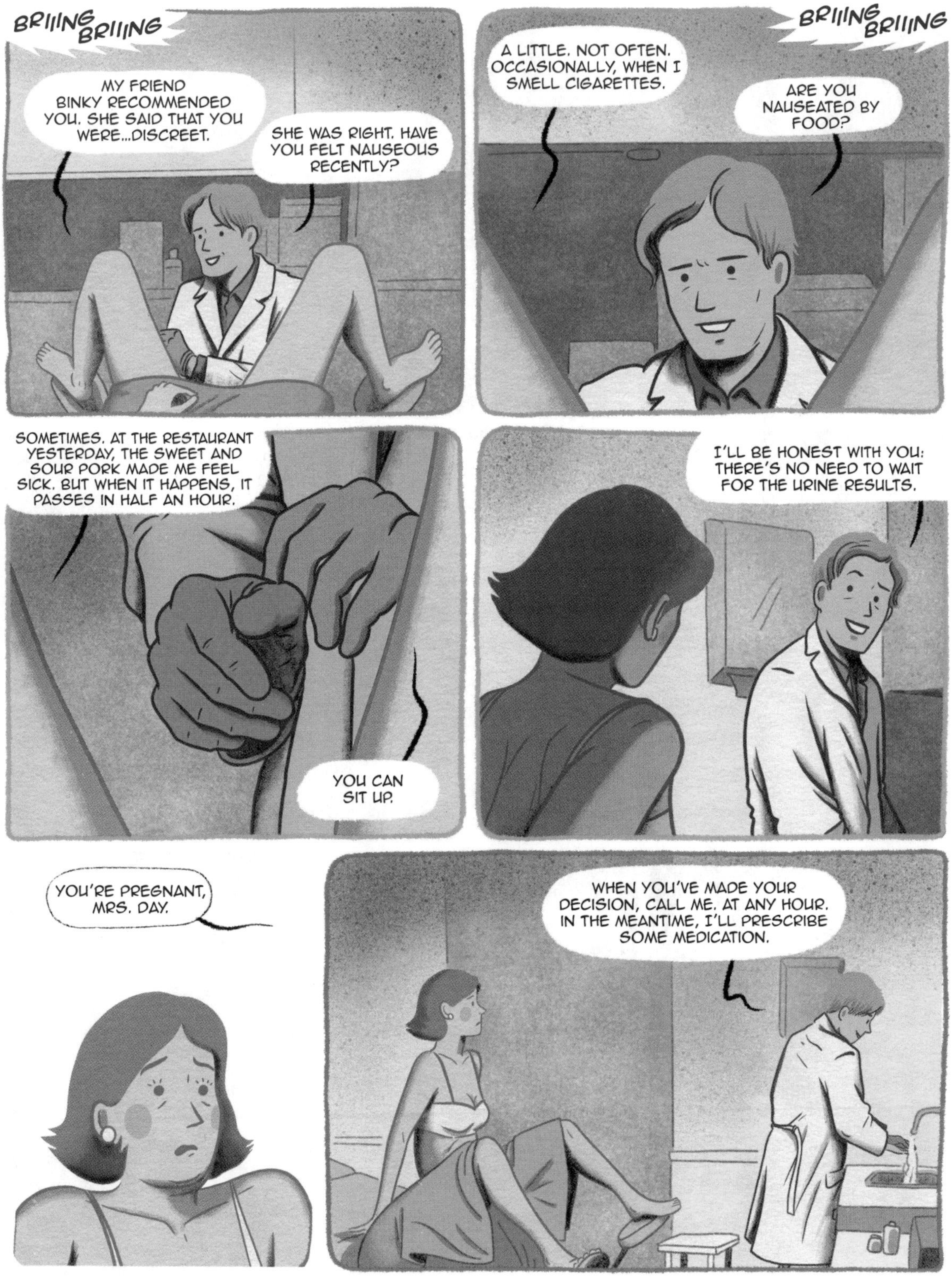
BRIIING BRIIING
MY FRIEND BINKY RECOMMENDED YOU. SHE SAID THAT YOU WERE...DISCREET.
SHE WAS RIGHT. HAVE YOU FELT NAUSEOUS RECENTLY?
BRIIING BRIIING
A LITTLE. NOT OFTEN. OCCASIONALLY, WHEN I SMELL CIGARETTES.
ARE YOU NAUSEATED BY FOOD?
SOMETIMES. AT THE RESTAURANT YESTERDAY, THE SWEET AND SOUR PORK MADE ME FEEL SICK. BUT WHEN IT HAPPENS, IT PASSES IN HALF AN HOUR.
YOU CAN SIT UP.
I'LL BE HONEST WITH YOU: THERE'S NO NEED TO WAIT FOR THE URINE RESULTS.
YOU'RE PREGNANT, MRS. DAY.
WHEN YOU'VE MADE YOUR DECISION, CALL ME. AT ANY HOUR. IN THE MEANTIME, I'LL PRESCRIBE SOME MEDICATION.

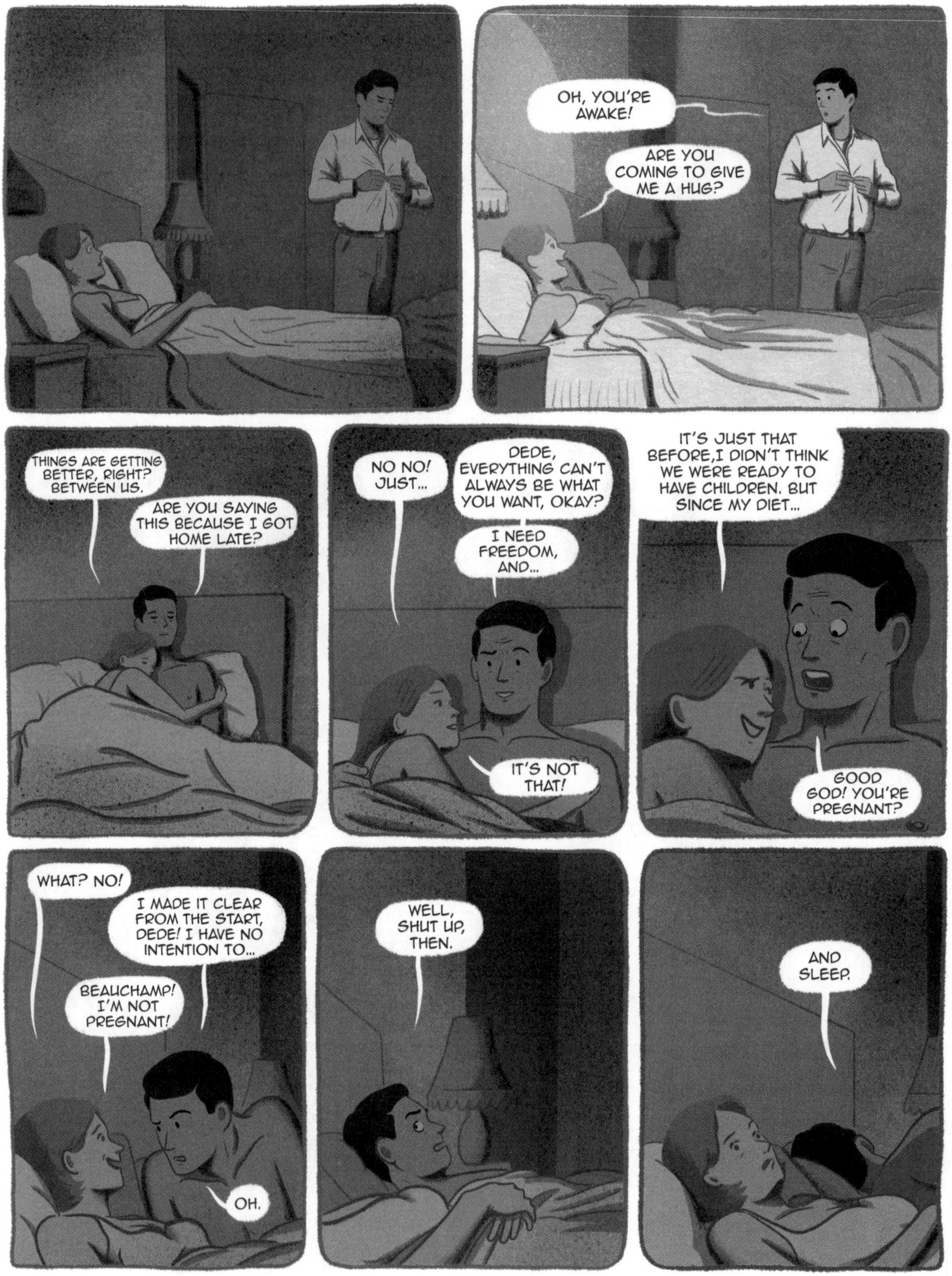
OH, YOU'RE AWAKE!
ARE YOU COMING TO GIVE ME A HUG?
THINGS ARE GETTING BETTER, RIGHT? BETWEEN US.
ARE YOU SAYING THIS BECAUSE I GOT HOME LATE?
NO NO! JUST...
DEDE, EVERYTHING CAN'T ALWAYS BE WHAT YOU WANT, OKAY?
I NEED FREEDOM, AND...
IT'S NOT THAT!
IT'S JUST THAT BEFORE,I DIDN'T THINK WE WERE READY TO HAVE CHILDREN. BUT SINCE MY DIET...
GOOD GOD! YOU'RE PREGNANT?
WHAT? NO!
I MADE IT CLEAR FROM THE START, DEDE! I HAVE NO INTENTION TO...
BEAUCHAMP! I'M NOT PREGNANT!
OH.
WELL, SHUT UP, THEN.
AND SLEEP.

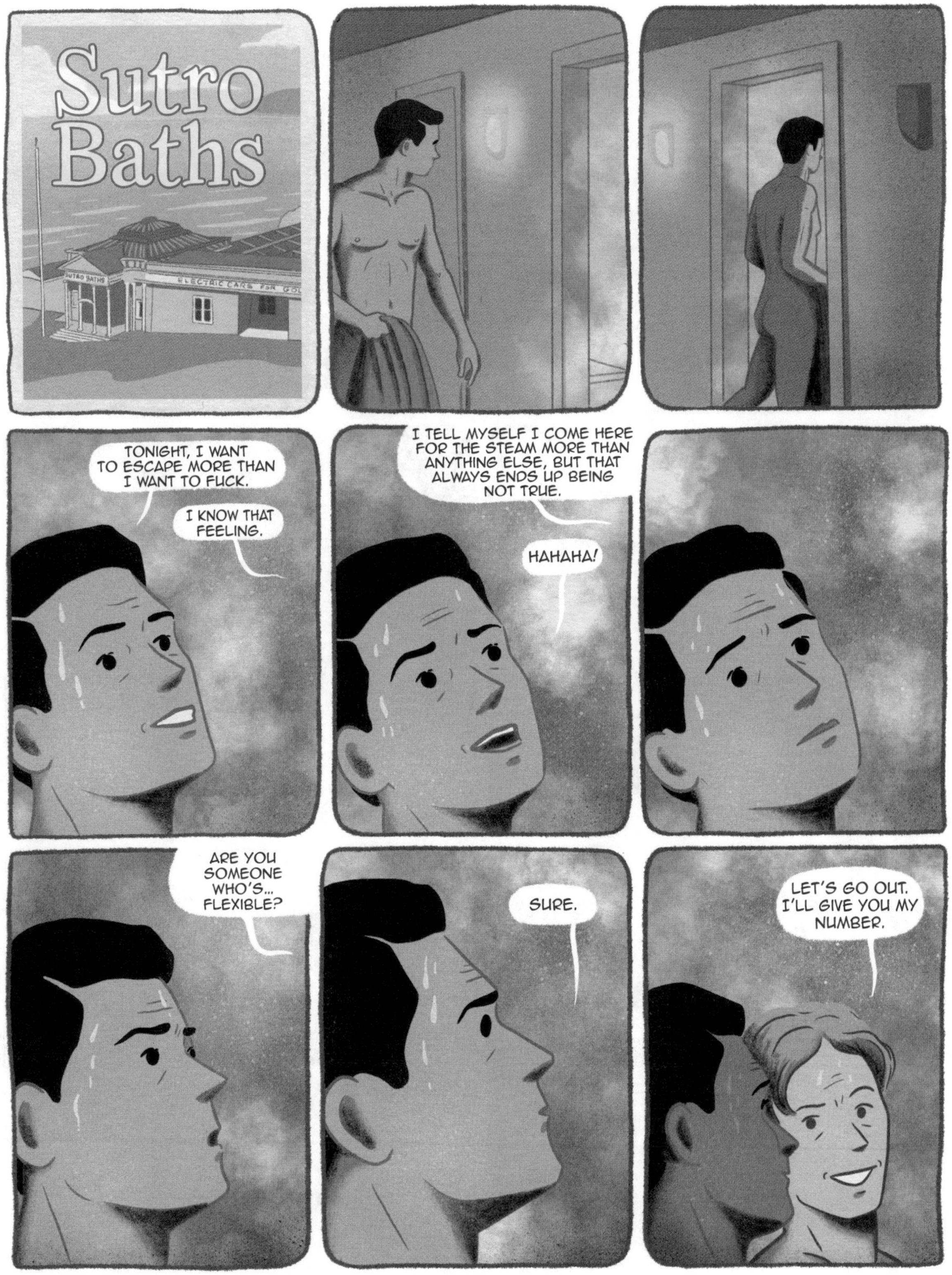
Sutro Baths
SUTRO BATHS
ELECTRIC CARS FOR
TONIGHT, I WANT TO ESCAPE MORE THAN I WANT TO FUCK.
I KNOW THAT FEELING.
I TELL MYSELF I COME HERE FOR THE STEAM MORE THAN ANYTHING ELSE, BUT THAT ALWAYS ENDS UP BEING NOT TRUE.
HAHAHA!
ARE YOU SOMEONE WHO'S... FLEXIBLE?
SURE.
LET'S GO OUT. I'LL GIVE YOU MY NUMBER.

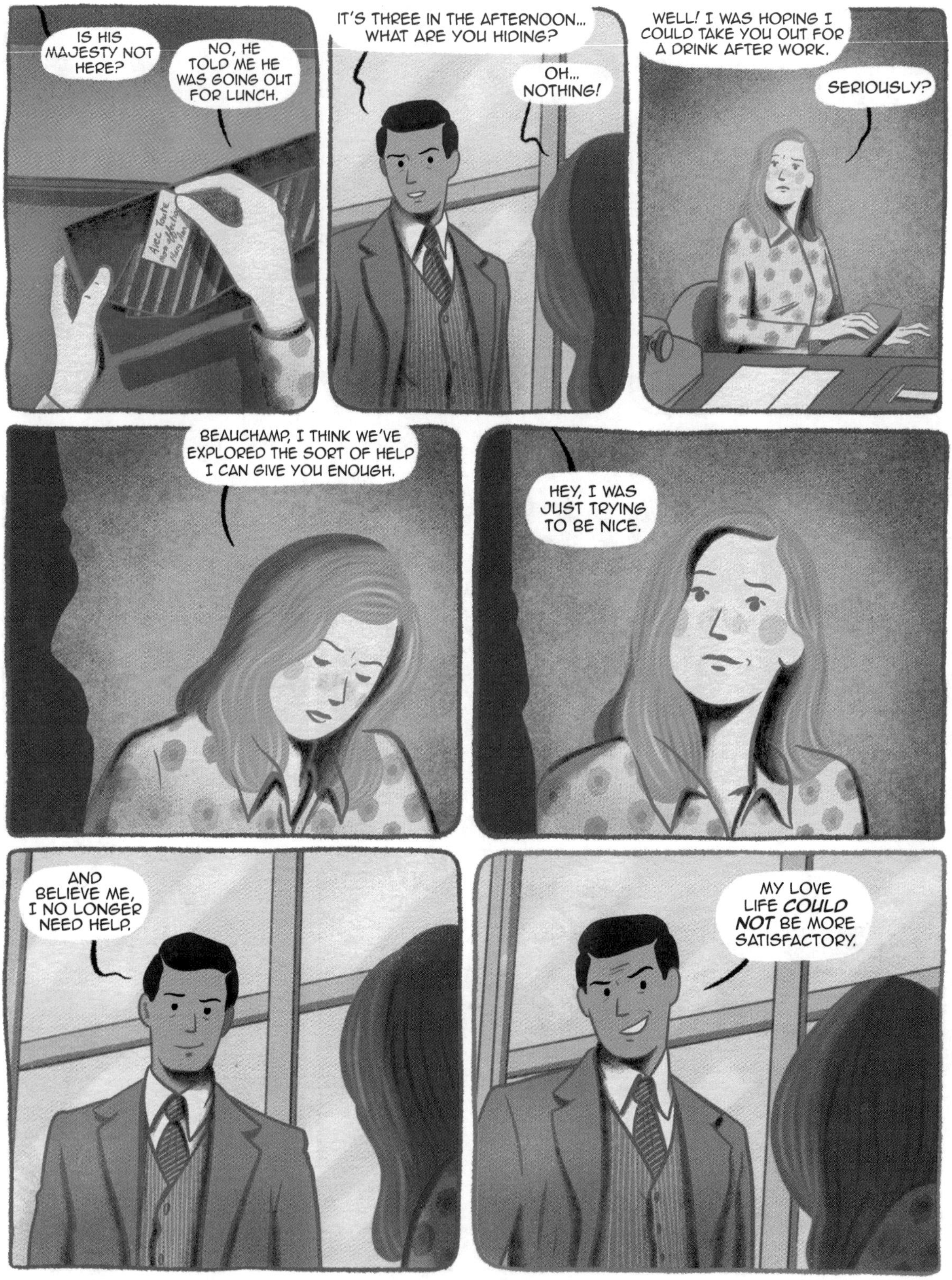
IS HIS MAJESTY NOT HERE?
NO, HE TOLD ME HE WAS GOING OUT FOR LUNCH.
IT'S THREE IN THE AFTERNOON... WHAT ARE YOU HIDING?
OH... NOTHING!
WELL! I WAS HOPING I COULD TAKE YOU OUT FOR A DRINK AFTER WORK.
SERIOUSLY?
BEAUCHAMP, I THINK WE'VE EXPLORED THE SORT OF HELP I CAN GIVE YOU ENOUGH.
HEY, I WAS JUST TRYING TO BE NICE.
AND BELIEVE ME, I NO LONGER NEED HELP.
MY LOVE LIFE ***COULD NOT*** BE MORE SATISFACTORY.

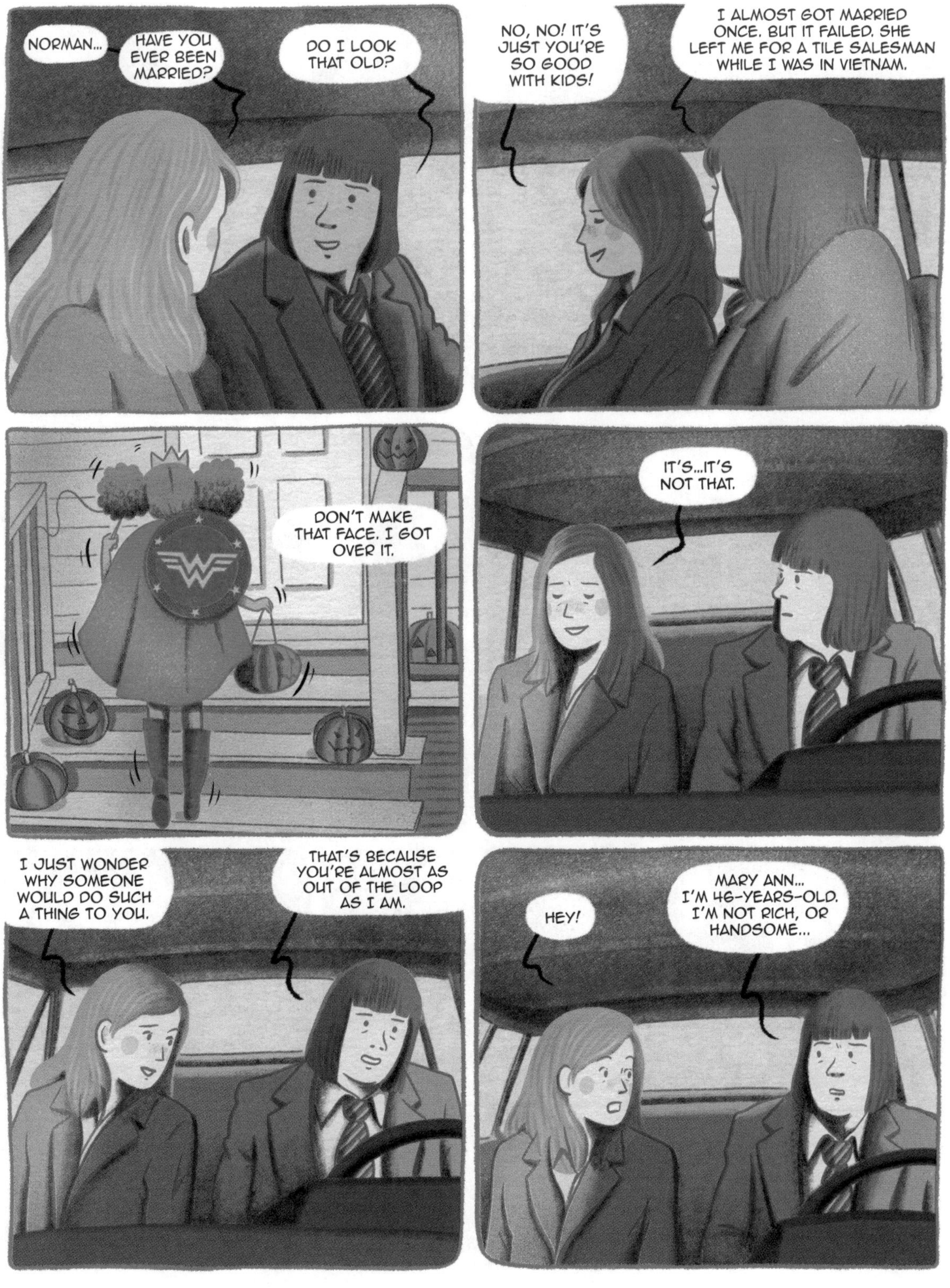
NORMAN...
HAVE YOU EVER BEEN MARRIED?
DO I LOOK THAT OLD?
NO, NO! IT'S JUST YOU'RE SO GOOD WITH KIDS!
I ALMOST GOT MARRIED ONCE. BUT IT FAILED. SHE LEFT ME FOR A TILE SALESMAN WHILE I WAS IN VIETNAM.
DON'T MAKE THAT FACE. I GOT OVER IT.
IT'S...IT'S NOT THAT.
I JUST WONDER WHY SOMEONE WOULD DO SUCH A THING TO YOU.
THAT'S BECAUSE YOU'RE ALMOST AS OUT OF THE LOOP AS I AM.
HEY!
MARY ANN... I'M 46-YEARS-OLD. I'M NOT RICH, OR HANDSOME...

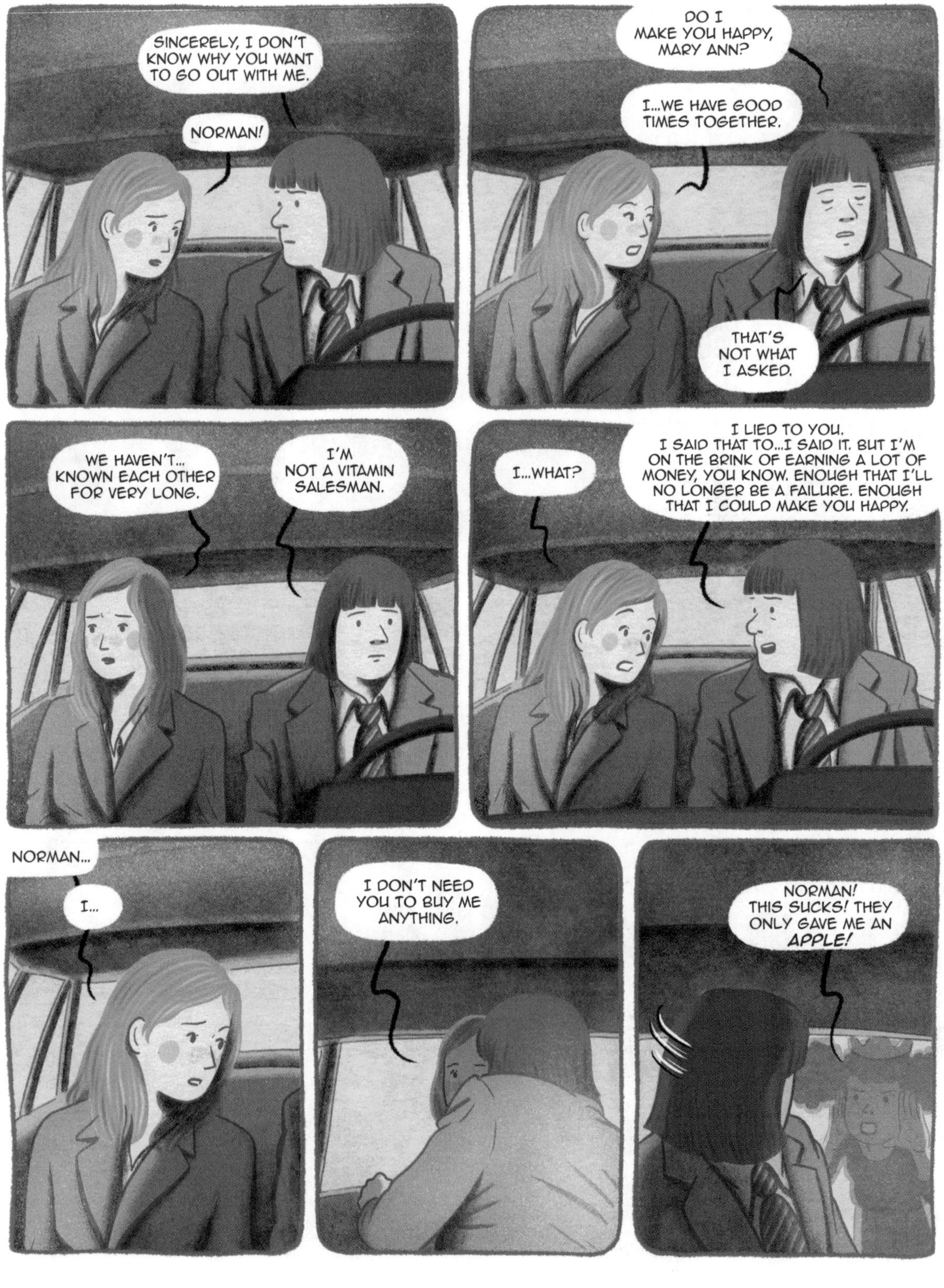
SINCERELY, I DON'T KNOW WHY YOU WANT TO GO OUT WITH ME.
NORMAN!
DO I MAKE YOU HAPPY, MARY ANN?
I...WE HAVE GOOD TIMES TOGETHER.
THAT'S NOT WHAT I ASKED.
WE HAVEN'T... KNOWN EACH OTHER FOR VERY LONG.
I'M NOT A VITAMIN SALESMAN.
I...WHAT?
I LIED TO YOU. I SAID THAT TO...I SAID IT. BUT I'M ON THE BRINK OF EARNING A LOT OF MONEY, YOU KNOW. ENOUGH THAT I'LL NO LONGER BE A FAILURE. ENOUGH THAT I COULD MAKE YOU HAPPY.
NORMAN...
I...
I DON'T NEED YOU TO BUY ME ANYTHING.
NORMAN! THIS SUCKS! THEY ONLY GAVE ME AN *APPLE!*

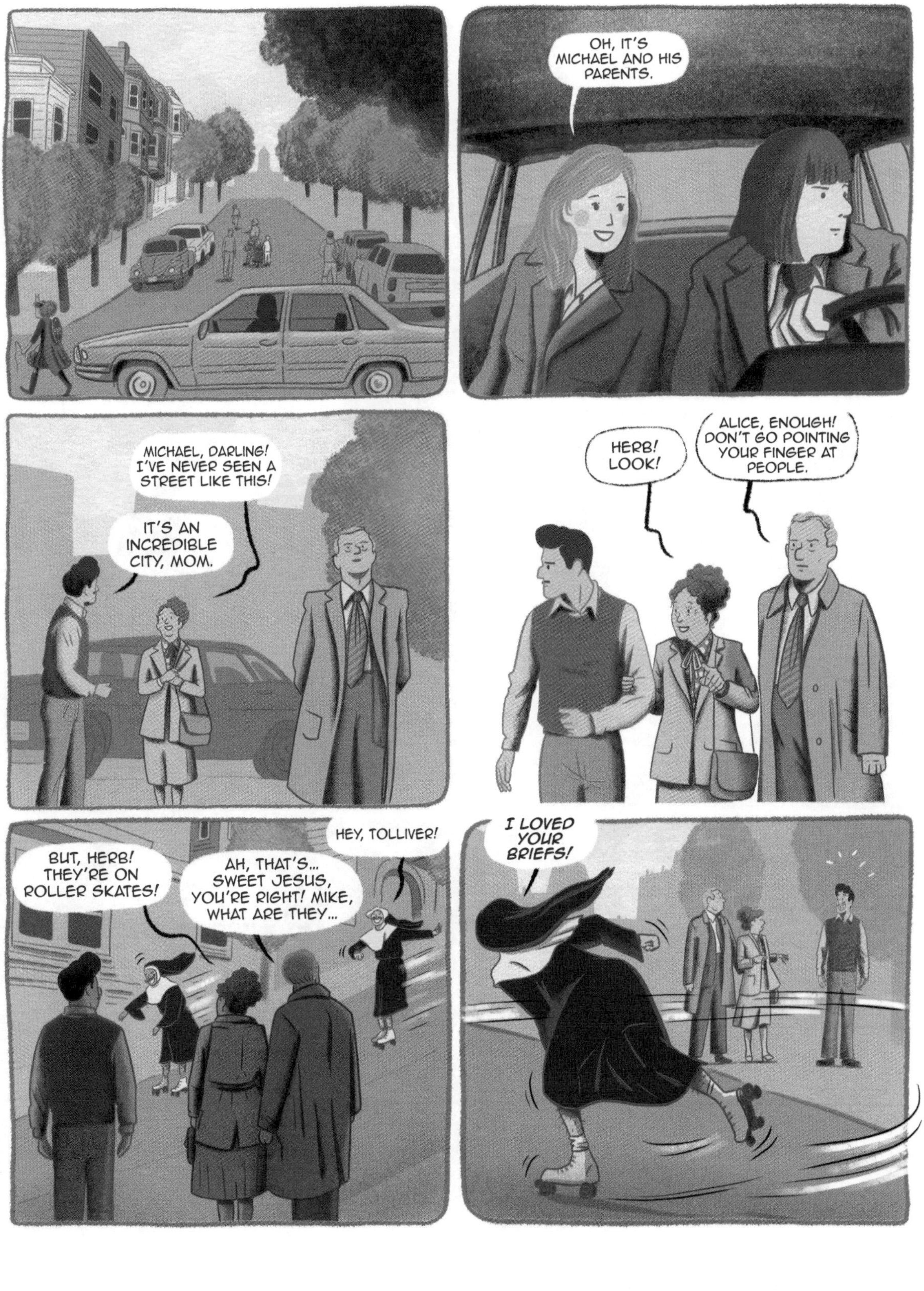
OH, IT'S MICHAEL AND HIS PARENTS.
MICHAEL, DARLING! I'VE NEVER SEEN A STREET LIKE THIS!
IT'S AN INCREDIBLE CITY, MOM.
HERB! LOOK!
ALICE, ENOUGH! DON'T GO POINTING YOUR FINGER AT PEOPLE.
BUT, HERB! THEY'RE ON ROLLER SKATES!
AH, THAT'S... SWEET JESUS, YOU'RE RIGHT! MIKE, WHAT ARE THEY...
HEY, TOLLIVER!
I LOVED YOUR BRIEFS!

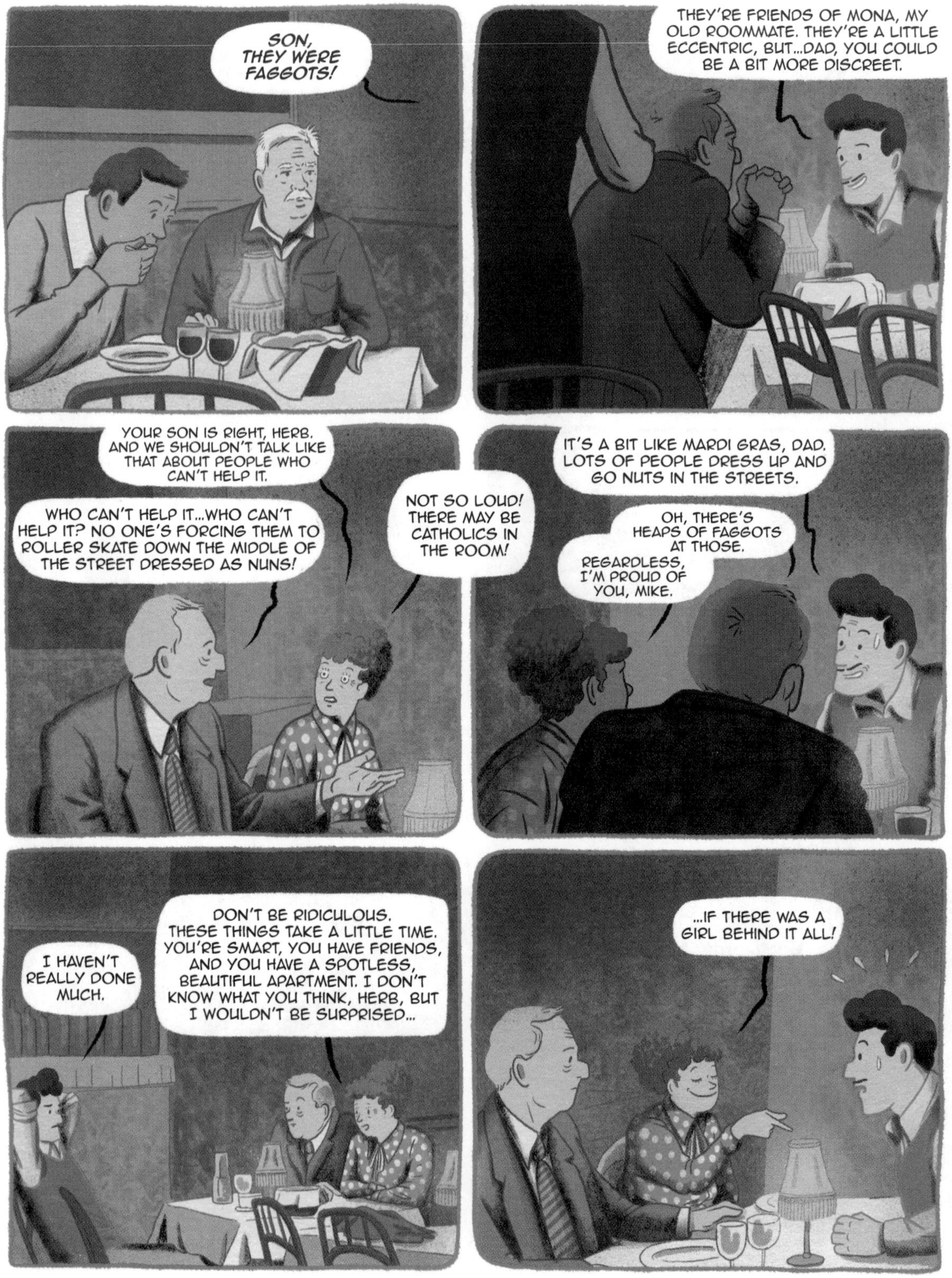
SON, THEY WERE FAGGOTS!
THEY'RE FRIENDS OF MONA, MY OLD ROOMMATE. THEY'RE A LITTLE ECCENTRIC, BUT...DAD, YOU COULD BE A BIT MORE DISCREET.
YOUR SON IS RIGHT, HERB. AND WE SHOULDN'T TALK LIKE THAT ABOUT PEOPLE WHO CAN'T HELP IT.
WHO CAN'T HELP IT...WHO CAN'T HELP IT? NO ONE'S FORCING THEM TO ROLLER SKATE DOWN THE MIDDLE OF THE STREET DRESSED AS NUNS!
NOT SO LOUD! THERE MAY BE CATHOLICS IN THE ROOM!
IT'S A BIT LIKE MARDI GRAS, DAD. LOTS OF PEOPLE DRESS UP AND GO NUTS IN THE STREETS.
OH, THERE'S HEAPS OF FAGGOTS AT THOSE.
REGARDLESS, I'M PROUD OF YOU, MIKE.
I HAVEN'T REALLY DONE MUCH.
DON'T BE RIDICULOUS. THESE THINGS TAKE A LITTLE TIME. YOU'RE SMART, YOU HAVE FRIENDS, AND YOU HAVE A SPOTLESS, BEAUTIFUL APARTMENT. I DON'T KNOW WHAT YOU THINK, HERB, BUT I WOULDN'T BE SURPRISED...
...IF THERE WAS A GIRL BEHIND IT ALL!

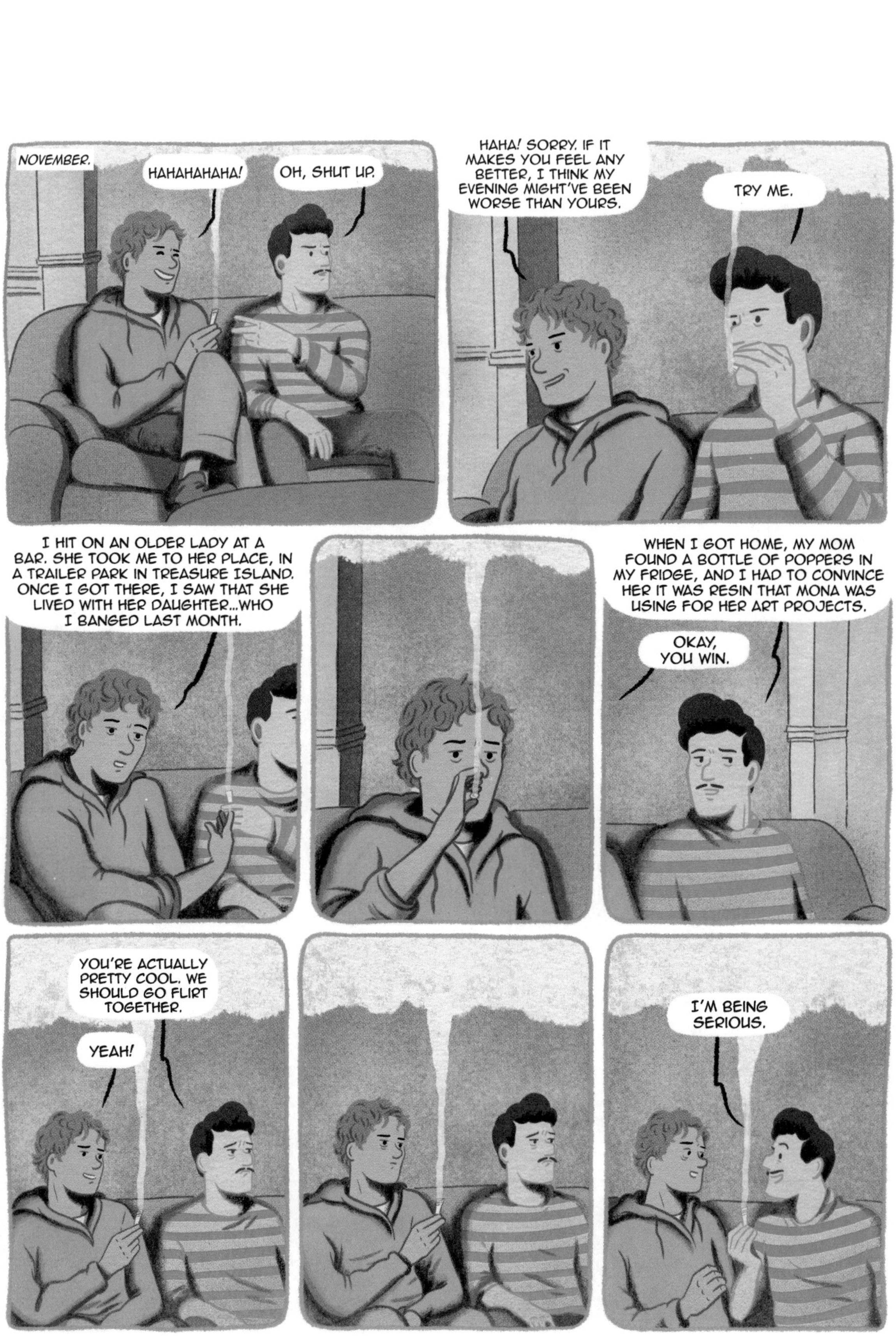

NOVEMBER.
HAHAHAHAHA!
OH, SHUT UP.
HAHA! SORRY. IF IT MAKES YOU FEEL ANY BETTER, I THINK MY EVENING MIGHT'VE BEEN WORSE THAN YOURS.
TRY ME.
I HIT ON AN OLDER LADY AT A BAR. SHE TOOK ME TO HER PLACE, IN A TRAILER PARK IN TREASURE ISLAND. ONCE I GOT THERE, I SAW THAT SHE LIVED WITH HER DAUGHTER...WHO I BANGED LAST MONTH.
WHEN I GOT HOME, MY MOM FOUND A BOTTLE OF POPPERS IN MY FRIDGE, AND I HAD TO CONVINCE HER IT WAS RESIN THAT MONA WAS USING FOR HER ART PROJECTS.
OKAY, YOU WIN.
YOU'RE ACTUALLY PRETTY COOL. WE SHOULD GO FLIRT TOGETHER.
YEAH!
I'M BEING SERIOUS.

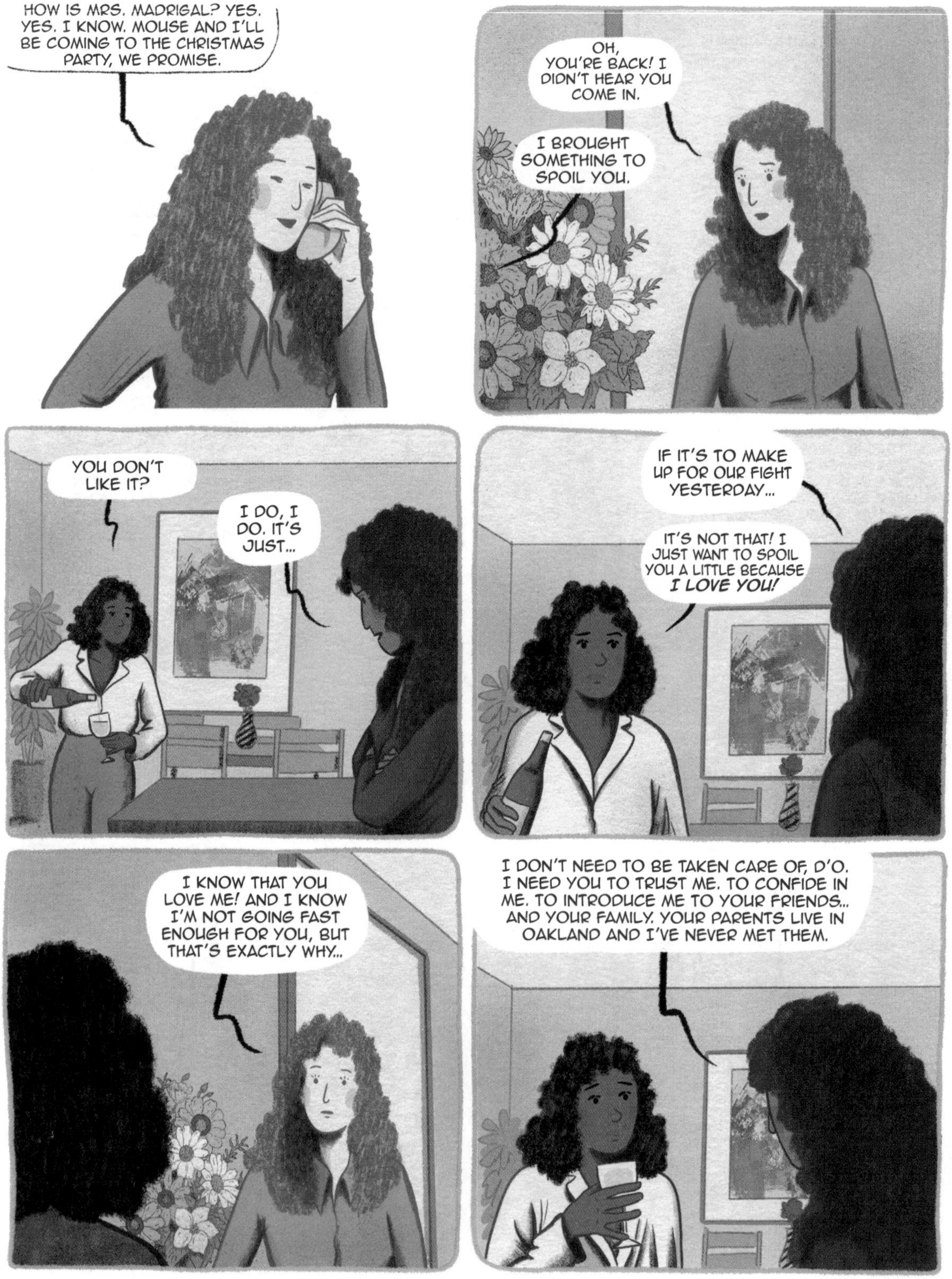
HOW IS MRS. MADRIGAL? YES. YES. I KNOW. MOUSE AND I'LL BE COMING TO THE CHRISTMAS PARTY, WE PROMISE.
OH, YOU'RE BACK! I DIDN'T HEAR YOU COME IN.
I BROUGHT SOMETHING TO SPOIL YOU.
YOU DON'T LIKE IT?
I DO, I DO. IT'S JUST...
IF IT'S TO MAKE UP FOR OUR FIGHT YESTERDAY...
IT'S NOT THAT! I JUST WANT TO SPOIL YOU A LITTLE BECAUSE *I LOVE YOU!*
I KNOW THAT YOU LOVE ME! AND I KNOW I'M NOT GOING FAST ENOUGH FOR YOU, BUT THAT'S EXACTLY WHY...
I DON'T NEED TO BE TAKEN CARE OF, D'O. I NEED YOU TO TRUST ME. TO CONFIDE IN ME. TO INTRODUCE ME TO YOUR FRIENDS... AND YOUR FAMILY. YOUR PARENTS LIVE IN OAKLAND AND I'VE NEVER MET THEM.

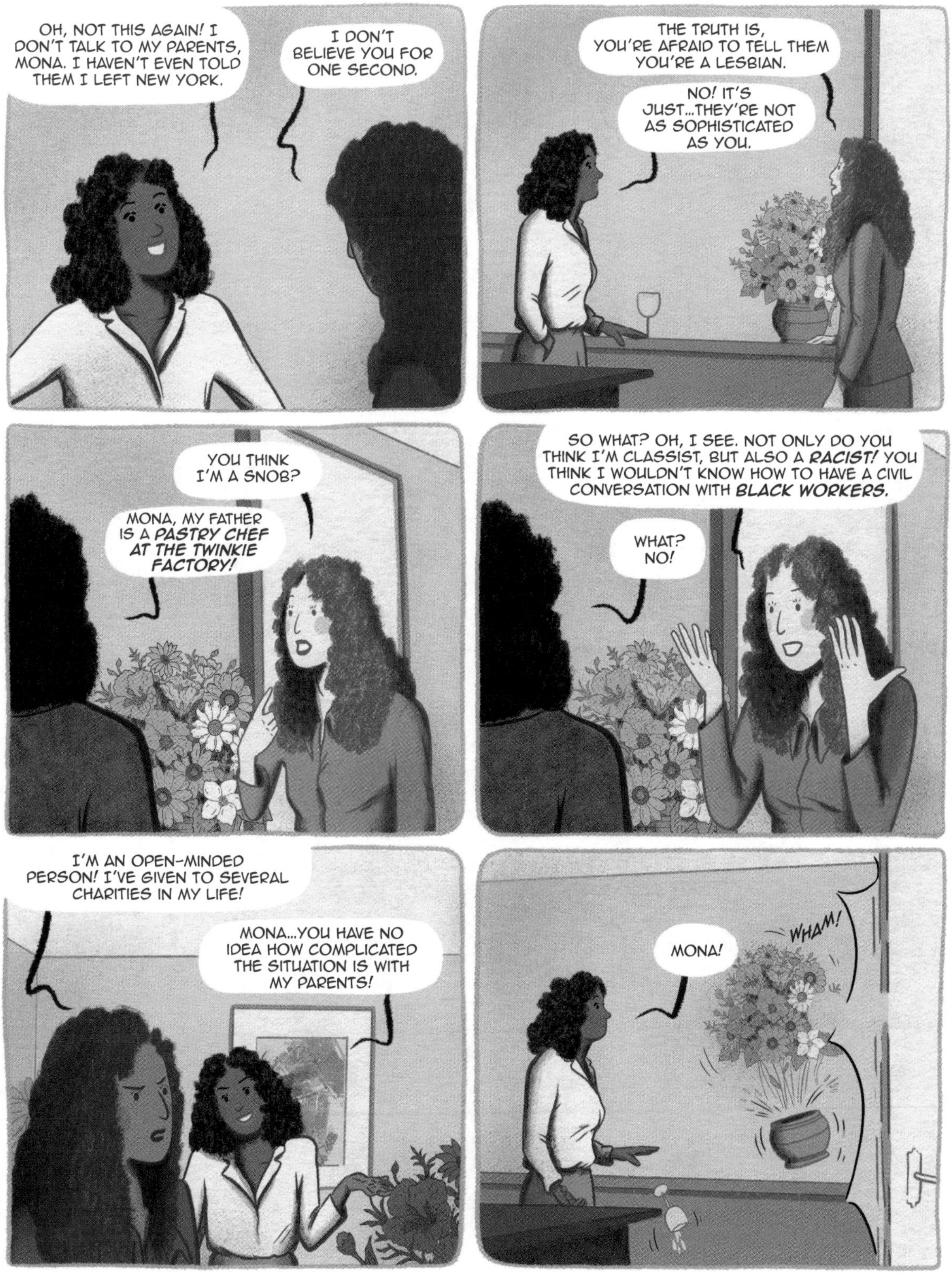
OH, NOT THIS AGAIN! I DON'T TALK TO MY PARENTS, MONA. I HAVEN'T EVEN TOLD THEM I LEFT NEW YORK.
I DON'T BELIEVE YOU FOR ONE SECOND.
THE TRUTH IS, YOU'RE AFRAID TO TELL THEM YOU'RE A LESBIAN.
NO! IT'S JUST...THEY'RE NOT AS SOPHISTICATED AS YOU.
YOU THINK I'M A SNOB?
MONA, MY FATHER IS A PASTRY CHEF AT THE TWINKIE FACTORY!
SO WHAT? OH, I SEE. NOT ONLY DO YOU THINK I'M CLASSIST, BUT ALSO A RACIST! YOU THINK I WOULDN'T KNOW HOW TO HAVE A CIVIL CONVERSATION WITH BLACK WORKERS.
WHAT? NO!
I'M AN OPEN-MINDED PERSON! I'VE GIVEN TO SEVERAL CHARITIES IN MY LIFE!
MONA...YOU HAVE NO IDEA HOW COMPLICATED THE SITUATION IS WITH MY PARENTS!
MONA!
WHAM!

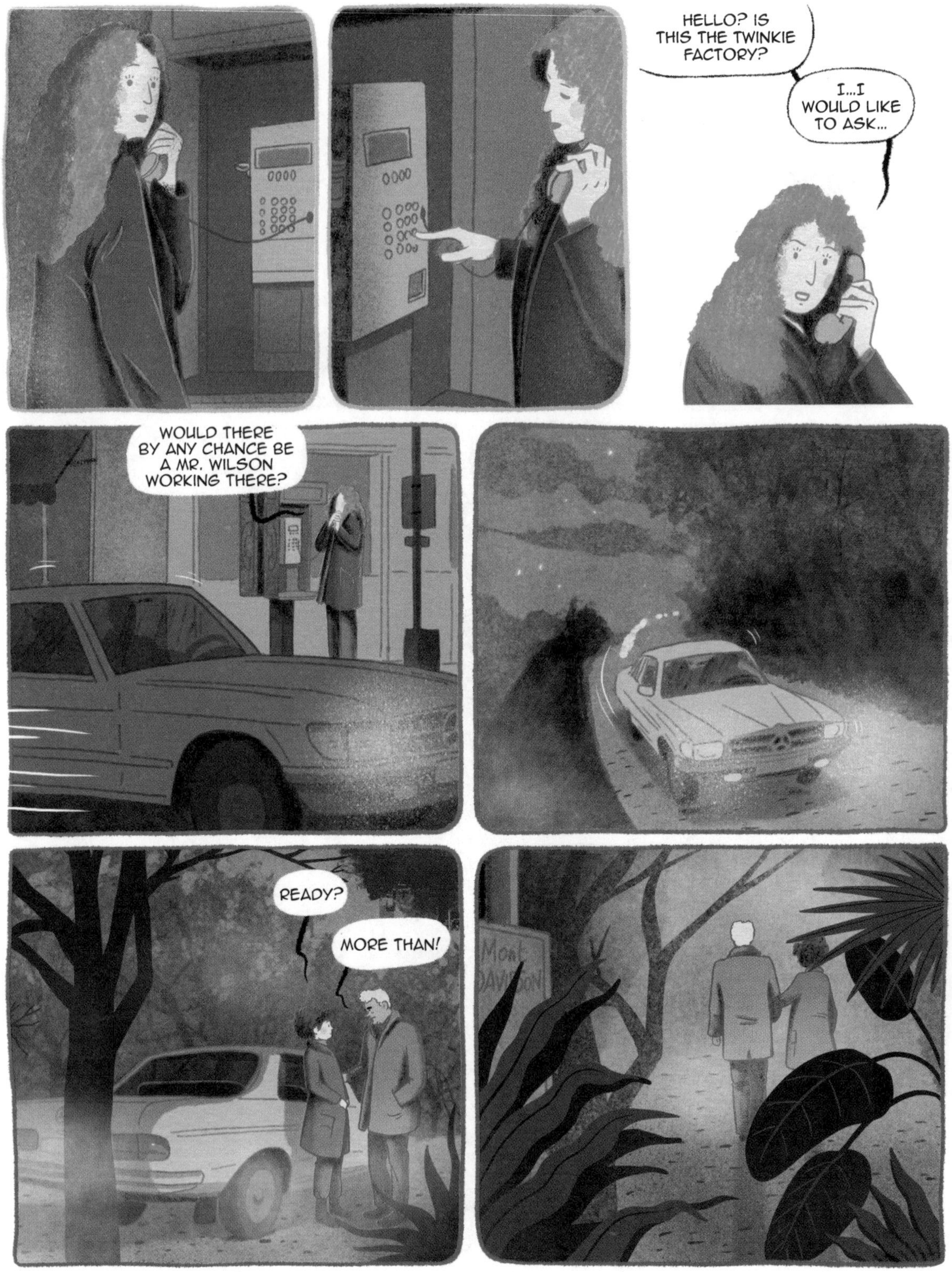
HELLO? IS THIS THE TWINKIE FACTORY?
I...I WOULD LIKE TO ASK...
WOULD THERE BY ANY CHANCE BE A MR. WILSON WORKING THERE?
READY?
MORE THAN!
Mont DAVIDSON

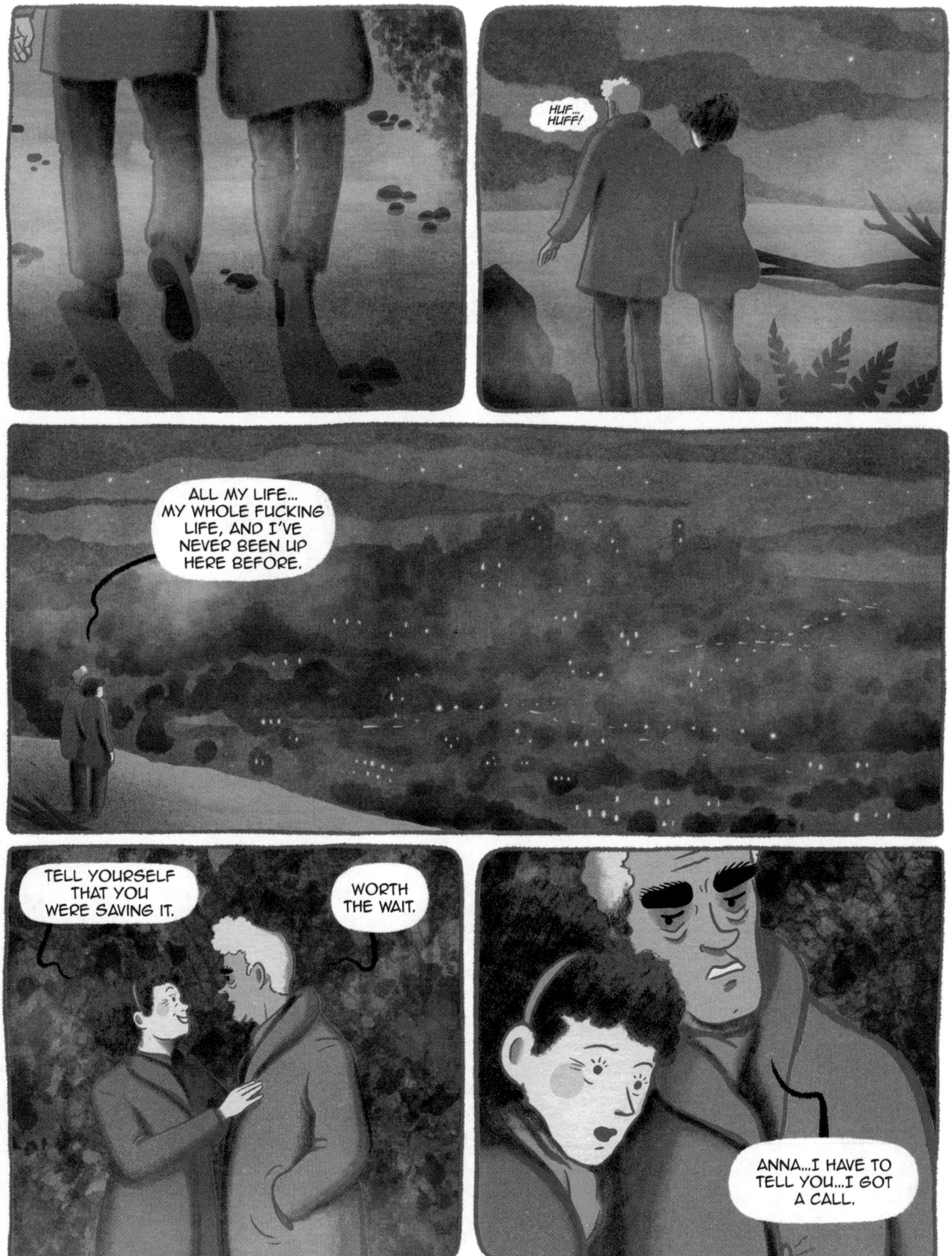
HUF... HUFF!
ALL MY LIFE... MY WHOLE FUCKING LIFE, AND I'VE NEVER BEEN UP HERE BEFORE.
TELL YOURSELF THAT YOU WERE SAVING IT.
WORTH THE WAIT.
ANNA...I HAVE TO TELL YOU...I GOT A CALL.

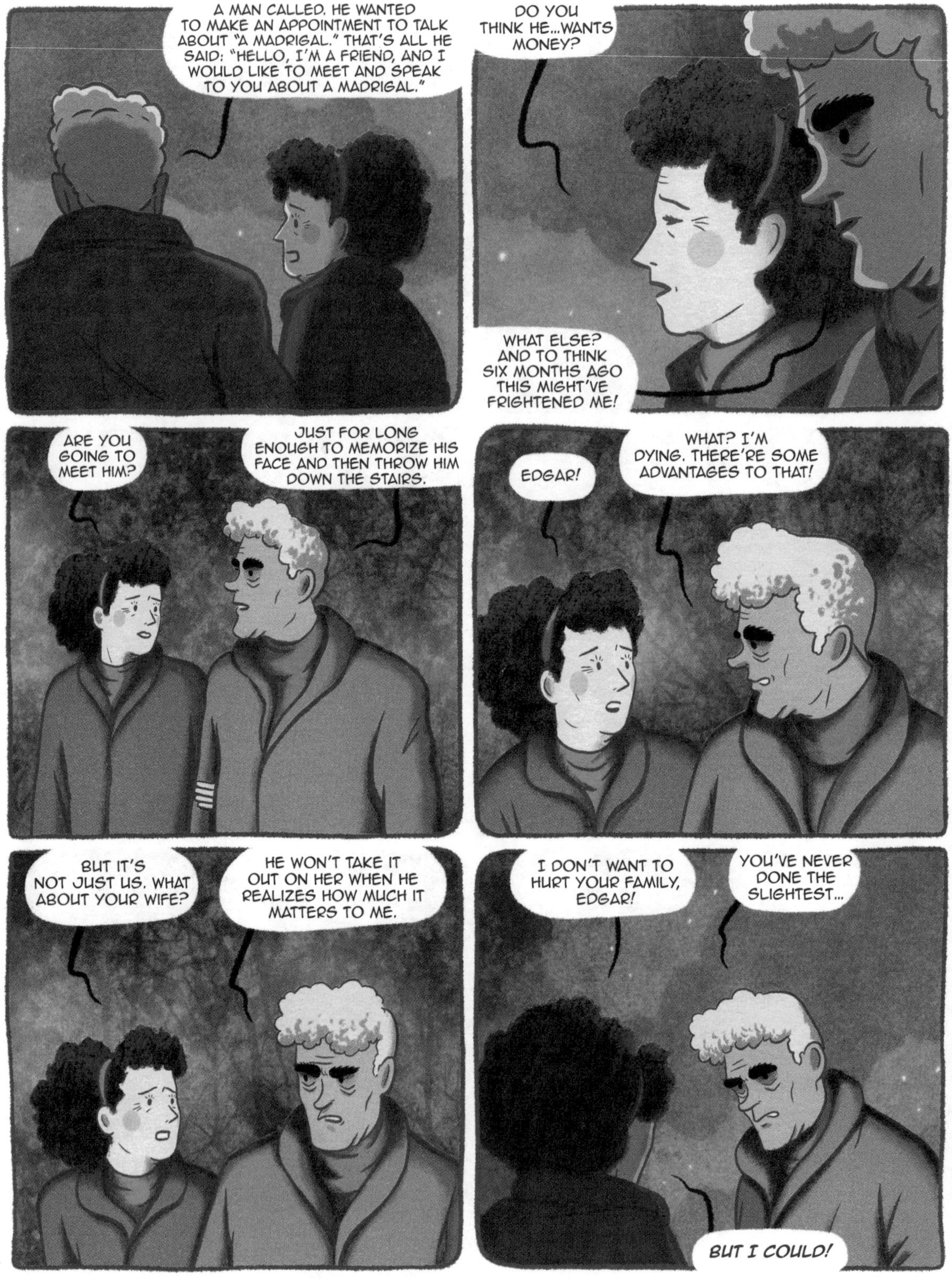
A MAN CALLED. HE WANTED TO MAKE AN APPOINTMENT TO TALK ABOUT "A MADRIGAL." THAT'S ALL HE SAID: "HELLO, I'M A FRIEND, AND I WOULD LIKE TO MEET AND SPEAK TO YOU ABOUT A MADRIGAL."
DO YOU THINK HE...WANTS MONEY?
WHAT ELSE? AND TO THINK SIX MONTHS AGO THIS MIGHT'VE FRIGHTENED ME!
ARE YOU GOING TO MEET HIM?
JUST FOR LONG ENOUGH TO MEMORIZE HIS FACE AND THEN THROW HIM DOWN THE STAIRS.
EDGAR!
WHAT? I'M DYING. THERE'RE SOME ADVANTAGES TO THAT!
BUT IT'S NOT JUST US. WHAT ABOUT YOUR WIFE?
HE WON'T TAKE IT OUT ON HER WHEN HE REALIZES HOW MUCH IT MATTERS TO ME.
I DON'T WANT TO HURT YOUR FAMILY, EDGAR!
YOU'VE NEVER DONE THE SLIGHTEST...
BUT I COULD!

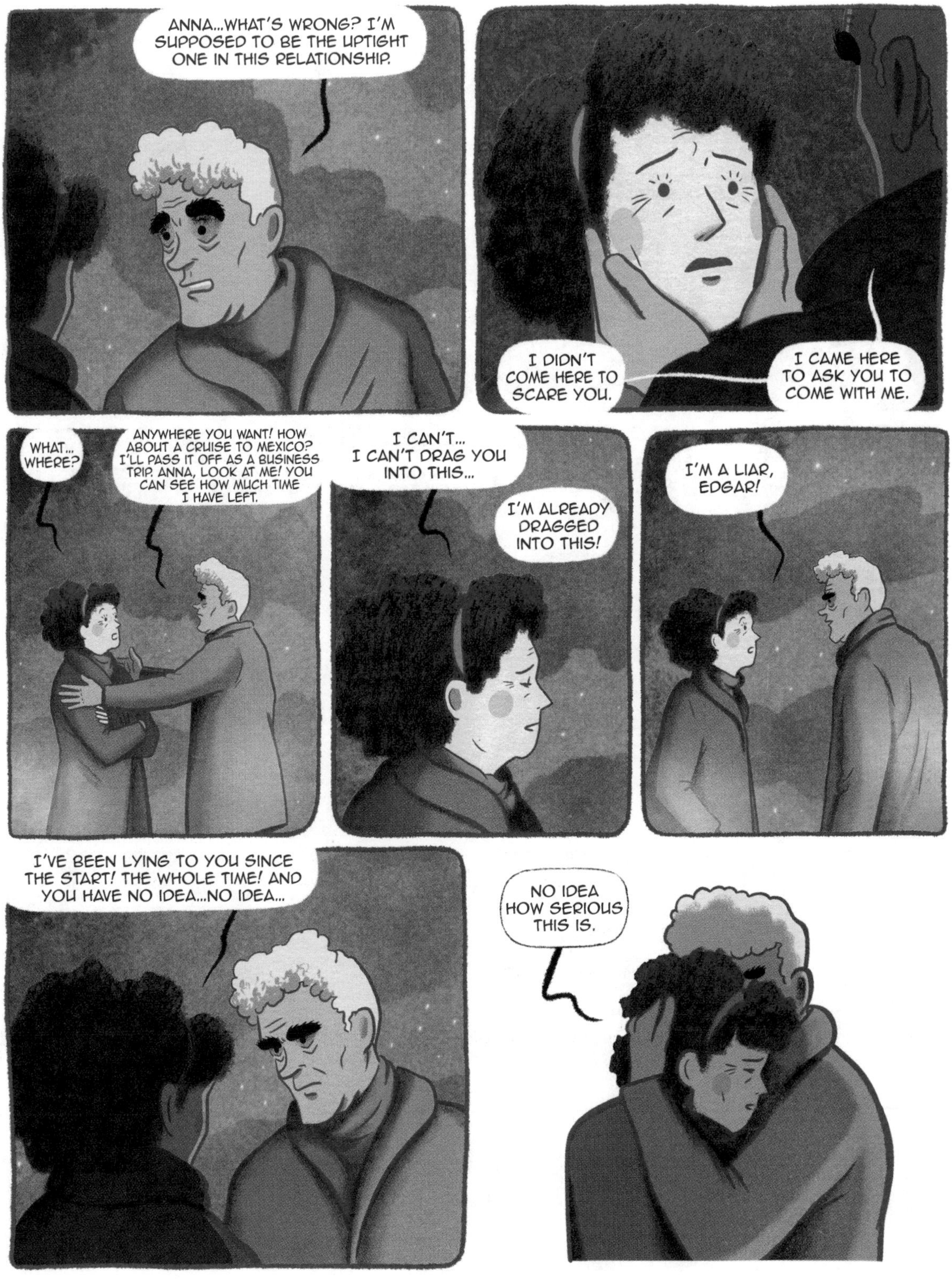
ANNA...WHAT'S WRONG? I'M SUPPOSED TO BE THE UPTIGHT ONE IN THIS RELATIONSHIP.
I DIDN'T COME HERE TO SCARE YOU.
I CAME HERE TO ASK YOU TO COME WITH ME.
WHAT... WHERE?
ANYWHERE YOU WANT! HOW ABOUT A CRUISE TO MEXICO? I'LL PASS IT OFF AS A BUSINESS TRIP. ANNA, LOOK AT ME! YOU CAN SEE HOW MUCH TIME I HAVE LEFT.
I CAN'T... I CAN'T DRAG YOU INTO THIS...
I'M ALREADY DRAGGED INTO THIS!
I'M A LIAR, EDGAR!
I'VE BEEN LYING TO YOU SINCE THE START! THE WHOLE TIME! AND YOU HAVE NO IDEA...NO IDEA...
NO IDEA HOW SERIOUS THIS IS.

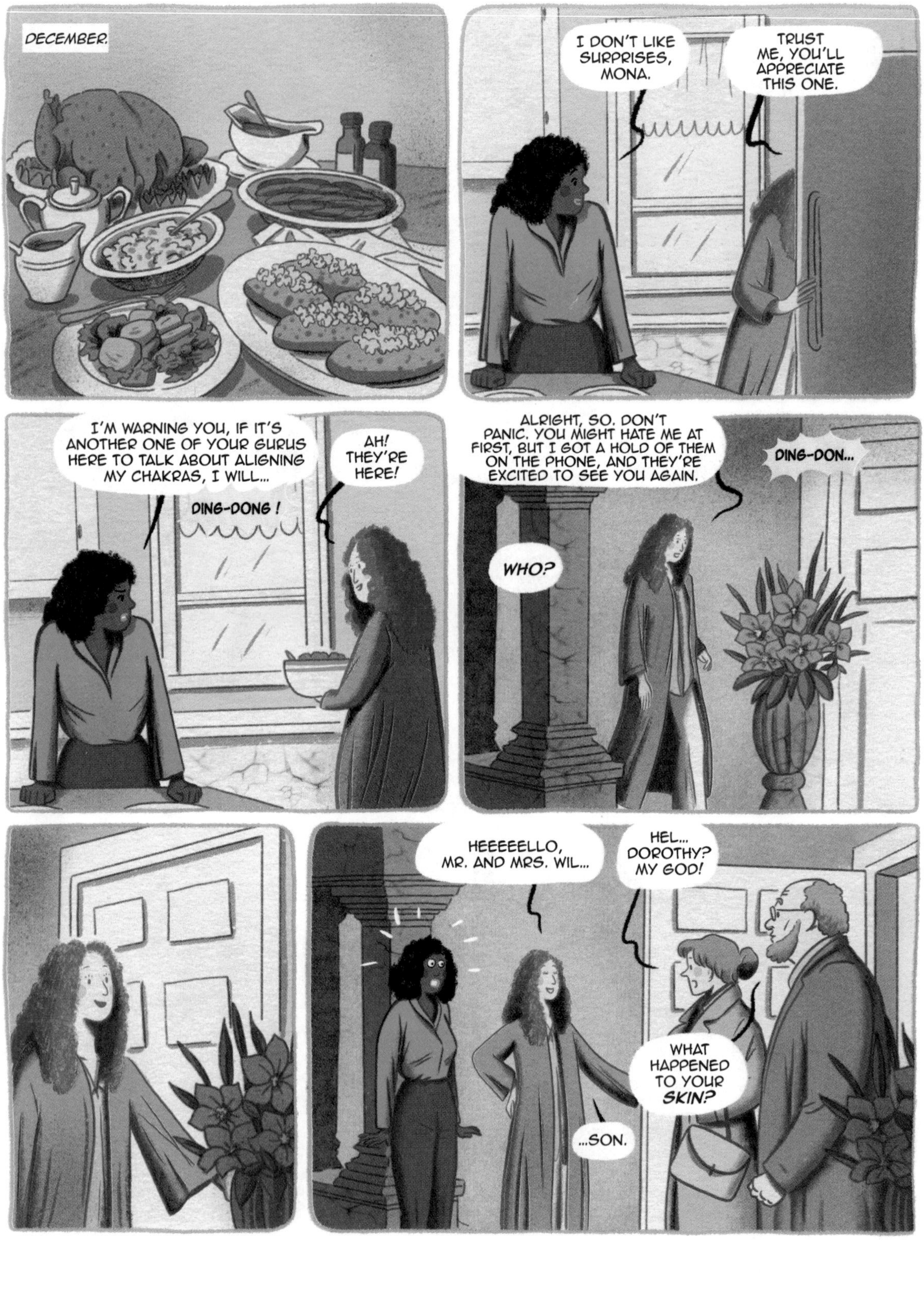
DECEMBER.
I DON'T LIKE SURPRISES, MONA.
TRUST ME, YOU'LL APPRECIATE THIS ONE.
I'M WARNING YOU, IF IT'S ANOTHER ONE OF YOUR GURUS HERE TO TALK ABOUT ALIGNING MY CHAKRAS, I WILL...
DING-DONG !
AH! THEY'RE HERE!
ALRIGHT, SO. DON'T PANIC. YOU MIGHT HATE ME AT FIRST, BUT I GOT A HOLD OF THEM ON THE PHONE, AND THEY'RE EXCITED TO SEE YOU AGAIN.
DING-DON...
WHO?
HEEEEELLO, MR. AND MRS. WIL...
HEL... DOROTHY? MY GOD!
WHAT HAPPENED TO YOUR SKIN?
...SON.

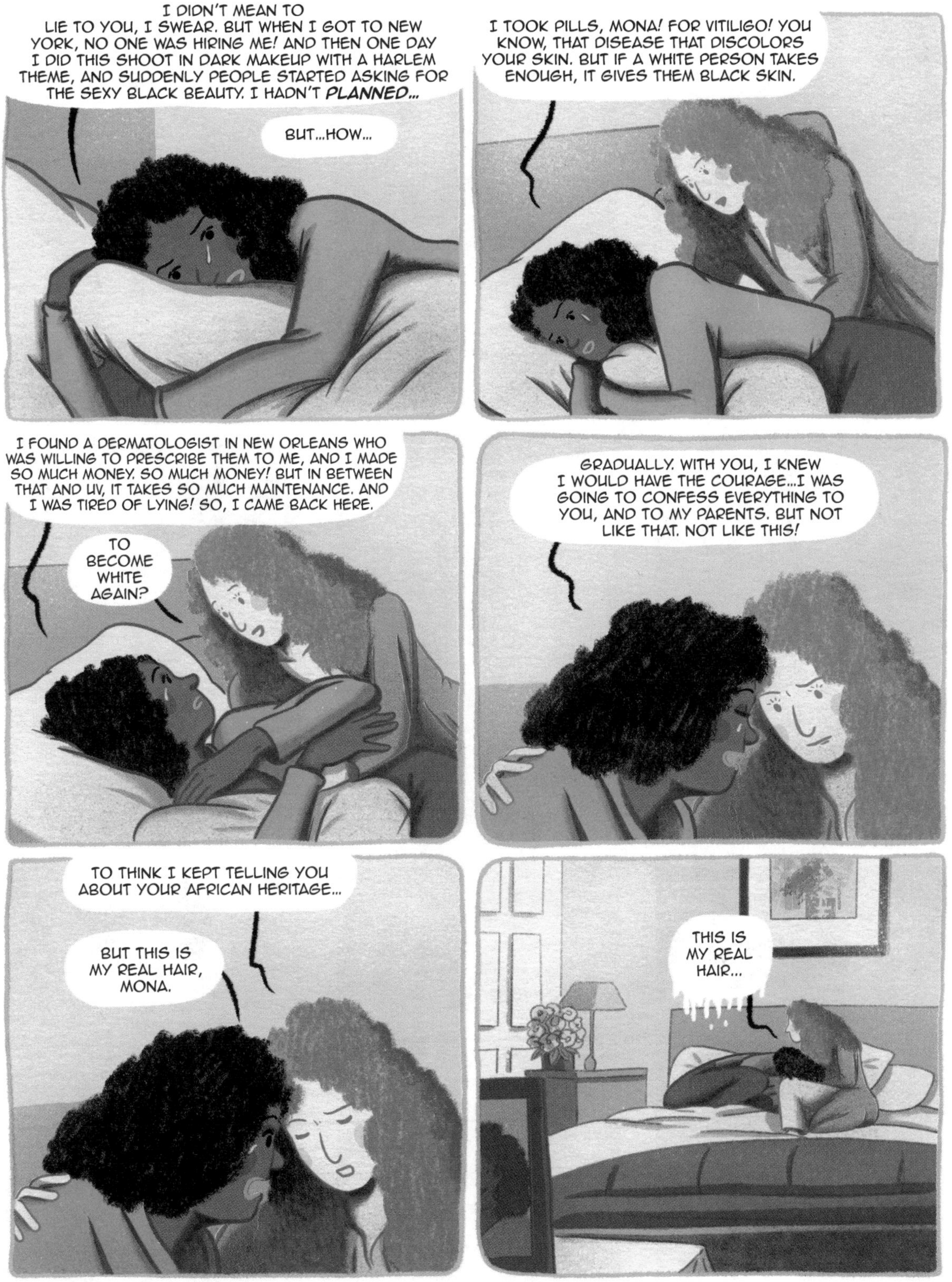
I DIDN'T MEAN TO LIE TO YOU, I SWEAR. BUT WHEN I GOT TO NEW YORK, NO ONE WAS HIRING ME! AND THEN ONE DAY I DID THIS SHOOT IN DARK MAKEUP WITH A HARLEM THEME, AND SUDDENLY PEOPLE STARTED ASKING FOR THE SEXY BLACK BEAUTY. I HADN'T ***PLANNED...***
BUT...HOW...
I TOOK PILLS, MONA! FOR VITILIGO! YOU KNOW, THAT DISEASE THAT DISCOLORS YOUR SKIN. BUT IF A WHITE PERSON TAKES ENOUGH, IT GIVES THEM BLACK SKIN.
I FOUND A DERMATOLOGIST IN NEW ORLEANS WHO WAS WILLING TO PRESCRIBE THEM TO ME, AND I MADE SO MUCH MONEY. SO MUCH MONEY! BUT IN BETWEEN THAT AND UV, IT TAKES SO MUCH MAINTENANCE. AND I WAS TIRED OF LYING! SO, I CAME BACK HERE.
TO BECOME WHITE AGAIN?
GRADUALLY. WITH YOU, I KNEW I WOULD HAVE THE COURAGE...I WAS GOING TO CONFESS EVERYTHING TO YOU, AND TO MY PARENTS. BUT NOT LIKE THAT. NOT LIKE THIS!
TO THINK I KEPT TELLING YOU ABOUT YOUR AFRICAN HERITAGE...
BUT THIS IS MY REAL HAIR, MONA.
THIS IS MY REAL HAIR...

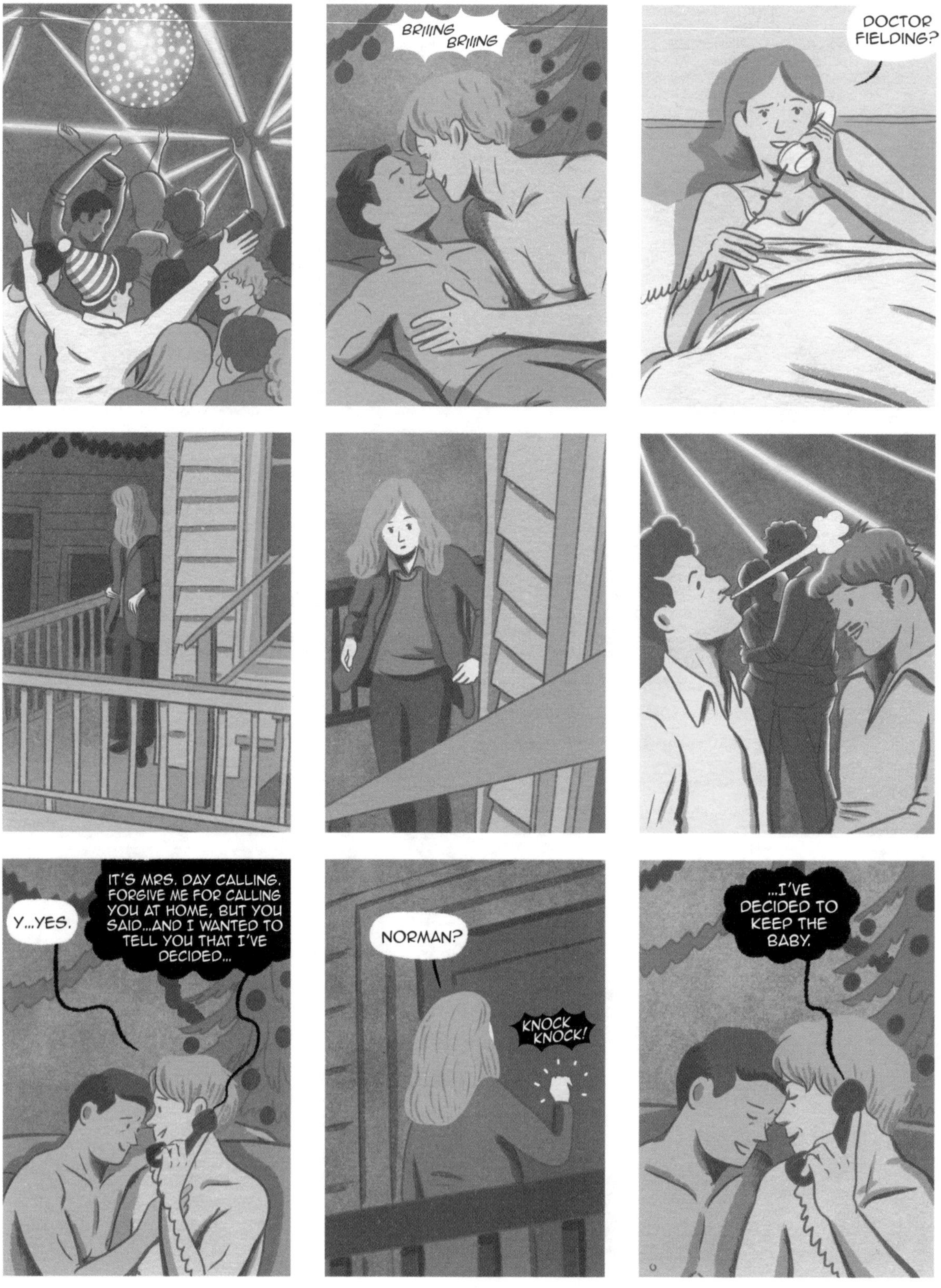
BRIIING
BRIIING
DOCTOR FIELDING?
Y...YES.
IT'S MRS. DAY CALLING. FORGIVE ME FOR CALLING YOU AT HOME, BUT YOU SAID...AND I WANTED TO TELL YOU THAT I'VE DECIDED...
NORMAN?
KNOCK KNOCK!
...I'VE DECIDED TO KEEP THE BABY.

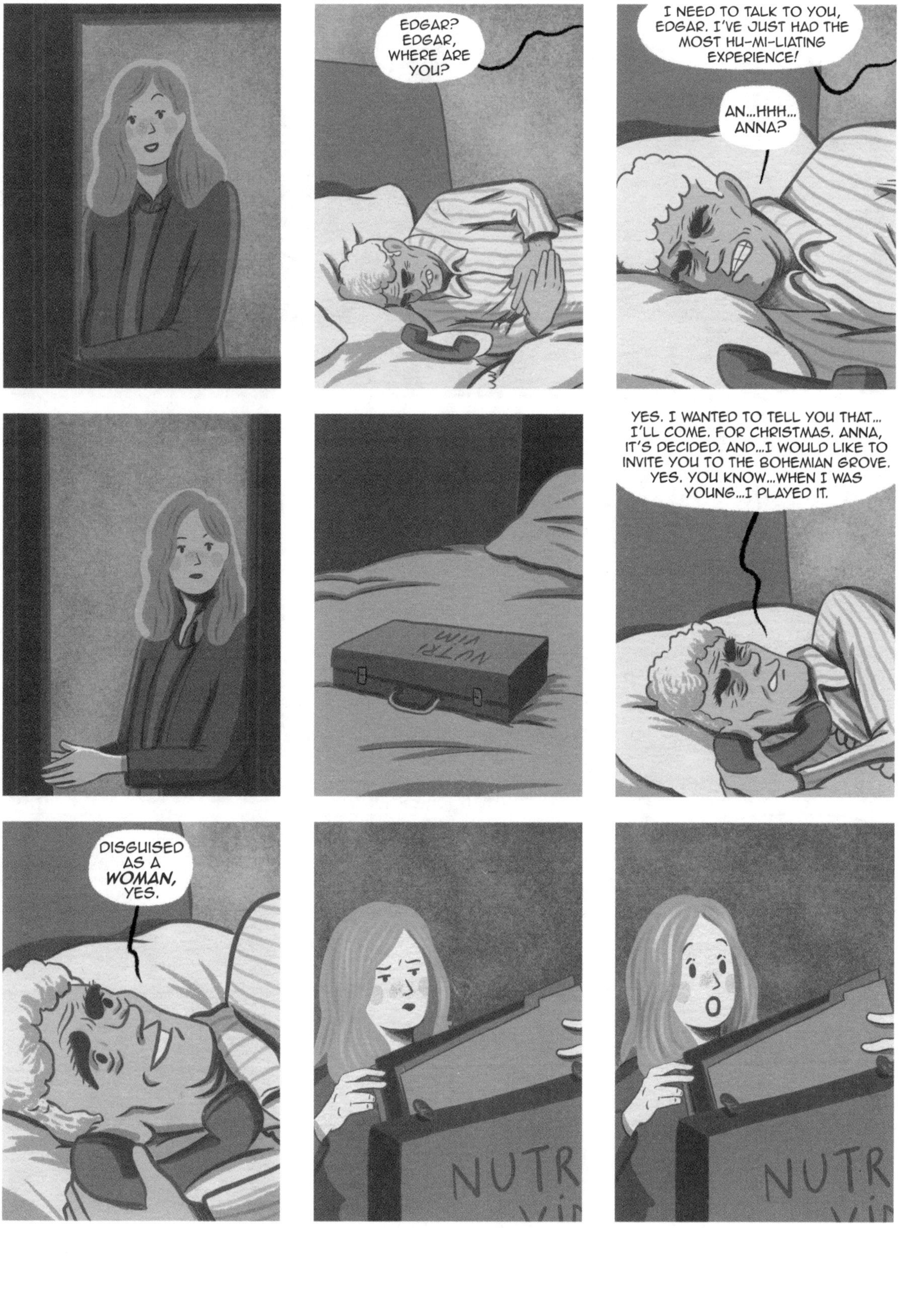
EDGAR? EDGAR, WHERE ARE YOU?
I NEED TO TALK TO YOU, EDGAR. I'VE JUST HAD THE MOST HU-MI-LIATING EXPERIENCE!
AN...HHH... ANNA?
NUTRI VIM
YES. I WANTED TO TELL YOU THAT... I'LL COME. FOR CHRISTMAS. ANNA, IT'S DECIDED. AND...I WOULD LIKE TO INVITE YOU TO THE BOHEMIAN GROVE. YES. YOU KNOW...WHEN I WAS YOUNG...I PLAYED IT.
DISGUISED AS A ***WOMAN,*** YES.
NUTR
NUTR

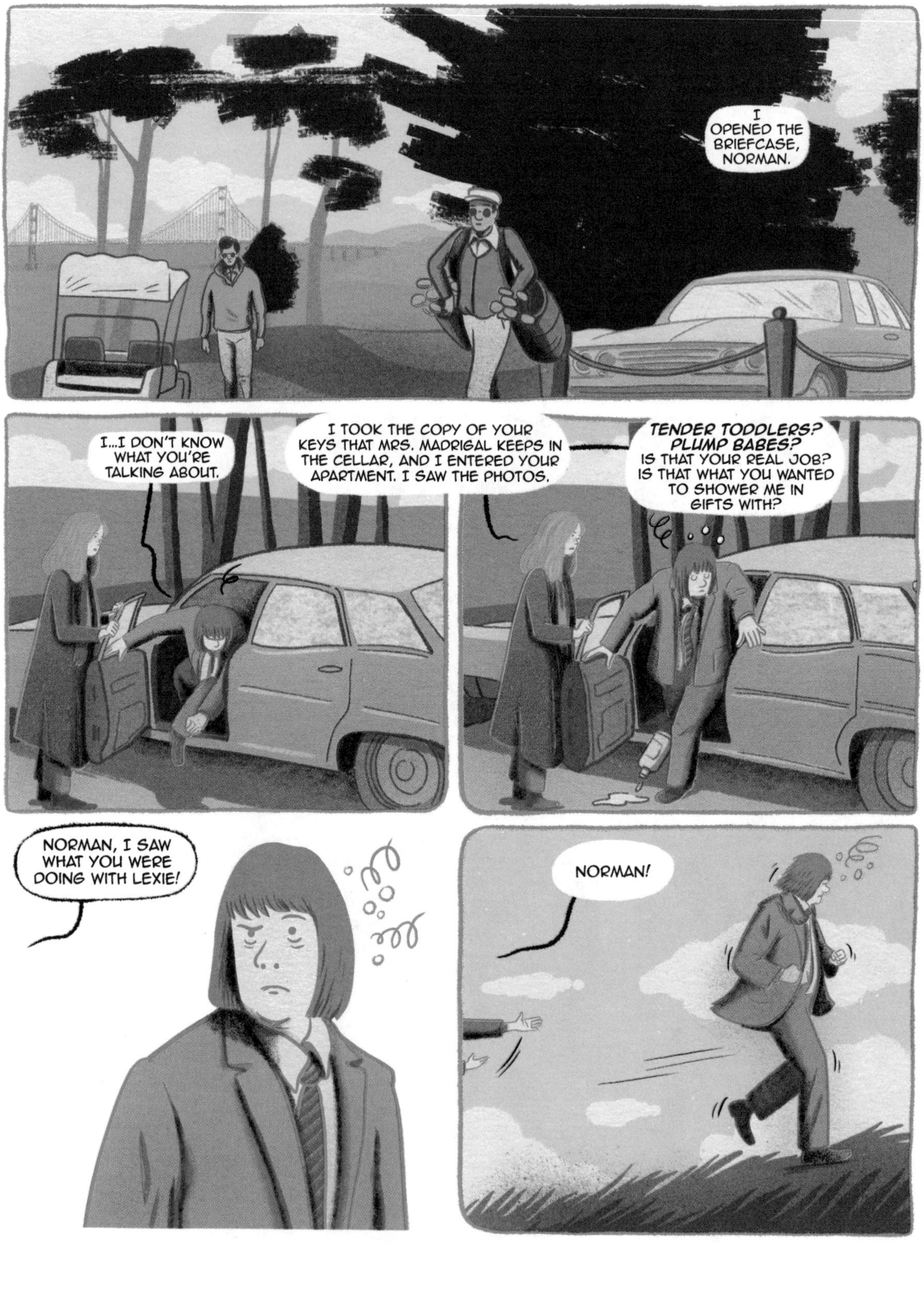
I OPENED THE BRIEFCASE, NORMAN.
I...I DON'T KNOW WHAT YOU'RE TALKING ABOUT.
I TOOK THE COPY OF YOUR KEYS THAT MRS. MADRIGAL KEEPS IN THE CELLAR, AND I ENTERED YOUR APARTMENT. I SAW THE PHOTOS.
TENDER TODDLERS? PLUMP BABES? IS THAT YOUR REAL JOB? IS THAT WHAT YOU WANTED TO SHOWER ME IN GIFTS WITH?
NORMAN, I SAW WHAT YOU WERE DOING WITH LEXIE!
NORMAN!

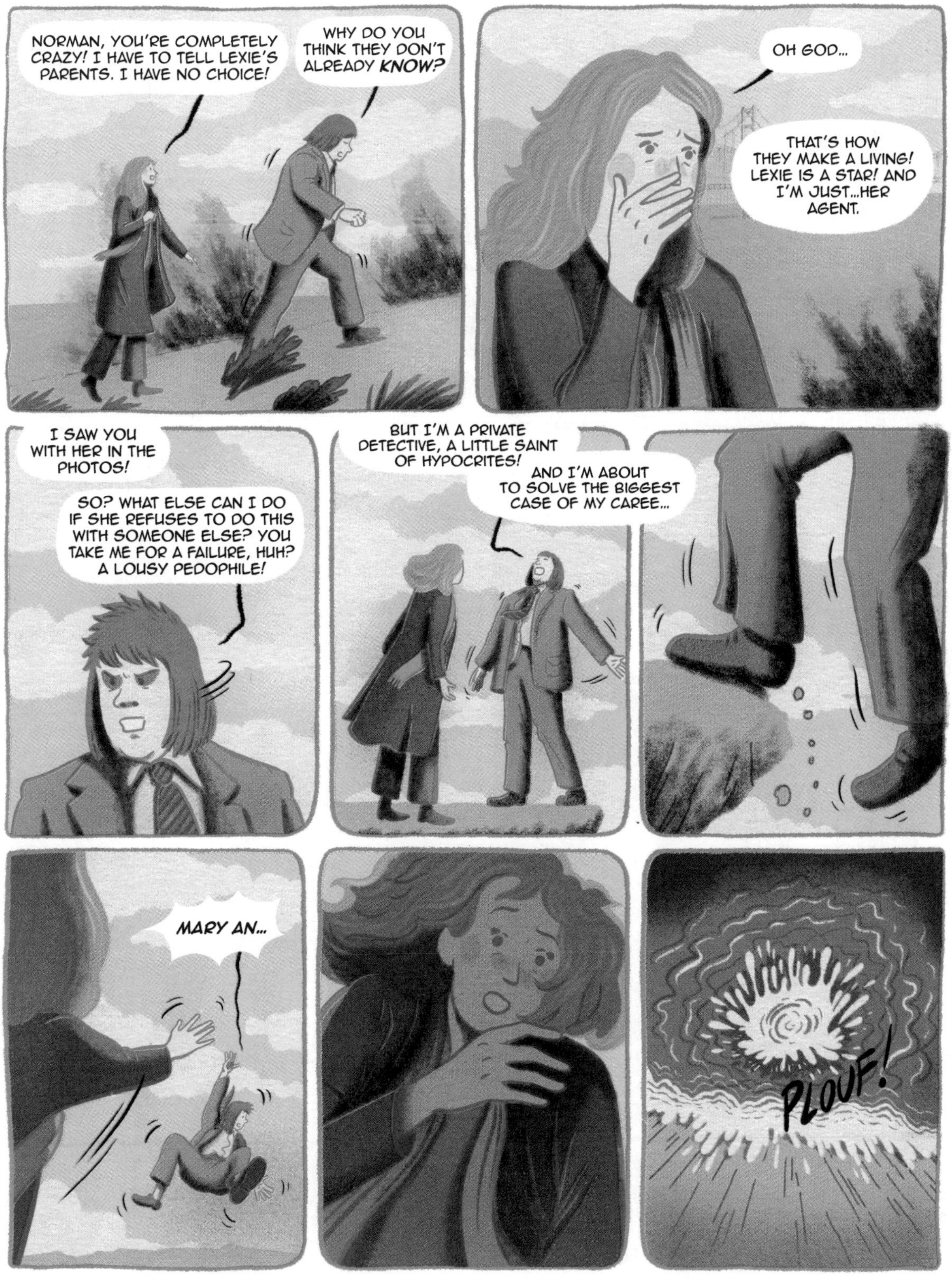
NORMAN, YOU'RE COMPLETELY CRAZY! I HAVE TO TELL LEXIE'S PARENTS. I HAVE NO CHOICE!
WHY DO YOU THINK THEY DON'T ALREADY KNOW?
OH GOD...
THAT'S HOW THEY MAKE A LIVING! LEXIE IS A STAR! AND I'M JUST...HER AGENT.
I SAW YOU WITH HER IN THE PHOTOS!
SO? WHAT ELSE CAN I DO IF SHE REFUSES TO DO THIS WITH SOMEONE ELSE? YOU TAKE ME FOR A FAILURE, HUH? A LOUSY PEDOPHILE!
BUT I'M A PRIVATE DETECTIVE, A LITTLE SAINT OF HYPOCRITES!
AND I'M ABOUT TO SOLVE THE BIGGEST CASE OF MY CAREE...
MARY AN...
PLOUF!

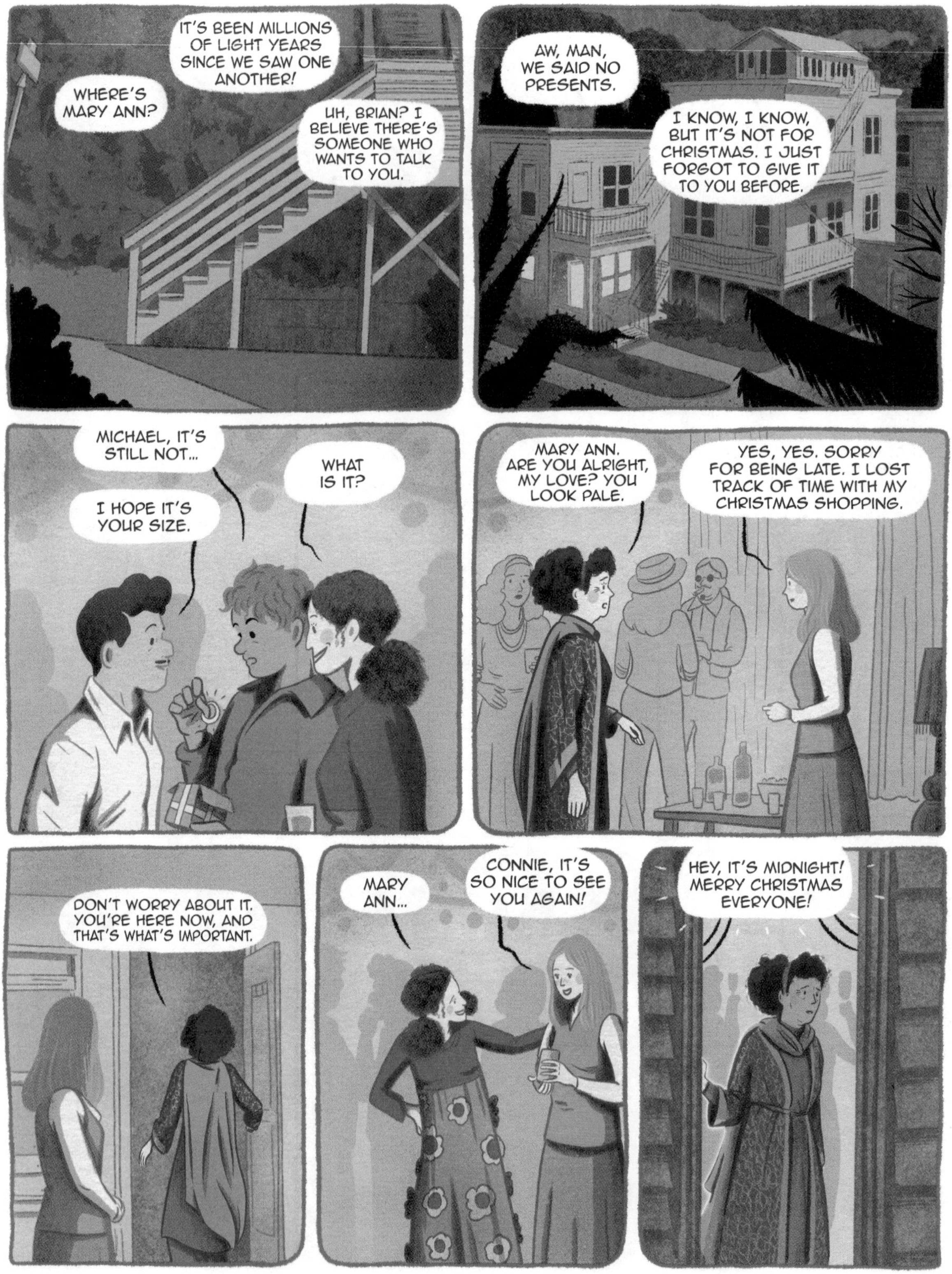
IT'S BEEN MILLIONS OF LIGHT YEARS SINCE WE SAW ONE ANOTHER!
WHERE'S MARY ANN?
UH, BRIAN? I BELIEVE THERE'S SOMEONE WHO WANTS TO TALK TO YOU.
AW, MAN, WE SAID NO PRESENTS.
I KNOW, I KNOW, BUT IT'S NOT FOR CHRISTMAS. I JUST FORGOT TO GIVE IT TO YOU BEFORE.
MICHAEL, IT'S STILL NOT...
WHAT IS IT?
I HOPE IT'S YOUR SIZE.
MARY ANN. ARE YOU ALRIGHT, MY LOVE? YOU LOOK PALE.
YES, YES. SORRY FOR BEING LATE. I LOST TRACK OF TIME WITH MY CHRISTMAS SHOPPING.
DON'T WORRY ABOUT IT. YOU'RE HERE NOW, AND THAT'S WHAT'S IMPORTANT.
MARY ANN...
CONNIE, IT'S SO NICE TO SEE YOU AGAIN!
HEY, IT'S MIDNIGHT! MERRY CHRISTMAS EVERYONE!

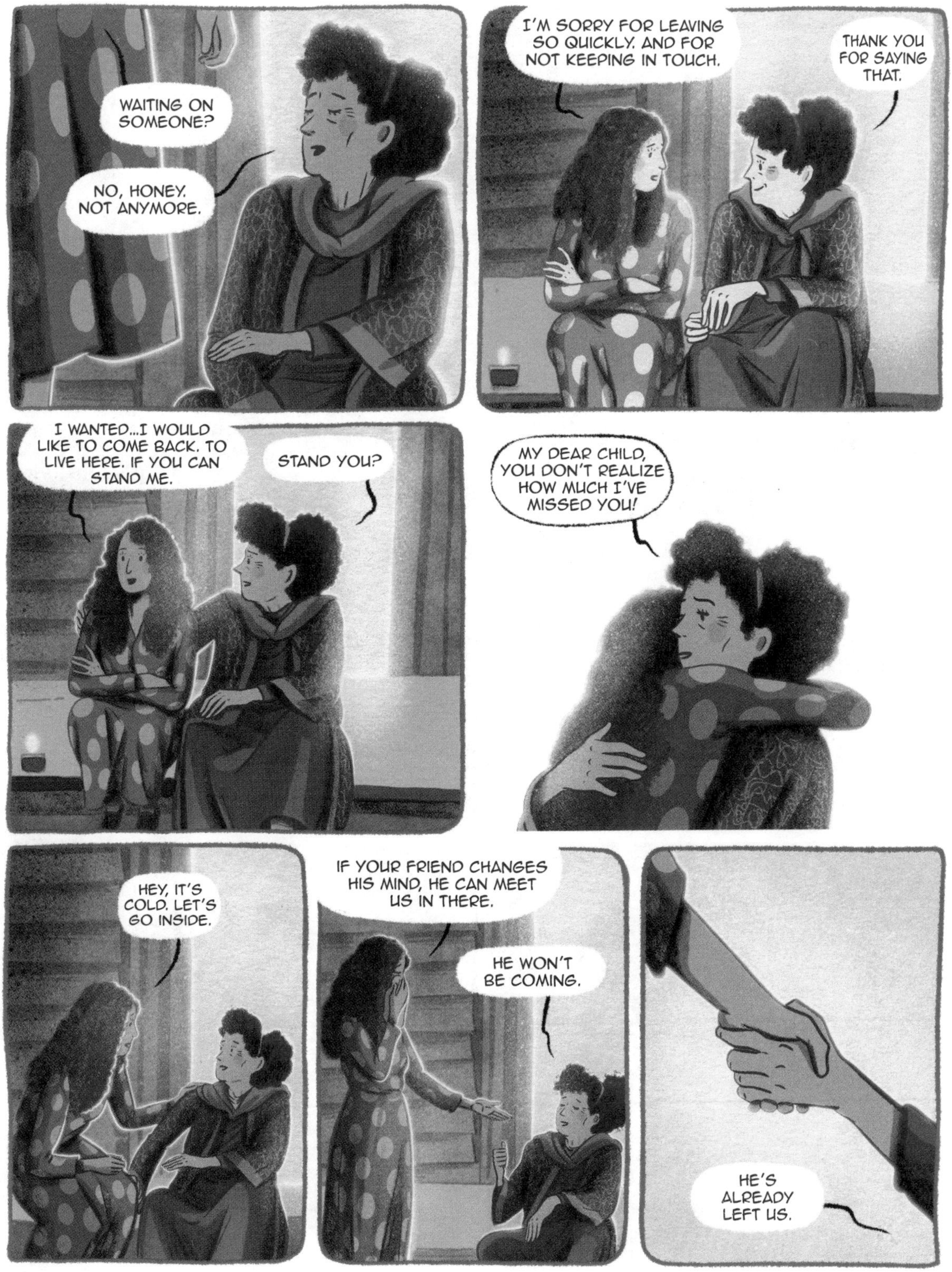
WAITING ON SOMEONE?
NO, HONEY. NOT ANYMORE.
I'M SORRY FOR LEAVING SO QUICKLY. AND FOR NOT KEEPING IN TOUCH.
THANK YOU FOR SAYING THAT.
I WANTED...I WOULD LIKE TO COME BACK. TO LIVE HERE. IF YOU CAN STAND ME.
STAND YOU?
MY DEAR CHILD, YOU DON'T REALIZE HOW MUCH I'VE MISSED YOU!
HEY, IT'S COLD. LET'S GO INSIDE.
IF YOUR FRIEND CHANGES HIS MIND, HE CAN MEET US IN THERE.
HE WON'T BE COMING.
HE'S ALREADY LEFT US.

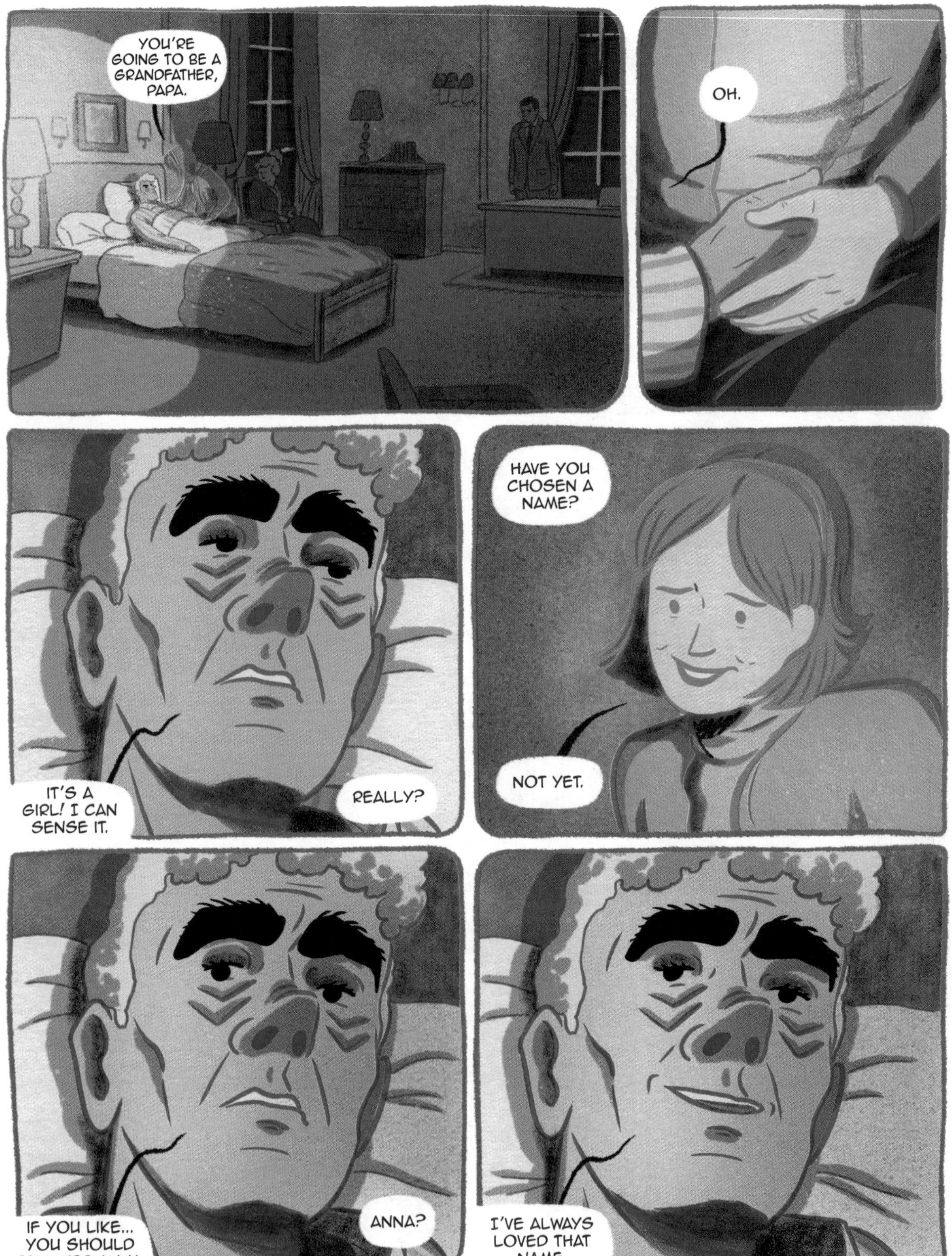

YOU'RE GOING TO BE A GRANDFATHER, PAPA.
OH.
HAVE YOU CHOSEN A NAME?
NOT YET.
IT'S A GIRL! I CAN SENSE IT.
REALLY?
IF YOU LIKE... YOU SHOULD CALL HER ANNA.
ANNA?
I'VE ALWAYS LOVED THAT NAME.

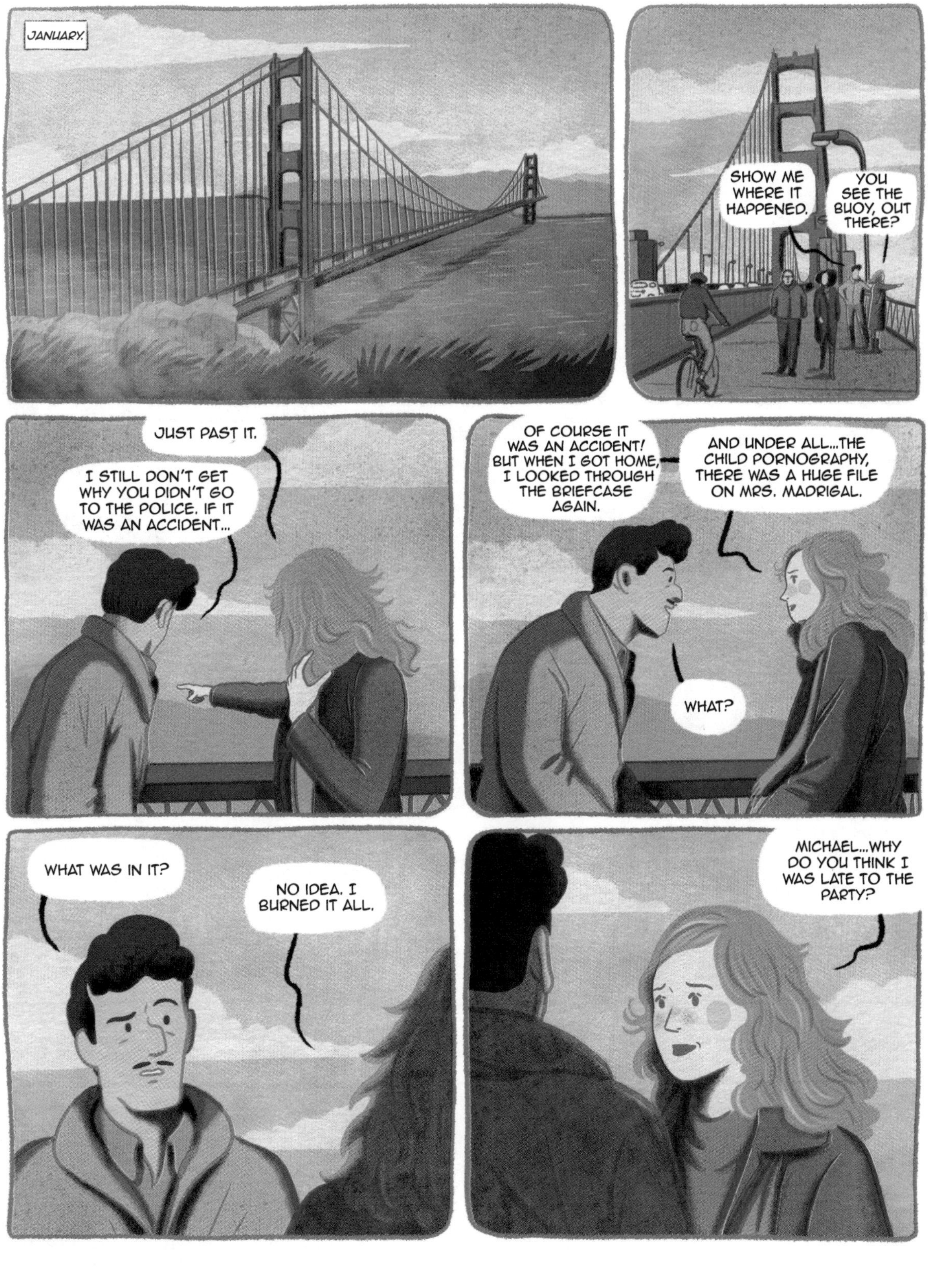
JANUARY.
SHOW ME WHERE IT HAPPENED.
YOU SEE THE BUOY, OUT THERE?
JUST PAST IT.
I STILL DON'T GET WHY YOU DIDN'T GO TO THE POLICE. IF IT WAS AN ACCIDENT...
OF COURSE IT WAS AN ACCIDENT! BUT WHEN I GOT HOME, I LOOKED THROUGH THE BRIEFCASE AGAIN.
AND UNDER ALL...THE CHILD PORNOGRAPHY, THERE WAS A HUGE FILE ON MRS. MADRIGAL.
WHAT?
WHAT WAS IN IT?
NO IDEA. I BURNED IT ALL.
MICHAEL...WHY DO YOU THINK I WAS LATE TO THE PARTY?

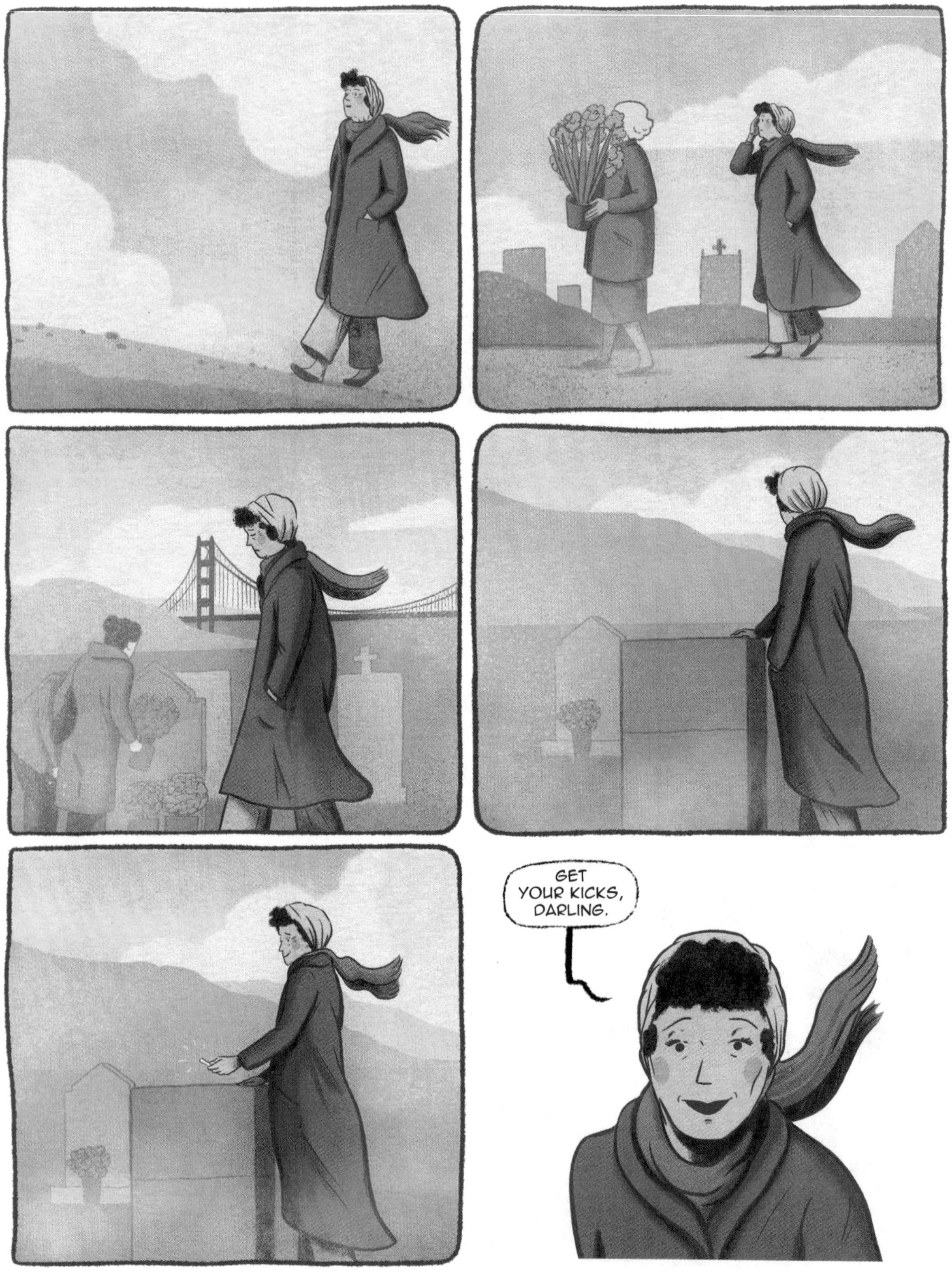
GET YOUR KICKS, DARLING.

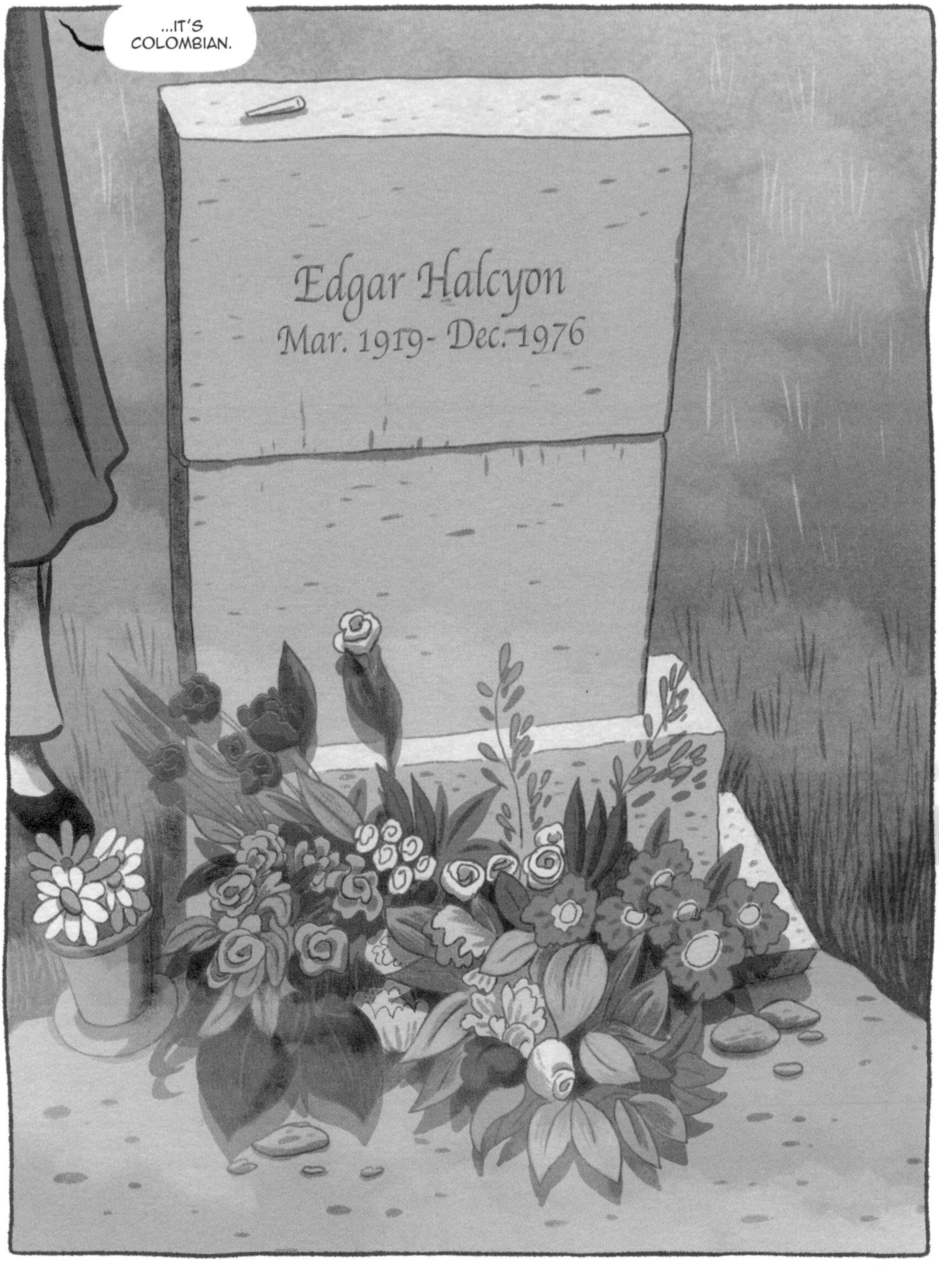
...IT'S COLOMBIAN.
Edgar Halcyon
Mar. 1919- Dec. 1976

Acknowledgements

Thanks to Celina for trusting me with this book,
and to Sandrine for having portrayed it so well.

And thanks very much, Mister Maupin, for your support.

Isabelle Bauthian

I give a big thank you to all the helping and benevolent
people present from far or near to the realization
of this work. Thank you, Celina, for offering me the
adaptation of this bestseller, thank you, Isabelle, for
having perfectly staged the universe of its author:
Armistead Maupin, thank you for your trust.

Sandrine Revel